# The Tree of Hands

# A Demon In My View

## Ruth Rendell

arrow books

Reissued by Arrow in 2006

2 4 6 8 10 9 7 5 3 1

Copyright © Kingsmarkham Enterprises Ltd 1984

Ruth Rendell has asserted her right under the Copyright, Designs
and Patents Act, 1988 to be identified as the author of this work

The Tree of Hand's first published in the United Kingdom by Hutchinson in 1984
A Demon In My View first published in the United Kingdom by Hutchinson in 1976

Arrow Books Limited
The Random House Group Limited
20 Vauxhall Bridge Road, London, SW1V 2SA

Random House Australia (Pty) Limited
20 Alfred Street, Milsons Point, Sydney,
New South Wales 2061, Australia

Random House New Zealand Limited
18 Poland Road, Glenfield
Auckland 10, New Zealand

Random House (Pty) Limited
Endulini, 5a Jubilee Road, Parktown 2193, South Africa

The Random House Group Limited Reg. No. 954009

www.randomhouse.co.uk

A CIP catalogue record for this book
is available from the British Library

Papers used by Random House are natural, recyclable products made from wood grown
in sustainable forests. The manufacturing processes conform to the environmental
regulations of the country of origin

ISBN 0 09 191580 5

Printed and bound in Great Britain by
Bookmarque Ltd, Croydon, Surrey

## About the Author

Since her first novel, *From Doon with Death*, published in 1964, Ruth Rendell has won many awards, including the Crime Writer's Association Gold Dagger for 1976's best crime novel with *A Demon In My View*, and the Arts Council National Book Award, genre fiction, for *The Lake of Darkness* in 1980.

In 1985 Ruth Rendell received the Silver Dagger for *The Tree of Hands*, and in 1987, writing as Barbara Vine, won her third Edgar from the Mystery Writers of America for *A Dark-Adapted Eye*.

She won the Gold Dagger for *Live Flesh* in 1986, for *King Solomon's Carpet* in 1991 and, as Barbara Vine, a Gold Dagger in 1987 for *A Fatal Inversion*.

Ruth Rendell won the *Sunday Times* Literary Award in 1990, and in 1991 she was awarded the Crime Writer's Association Cartier Diamond Dagger for outstanding contributions to the genre. In 1996 she was awarded the CBE, and in 1997 was made a Life Peer.

Her books have been translated into twenty-five languages and are also published to great acclaim in the United States.

Ruth Rendell has a son and two grandsons, and lives in London

# By Ruth Rendell

# The Tree of Hands

*For Francesca, my godchild, with love*

# Book One

Book One

# 1

Once, when Benet was about fourteen, they had been in a train together, alone in the carriage, and Mopsa had tried to stab her with a carving knife. Threatened her with it, rather. Benet had been wondering why her mother had brought such a large handbag with her, a red one that didn't go with the clothes she was wearing. Mopsa had shouted and laughed and said wild things and then she had put the knife back in her bag. But Benet had been very frightened by then. She lost her head and pulled the emergency handle that Mopsa called the 'communication cord'. The train stopped and there had been trouble for everyone involved and her father had been angry and grimly sad.

She had more or less forgotten it. The memory of it came back quite vividly while she was waiting for Mopsa at Heathrow. Though she had seen Mopsa many times since then, had lived under the same roof with her and seen how she could change, it was the scarved, shawled, streamered figure with its fleece of shaggy hair that she watched for as she waited behind the barrier among the tour guides with their placards, the anxious Indians, the businessmen's wives. James wanted to come out of the pushchair, he couldn't see down there and he wasn't feeling well. Benet picked him up and set him on her hip with her arm round him.

It ought to have been exciting, waiting here. There was something dramatic about the emergence of the first people from behind the wall that hid Customs, almost as if they had escaped into freedom. Benet remembered once meeting Edward here and how wonderful that first sight of him had been. All those people streaming through, all unknown, all strangers, and then Edward, so positively and absolutely Edward that it was as if her were in colour and all the rest in black and white. Waiting for Mopsa wasn't like that. Waiting for Edward, if such a thing were conceivable, wouldn't be like that now. There was no one in her world that waiting for would be like that except James, and she couldn't see any reason why she and James should be separated. Not for years and years anyway. She dug in her bag for a tissue and wiped his nose. Poor James. He was beautiful though, he always was, even if his face was wan and his nose pink.

A couple came through, each pushing a tartan suitcase on wheels. The woman behind them held a small suitcase in one hand and a small holdall in the other. It would be hard to say which was carry-on baggage and which had been checked. The cases matched; they were of biscuit-coloured stuff you couldn't tell was plastic or leather. She was a drab colourless washed-out woman. Her pale wandering eyes rested on Benet and recognized her. It was that way round – otherwise would Benet ever have known?

Yet this was Mopsa. This was her mad mother who was kissing her, smiling and giving a dismissive wave of the hand when James, instead of responding to her, buried his face in Benet's shoulder. This was Mopsa in a dowdy grey suit, a pink silk blouse with a gold pin at the collar, her hair cut brusquely short and faded to tarnished silver.

Benet put the cases on the pushchair, using it as a baggage trolley. She carried James who snuffled and stared, round-eyed, curious, at this new unknown grandmother. Mopsa had developed a brisk springy walk. Her carriage was erect, her head held high. In the past she had some-times slouched, sometimes danced, swanned and swayed in her Isadora Duncan moods, but she had never walked briskly like an ordinary woman. Or perhaps she did when I was very young, thought Benet, trying to remember a girl-mother of twenty years before. It was too long ago. All she could recall now was how she had longed for a normal mother like other girls had and took for granted. Now when she was twenty-eight and it no longer mattered, it seemed she had one. She stopped herself staring. She asked after her father.

'He's fine. He sent his love.'

'And you really like living in Spain?'

'I don't say it hasn't its drawbacks but Dad hasn't had a sign of his asthma in three years. It keeps me fit too.' Mopsa smiled cheerfully as if her own illness had been no more than a kind of asthma. She talked like one of those neighbours in Edgware had talked. Like Mrs Fenton, Benet thought, like a middle-aged housewife. 'I feel a fraud coming here for these tests,' Mopsa said. 'There's nothing wrong with me any more, I said, but they said it wouldn't do any harm and why not have a holiday? Well, I'm on holiday all the time really, aren't I? Are we going in the tube? It must be seven or eight years since I went in the tube.'

'I've brought the car,' said Benet.

In her teens, she used sometimes to say over and over to herself, I must not hate my mother. The injunction had not always been obeyed. And then she would say, But she's ill, she can't help it, she's mad. She had understood and forgiven but she had not wanted to be with her mother. When she went away to university, she had resolved that she would never go back and, except for short holidays, she never had. Her father had retired and her father and mother had bought themselves a little house near Marbella. Mopsa's face and the backs of her hands were tanned by the sunshine of southern Spain. Benet shifted James on to her other hip and he snivelled and clung to her.

'He's got a nasty cold,' said Mopsa. 'I wonder if you ought to have brought him out with a cold like that.'

'I'd no one to leave him with. You know I've just moved house.'

There was a baby seat in the back of the car in which James usually sat contentedly. Benet strapped him in and put Mopsa's cases in the boot. She would have been grateful if her mother had offered to sit in the back with James but Mopsa was already in the passenger seat, her seatbelt fastened, her hands, in rather clumsy black leather gloves, folded in her lap. It didn't seem to occur to her even to talk to James. He was miserable in the back, sneezing sometimes and grizzling quietly. Benet talked to him as she drove, pointing out people and dogs and buildings, anything she thought might be interesting, but she soon became aware of Mopsa's resentment. Mopsa wanted to talk about her own troubles and her own hopes, about Spain and their house and about what she was going to do while in London. Something struck Benet that she had never thought of before, that one always assumes that when mental illness is cured or alleviated one will be left with a nice person, an unselfish, thoughtful, pleasant, sensible person. But of course this wasn't so. Why should it be? Underneath the psychosis there might be just as well be normal nastiness as normal niceness. Not that Mopsa was nasty, far from it. Perhaps what she meant was that Mopsa was, had been, used to be, mad – but when the madness lifted, it revealed a solipsist of a very high order, someone who believed the world to revolve around herself.

The house in Hampstead, in the Vale of Peace, still seemed an alien place to return to. It was only three days since Benet had moved in. Benet slid the car into the narrow lane between high banks which led into this hamlet on the edge of the Heath. For half her life, since the day she had come with friends to the fair that is always held on public holidays just off the Spaniards Road, she had dreamed of living here. Then, when it need not be fantasy any longer, when it was possible, she had planned for it. But Mopsa seemed never to have heard of this celebrated enclave, enbowered by chestnuts and sycamores and Monterey pines, where blue plaques honoured poets dead and gone, a painter, an impresario or two. That Shelley had sailed paper boats on the pond and Coleridge had begun, while sitting on a log on the green, another magical epic never to be completed, were items of literary lore that had never reached her. Getting out of the car, she eyed

Benet's tall and narrow Victorian villa with something like disappointment. What had she expected? An art deco palace in the Bishop's Avenue?

'Well, I don't suppose you wanted anything too ambitious, just you and the baby on your own.'

James wasn't really a baby any more, Benet thought, unlocking the front door. He was a year and nine months old, saying a good many words, understanding more. He clambered up the flight of steps, happier now he was home, probably remembering the treasures awaiting him, the toys that littered the floor of the big basement–kitchen–playroom. Mopsa stepped over him to get to the door. Benet wondered how soon it would be before she began on his fatherless state. Or was she, in spite of the enormous improvement, not quite enough, never to be quite enough, of the conventional suburban middle-aged woman for this to weigh with her? Benet hardly expected to escape without a mention of Edward, the disadvantages of illegitimacy, the threat to a boy's normalcy of growing up only with a mother. She ought to be glad, she told herself, that it was Mopsa who had come and not her father. He was still expressing shocked disbelief over James's very existence.

The house was not yet set to rights. Boxes and crates of still-unwrapped ornaments, kitchen utensils, china and glass and the unending hundreds of books were ranked along the hallway. Leaving for the airport, Benet had come from her task of setting books on the shelves she had had built in the room that would be her study, from attempting some sort of cataloguing system. Spread across the floor in all its sixteen foreign language editions lay her best-selling novel, the source of her affluence, of this house, *The Marriage Knot*. She closed the door to keep James from rampaging among the welter of paperbacks.

Though James seemed even farther from rampaging than he had been in the car. Instead of doing what Benet had expected and rushing back to his newest toy, a xylophone with its octave painted in colours of the spectrum plus one in gold, he had taken himself to his small wicker chair and sat in it, sucking his thumb. His nose had begun to run, and when Benet picked him up, she could hear his breath moving in his chest. It wasn't wheezing exactly, just a sound of his breath moving where there should be no sound. It was warm and cosy in the big basement room, and on a sunny day like this one, bright enough. Benet had had all the kitchen part-fitted with oak units and the floor carpeted in Florentine red and a big cupboard built for James's toys.

Mopsa, having deposited her cases on the bed in the room Benet had got ready for her, came downstairs quite jauntily and said, 'Now I'll take us all out for some lunch.'

'I don't think I ought to take him out again. He doesn't seem very well. We can eat here. I meant to give you lunch here.'

Mopsa showed her displeasure. 'It isn't *cold* even by my Spanish standards.' She laughed, a metallic, rather cracked sound not unlike that made by striking the lowest key of the xylophone. 'You must be a very devoted mother.'

Benet made no answer. She too was amazed by what a devoted mother she had become. Of course she had meant to be that. In having James, in purposefully setting out as an unmarried woman to have a child, she had planned a perfect devotion, an ideal childhood, the best of love and of material things. She had not guessed how little she need have calculated, how absolutely committed to him she would be within a moment of his birth.

She made lunch – soup, wholemeal bread, duck pâté and salad for her and Mopsa, scrambled eggs, fingers of toast and chocolate ice cream for James. Up at the other end of the room, in the window seat with the little front garden and the stone garden wall rising up behind it, Mopsa sat reading the paperback she had brought with her on the plane. She hadn't attempted to take James on to her knee. Benet repressed her indignation, told herself not even to feel it. James's favourite lunch didn't tempt him beyond a few mouthfuls.

'He needs a good sleep,' said Mopsa.

Probably she was right, though Benet thought she said it more from a desire to be rid of him than for his own benefit. James's bedroom was the room in the house she had seen to first, the only one without a still-unemptied crate in it. Benet put his favourite toy, a squashy tiger cub with dangling limbs, into his hands and laid him gently in the cot. James didn't like being put down to sleep in the daytime and usually if this was attempted sat bolt upright at once, putting up importunate arms. This time he lay where he was put, clutching the tiger. His face was flushed as if he might be cutting those awaited back molars. Benet thought there couldn't be much the matter with him. She had had him immunized against every possibly threatening disease. His chest had always been a bit troublesome when he had a cold. It growled now when he breathed in. She sat with him for five minutes until he slept.

'I didn't imagine you'd have all that much maternal feeling,' Mopsa said. She had been up to the chaotic living room and found bottles that hadn't yet been put away and poured herself some brandy. She had never been a hard drinker, never approached alcoholism, but she liked a drink and it sometimes affected her strangely. Benet remembered, from years back, her efforts and her father's to deflect Mopsa from the sherry bottle. Mopsa smiled her vague silly smile, parted lips trembling. 'It's often the case that you don't want them but you come to love them when they arrive.'

'I did want James,' said Benet, and to effect a change of subject, one she knew her mother would be happy to embark on, 'Tell me about these tests you're having done.'

'They haven't got the facilities to do them in Spain. I always did say there's some enzyme or something that's missing in me, that's all it is, and now it looks as if they're coming round to my way of thinking.' Mopsa had for years denied that she was ill at all. It was others who were ill or malicious or lacking in understanding of her. But when realization that she was not normal was inescapable, when in lucid periods she looked back on nightmares, she had come to lay the blame not on psychosis but on a defect in her body's chemistry.

'Take the case of George III,' she would say. 'They thought he was mad for years. They subjected him to hellish tortures. And now they know he had porphyria and just giving him what his body lacked would have made him sane.'

Perhaps she was right. But whatever vital substance she might lack, it now seemed that the deficiency had lately and by natural means made itself good. As Mopsa talked lucidly, and with a good deal of intelligent grasp of detail, of the tests and the complicated processes that would follow them, Benet thought her saner than she had been since she herself was a child. Even the glaze that lay on her greenish-blue eyes seemed to have lifted and been replaced by a more normal inner light.

Mopsa was looking round the room. 'Where's your television?'

'I haven't got it.'

'You mean you haven't got a set at all? I should be lost without the TV, not that it's very good in Spain. I was looking forward to English TV. Why haven't you got it? It can't be that you can't afford it.'

'I write when James is asleep, so that means I mostly write in the evenings and television wouldn't be much use to me.'

'He's asleep now. Do you want to do some writing now? Don't take any notice of me. I'll keep quiet and read my book.'

Benet shook her head. The peculiar conditions necessary for writing – some measure of solitude, a contemplative atmosphere, a certain preparation of the mind – she felt unable to explain to anyone not involved in the process, least of all Mopsa. Besides she was in the highly unusual position of someone who had written down some reminiscences and observations – in her case the time in India with Edward – made them into fiction largely for her own amusement and suddenly finds she has produced a bestseller. An immediate and enormous bestseller. Now she had to write something else, if not to match *The Marriage Knot*, at least to put up a creditable showing beside it. She was the author of what might prove to be a one-off success faced with the hurdle of the 'second book'. It didn't come easily even when she was feeling tranquil and James slept.

That reminded her, he had been asleep for nearly two hours now. She went upstairs to look at him. He was still sleeping, his face rather flushed and his breathing rough. She could see Edward in his face, especially in the curve of his lips and the modelling of his forehead. One day, when he was grown up, he would have those 'English gentleman' looks Edward possessed, flaxen hair, steady blue eyes, strong chin – and perhaps something more than just looks, something more than his father had.

Waiting for him to wake, she stood by the window and watched the setting sun. The sky would become red only after the sun had gone down. Now it was a dark gold, barred with grey, the waters of the Vale of Peace pond sparkling with points of light. A row of Monterey pines on the farther bank stood black and still against the yellow and grey marbling. A good place to live, a fine place for James to grow up in. She had chosen wisely.

Was there some feature of that view, the row of pines perhaps, the sunset, or simply thinking of childhood and an environment for it, that brought back that awful afternoon with Mopsa? She hadn't thought of it for years. Now she remembered it very clearly, though it was nineteen or twenty years ago, but did she remember what had really happened? It had been the first manifestation of Mopsa's madness, her paranoid schizophrenia, that Benet had known. She was eight and the cousin who was with them only three or four. Mopsa had taken them into the dining room of the house they lived in in Colindale and locked the door and bolted it and then phoned Benet's father at work to say she was going to kill the children and then herself. Or had Mopsa only threatened to remain shut in there with the children until some demand of hers was met? The true version was something between the two probably. Why, anyway, would a dining-room door have a bolt on it? But Benet could very clearly remember Mopsa taking knives out of a drawer, the little cousin screaming, Mopsa pulling heavy pieces of furniture, a sideboard, some other sort of cabinet, across the french windows. Most of all she remembered the door coming down, splintering first, and her uncle breaking through, then her father. They had brought no outside aid; shame and fear of consequences had no doubt prevented this. No one had been hurt and Mopsa had become quite calm afterwards so that one wouldn't have guessed anything was wrong with her. Until she had started the compulsive stealing, that had been the next thing. It became impossible to say you wanted anything – anything within reason, that is – without Mopsa stealing it for you. Benet remembered her father admiring a record he had heard in someone's house, a popular, even hackneyed classical piece, Handel's *Water Music* most likely. Mopsa had gone to great pains to find that identical recording in a shop, and when she had found it, she stole it, though she could easily have afforded to buy it. She stole to make gifts to those she loved and the element of risk involved in the theft rendered her gift, so some psychiatrist had said, more valuable in her own eyes. Since then the manifestations of her condition had been many and various: sporadic violence, divorcement from reality, inconsequential 'mad' acts . . .

James turned over, sat up and gave an angry yell, rubbing his eyes with his fists. His cries turned to coughing with a rattle in his chest. Benet picked him up and held him against her shoulder. His chest was a sounding box that made almost musical notes. An idea which had been taking shape of asking people round for drinks – a way of passing the evening and quite a good way now Mopsa was behaving so rationally – no longer seemed feasible. James had a bad cold and would need her attention all evening.

The house felt very warm. She was glad she had had the

central heating system overhauled before she moved in. Mopsa, unpacking her case, her bedroom door open, looked the epitome of a sensible, rather ordinary, housewife. No doubt it was a part she was acting, had perhaps been acting for years. Roles of various kinds had been common with her in the past, all of them seemingly having coalesced into this form. Or was this the real Mopsa, emerging at last from shed layers of psychotic personae?

Now it was even as if her true name, the mundane Margaret, would have suited her better than that which evoked connotations of wildness and witchcraft, ancient familiars, ducking stools, eye of newt and toe of frog. It was not from *Macbeth* though but *The Winter's Tale* that she had named herself when playing the part of Mopsa in a school production at the age of fifteen. Familiar with it as a mother's name, as others might be with a Mary or Elizabeth, Benet nevertheless suddenly saw it as fantastic, incongruous, something that should have been disposed of at the same time as that fleece of blond hair. Mopsa's face, a thin and pointed face, always witchlike, though in Benet's childhood that of a young and beautiful witch, had undergone some blurring of the features that was perhaps part of an ageing process. The jawline was no longer hard and sweeping, the lips were less set. The dowdy haircut made her look very slightly pathetic but possibly no more so than any woman of her age who had no particular purpose in life and was not very well or much loved or needed.

Benet was surprised to find her down in the kitchen making tea for herself. Mopsa generally expected to be waited on wherever she was. Once James was better, Benet thought, they would all go out together. He was almost old enough to be taken to places of interest, to begin anyway. Lunch somewhere nice after Mopsa had been for her hospital appointment and then if the weather were as good as it had been that day, they might go to Hampton Court. Little children became ill and well so quickly, she had already learned that. It wasn't going to be easy getting through this evening. In a day or two she might come to find hiring a television set essential.

'When is his bedtime?' Mopsa said.

'About six-thirty usually but it obviously isn't going to be tonight.'

'You spoil him.'

Benet made no answer to that and Mopsa began to talk of the complexities of getting to the hospital where the first tests were to be carried out. It was such a long way and the underground system had 'all changed' since she had lived in London. She studied a tube map and a street guide. Benet said of course she would take her by car, and if James wasn't well enough to come, she would find someone to sit with him.

When she had been living in her flat in Tufnell Park, a baby-sitter had sometimes been arranged but that was from the block of flats next door where teenage girls abounded, all wanting to earn. Here it was different. She knew no one. She didn't even have friends with small children except Chloe who was currently away on holiday.

Mopsa, never lacking in intuition of a kind, went part of the way towards reading her thoughts. 'Can't you find someone now? I should like us to go out to eat.'

'I couldn't leave him.'

Benet decided to ignore Mopsa's sullen look. Anyway it was becoming a question not of whether she should stay with James or leave him but of taking some more positive step. His forehead felt hot and damp. His breath strained and sometimes a honking sound came from his chest. He had made an attempt to play with the xylophone but had soon come back and climbed on to Benet's lap, the difficulties he was having with breathing making him break into miserable choked cries.

'I'm going to have to ring the doctor.'

'It's seven o'clock. Surely you wouldn't bother an over-worked man like that just because the baby's got a cold.'

'It's a woman,' Benet said and she said no more. In the old days it had always been useless getting cross with

Mopsa, still less losing one's temper. It threw her at once into a desperate frenetic panic. That was years ago now but old habits died hard. Benet reached for the phone and as she did so it rang.

'That'll be your father.'

It was. Mopsa looked complacent. Signs of care and attentiveness towards herself always disproportionately gratified her.

'Hallo, Dad, how are you?' Benet had to move the mouthpiece away from James's loud unhappy crying. 'Sorry, that's poor James giving tongue. He's got a cold.'

Though there had never been anything so dramatic as casting her off from the bosom of the family, though in fact no positive denunciation of her had ever been made, her father had been shocked and outraged by her pregnancy and the birth of James. The situation was made worse by her being an educated person and now a well-off one, living in a society where much was on offer to prevent the births of children outside wedlock. He had never yet actually referred to James by name. When James, as had lately happened, became interested in the telephone and wanted to speak to whomever was on the line, his grandfather had been embarrassed and had spoken gruffly, had barked out a series of hallos and goodbyes and positively panted to get back to Benet. Now when she explained about James's cold, he said only, 'Ah, well.' An awkward pause followed. 'How's your mother? Got there all right, did she?'

'She's fine. Do you want to speak to her?'

The pause was briefer this time but it was there. No doubt John Archdale had loved his wife once. Since then he had had a lot to bear. It wasn't her fault, she was to be pitied, she was just as helplessly ill as if she suffered from multiple sclerosis, but now, instead of love, what he felt was duty; he bore a cross that yearly grew heavier. At the moment he was probably having a little well-earned respite with those expatriate cronies of his, a game of bridge, a drink in the bar of the Miramar. The sound of his wife's voice would not make that evening pleasanter. Benet could do nothing.

'I'll just have a word,' he said.

From time to time in the past, Benet had heard her mother hurl at him a variety of epithets of which 'bag of shit' and 'filthy murderer' was among the mildest. Now Mopsa took the receiver and spoke into it in her sensible housewife role.

'Hallo, dear.'

There was a short interchange. Benet couldn't help feeling indignant that James's name wasn't once mentioned. He was quiet now – that is, he had stopped crying – and leaned heavily against her, the rasps of breath louder than ever.

'Yes, quite a nice flight. One thing you can say for air travel, it doesn't go on for long, it's soon over. I was met and brought here in style. Yes, in the morning, ten in the morning. You'd better phone again tomorrow, hadn't you? I'll say goodbye then.'

She put the phone down and stood staring at Benet with James in her lap. That trembly look, rather as if she were going to cry, which Benet knew of old as presaging a change of mood, had settled on her face. Suddenly Mopsa began to speak in a high and rapid, though not mad, voice.

'I wasn't a good mother to you, Brigitte. I know that. I neglected you – well, I didn't pay enough attention to you. I was ill, you see, I was ill long before you and Dad realized. It was this hormone or whatever it is that's missing, it was missing then, it was affecting me. I wasn't a good mother. I was a lost soul, you see. Can you forgive me?'

Emotional outbursts from Mopsa always embarrassed Benet. She felt awkward, farouche, not least because of the use her mother always fell back on, in times of stress particularly, of the hated given name which, for once following in Mopsa's footsteps, she had divested herself of immediately she left home. Benet was rather angular, long-legged, with pointed features and straight dark hair. How could she have borne to suffer afresh, with a new set of friends, the inevitable mirth and amazement consequent upon being called after Bardot?

She was embarrassed but she had to conquer that embarrassment for poor, pathetic Mopsa's sake. And Mopsa stood there waiting, hungry for love, for reassurance, her breathing fast and nearly as shallow as James's.

'Can you forgive me, Brigitte?'

'There's nothing to forgive. You were ill. Besides, you weren't a bad mother.' Holding James, pressing him against her shoulder, Benet forced herself to get up and put the other arm round her mother. Mopsa was trembling, she quivered like a nervous animal. Benet held her arms round her mother and round James. She kissed Mopsa's cheek. The skin was hot and dry and slightly pulsating. But Mopsa's water-blue eyes were clear and steady and sane. 'I haven't anything to forgive, believe me,' Benet said. 'And now let's forget it, shall we?'

'I'd do anything in the world for you, anything to make you happy.'

'I know.'

Benet sat down by the phone again, settled James on her lap and dialled the doctor's number.

# 2

'He's got croup.'

An onomatopoeic word, roughly the sound James made when he breathed. Benet knew by the immensity of her relief – she could have thrown her arms round Dr McNeil's neck – how worried she had been.

'I thought that was something Victorian children got.'

'They did. Children still do. Only we can do more for them these days.' Causing Benet's relief to plummet like a lead weight, the doctor said, 'I'd like him to go to hospital.'

'Is that absolutely necessary?'

'To be on the safe side. They'll have the equipment. I don't suppose you could achieve a steam-filled room here, could you?'

Dr McNeil was sixty, she was due to retire in a week or two. Was she old-fashioned? Benet wondered. A steam-filled room? She imagined a shower turned on full, crashing nearly boiling water into a bath, the door and window of the bathroom shut. But one of the bathrooms here didn't have a shower at all and the other had one that was hopelessly furred up, waiting for a replacement.

'What exactly is croup?'

'If you had it, we'd call it laryngitis.'

Benet left the doctor to make phone calls. She carried James down into the kitchen where Mopsa, very practical in apron and rubber gloves, was washing up cups and saucers. Relief had returned. Croup was only laryngitis.

'I'll come with you,' Mopsa said.

Benet would have preferred her mother to stay here but she didn't know how to say so. And perhaps Mopsa shouldn't be left alone, especially at night and in a strange place. It was unfortunate Mopsa happened to be here at this particular time. Benet could not help reflecting that, when people said they would do anything in the world to make you happy, they never meant things like keeping in the background, not interfering, acceding to your small requests.

At any rate this time Mopsa sat in the back of the car, holding James. The night was clear but moonless. Benet realized suddenly that it was Hallowe'en. She carried James, wrapped in a big fleecy blanket, into the big old vaulted Gothic vestibule of the hospital and then they were sent up to the ward in the lift.

Not very familiar with hospitals – she had been in one only once and that when James was born – Benet had expected a long ward with beds close together and ranged along both sides. But Edgar Stamford Ward was all small rooms with a wide corridor down the centre. The building, she had heard, had once been the old workhouse, but this part must have been gutted to make the children's department, for nothing nineteenth century remained except for the windows with their small panes and pointed arches. In James's room, a tent over a cot into which steam was being pumped awaited James. The nurse called it a croupette. He had been in it for about ten minutes, protesting at first, then lying quietly and clutching Benet's hand, when the doctor arrived to look at him. In the doorway he took off his hospital jacket and laid it across the sister's desk.

'They get white-coat phobia if we don't do that,' he said. 'Won't even go in the butcher's with you.' He smiled. 'My name's Ian Raeburn. I'm one of the registrars here.'

There was a bed beside the cot. She was sitting on it. She had noticed it was made up with sheets and blankets.

'Can I stay here with him?'

'Sure you can if you want. That's what the bed's for. And you've got a bathroom next door. We're rather proud in here of encouraging parents to stay – a change from the bad old days.'

25

'I'd like to stay.'

Mopsa said in a small lost voice, 'What about me?'

'I'll leave you to decide about that,' said Dr Raeburn. 'I think you'll find James will be easier now he's in the tent.'

The fingers clutching her finger had not slackened. 'You can have a taxi back, Mother. I'll come down with you and call you a taxi. You'll be all right.'

Mopsa's face had grown soft, putty-like, tremulous. Her lips shook. The bedroom was very dimly lit, a single low-wattage bulb gleaming from a fitting on the wall above the washbasin, and in this gloom the glazed look had come back into her eyes. It was the first time since her arrival that Benet had seen that look.

'I'm never left on my own. It was bad enough being alone in the plane, I mean, without anyone I know. I can't be all on my own in a strange house.'

'It would only be for one night.'

'Why do you have to stay with him? He's asleep, he won't know whether you're there or not. Parents never used to stay in hospitals with children, it was unheard-of, the staff wouldn't have put up with it.'

'Things have changed.'

'Yes and for the worse. Your father wouldn't have let me come if he'd known you were going to leave me on my own, Brigitte. I'll be ill if you leave me on my own.'

Benet carefully disengaged her finger from James's grasp. He did not move. She was filled with an intense dislike of Mopsa, something that verged on hatred. When her mother was rational like this, though exhibiting all the signs of solipsism – indifference to others' wishes, deep selfishness – the feeling that all her madness was an act put on to gain attention was inescapable. Of course it wasn't, it was as real as a physical paralysis. And if it were an act, wasn't that in itself a sign of madness, that anyone would take an act so far?

I must not hate my mother . . .

'You'll be quite safe. There are bars on the ground-floor

windows, there's a phone on each floor. It's not exactly a rough area, is it?'

'I'm not going without you, Brigitte. You can't make me. I can sleep in the chair here. I can sleep on the floor.'

'They won't let you,' Benet said. 'They'll only allow parents. Look, I'll drive you home and then I'll come back here. I'll come home again first thing in the morning.'

'I have to go for my tests first thing in the morning.'

Mopsa's face was stubborn and set. All the pointed, sharp witch look had come back. Her clouded eyes were fixed not on Benet but on a point in the far corner of the room. Benet looked at James. He was asleep and the vaporizer was gently and steadily puffing steam into the croupette. She picked her coat off the bed. She thought she saw surprise, perhaps a little more than that, in the ward sister's expression when she said she wouldn't be staying overnight. Mopsa, who had spent long stretches of her life in hospitals, wasn't happy here. She darted wary glances from side to side as they walked towards the lift, especially at the sign pointing in the direction of the psychiatric clinic.

The house had a welcoming feel in spite of the crates still waiting to be unpacked. It was warm and bright and comfortable. Yet for Benet the night was almost a sleepless one. She could not rid her mind of the image of James waking up in that steamy hothouse and finding her gone. What use was she to her mother? Mopsa had taken a sleeping pill the moment they got back to the Vale of Peace, had fallen asleep ten minutes later and had been sleeping ever since. Passing her door at six in the morning on her way to make tea, Benet heard Mopsa's regular breathing with a hint of a snore in it.

She phoned the hospital, spoke to the staff nurse on Edgar Stamford Ward and was told James was much the same. He had passed a restless night. The staff nurse didn't say if he had called for Benet or cried for her and Benet could not bring herself to ask. She knew he must have done. He had never before been parted from her. If only

Mopsa's tests were being done at the same hospital! Instead she was going to have to drive her miles across the sprawl of north London suburbs and fight her way back again through the traffic before she could go to James. For the first time in her relationship with James, she felt guilt, she felt she had failed him.

Mopsa appeared at eight, dressed in the skirt of the grey suit and a harebell-blue angora jumper with a string of pearls round her neck. This morning she was not so much the sensible housewife as the svelte businesswoman. Even her hair, probably from the position in which it had been pressed into the pillow, looked less uncompromisingly chopped off. Discreet make-up, pinkish and mauvish, lessened the years and the ducking stool image. She didn't ask about James and Benet didn't tell her she had phoned the hospital. She was full of the prospect of her tests. Did she look all right? Should she wear her blue raincoat or the jacket of the suit or both?

James might not have existed. Benet felt an actual physical pain at this neglect of him, she couldn't eat, she was choked with resentment at Mopsa's attitude and with love for him. She wanted to get hold of Mopsa and shake her and shout into her face, this is my child, this is my son, don't you realize? It would be useless, it would be cruel and pointless.

I must not hate my mother . . .

Once they were in the car, driving along Hampstead Lane, she found a practical calm voice.

'I'm going to leave you at the Royal Eastern and go to James. You must either take a taxi back home or to the hospital where James is. It's quite simple and you'll be fine. I've written down both addresses for you.'

She waited for the storm of protest but none came. Mopsa was in euphoric mood, anxious to please, graciously prepared to be unselfish. Of course she would have a taxi, of course she would be all right. She was sorry she had insisted on Benet's coming back with her the night before, but things felt different at night, didn't they? On a bright morning like this one you could hardly believe how bad you had felt at night, how disorientated and alone and afraid.

Benet came back by the same route, the same short cut through back streets, as that by which she had taken Mopsa to the Royal Eastern Hospital in Tottenham. The traffic piled up as she was waiting to turn out of Rudyard Gardens into Lordship Avenue – there were roadworks in progress at the junction – so, taking her place in the slow-moving queue, she was able to look around her at this district where she had once lived.

It was very much changed. The trees in Rudyard Gardens had been pollarded and had become an avenue of beheaded trunks. The rows of houses were no longer inhabited, their doors and windows boarded up with sheets of corrugated metal. Mopsa would have called it a slum. On the far side of Lordship Avenue the sun shone out of a hard blue sky on to the blocks and terraces and single tower of a housing estate called Winterside Down. When she and Mary and Antonia had shared their attic in Winterside Road, the estate had not yet been built. There had only been their road overlooking a stretch of desolate land extending from the gasworks to the canal.

Her car and the three ahead moved slowly up to the junction. A black Dobermann pinscher was strolling over the pedestrian crossing. It reached the Rudyard Gardens side and the traffic began to shift again. Just at this point, Benet remembered, she had used to catch the bus that took her down into the City and the offices of the magazine she had been working for. If it hadn't been for James, for hurrying to be with James, she would have turned into Winterside Road and parked the car, for just as the traffic began to move she saw someone she knew. Tall, heavily-built, fair, getting on for forty now probably – what was his name? Tom something. Tom Woodhouse. He had had the garage next to the house where their flat was and once or twice she had rented a car from him. Benet wound down the window, called his name and waved but the traffic roar drowned her voice. She watched him in her rearview mirror as he went across the zebra crossing and got into the cab of a parked van.

James wasn't in the croupette or even in his room but in the children's playroom chalking on a blackboard. When Benet came in, he didn't run to her or hold out his arms but only smiled a radiant and somehow mysterious smile as if he and she were together in some secret conspiracy. He said to a small girl: 'That's my mummy.'

'We'd like him to have one quiet night in here before he goes home,' the sister said.

Mopsa arrived at twelve. She looked pleased with herself, almost jaunty. They had done no tests on her at the Royal Eastern, only examined her and questioned her and made a new appointment for three days' time.

'I shall risk it on my own in your house tonight.'

'It would be a great help if you could.' Benet felt absurdly grateful. 'It's very brave of you.'

Suddenly Mopsa had become the sensible no-nonsense woman who stayed by herself in strange houses night after night. 'I shall take a pill. I shan't know a thing till morning.'

James ran about playing all day. By six he was asleep, rather pale, breathing heavily, exhausted. One more night and he could go home.

'I ought to be there now,' said Mopsa, looking at her watch. 'I expect your father's been phoning. I expect he was worried when I wasn't there.'

'I'll come down with you and help you find a taxi.'

'I thought I might drive your car.'

It was dark. The streets here were narrow and congested. Mopsa had held a driving licence for thirty years but not driven for the past fifteen.

'I'd rather you practised in daylight first,' Benet said.

Mopsa argued about it while putting her coat on, she argued about it in the lift, surprisingly giving way without another word when Benet said she had left the car keys up in the room and the spare set at home. The night was black and damp with a smell of gunpowder in the air. Children had been letting fireworks off in advance of Guy Fawkes Day. Mopsa waved from the taxi window, she leaned out and waved as if she were going away for ever.

James's crying awoke Benet after about three hours. She had been dreaming of Edward, the first time she had dreamed of him for months. She was telling Edward she was going to have a child, his child, and no, she didn't want an abortion, she wanted the child, and the alternative was not marriage, she didn't want to marry him or even be with him any more . . . It had been very much like that, things in reality had been very much like that dream. Waking up was a shock because she had thought the dream was real. James was sitting up inside the croupette, crying and sobbing.

Benet picked him up and held him and he stopped crying, though his breathing was rough again. She wondered if this would count against a 'quiet' night. The next doctor or nurse to look in would probably ask her and she couldn't lie to them, for James's sake she wouldn't dare. The room was not dark, it was still lit by the single dim wall light. It was very quiet for a hospital, silent but for a distant faint metallic clattering. She started thinking about Mopsa. She was aware that it was a mistake to admit anxieties into her mind at this hour, but, once there, they stuck, they refused to go away. Had she been wrong to let Mopsa go off alone? Suppose she hadn't been able to find the doorkey? Or once she was in, suppose the lights had fused? Benet was sure her father would never have allowed Mopsa to be alone. And if Mopsa had got into the house safely, had answered the phone and spoken to him, was he too lying sleepless down there in the south of Spain, worrying about his wife, furious with his daughter, thinking of all the things that might happen?

James was sleeping now against her shoulder. She laid him back in the cot inside the tent and put her hand through the opening in the zip so that he could hold it. When the nurse came in at four he was still sleeping and Benet said nothing about the disturbance of two hours before. She went to sleep herself, she had no more dreams. The room was beginning to lighten, a grey dawn showing through the slats of the blinds, when next she woke. A siren had awakened her, and when she knelt up and looked out of the window, she saw an ambulance passing with its blue light on.

As soon as it got to eight Benet thought she would phone the house in the Vale of Peace. It was not yet half-past seven. Mopsa was not a late riser, she was always up and about by eight. Inside the steamy tent James slept, lying on his back, the vaporizer puffing away. They would let her take him home before lunch. Then a week or two for convalescence, and once Mopsa had gone back, there was no reason why the two of them, she and James, should not go away for a holiday. Why not? She could afford it now. She could afford any amount of holidays, or tax-deductible working trips, as her accountant called them.

'You don't have holidays any more, Miss Archdale.'

They could go somewhere warm, North Africa, or the Canaries. James wouldn't get croup there. Her American publishers wanted her to go to California as part of a promotional trip and she could pay a visit to Universal Studios where they had begun shooting *The Marriage Knot* . . .

James had opened his eyes. He was moving his head from side to side, rubbing his eyes with his fists. The floppy-legged tiger cub lay sprawled on the pillow beside him. Benet ran the drumstick down the painted octave of the xylophone, *do-re-mi-fa-so-la-ti-do*. Usually that alerted him. He would reach for the stick and want to play the notes himself. She unzipped the tent. He put out his arms and said, 'Mummy,' but he didn't raise his head from the pillow.

Benet lifted him on to her lap. His forehead was hot and he was breathing the way he had done the evening she had brought him in. He very obviously wasn't over it yet; he was less well than he had been the day before.

'You're my poor lamb, aren't you? It's giving you a really hard time.'

The nurse came in with a thermometer. Benet left James with her and went down the corridor to the pay phone. The time was just on eight. In the house in the Vale of Peace there was a phone on each floor, you didn't have to run downstairs or up when the phone rang. Benet dialled her own number, wondering what kind of storm would break when she had told Mopsa that James was going to have to stay in hospital for more days and more nights and she was going to have to stay with him.

The phone started ringing. It rang and rang. Benet put the receiver back and tried again in case she had misdialled. Still there was no answer. It was early yet, it was possible Mopsa was still asleep.

Breakfast had arrived. Cornflakes, a boiled egg and bread and marmalade for herself, milk, baby cereal and an orange for James. James wouldn't eat. He clung to her, clutching her round the neck while she tried to eat cornflakes. The day sister came in, said she would like him to be in the croupette, would Benet please try and keep him in the croupette, and Dr Raeburn would be along to see him in about an hour.

James pushed the milk away with his arm, spilling it over Benet's jeans. She got him to lie down inside the tent by inserting the upper half of her own body in with him. The vaporizer puffed away steadily.

'He's got a little temperature,' the nurse said, filling in his chart. 'It would be good for him to have a little sleep.'

Finally he did sleep and she went back to the phone. She dialled her own number and it started to ring. She was aware of a tight feeling of anxiety beginning to knot inside her. The phone rang ten times, fifteen times. She put the receiver back and she didn't dial again because there was a woman in a dressing gown with a bandaged leg waiting to use it. Benet recalled how, when she herself had been about thirteen, Mopsa had disappeared without warning and been found two days later wandering in Northampton (in a sleeveless dress) having apparently lost her memory. No one ever found out how she got there or where the dress, which was not one of her own, had come from.

Mopsa might never have gone back to the Vale of Peace last night. As soon as she was out of sight, she might easily have altered the directions to the taxi driver. Benet wondered if she should phone the police, then dismissed the idea as extreme. Later in the day, especially if James got up and played with the other children as he had been doing, she would take the opportunity to rush home for an hour.

Mopsa had seemed so sane, so ordinary, so normal. But perhaps she had always been at her sanest, or appeared to be so, before a bout of madness. If she hadn't gone to the Vale of Peace, where would she go? She knew no one in London now except those old neighbours, the Fentons, and very likely they too had moved away by now.

The woman with the bandaged leg finished her call and Benet dialled again. There was no reply. Benet found it impossible to imagine her mother going for a walk or getting a taxi to come here, but how well did she know her mother? What did she know of her except that she was totally unpredictable? Once Mrs Fenton had found her lying in a bath in reddening water, her wrists cut . . .

It took Benet a long time to get hold of a London telephone directory E–K but at last she did and found the Fentons' number. They were still there at number 55 Harper Lane, or Mrs Fenton was. The number was listed in the name of Mrs Constance Fenton, so perhaps her husband had died in the meantime. Benet dialled her own number again and, when there was no reply, Mrs Fenton's. A young woman's voice answered.

'That was my daughter,' Constance Fenton said when she came to the phone. 'I've got my daughter and my son-in-law and my grandson staying with me till their house is ready.' She was a woman who had the rather pleasant habit of talking to you as if the last time you had conversed had been yesterday and not ten years ago.

Benet asked her, warily, tactfully, if by any chance her mother was there.

'Your *mother*?'

Then Benet knew at once Mopsa wasn't there, hadn't been there. Constance Fenton wanted to know all about Mopsa. Was she in London? When was she coming to visit? What a delightful surprise it was, how much she looked forward to seeing Mopsa!

'I know she'll be in touch with you very soon,' Benet said. She put the phone down. She had begun to feel sick with dread. Mopsa might be anywhere, a danger to herself and others.

# 3

The Chinese bridge spanned the canal from Winterside Road to the path that crossed the green lawns and penetrated the estate. Barry had wondered why they called it Chinese until he had seen one just like it on an old willow-pattern plate round at Iris's. Winterside Down was a little world that had everything in it you wanted and plenty you didn't. The streets were all named after people from the Labour Party's past. There was a square in the middle of it called Bevan Square with a shopping precinct, a sub-post office, a unisex hair stylist, a video centre and a Turkish takeaway. Most of the people were of Greek or Irish or West Indian origin, though there were some Indians too. It was all quite new, the oldest houses only six years old, and it hadn't yet settled down. They had built one tower block and then apparently decided people didn't want tower blocks and were frightened of living in them, so that single tower stood out of the middle of Winterside Down like an enormous lighthouse, surrounded by the pygmy houses that people did want to live in.

The Isadoros lived in two, they were such a big family. The council had put an arch between the hallways so that you could go through from one house to the other without going outside. Carol's was just an ordinary single house, part of a terrace, one of the oldest. When you came into Winterside Down by way of the Chinese bridge, the first part of the estate you saw was the back of that terrace, and if Carol was at home, you could see her lights on. It seldom happened that Barry came home later than Carol, but if he did, or thought he was going to be later, he would look for her lights as soon as he came to the crown of the bridge.

Her house was the eighth from where the path came into Summerskill Road. He would count, two-four-six-eight, and if the lights were on feel a surge of joy, a leaping of the heart.

Mostly he got home first. It had been home to him for the past six months, not the kind of place he would have chosen to live in, but home because Carol was there. When she worked evenings at the wine bar, he didn't come the Chinese bridge way but by the main turn-in from Lordship Avenue. Sometimes the Isadoros looked after Jason in the daytime and sometimes his grandmother, Iris, did or, rarely, his aunt Maureen. Barry called round at Iris's place on his way home, but Jason had fallen asleep watching the TV and Iris had put him to bed. He might as well stop the night, why not? She was having him in the morning anyway.

Barry walked home across Bevan Square. He went into the tobacconist, open till eight, and bought twenty Marlboro. He had never used to smoke, but being with Carol so much and Carol's family, he was on to twenty a day now. The square was paved in pinkish-red with flowerbeds surrounded by low brick walls and with a statue in the middle of it that looked like a piece of car bodywork from a scrapheap but was by quite a famous sculptor and called *The Advance of Man*. A smell of garlic and fat hung about the Turkish takeaway. The eldest Isadoro girl and a boy Barry didn't know sat on one of the flowerbed walls, eating kebab and chips out of paper cones.

It was dark, the place painted with the brownish-yellow light from the sodium lamps that stood on concrete stilts above Winterside Down. The light turned everything to khaki and yellow and black. Of the boys who huddled or lounged over their motorbikes all round the statue, one had red and yellow hair in a crest like a hoopoe's and another had dyed his blue, but the light turned all to yellow-brown and glittered like crumbling gold leaf on their black leathers. Those boys were not much younger than Barry, they were almost his contemporaries, but he felt immeasurably older than his twenty to their seventeen or eighteen. In taking on Carol, in becoming, so to speak, the father of a ready-made family, he had leaped half a dozen years.

Her husband's photograph, in a plastic frame from Woolworth's, stood on the shelf over the living-room radiator. It was the only photograph in the house. Dave. He was dead, killed when the lorry he had been driving went over a mountainside in Yugoslavia. A tall, thin, dark-haired man, Dave had been, with blue eyes and an Irish mouth. Barry didn't look like him but they belonged to the same type, Carol's type. Soon after they had first met and he had gone home with her, Carol had told him he was her type and shown him the photograph of Dave.

Barry dusted the photograph. He dusted the few ornaments in the room and the phone and the back of the television set and then he got the vacuum cleaner out and vacuumed the bit of carpet that had been Iris's before she went mad (as she put it) and had wall-to-wall. He kept the house clean for Carol, it was the least he could do. Before he had moved in, it had been a tip which was only what you'd expect in the home of someone who had three kids and two jobs.

There was nothing demeaning or emasculating to Barry in house-cleaning. His mother, had she known, would have sneered and called it woman's work. But Barry belonged to a generation in which the girls resented menial tasks even more than the boys. He might take it for granted that his mother cleaned and washed and polished but not the woman he lived with. Why should she? She worked as hard as he did.

He cleaned the hall as well and stripped the bed and changed the sheets. The only nice furniture in the house was in this bedroom, Carol's bedroom and now his too. The cupboard which Dave had built in when they first moved here and the house was new had its doors made of mirror. It was on the wall facing the bed. Carol liked to sit up in the mornings and look at herself. It brought her a childlike pleasure that warmed Barry's heart to look at herself in mirrors.

Barry put the sheets and pillowcases into a plastic carrier with a pile of smelly napkins of Jason's and took the lot round to the laundrette in Bevan Square. Blue Hair and Hoopoe and the rest of them were still there but clustered now round an old American car, a Studebaker, parked on the edge of the precinct with its windows open and its radio playing loud rock music. Barry felt old, but in a way he felt proud too and responsible. He and Carol had met in a laundrette, though not this one. His mother's washing machine had broken down and he had taken a couple of pairs of jeans to do himself. Carol had come in with two loads. She had had Ryan and Tanya home for the weekend and Four Winds didn't like it if you sent the kids back with a lot of dirty washing.

Those two big children – he had thought they were her brother and sister. He had thought her the same age as himself or younger. It wasn't possible she was twenty-eight. Maureen said Carol had a face like a doll and in a way that was true, but dolls were made that way, to look like beautiful children, that was the idea, wasn't it? Carol's face was round and her upper lip very short, her skin pink and white china and her hair the kind of golden curls that cluster baby-like over forehead and temples, ring curls, coin curls, damp-looking like a child's. And her sea-blue eyes had met his and she had smiled.

He fell in love with her, he often thought afterwards, even before she spoke. When she did speak, it was to see if he had any change for her second machine. He hadn't – who ever has enough in a laundrette? But he told her where change was to be come by.

'Get your sister to go next door but one to the paper shop. They've always got change.'

She looked at him sideways, charmingly. She lowered her long dark curling lashes.

'Flattery could get you a long way, d'you know that?'

He hadn't known what she meant, and when she

explained, he couldn't believe it. It was hard for him to believe his luck too, that he had met Carol and she liked him. Two days later he was in her house and he was asking who the man in the photograph was and she was saying: 'You're the same type really. I always say that's *my* type.'

Rolling up the clean sheets, stuffing them back into the bag, he set off home to wait for her. After six months he still got exciting thinking about her coming home, waiting for the sound of her key in the lock. Still? It was stronger now than it had been at first. Best of all, he liked coming home at night over the Chinese bridge – on whose wooden parapet he had joined the other graffitists and printed in aerosol paint: *Barry loves Carol* – and counting the houses and seeing the lights in the eighth one and knowing she was there, longing for him as he was longing for her.

Just before eleven-thirty he thought he heard a car outside but he must have been mistaken because Carol never had a taxi or a mini-cab, they couldn't afford it. It was coincidence, that was all, that a minute or two after he heard the car Carol's key turned in the lock. He had been watching television and he turned it off as she came in.

She had had quite a bit to drink. Who wouldn't have, working six hours in a wine bar? It was only human nature. Her cheeks were flushed pink and her greeny-blue eyes very bright. She came a little way into the room and took an extravagant pose, lifting up her arms, turning slowly round to twirl the skirts of the black and white zig-zag striped dress above her red boots.

'That's new,' said Barry. 'Where did you get that?'

Carol began to laugh. 'Nicked it. How about that?' She pulled him into the armchair and sat on his knee. 'Mrs Fylemon went out to have lunch with her mum so I whipped round quick with the Hoover and got done by two and then I got on the bus and went down Shopper's Heaven. There's this new boutique I've had my eye on. They only let you take two things in the changing room with you. The girl said how many had I got there and I said two though I'd got three. I'd put a black one on the hanger over this one. I put this one on and my jumper and skirt over it and I didn't hang about. I took the other two back and said they were too big and just sailed out though I was laughing inside fit to kill myself.'

'That was clever,' said Barry admiringly. 'I wouldn't like you to get caught, love.'

Carol stroked his hair, and rubbed his nose with her nose. 'I won't get caught. I'm too careful.' Her fingers moved over the nape of his neck. 'Dennis Gordon was in Kostas's. He kept on about my dress, wanted to know if I'd ever done any modelling. Modelling, I said, what's that supposed to mean?'

'You don't like him, do you, Carol?' said Barry.

'He's okay. I don't fancy him if that's what you mean. He was a pal of Dave's. He reminds me a bit of Dave, him being on the lorries too. D'you know, he told Kostas he makes so much doing the Turkey run he can't afford to live here really, he ought to live in one of them tax havens. How about that?'

'I wish he would. I wish he'd go and live in Jersey or Ireland or somewhere.'

'I believe you're jealous, Barry Mahon!'

'I'm not ashamed to admit it. Wouldn't you be jealous of me?'

She snuggled close to him, put her lips against his ear. 'I reckon. Let's go to bed, lover.'

His voice grew hoarse. 'I won't say no to that.'

On the stairs she remembered Jason.

'Stopping the night with your mum,' said Barry.

That was a relief to her. She danced into the bedroom and peeled the new dress over her head. Underneath it she wore only tights, black, see-through. Carol seldom wore a bra, she didn't need to, her breasts were as firm as the buds of large white flowers.

'You're going to marry me, aren't you, Carol?' he said, holding her, touching the warm, damp, creamy flesh. The bedlamp was on, the clean sheets turned back.

'Maybe,' said Carol, teasing. 'I reckon. Some day. You've got a pretty face and Christ knows you're a great stud.'

'But you do love me?'

'Haven't I said?'

Barry had had quite a lot of girls before he met Carol but he might truthfully have said that, before he made love to her, he had never made love. It was something different, it was something he hadn't known there could be. And it was not without its frightening side, for the passion he felt and its fulfilment brought him not so much satisfaction as awe. He lost himself in Carol and found something he couldn't name. He underwent a mystical experience such as he imagined you might feel under the influence of certain kinds of drugs of a curious mind-altering intensity, but this experience had no side-effects except to heighten his love.

When, afterwards, they composed themselves for sleep, Carol curled up against him and held his hand in her hand between her breasts. He was supremely happy then, he was happier than he had ever been in his life.

# 4

When she had tried to phone Mopsa again and there was still no answer, Benet walked back to James's room and found Ian Raeburn with him. Once more he had taken off his white coat so as not to create a phobia in James. He had his stethoscope held against the small, rapidly rising and falling chest.

'He seems to have got a secondary infection,' he said, emerging from the glistening folds of the croupette. 'It's not responding to the antibiotic. I'm sorry to disappoint you but you won't have him home for a while yet.'

Benet had known it but it was still a blow to have it confirmed. She sat down on the bed and put one hand up to her forehead.

'You're not worried, are you?' he said.

'Oh, not about James, no. I know he's being looked after here. It's my mother. My mother's staying with me and she's not very well and she really shouldn't be left on her own.'

But she had left her and where was she now? He asked no questions about Mopsa. Perhaps he had already discerned it was mental instability she was talking about.

'Couldn't you find someone else for your mother to stay with? To take a load off your mind?'

The Fentons? Could she ring Constance Fenton and ask her to have for Mopsa for a day or two? It would have to be fixed so that Mopsa didn't know it was a put-up job. What was the use of even thinking of such a thing when she didn't know where Mopsa was? Ian Raeburn was looking at her, not a doctor-to-patient's-mother look at all. Benet thought she recognized that look as of a man taking an interest in her as a woman. No man had done that for two-and-a-half years, there hadn't been the opportunity or, on her part, the wish for it. He was rather a personable man, she noticed for the first time – tall, thin, inclined to be but not markedly sickle-faced, his hair a reddish-blond. She wondered what he was going to say.

'You are *the* Benet Archdale, aren't you?'

'I suppose so. Yes, I am.'

So much for his being interested in her as a woman. She almost laughed.

'I liked your book very much. It must be the worst cliché a writer hears when people say they don't have time for reading. I made time to read it and I hope my patients didn't suffer.'

She was so warmed and delighted by what he said that it carried her for a few moments above her worries over Mopsa and James. It was somehow as gratifying as getting her first good review had been. She smiled with pleasure. How could she have been so foolish, so female in the worst possible way, as to fancy she would have preferred sexual attention to *that*?

'How do you come to know so much about India?'

'I was there for six months with James's father. He was planning a series of articles about an Indian mystic.' She began telling him about Acharya the Learned One and his 40,000-mile walk.

A nurse came in to say he was wanted. Could he come now? Benet had forgotten to ask him if it would be all right for her to go home for an hour to look for Mopsa. But now she could see that this would in any case be impossible for her. James couldn't be left. He lay on his back, listlessly holding the tiger cub. His eyes were wide open, unblinking in their distress at the shallow noisy breaths he was forced to take. At this time yesterday she had been in the children's playroom with him while he trundled a wheelbarrow full of bricks and drew on the blackboard.

They said now that he had a virus infection. There was a drug to treat it but it was very new and still only in use in certain teaching hospitals. It might be thirty-six hours before James began to respond to the drug. After a while he cried to be taken out of the tent. Benet lay on the bed and held him against her, rocking him gently. It was wrong to keep him out of the tent. The more he was kept in there, even against his will, the more quickly he would recover. And he must recover soon, he must be up and about and playing by tomorrow so that she could put an end to the imprisonment that kept her from her responsibilities to Mopsa. Somehow she knew that one day he would see it that way too, he would share in the burden his mother and grandfather had. She imagined him a teenager, becoming responsible, and talking to him about his grandmother, teaching him to understand.

If Mopsa were still alive when James was a teenager. If she were still alive now . . . He fell asleep, lying against her, and she put him gently back into the tent, hating that breathing of his, physically hurt by it. But he was sleeping and the vaporizer was steaming up the tent and the anti-viral drug had begun its work. She left him and went back down the corridor to the phone.

A young woman with a child on her lap was using it. The playroom door was open so she went in and sat on one of the chairs for five-year-olds that were set round the table. There was a Wendy house in the playroom, a bookcase of books, boxes of toys, a cage with two gerbils in it and, all over the walls, posters and drawings and collages. Paper cut-out witches riding up the window panes on paper cut-out broomsticks reminded her of Mopsa, though she needed no reminding. On the inside of the door a dozen or so children had written, or had had written for them, their names underneath the heading: *We have had our tonsils out*. The dominating collage was a piece of bizarrerie, the brainchild evidently of someone with a B.Ed and flair, a mural whose paper base sheet filled half a wall.

Benet, when she had seen it the day before, had immediately dubbed it a tree of hands. She had liked it then, it had even made her smile. Now it seemed to her sinister,

Daliesque, haunting, something about which one might have bad dreams. On the white paper base sheet had been drawn a tree with a straight brown trunk and branches and twigs, and all over the tree, on the branches, nestling among the twigs, protruding like fungus from the trunk, were paper hands. All were exactly the same shape, presumably cut out by individual children using a template of an open hand with the fingers spread slightly apart. And the children must have been allowed to decorate them as they pleased, for some were gloved, some tattooed, some ladies' hands with red nails and rings, one in mittens and another in mail, mostly white but some black or brown, one the stripped bone hand of a skeleton. And now to Benet all those hands seemed to be held upwards, to be straining upwards in silent supplication as if imploring mercy. They reached out from the tree begging for relief or freedom or perhaps for oblivion. They were horrible. There was an essentially mad quality about them. She found that she had got up from the low chair and gone close to the tree of hands to stare at it with fascinated repulsion. As soon as she realized how hypnotically she was staring, she pulled herself away and went out into the corridor to the phone which was now free.

The repeated hollow ringing had a dull meaningless sound. Benet listened to the ringing, she let it ring on and on. An idea had come to her that Mopsa might simply have decided not to answer the phone but she would have to if it rang long enough. She let it ring forty times, fifty times, until going on any longer became absurd.

The best that could have happened to Mopsa was that the change of scene, the new ways, being abandoned to look after herself, had been too much for her and she had wandered off in the manner of the Northampton escapade. Looking out at the clear hard blue sky and the racing wind, Benet hoped she hadn't done it in her nightgown. But that was the best. There were other options. The overdose of sleeping pills and the rest of the brandy or the sleeping pill ten minutes before she took a bath or the barricading of herself in one of the rooms with a can of paraffin and a box of matches. Surely there hadn't been any paraffin in the house or matches either for that matter . . .

If she phoned the police, they would want her to go to the police station and fill in a 'Missing Persons' form. Of course she could ask them to come here and collect her key and let themselves into the house in the Vale of Peace. But would they do that? She must try, that was all. As soon as Mr Drew, the ear, nose and throat specialist, had been to see James, she would go back down the corridor and phone the police.

He came at two, accompanied by Ian Raeburn and a couple of house officers. Mr Drew was shortish, thick-set, wearing a brown tweed suit and gold-rimmed glasses. James began crying at the sight of the white coats which the house officers hadn't remembered to take off. When he cried, it made him choke.

Drew was one of those doctors of the old school who never tell a patient or a patient's next-of-kin anything if they can help it. If they can't help it, they talk to them as if they were illiterate half-wits or simple-minded peasants. He said nothing at all to Benet, talked to Ian Raeburn in polysyllabic words of Greek aetiology, and walked out leading his little procession. James put out his arms to be picked up but the nurse said he had to stay inside the croupette. The hectic flush had faded from his cheeks and he had become pale again. His pulse was taken and Benet asked what it was.

Was there ever a nurse born who would answer that question? 'He's not a very well little boy, are you, sweetheart?'

When they were alone again, Benet put her hand inside the tent for him to hold. Her hand did not interest him. He let her take his, he suffered her touch. All his energies, all his will, seemed concentrated on maintaining his own breathing. Benet held his hand and came as close to him as she could. To leave him and phone the police, to leave

47

him even for those few short minutes, she could see was out of the question. If Mopsa were wandering, she would be found, and if she were dead – well, she was dead and it was too late. Benet took James's wrist and began to count his pulse beats, looking at her watch. A hundred, a hundred and ten, twenty, forty, sixty, eighty . . . He couldn't have a pulse rate of a hundred and eighty a minute, she must have counted wrong. His forehead was cool and dry, his temperature was normal.

So perhaps he was not so very ill. The first infection had passed off quickly so it was very likely this secondary one would too. If only he wouldn't breathe in that awful way, puffing like a little weak, feverish, anxious bellows, the way she had never heard anyone breathe before. The door opened, the procession came back, Mr Drew leading it.

'Now then, this is James, isn't it? And you are the mother? I'm going to have to do a little operation on James to relieve his breathing.'

Benet stood up. She felt as if a heavy stone, for some while lodged in her throat, were slowly rolling down through her body.

'An operation?'

'Nothing too serious. Just to relieve the breathing. For a few days he'll be breathing through his neck instead of his nose and mouth.'

The stone rolled out of her, leaving her with a sick, dry, bruised feeling. 'Do you mean a tracheotomy?'

Mr Drew looked at her as if she had no business to know the word, much less utter it. It was Ian Raeburn who answered.

'It will be a tracheotomy, yes. The larynx in a child of James's age is very narrow, only about four millimetres across. If you get a millimetre and a half swelling on one side and a millimetre and a half on the other you haven't much space left to get air through. Now James's larynx is closing up and we aren't able to dilate it sufficiently with the ventilator.'

A nurse came up with the form for her to sign consenting to the operation. Her hand wasn't very steady.

'Mr Drew is very experienced,' Ian Raeburn said. 'Only a week ago he had to do a tracheotomy on a child with diphtheria, so he's had some recent practice.'

'Can I be in the operating theatre with him?'

'He'll be under anaesthetic, he won't know whether you're there or not. Mr Drew would say he doesn't want two patients on his hands.'

It took her a moment to understand what he meant. 'You mean I might be sick or I might pass out?' She tried to smile. 'It's possible. How does one know?'

He took her hand and held it. He held it tightly. 'You can be just outside. It won't take long.'

The nurse unzipped the tent and lifted James out. Benet put out her arms to him, was about to say she would carry him herself when the door swung open and Mopsa walked into the room. Benet stared at her, stunned. She looked serene and happy, years younger. Her hair was covered by a pink and red scarf and she wore a rather dashing bright red coat.

'I've been trying to get you on the phone,' Benet said. 'I've been trying for hours.'

'Have you really? I heard the phone ringing when I first woke up and then I thought it couldn't be you, you'd be too occupied with him to bother about me. So I thought I'd find your spare car keys and come down here and get your car and practise driving. And that's what I did. I've been doing it all morning. I'm quite an expert now.'

Benet said nothing. It was better not. It was always best to control one's temper with Mopsa. She turned away, first managing a strained smile. Her mouth felt dry and there was a pain pressing on the bone above her eyes. James, his skin bluish, was taking a breath every second now. For one brief instant she thought of, she pictured, that tiny narrow passage, no thicker than a darning needle, a thread, the stem of a daisy, through which all the air for James's lungs and brain and heart must pass, and then she pushed the thought away with such force that she made a little sound, a stifled 'ah!' Mopsa looked at her. They were going up to the operating theatre in the lift, all of them.

'Croup? He has to have an operation for croup? I can't believe it. There must be something they're not telling you.'

Ian Raeburn said, 'There is nothing more complicated than a swollen larynx.'

Benet noticed a harsh, even ragged, edge to his voice she hadn't heard there before. Did he too find Mopsa almost unbearably irritating? He went between the double doors into the theatre and the nurse carrying James went with him. Mr Drew was already there. Benet wondered if she should have insisted on going in there with James. He would be having the anaesthetic now though, it would soon be over . . . There was a kind of waiting room here, comfortless like all waiting rooms, with armless chairs and unread magazines. Four floors higher than the children's ward, it overlooked a panorama of roofs and spires. The old workhouse windows showed a spread of the top of London with a horizon of Hampstead Heath, so green it hurt the eyes. The sunshine looked warm because it was so warm inside, a still, constant hospital heat, smelling faintly of limes.

'He's going to be all right, isn't he?' Mopsa said. 'I mean he's not in danger?'

Benet felt sick. 'As far as I know, this is just routine. I don't really know any more about it than you do.'

'Mrs Fenton's sister had one of those trach-whatever-they-are things done. She had cancer of the throat.'

I must not hate my mother . . .

'Your father phoned when I got back last night. He was very worried about me. He'd been phoning all the evening. I didn't say anything about James. I thought it best not to.'

Pointless to argue about that. A waste of time even to attempt to find out why Mopsa thought it best not to. Benet picked up one of the magazines but the print was a black and white pattern, the illustrations meaningless juxtapositions of colours. She found herself thinking of the tree of hands, all the hands upraised, supplicating, praying.

The double doors opened and Ian Raeburn came out. He stood there for a moment. Benet jumped up, still holding the magazine, her nails going through the shiny paper. His face was as grey as James's had been. He took a step towards her, cleared his throat to find a voice and began apologizing, saying he was sorry, they were all sorry, beyond measure sorry. He stopped and swallowed and told her that James was dead.

The floor rose up and she fell forward in a faint.

# 5

Every other Saturday, Carol was allowed to have Ryan and Tanya home and sometimes they stayed overnight. It was usually Barry who went over to Four Winds at Alexandra Park to fetch them. Carol liked to have a lie-in on Saturdays. She had a bath every morning anyway, it was a rule of life with her, but on Saturdays she made a special ritual of it, putting avocado-and-wheatgerm bubble bath in the water and rubbing body lotion on herself afterwards, washing her hair and giving it a blow-dry and painting her nails. There wasn't a mark on Carol's body from having had three children. It was white and firm with taut muscles. The only scar of any kind Carol had was a curious curved pit on her back just below the left shoulder blade. She told Barry how she had come by it.

'My dad did that when I was a kid. He was always belting us up, me and Maureen. I reckon we deserved it, kids can be a real pain in the arse. He went a bit too far that time though, didn't he? That was his belt buckle done that, cut right through to the bone.'

Barry had been horribly shocked. He would have liked to have got hold of Knapwell, wherever he was – he had walked out on his family when Carol was ten – and cut him to his bones with a steel buckle. He loved Carol even more for her generosity of spirit, her ability to forgive. Though how she could say any child deserved that, he didn't understand. Carol didn't like children much, he was forced to admit that. It was her misfortune really that she had had three of her own. Sometimes Barry worried that she might not want any more when he and she were married.

The Isadoros were having Jason for the whole weekend and maybe they would keep him over the Monday. Beatie Isadoro's youngest was about his age, a khaki-skinned fat girl with red kinky hair. Beatie was an Irishwoman from County Mayo but her husband was Jamaican and they had produced some interesting colour combinations among their seven children. Because she had plenty of room in her two adjacent houses, Beatie ran a kind of unofficial nursery and the older girls were expected to help when they weren't at school. Beatie wasn't registered with the council as a childminder or anything like that, but that was rather an advantage since it meant she didn't charge as much as a registered childminder would have. To Barry the houses seemed full of kids, twenty or thirty of them, though there probably were not so many as that. He paid up, six pounds for the two days, which he thought exorbitant but Carol said was cheap at the price.

Karen and Stephanie and Nathan Isadoro were watching a film on the video, *The Texas Chainsaw Massacre*. Barry was squeamish and didn't look. There was a little fair-haired boy strapped in a pushchair and screaming his head off. No one took any notice of him and the video viewers didn't even turn their heads. The Isadoros' home always had a curious smell about it – a mixture of pimento, babies' napkins and hot chocolate.

Barry collected Tanya and Ryan and took them back to Summerskill Road. Carol was ready by then, wearing the tweed culottes Mrs Fylemon had given her, and a cream wool polo-neck sweater that showed off her figure. She had made up her face in a very clever way so that it looked luminous and glowing and not really made up at all. Her hair was in soft floppy curls and a true natural gold. Barry knew for a fact she didn't tint it. They all went shopping at Brent Cross and had lunch in a hamburger place and then to the cinema to see a space fantasy film. Barry organized all that. Before he had come to live with her, Carol often hadn't bothered to take the kids out, she had told him. It had all got on top of her and she hadn't been able to cope.

He had more or less taken charge of the children insofar as they needed to be taken charge of. He thought they liked him.

Waiting for the bus home, Barry hoped people would look at them and think Carol was his wife and the kids his. He was young enough to hope that. Carol would catch sight of herself in shop windows and make a face because Ryan came nearly up to her shoulder, and she would say to Barry, 'I must have been off my nut having him so young. Do you realize I could be a bloody grandmother before I'm forty?'

It made Barry laugh to think of Carol being a grandmother. He put his arms round her and started kissing her there in the street and forgot about the kids watching them.

Next day they had to go back to Four Winds. Tanya never wanted to go. She always screamed and stamped and sometimes she clung to Carol and had to be prised off. It made Barry wonder why they had to be in care if they were so happy in their home and with their mother.

'You can *ask* the council to take your kids into care, you know,' Carol said. 'It doesn't have to be that they take them away from you. I couldn't cope after Dave died. I had to do something about the kids. I was desperate.'

Less than two years after Dave's death, she had Jason. Barry had never asked her much about that, he didn't really want to know, he preferred to be in ignorance. He could probably even have convinced himself that Jason was Dave's child. Only one day, when Carol was telling him off and calling him a little bastard, Iris said, 'You didn't ought to call him that, Carol. It'd be one thing if he wasn't one but he is, isn't he?'

When they were married, Barry thought, they could apply to take the kids out of care. Carol could give up work too or at least she could give up working in the wine bar. Barry was ambitious. He had a good job as cabinet-maker and carpenter in a two-man business operating from Delphi Road. Or it would be a good job when this recession came to an end and things picked up a bit. They'd be able to move out of Summerskill Road then and maybe buy a place somewhere and be a real family. Sometimes Barry had a dream that was really a vision, it was so clear and solid, of a room in their house in the future, all of them sitting round the table eating Christmas dinner, all happy and wearing paper hats and laughing, and Carol in a sea-blue dress with their new baby on her lap.

Barry knew it couldn't all be roses. There were the children for one thing, they weren't his and they never could be, and that wasn't just nothing, that wasn't something you could just dismiss. And there was Dave, always there, always smiling out of his plastic frame. Carol might look about seventeen but she wasn't, she was eight years older than him and that much more experienced and sophisticated. And there was one other thing that troubled him sometimes.

He was a gentle person, a bit too soft, he sometimes thought. He couldn't stand seeing a kid get hurt. You had to smack them if they went too far, he knew that, but not hard and always on the leg or the behind. So when he saw Carol strike Tanya with a back-handed blow across the little girl's face and head, using all the strength of her arm, strike her again and again after that, wielding her arm like a tennis player, he saw red and pulled Carol off and hit her himself to calm her down. That was the only reason he did it, to calm her down, like he'd been told you had to with hysterical people. There was no passion in it for him, no uncontrolled violence. He took her by the arm, and because he was young and strong, he held her hard, and struck her a sharp blow across the face.

It was her reaction that troubled him. She stopped screaming at the child, she was quiet and that was all right. It wasn't that. She cringed a little but she didn't put her hand up to her face where his blow must have stung. He had the curious sensation – and he didn't know how he knew this then, he had no real evidence for it – that she was waiting for him to hit her again, that she *wanted* him to hit her again. She stood there in front of him, vulnerable, exposed, her hands hanging a little way from her body, breathing shallowly, her lips parted, sweat on her skin, waiting for more.

Of course he hadn't hit her again. He had told her he was sorry, he loved her, he wouldn't hurt her, but he had had to do it to stop her when she was out of control like that.

'I didn't mind,' she said and she gave him a curious sidelong look, a look that was sly and also faintly irritable.

That night, when they made love, she tried to get him to strike her. It was a while before he realized, he didn't know what she was doing, provoking him with her teeth and nails, jumping from the bed to run across the room and stand pressed against the wall with her arms covering her body, then kicking him when he came near, hissing at him, darting her head like a snake. She had to tell him because he didn't understand.

'Hit me, lover, hit me as hard as you can.'

He couldn't. He forced himself to pat her face, tap her shoulders a little harder with his fingers. That wasn't what she wanted. She wanted blows, she wanted pain. Why? How could she? You would have thought she had suffered enough of that from that father of hers. Barry struck her. He beat her hard but only with his hands. He hated it. He had to tell himself it wasn't Carol, it was someone he hated, and he shut his eyes to do it.

She never asked him for anything like that again. He tried to forget it, to put the memory of it out of his mind, and he nearly succeeded. Sometimes he thought that perhaps he had only dreamed he was beating Carol just as he had dreamed of seeing her strike Tanya. Since then, though, their love-making had been more strenuous, more savage really. Barry didn't mind that. It was a change to find a woman who preferred it that way. But then Carol wasn't like other women. She was one in a million . . .

After the children went back, they were alone. They went to bed. That was what they always did when they got the chance. When there were people there who were just going or when they were soon to be rid of the kids, Barry always had this sense of mounting excitement and, looking at Carol, he knew she had it too. It was all they could do to wait till the door closed. And yet such was the pleasure of anticipation that sometimes he hoped leave-takings would be prolonged or children's departure delayed so that he might be kept a little longer on this pinnacle of breathless expectancy.

Once they were alone they fell into each other's arms, desperate by then for love, kissing and licking and biting and holding, laughing for no reason unless it was at their own thraldom. In that big bed with Carol there was no one else in the world for him, no one and nothing beyond the invisible dome that seemed to enclose the bed. Carol told him that once or twice she had watched them in the big mirror, it excited her more, but he never had. His love was here and now, not even at that small remove.

They slept. They awoke in darkness, still embraced, damp and cool with their own and each other's sweat. Carol got up first and washed and put on the black and white zig-zag dress. She painted her face with brushes, big ones for the foundation and the blusher and small fine ones for the eyelids and brows and outlining her lips. She combed her hair and wound the little tendril curls round her fingers. They were going out for a drink with Iris and Iris's Jerry.

A big full moon was up, bright as a floodlight, competing with the harsh yellow that overhung Winterside Down. They went by way of the Chinese bridge where Barry's graffiti still proclaimed his love and where it was light enough to see their own faces reflected in the calm glistening water of the canal. Their faces gazed back at them as from a mirror in a room which is dark but nevertheless faintly lit by light showing through an open door. Carol dropped her cigarette stub into the water. It was just heavy enough to fracture their images and, for a brief moment, distort them so horribly that Barry stepped back, removing his own. He had seen Carol's beautiful face shudder and collapse and melt until it became a rubber mask representing some cartoon character, voracious, lecherous and coarse, while his own was a gargoyle with bloated lips and rolling wobbly eyes.

He put his arm round her, rubbed her cheek with his and kissed her lips. Carol put sealant on her lips so that you could kiss a hundred times without the lipstick coming off. They held hands walking down Winterside Down, past Maureen's house with its curtains like fancy white lace aprons and the polished car outside. Iris and Jerry were already in the Old Bulldog, they had probably been there since it opened. Jerry was a smallish, fattish, pink-faced man, a heavy drinker but showing few signs of this. He was never drunk. His eyes looked as if they had been stewed in brine, they had a soggy yet shrivelled look, and his clothes smelled as if they had been rinsed out in gin. His favourite pastime next to going to the Old Bulldog was watching television with a tumbler of gin and water beside him.

People said Iris had once been even prettier than Carol. Barry found that hard to believe. She was fifty, thin as a skeleton and with long bony legs. She wore her dyed yellow hair shoulder-length to make herself look younger, and she always had very high-heeled sandals on, summer and winter, to show off her high insteps and her thin ankles. Barry guessed she had had a hell of a life with the brutish Knapwell. Yet she was always cheerful, carefree, making the best of a bad job. She smoked forty or fifty cigarettes a day and had a cough which turned her face purple with the strain. Iris couldn't get down to anything without a cigarette.

'Let me just get a fag on,' she would say, or 'I'll have to have a cig first.'

Since Knapwell went, there had been (according to Carol) a man called Bill and one called Nobby, but they hadn't lasted long and Jerry had been Iris's companion for years now. He was a mysterious man who seldom spoke, showed no emotion, seemed to have no family of his own, and who preserved towards everything but gin and the television a sublime indifference. Even his real name was a mystery, for he had begun to call himself Knapwell within a year of moving in with Iris. He worked for Thames Water which made Barry laugh, considering Jerry's tastes. Iris had a job in a small garment factory housed in what used to be the old Prado cinema.

Barry had a Foster's and Carol a gin and tonic. She and Iris talked about childminding arrangements for the coming week. Maybe Maureen could be roped in for one day.

'You have to be joking,' said Iris. 'Maureen's doing up her lounge. She's been all day stripping.'

'I'll have to take on another evening at Kostas's, that's all,' said Carol. 'It's costing me a fortune.'

Jerry got up. 'You going to have the other half?' he said to Barry as if his lager hadn't been the entire contents of a can but out of a bottle or jug. Knowing what they would want, he didn't waste words on the women.

'Let me get a fag on,' said Iris. She smoked in thoughtful silence. Carol talked about taking on extra work. That troubled Barry who had been feeling happy and contented. He longed to earn more, make a lot of money, so that instead of working longer hours Carol could give up altogether and stay at home with the kids. 'There's always the council,' Iris said suddenly. 'You could try them, see what they come up with.'

Barry didn't know what she meant for a minute but he could see Carol did. She took one of her mother's cigarettes, lit it from Iris's.

'It may come to that. It just may.'

'I'd like to do more myself,' said Iris. 'You know I'd bend over backwards to give you a helping hand. But if it means giving in my notice, I have to draw the line. I couldn't let Mr Karim down. I've been there seven years or it will be come New Year and he, like, relies on me, doesn't he, Jerry?' She didn't even wait for the confirmation. She knew it wouldn't come. 'You'll have to play it by ear, I reckon,' she said cheerfully. 'Just go on from day to day.'

'I couldn't cope before, and if I can't again, they'll have to step in.'

Barry understood then. 'It's not going to come to that,' he said. He felt that his voice was firm, authoritative, manly, the ruling voice the women were waiting for. 'We'll manage. *I'll* manage.'

Carol had been holding his hand. She put her other arm round him, over his chest and held his shoulder. She leaned her head against chest. 'You're lovely,' she said. 'You're so strong. Isn't he lovely, Mum? He reminds me of Dave. Doesn't he remind you of Dave?'

'He does a bit,' said Iris.

Barry knew there could be no higher praise. Feeling Carol's soft warmth against him, a thread of excitement moved in his body. He began to look forward to the evening's end, to their parting from Iris and Jerry on the pavement under the white moon, for him and Carol once more to be alone together.

# 6

The days blended into one another without demarcation, without date, without weather, almost without light or dark. She lay, then sat, in her bedroom, the big room in the very top of the house in the Vale of Peace. Mopsa brought her food on trays, but when she saw Benet didn't want to eat, could not eat, the food was replaced without demur by cups of tea, of instant coffee and, in the evenings, their coming preceded by no inquiries, tumblers of brandy and water.

Life had stopped. At first, because what had happened was unbelievable, it could not have happened, little children in the 1980s do not die – because of that, there was only shock which stunned and numbed. For a good deal of the stunned, numbed phase, Benet had been kept in hospital herself. In that same state, armed with sleeping pills and tranquillizers, she had been sent home to her chaotic house and Mopsa. There the shock began to wear off. It was like the anaesthetic wearing off after you have been to the dentist and the pain starts. Only no physical pain Benet had ever known was like this. Even when she was giving birth to James and had shouted out, her cries had been part pleasurable, compounded of effort and intent and joy as well as pain. Now she found herself holding both hands tight over her mouth to keep herself from screaming out her suffering. She sat or paced the room because when she lay down she could not keep from twisting and turning and digging her nails into the soft parts of herself. One afternoon she stuck a pin into her arm to have a different focus of pain.

Because she had no idea of time or its passing, it seemed

to her that she had been a year in that room at the top of the house, tended by Mopsa, with Mopsa coming every hour to the door. Perhaps it had been no more than two days. She took a lot of barbiturates and a lot of Valium. The sleeping pills she put down the lavatory and pulled the flush on them. The oblivion they brought was not worth the awfulness of waking up, appreciating the light of morning, listening for the first morning sounds from James next door – and realizing there would be no morning sounds from him, there never would be. Never never never never never.

The Valium stopped her wanting to scream or wanting to put her hands over her mouth to stop the scream. It made her, while sitting quiet and still, consider in a low muddled way methods of suicide. She threw those pills away too. She stood by the window, high above the Vale of Peace, looking at a large white moon like a radiant pearl. Two years before, James had not existed, yet she was the same person she had been then, not much older, unchanged in appearance. She looked into the mirror and saw the same familiar regular features, almond-shaped dark eyes, high cheekbones, full folded lips. The dark brown, longish, implacably straight hair was the same and the clear sallow skin. Why then could she not be as she had been before he came into her life? It was such a short time ago. How could she have been so unimaginably affected, so transformed, in less than two years by another person and that person scarcely able to speak?

She did not want to think of him as a person, as himself, of the things he had done and said. That was the worst. That way unbearable panic lay, the kind of panic that comes from knowing one more step in that direction and the mind will break. She went downstairs, all the way down the long flight that wound through the middle of the house, and came into the basement room and sat in the window looking up at the garden wall and the street. She felt she would never go out there again. It was impossible to imagine going into the open air, walking, confronting other human beings.

Mopsa was at the kitchen end of the room, apparently making a cake. What was the use of it? Who would eat it? Mopsa wore an apron Benet had never seen before, a pink-and-white check gingham apron with straps that crossed over at the back. She had cleared every trace of James out of that room. The doors of the toy cupboard were closed. The highchair was gone. Upstairs Benet had closed her eyes while passing James's bedroom door on her way to the bathroom. She had been afraid it might be open and its contents showing. Now she knew she need not have bothered to close her eyes. Mopsa would have seen to those things. Dimly, through that timeless time up there, she had perceived that Mopsa had been seeing to things, had seen to everything.

The things she could not name even in her own thoughts. The registration of death. The undertakers. The funeral. To herself she named them, shivering long and inwardly, with a euphemism she had once despised: the formalities. Poor mad Mopsa, who was mad no longer, who had taken up this terrible challenge better than the sanest of women, had seen to . . . the formalities. Vaguely, up in that high room, that dark tower, Benet had been aware of Mopsa going out, of the car starting, of doors closing and opening, of Mopsa returning, of Mopsa *bustling*, busy in her record-ing angel, amanuensis, indispensable role. And now, having turned to look at her daughter and give her a small, sad, pitiful smile, she was making a cake, beating eggs with a hand whisk into a creamy concoction in a glass bowl.

Mopsa had been – wonderful. That was the word one always used of someone who did what she had done in this situation – wonderful. Often Benet had heard the phone ringing. Mopsa had answered it, though Benet never heard what she said. It rang now. Mopsa rested the whisk against the side of the bowl and went to the phone and took up the receiver. She spoke to Antonia as if they were old friends, though to Benet's knowledge they had never met.

Her tone was chatty, pleasant, in no way tragic. Benet would certainly phone Antonia, Mopsa said. As soon as she was up and about and fit again, she would phone her. Yes, Mopsa would pass on the message.

Benet addressed the first question to her mother she had put since she had come home from the hospital. Her voice which had been silent for so long sounded strange to her. She walked over to Mopsa, her legs feeling weak as if she were convalescent.

'Have there been many phone calls?'

Mopsa was sifting flour through a sieve. She worked neatly, without spilling. 'Half a dozen. Quite a few. I didn't count them.'

'What have you told people?'

'I've told them you're not well enough to speak to anyone. I've told them you're confined to your bed and can't be expected to talk.'

It was the correct response, it was the prescribed, ideal, merciful way for anyone in Mopsa's position to behave. Benet felt, creeping into the immense wide cold sea of her misery, a trickle of unease. She ignored it. It was nothing. Unease was nothing any more, of no importance, and never would be.

'Have you spoken to Dad?'

'He's phoned every evening nearly.' The complacent look touched the corners of Mopsa's mouth. 'He sent you his love.'

Poor Mopsa who was unstable, ill really, not like other women, other people's mothers. A line came into Benet's mind – there's a part of my heart that's sorry yet for thee . . . She said quietly, 'It must have been very hard for you to tell him.'

The thin custardy stuff was poured into the tin. Mopsa had an air of frowning concentration. When it was done she expelled her breath with a puffing sound. She was like a schoolgirl making a cake for a home economics exam. She was like someone who had never made a cake before. Perhaps she hadn't. Benet couldn't remember cakes in

Mopsa's crazy days. She put the cake into the oven and slammed the door as if slamming it on something she would never return to, the final closing of the door of a house she was quitting for ever.

She turned to Benet, wiping clean hands down the front of her apron.

'Oh, I didn't tell him, Brigitte. I couldn't *tell* him. He doesn't ask, you see. It's an embarrassing subject for him. He might have got over it if things had been different. But since he doesn't ask, there's no point in telling him, is there?'

'He will have to know sometime.'

Mopsa didn't say anything. She looked levelly into Benet's eyes. At that moment, in her apron, a smudge of flour on one cheek, her hair silvery-gold with pins fastening it, she was exactly like other people's mothers.

'Have you told anyone?' Benet said.

A hand went up and touched the flour smudge, a finger rubbed and flicked at it. Mopsa's stare shifted from Benet's face to the light switch on the far wall.

'You haven't told anyone at all, have you?'

Mopsa began to mumble. 'I couldn't, Brigitte. I didn't want to upset myself. It's bad for me to be upset.'

Benet shouted at her: 'Who do you suppose is going to eat that bloody cake?'

She ran out of the room and up the stairs. Behind her she could hear Mopsa starting to snuffle and cry. She didn't go back. She went on up the stairs, a feeling of pressure on the top of her head, a throbbing behind her eyes. She passed the open door to Mopsa's bedroom and the photograph on Mopsa's bedside table caught her eyes. It was a photograph of Edward. What was Mopsa doing with a photograph of Edward? Benet hadn't even known she possessed one. It was a head and shoulders shot, rather fuzzy, enlarged from a snap.

She went up the last flight and entered James's bedroom. The cot was still there and the bare mattress. Apart from that, there was nothing to show the room had ever been occupied by a child. From the window you could see the row of pines behind the pond, the green strip of the Heath, a large white empty sky. She shut herself in her own bedroom. Should she tell Edward about James? Was there any point? He had only seen him once and that when he was two days old. He had come into the hospital and seen him and Benet and not known what to say.

'You have utterly humiliated me' was what at last he did say. He had glanced at the child and looked away.

'It would have been better if you hadn't come, Edward. You shouldn't have come.'

She felt as bad about things as he did, in her own way. It *had* been wrong to use him, it *had* been wrong to set out to have a child by him when she had no intention of marrying him or even continuing to live with him. But it had not seemed like that at the time, it had seemed the obvious thing, even the moral thing. With that decision made, with the baby in her arms, even then she had not been able to ignore Edward's beauty, a beauty that inevitably moved her. She had thought, why can't that alone be enough for me, though I know there is nothing else, scarcely anything else to him at all? The world was full of men bound to women for no more reason than that those women were beautiful. Why couldn't it be the other way round and be so for her?

He sat on the side of her bed and once more asked her to marry him. She said no, no, she couldn't, please not to ask her again, it was impossible, they would both be unhappy, all three of them would be unhappy. He had got up and gone and she had never seen him again.

From somewhere or other, Mopsa had acquired a photograph of him and had it framed and put it by her bed. As if he were her son. Did it matter why? Did it matter, come to that, that Mopsa had not told anyone of James's death? Did anything matter?

Strangely, she remembered dreams she had had which she had not known were dreams at the time but had believed, while she was living through them, to be real.

Suppose she were dreaming now and due to wake and find it had been the most terrible nightmare of her life but still only a nightmare, find that it was morning and James was waking up in the room next door?

She went back in there and looked at the neat bareness Mopsa had made of it. Grief fills up the room of my absent child, lies in his bed, walks up and down with me . . .

Next morning there was a note from Mopsa on the hall table. *I have gone to lunch with Constance Fenton,* it read. *Back about four.* Mopsa hadn't bothered to leave her notes on other days. Or had she? There was a small wastepaper basket under the table. It was full of screwed-up pieces of paper. Benet began flattening them out. They were all notes from Mopsa, daily notes. *I have gone to the hospital. I have gone to the registrar. I have gone to see Sims & Wainwright.* Benet did not want even to guess who Sims & Wainwright might be. She was touched, she felt guilty, that Mopsa had written all those notes and, seeing them ignored, had patiently retrieved each one and thrown it away before writing the next.

She opened the door of the room that was to be her place to work in, the room Mopsa inevitably called the study. What else, after all, could you call it? When last she had been in there, books had lain in heaps all over the floor. Mopsa had put them away. She had put them on the shelves, in no sort of order, some of them even upside down. And into the roller of the typewriter she had inserted a clean fresh sheet of paper as if inviting Benet to begin work. Benet wondered if she would ever work again. The idea seemed grotesque. How could she, in her own devastation, ever hope to render on to paper the emotions of others?

In the basement room she sat by the window. A woman went by, then a child with a dog on a lead. Benet made herself a cup of tea for something to do and drank it to pass the time. The time until what? She wondered about the rest of her life, how she could contemplate it, what she could possibly do with it. After a while she put a coat on and went out of the house and on to the Heath. It was a cold day with a cold wind blowing. The air was as clear as if this were some remote unspoiled place on the edge of the world where pollution and fog and fouled atmosphere never came. Acres of London roofs and spires and towers lay below her clear as a painting on glass, only faintly blurred with blue at the horizon. Clouds lay over Highgate and the north, piled, frothy, full of rain. She went back.

The phone rang three or four times. She didn't answer it. She ate a very small piece of bread and butter and half an apple, afraid she would be sick if she ate any more. After that she went back to the window and sat there, wishing she hadn't thrown Ian Raeburn's sleeping pills away. She sat and thought about James because there was nothing and no one else to think about. She had written a book and had a child and now the child was dead and she would never write again. It seemed like something that was happening to someone else because it was too bad, too terrible to be happening to her. Yet it was. The someone else was she herself and it was all for her alone . . .

Above her, beyond the window, against the pavement, she heard her own car draw up. She knew the sound of that car. Mopsa was back. It was only just gone three.

She didn't look. It was only Mopsa. The front door closed and footsteps sounded along the passage above her head. A moment ago Benet would have said that she could never wish passionately for anything again but she found herself wishing passionately that Mopsa was not with her, that Mopsa would go home, that she might be alone. It was kind of Mopsa, it was motherly, it was what mothers did – but it would be better if Mopsa were gone. At least, if not better, it would somehow be less intensely, grindingly, awful.

Mopsa came into the room. She was holding a child by the hand, a small boy. She said rather stupidly, 'Were you asleep, Brigitte? Did we wake you up?'

Benet had eyes only for the child. Apart from the girl

walking the dog, this was the first child she had seen since James's death.

'Who is that?' she said. It was her voice but it sounded to her like someone else's, coming from another part of the room.

'Don't you like him?' Mopsa said.

That seemed to Benet one of the most absurd remarks she had ever heard. It was meaningless, not something you asked in connection with a child. A dog perhaps . . .

'Who is he?'

Mopsa had begun to look frightened. The wary, alert animal look was on her face. The little boy still held on to her hand in a docile way. He seemed about two or a little younger, James's age perhaps, but big and sturdy. Under a dirty red quilted jacket with a dirty white nylon fur lining, he wore blue denim dungarees, green-and-brown striped socks and sandals of red moulded plastic. His hair was fair, almost white, a thick thatch of it. He had bright shiny red cheeks and big coarse features. You could already see the man he would become in those features, in the strong nose and the rather bloated sore-looking lips. Benet thought him the ugliest child she had ever seen.

'He's Barbara Lloyd's little boy,' Mopsa faltered.

'I don't know any Barbara Lloyd.'

'Yes, you do, Brigitte. You'll remember when I tell you. She's Barbara Fenton that was, Constance's girl. She married a man called Lloyd who's something in computers. They're living with Constance until their house is ready.'

Then Benet did remember. Not so much Barbara Fenton whom she must once have known by sight if not to talk to, but the phone conversation she had had with Constance a thousand years ago, when things were all right, when she was happy, when James was alive and she was stupid enough to be worrying over Mopsa. Constance had told her then that she had her daughter and son-in-law and grandson staying with her.

'What's he doing here with you?'

'I said I'd mind him for them for a little while. They were desperate.'

The little boy had freed himself from Mopsa's grasp. He took a step forward in this strange place, looked about him, then up at Benet, back at Mopsa, his face beginning to work in that open, unrestrained way children's faces do. His mouth made a square shape and he started to cry.

'Oh dear, oh dear,' said Mopsa. 'Oh dear.' She was saying it to herself, not to him. She bent to pick him up. In her arms he struggled and screamed.

Benet went upstairs to her bedroom.

It was dark when she came down again. She hadn't heard the car go. She looked and saw that the car was still there. The boy was still there too and he was sitting in James's highchair. Mopsa had given him a scrambled egg and fingers of bread and he was using his fingers and a spoon to eat it. Mopsa herself sat up at the table beside him with a cup of tea in front of her.

'Isn't it time you took him home?' Benet said.

She could tell her mother was hiding something. Mopsa was tense with nervousness.

'Why did you have to have him anyway?'

'Someone had to. The lady he was going to stay with, she's his godmother, she fell over and broke her leg.'

'He's got a mother and father and grandmother, hasn't he?'

'They were booked up for this holiday. They've been booked up for weeks.'

Benet felt cold. 'Mother, what holiday? What do you mean?' She recalled something Mopsa had said. 'What did you mean "going to stay with"?'

Mopsa faltered. 'He was going to stay with his godmother.'

'Yes, you said. Do you mean he's come to *stay* here?'

Mopsa bit her lip. She was half smiling while she did so, like a naughty child. She gave Benet a sly sidelong look.

The boy was eating his egg and bread, concentrating, apparently enjoying his meal.

'Where does one go on holiday in November?'

'The Canary Islands,' said Mopsa.

Closing her eyes, Benet held on to the arms of the chair. She counted to ten. She opened her eyes and said to Mopsa, 'You mean they are going to the Canary Islands and you've said you'll look after this child while they're away? You've actually offered to do that? For how long? A week? A fortnight?'

A very small low voice whispered out from Mopsa's faintly tremulous lips, 'A week.'

Benet stared at Mopsa uncomprehendingly. It was not possible. How could anyone be like Mopsa? She would never get used to her, never accept her, never understand. How could Mopsa do what she had done, attend to everything, be caring and attentive and responsible, yet also be so brutally insensitive and thoughtless and cruel? To bring that child here where her own daughter had lost her child, a child of the same age and sex! How could she? How could anyone?

I must not hate my mother . . .

Mopsa had tied a table napkin round the boy's neck for a bib. She was pouring milk into a mug for him and he put out his hands for it, making what Benet thought of as idiot sounds, not words. This was just the sort of child that hefty lump Barbara Fenton would have had. Benet thought she could even trace Barbara's big prominent features in his. Suddenly Mopsa began to talk, to recount in detail the plight of Constance Fenton and the Lloyds, how when she had arrived they had resigned themselves to having to forgo their holiday and lose the advance payment they had made for a reduced-cost flight. Barbara had been crying. It was to have been the first holiday she had had in five years. What could Mopsa do? She hadn't wanted to do it, she dreaded the thought, but she owed it to Constance, Constance had been so good to her in the past. And she hadn't been thoughtless, she had known how Benet would feel.

71

But Benet was mostly up in her own room, wasn't she? It was a big house. Benet need hardly see him. She, Mopsa, would do it all on her own, have him to sleep in the same room with her, take him out . . .

Benet got up. She looked through the E–K phone directory. Mrs Constance Fenton, 55 Harper Lane, NW9.

'What are you doing, Brigitte?'

'Phoning Mrs Fenton to tell her we're sorry but we're not a nursery, we don't board kids, and we're returning her grandson to her in half an hour.' Her finger in the dial, the first digit spinning.

'They won't be there, they'll have gone by now.'

'I don't believe you, Mother.'

She listened to the bell ringing. She was beginning to be angry. It was, at any rate, a change of emotion, it was different. The bell went on ringing. No one was going to answer it. Mopsa was right, they had gone.

The boy had got down from the highchair, his face still sticky with food. He was moving about the room, looking for something to do. There was nothing for him to do, there were no toys, no books, crayons, no television. He went into the kitchen area and opened a cupboard door. He paused, looked over his shoulder to see if anyone was going to stop him, and, when he saw they weren't, began removing from the cupboard on to the floor a saucepan, another saucepan, a sieve, a colander.

'I'm going out,' said Benet. 'I'm going for a walk on the Heath.'

'It's pitch dark, Brigitte. I'm sure it isn't safe.'

'That's all right. Maybe I'll get murdered.'

Normally she would have regretted saying anything that made Mopsa's face change like that, quiver like that, made her hands go up to cover her wobbly mouth. Now she didn't care. She went out into the cold clear night under a moon that had just begun to wane from the full.

# 7

It wasn't until the following day that she asked his name. He was a child, he was in her house, none of it was his fault. She was going to have to see him and occasionally – though as seldom as possible – be with him. She had to know what he was called.

Mopsa looked foolish. This was not her witch or her frightened hare but her village idiot look. She smiled slyly.

'I don't know.'

They had been out, Mopsa and the boy. She had taken him somewhere in the car. The thought came to Benet that he must have sat in the back in James's baby seat. At least she hadn't seen it. She had decided she wouldn't go out in daylight again. After dark, yes, but not by day. They had been shopping and brought back their purchases, whatever those might be, in carrier bags from Mothercare and Marks & Spencers. The boy whose name Mopsa said she didn't know was taking off his dirty red coat and trying to undo the fastenings on his sandals.

'Yes, you do,' Benet said. She thought her voice sounded like that of a psychiatric nurse. 'Of course you know his name.'

Mopsa squatted down to help him with his sandals. She looked up at Benet in a very shifty, sly, covert way. She held her head on one side as if assessing what Benet's reaction would be to the reply she intended to make. Benet wondered what sort of people Constance Fenton and her daughter could be to entrust this child to Mopsa's care. She was mad. Couldn't they see that? She was unfit to be in charge of a child. And Constance Fenton knew it, she knew Mopsa's past. In the circumstances, should she,

Benet, allow Mopsa to be responsible for him? That thought with all its implications was something else she wasn't going to think about.

'Come on, Mother. What is his name?'

'It's James.'

Benet said no more. She went upstairs. She didn't cry. She hadn't cried since they told her James was dead. Crying seemed an inadequate thing, not big enough for a great grief.

They had had to tell her twice. Ian Raeburn told her and she had fainted, and when she came round he was there with a sister and they both had to tell her again. James had stopped breathing before the anaesthetist reached him. His airway had closed. If Mr Drew had perhaps taken this emergency measure – this very rare emergency measure in the case of a child – half an hour before, if they could have foretold the ventilation would cease to work, if . . . if . . .

'You ought to sue them for negligence,' Mopsa had said.

But there had been no negligence, only mischance, only a human error of timing. And what was she supposed to achieve by an action? Compensation for the loss of James? She wasn't poor, she didn't want money or consolation or revenge. She wanted James again and no one could give him to her.

She lay down on her bed, thinking of what Mopsa had said, of the stream of insensitive, outrageous things that issued from Mopsa's slyly smiling, tremulous mouth, telling herself not to hate her mother, to bear with her, to try to understand. How can the sane understand madness? She wondered now how on that first day she could have thought Mopsa 'cured' or even improved.

After a while she sat up and reached for the phone and dialled Constance Fenton's number. By now she knew it by heart, she had dialled it so many times. Much of what Mopsa told her she refused to believe. Mopsa lied if there was the slightest risk of anything unpleasant for herself, anything that might cause a hint of uneasiness to herself, attaching to the telling of the truth. Lies made life smooth so she told them as a matter of course. Benet knew that the whole tale of the Fentons going to the Canaries might be a fabrication. Instead of a week in the Canaries, they might be spending three days in Blackpool. They might never have gone away at all. The phone rang and rang. They might have gone away – and this would be the worst – not for a week but a fortnight. The phone went on ringing and Benet put the receiver back.

She began to think that it was perhaps wrong to leave that child in Mopsa's charge. When she had first understood that the boy was there to stay, that he was staying in her house for a week, she had considered going away to an hotel. She was still thinking of it, but no longer very seriously. It would be an irresponsible thing to do. She couldn't leave Mopsa and she dared not leave a child alone with Mopsa. As much as his presence distressed her, she couldn't leave Mopsa to him and him to Mopsa. The memory was strong and sharp of herself and her small cousin locked in that dining room, of the barricaded door and windows, of the knives.

Mopsa had dressed the boy in new clothes. Or at least in different ones. They looked new. It took Benet aback rather to see that at his age he was still incontinent. She could see the bulky outline of a napkin through his blue velvet jumpsuit. He sat in the small wicker chair which had been James's and which, like the highchair, had been hidden by Mopsa until yesterday. What would be next? Benet found herself briefly standing aside in an unexpected cold detachment. James's toys? His clothes even? What would be next?

'Jay,' he said. 'Jay. Jay wants drink.'

So he could talk and he was called James. Well, it was a popular enough, even common, name. Mopsa came bustling in with apple juice in a feeding bottle. At least that wasn't James's, she must have bought it. A feeding bottle was something he had never used. The same snobbery which had caused Benet to recoil from the sight of the napkin now made her look askance at this big child, this very masculine-looking, hefty boy, sucking on a teat.

When he had finished the bottle, he returned to his favourite pastime of turning out the kitchen cabinets. He worked with an air of intense concentration, frowning and keeping his lips firmly compressed as he brought out pots and pans and bowls and dishes, examining them, fitting one into another. He came upon an egg beater, turned the handle and made the whisk blades spin and looked up at Mopsa with a broad grin of satisfaction.

'May I have one of your sleeping pills?' Benet said to Mopsa. 'I threw mine away.'

Mopsa said they were in her bedroom on the bedside table and Benet was to help herself. Benet found the bottle of Soneryl between a container of Mogadon and the inevitable Valium behind Edward's photograph. She looked at Edward's face and he looked resolutely away into the distance. The face was intelligent and sensitive as well as handsome. It looked as if its possessor would say and think and feel wonderful things. An air of mystery hung about it as it does over all still and silent beauty. The extraordinary thing was that there was so little underneath and what there had been was so commonplace. It hurt her to think that and to remember it had taken her three years to find it out.

She took the Soneryl quite early and had a long night's sleep. Where the boy was sleeping she didn't inquire. The house had five bedrooms and in any case there was a second bed in Mopsa's room. Mopsa took him out and of course they must have used James's pushchair. Next day she had to go back to the Royal Eastern Hospital for further tests, and Mopsa asked would Benet look after him just for three hours? Benet said she had seen that coming. Sooner or later she had known that would happen.

'I haven't much choice, have I?' she said.

Mopsa was looking tired. She had dark bags under her eyes and hollows in her cheeks. Looking after a two-year-old was too much for her. Benet wondered if she had been up in the night with the boy, if he woke up in the nights and cried and wanted his mother and Mopsa had to deal with that. She didn't feel much sympathy, she had no room for pitying anyone but herself.

The boy was back in his denim dungarees today and his red plastic sandals. Benet thought she had seldom seen a nastier kind of footwear for a child. It made her wonder afresh about Barbara Lloyd. The boy clambered up and down the staircases. He seemed safe enough on them, climbing up on all-fours and down by sliding on his bottom. He spoke very little, never for the mere pleasure of making comprehensible sounds. When he wanted something, really wanted it, he expressed himself in the third person, calling himself Jay. Never James or Jim or Jem but always Jay. He was extraordinarily self-contained and somehow self-sufficient. Benet, hunched up in her window chair in the basement, had to acknowledge that he was no trouble.

She hadn't seen him for half an hour so she bestirred herself unwillingly and went upstairs to look for him. He had got into the study room. There he had found a half-empty box of heavyweight A4 typing paper, helped himself to a dozen sheets and was drawing on them with a blue ink felt-tipped pen. He sat on the floor with the paper spread out in front of him and resting on the stiff cover of Benet's book of days. Whether this was by accident or design it was impossible to tell, but it was obviously a sensible thing to do. And although he had got a lot of ink on his hands and arms and dungarees and the book of days, the drawings he had made were not scribbles, they were recognizable drawings of things, of a man, a woman, a house, of something that looked like a bridge.

Benet picked up one of the pictures and looked closely at it. She was astonished. It seemed to her more like something one would expect of a six-year-old and she remembered children's drawings on the wall of the playroom where the tree of hands poster was. The memory of sitting in that playroom came back to her with a pain so sharp that she dropped the drawing and turned away, clenching her hands.

The boy said, 'Jay wants drink.' He was trying to put the cap back on the felt-tipped pen.

Benet did it for him. She picked him up to carry him upstairs, performing this action almost without thinking, automatically. Immediately she wanted to drop him again, she had such a sensation of recoil. But she couldn't do that. He was a person, he had his feelings, and none of it was his fault. She took him upstairs and filled a bottle with apple juice for him.

When Mopsa came back, Benet suggested they should rent a television set. The boy had obviously been used to watching television. When he had first come, he had gone about the room looking for it in much the same way as Mopsa had on her first day. 'It would make things easier for you,' Benet said.

Why wasn't Mopsa more enthusiastic? Benet had expected a delighted response, even a suggestion that they should all go out in the car now and see about it. But there had been a worn look about Mopsa since her return, something almost frightened or hagridden, rather as if, while she was away, she had seen or heard something to dismay her. Yet whatever processes had been gone through at the Royal Eastern, they had been routine and simple and not alarming. She told Benet that and Benet believed her. She screwed up her face, making a muzzle mouth.

'You don't like television.'

'I shan't watch it. You and your little charge can have it upstairs in the living room.'

Still there was no show of enthusiasm and Benet said no more about it, but Mopsa must have taken to heart what she had said for a television set appeared, was brought over from a rental centre in Kilburn and installed in the living room. Its big grey pupil-less eye gleamed out from the corner among the still-unpacked crates. At half-past four Mopsa and the boy ensconced themselves on the settee in front of it, Mopsa with a cup of tea and the boy with apple

78

juice, this time in a cup. Benet went past the open door and looked at them, but did not go inside.

Afterwards she dated what happened from the arrival of the rented television set. That seemed to mark the demarcation line between the wretched limbo she had lived in and what came after it, a time of discovery, of stupefaction, of fear. Yet for a day or two after the television came, nothing much did happen and it would all have happened whether the television had come or not.

For a long time, petrified as a cameo in her mind remained that glimpse, that picture, of skinny, witch-like, galvanic Mopsa, sitting on the edge of the sofa – the way she always sat, poised, tense, as if ready to spring – and the little boy beside her, as snug in stretchy velour as a puppy in its skin, his thumb in his mouth, his other hand firmly holding on to a thick blue pottery mug. This image later seemed to her the last image in a cycle of despair or one that stood at the beginning of being afraid.

That night she did without the Soneryl. She dreamed of the tree of hands. James and she were walking on the Heath. She was pushing the empty pushchair and James was walking beside her, holding her hand. In life they had never been on the Heath together but this was a dream. They crossed a clearing by a sandy path and came into another piece of woodland, sunlit, high summer, the trees in fresh green leaf except for one in the centre of the copse which grew hands instead of leaves, red-nailed hands, gloved hands, hands of bone and hands of mail.

James was enraptured by the tree. He went up to it and put his arms round its trunk. He put his own hands up to touch its lowest hands. And Benet was reaching up to pick a hand for him, a lady's white hand with a diamond ring on it, when his crying penetrated the dream, broke into it, so that the tree grew faint, the sunshine faded and she was awake, out of bed, going to James.

Before she saw the empty room, she remembered. Her body twisted and clenched itself. She closed her eyes for a moment, made the necessary effort and went down the top flight to where the crying was coming from, the small bedroom next to Mopsa's. The room was in darkness. The boy stopped crying when she put the light on and picked him up. Had he been used to light in his room? Had light perhaps come into where he slept from a street lamp?

She switched on the bedside light, covering the shade with a folded blanket. Sucking his thumb, he fell asleep while she stood and watched him. She found now that she was really looking at him properly for the first time and found, too, that his face reminded her of someone. Who that someone was she didn't know. But this boy was very very like some adult person she knew or used to know. Generally speaking, the 'prettier' the child, the less he or she resembles an adult. Prettiness, loveliness in very young children is equated not with any individuality of looks but with a conformity to an ideal babyhood appearance, a kind of amalgam of a Raphael cherub, Peter Pan and a Mabel Lucy Atwell infant. The sleeping boy looked quite unlike any of these. His nose was straight and bold, his chin long, his mouth full and symmetrically curved, his eyebrows already marked in sweeping lines. You could see exactly what he would look like when he was grown-up, a craggy-faced fair man, tall and big-built, ugly till he smiled. Some grown man she knew must be like that, or some woman with thick lips and blond hair. Not Constance Fenton. Barbara Lloyd? She didn't think so. She had forgotten what Barbara Lloyd looked like, but now Barbara's face came clearly back to her, moon-like with low forehead and tip-tilted nose. He probably looked like his father whom she had never seen. There was something faulty in that reasoning. He reminded her of someone she *had* seen, someone she knew.

She knew she would get no more sleep. In a dressing gown, wrapped in a blanket, she sat in the study room among the books, the boy's remarkable drawings on her lap, willing the morning to come, yet not much wanting the morning. At about five she made herself tea.

It didn't start to get light until after seven-thirty. A cold grey twilight seemed to flow out of the cloudy sky, the green Heath, the pond, into the Vale of Peace. There had been no sign of the sun for many days. A boy was delivering newspapers from a canvas bag on his cycle handlebars. Benet watched him. It came to her that she hadn't seen a newspaper for several weeks.

The boy was due to go home on Wednesday and it was Sunday now. Benet went out by herself. She walked down to South End Green. The world was green and grey and chilly, a feeling in the air of November hopelessness, but at the same time it seemed unreal, spaced away from her at a remove and she encased in a capsule of glass. She found a newsagent's open and bought a Sunday paper but she didn't read it. She took it home and put it on the table in the basement room, but still she didn't read it and later on she couldn't find it. Mopsa must have removed it to her bedroom.

Mopsa and the boy watched television. Benet sat with them. She looked for things to do that she had never done with James, walking on the Heath, sitting in the study, watching television. Mopsa seemed uneasy to have her there – perhaps she was troubled by Benet's inconsistency in saying she would never watch television and then doing so – but she became easier once the news headlines had been read.

Brezhnev, the Soviet leader, had died and there was a lot about his funeral. Benet watched for about ten minutes. The boy was holding on to a white rabbit toy Mopsa must have bought him. He sat with his knees slightly apart, holding the rabbit but having absent-mindedly taken it from his mouth like a man with a cigar. His lips were compressed, his eyes fixed on the screen. Benet got up and went upstairs to the boy's room. There was nothing in the room but the bed he had been sleeping in and a small chest of drawers. She looked in those drawers but they were as empty as when she had bought that chest a year before. No suitcase had been sent with him, none of the inevitable carrier bags and holdalls of clothes and toys and paraphernalia that accompany small children whenever they travel. On top of the chest lay the Mothercare and Marks & Spencer carriers Mopsa had brought home. The clothes in them had been new. Mopsa had bought them. In one of the bags an unworn garment still remained, a pair of brown velour pants.

His clothes might be in Mopsa's room. Benet looked in Mopsa's room but there were no children's clothes anywhere. The *Sunday Times* that she had bought that morning lay curiously tucked between the two pillows on Mopsa's bed. She wouldn't have seen it if she hadn't opened the drawer in the bedside table and, in doing so, very slightly rucked up the bed cover.

Holding the newspaper, she began to go downstairs again. The boy's screams broke out of silence, they sounded as if they came from someone terribly injured. Benet ran down the stairs, seeing Mopsa's eyes, remembering the barricaded room and the knives. She opened the living-room door. The television had been switched off and the boy stood in front of it, screaming in distress, weeping bitter tears, belabouring the screen with his fists.

'What on earth is the matter?'

'He didn't like me turning off the TV.'

'Why did you?' Benet had to shout above his crying. She picked him up and tried to soothe him. He sobbed and beat her shoulder.

Mopsa didn't answer her. She was wearing her defiant, insouciant, nothing-really-matters face.

'What a silly noise,' she said to the boy. She got up and turned the television on again, altering the channel, Benet noticed, before she did so. A picture came, a pair of shire horses pulling a plough across a meadow.

The boy struggled to get down. He went up to the set and did a curious thing. He put his fingers on the screen and then round the rim of the screen as if he were trying to open it, to get inside or find something that was inside. That was what it looked like to Bent. He gave up the attempt after a moment or two and his oddly mature face, his little man's face, looked sad, resigned. He sat down again, not on the settee beside Mopsa but on the floor quite near to the television and he leaned forward, watching it intently.

Benet took the newspaper downstairs. There was a lot in it about Leonid Brezhnev. She was more interested in reading the home news but she couldn't find much of that and presently she saw why not. Pages three and four were missing. Someone – Mopsa – had cut them out.

If Benet were to ask her why, she would only deny it. And although she knew Mopsa must have done it, she could not absolutely prove it. It might have happened in the newsagent's – there was the remote possibility of that. The phone began to ring. She thought she had better answer it, though it was nearly two weeks since she had answered the phone. She had to start answering the phone again sometime. She had to start doing the explaining that Mopsa had failed to do, been afraid to do.

The voice was her father's. How was she? Was she recovered from the flu? How was Mopsa?

'She's fine,' Benet said and she added with a vindictiveness she almost at once regretted, 'She'll be home very soon.'

He hadn't asked about James. What would she have said if he had? She had felt antagonistic towards him because he hadn't asked about James, though James was dead, though she could not have answered if he had asked. He should have asked, it was cruel of him not to, crueller than he knew. She went up to fetch Mopsa. The boy was still sitting on the floor, still staring at the screen, though the horses were long gone and replaced by a man in sequins tango-ing with a microphone.

Benet heard her mother talking on the phone like a young girl in a bygone time, the Twenties perhaps, who had been rung up by some undergraduate or subaltern she had met at a tennis party. She sounded coy, petulant, flirtatious. With this man she had been married to for thirty years, she was coquettish, provocative. She giggled and gave a little scream of delight. Benet put on her coat and tied a scarf round her head and went out. She walked up the hill and down Heath Street and looked at a display of *The Marriage Knot* in paperback in the window of the High Hill Bookshop. There was a photograph of herself set in the midst of the arrangement. It had been taken when she was pregnant, though there was no sign of this through the folds of the dark loose dress she wore.

Go back two and a half years, she told herself, go back to the time before he was conceived. Go back to that. He was never conceived, it never happened. You didn't say to Edward, I'm going to have a baby but that makes no difference, it still won't work, it doesn't change things. You said a straight goodbye: Edward, it's over, we've come to the end. There was no baby, there never was. Hadn't Edward himself said there couldn't be?

'I don't believe you, Benet. You're lying. You wouldn't do that, even you wouldn't do that . . .'

She bought herself a cup of coffee and a sandwich and sat alone in a corner watching the people who were all in couples or in groups. It was strange, she thought, that you couldn't see she was pregnant in that photograph. James had been born three months later but you couldn't see she was pregnant. It was almost an omen.

They were both in bed asleep when she got back. She looked for the missing pages from the *Sunday Times* but she couldn't find it. Probably it also was in Mopsa's room, under the mattress perhaps.

Mopsa had two more visits to pay to the Royal Eastern, one on Monday morning and one on Friday. She left the boy with Benet and went off at nine-thirty. Benet sat him on the floor in the basement with some sheets of paper in front of him and three felt-tipped pens in different colours. He was wearing the brown velour pants and a yellow jersey and his bright pale yellow hair, newly washed, stood out like a sunburst. After a while he asked for a drink, calling himself Jay, or something that sounded more like Jye.

What words he did speak were uttered in unmistakable cockney. Barbara Lloyd herself probably talked cockney, she had left school at sixteen, Benet thought unfairly. Who knew what sort of background this husband of hers came from? Benet knew she was being mean-spirited and snobbish. She couldn't help it. Despair and desperation had returned to her in the night and clung to her like heavy wet clothes.

When the phone rang, she considered letting it ring. It wouldn't be her father this time. It would be Antonia or Chloe or Mary or Amyas Ireland or someone she would have to tell the truth to.

The boy looked round and said, 'Phone ring.'

'I know. I can hear it.'

'Ring ring,' said the boy and he made *brrr–brrr* sounds like a telephone bell.

Benet picked up the receiver, steeling herself.

'Is that you, Benet? This is Constance Fenton. Is your mother all right?'

'Yes. Yes, I think so. Quite all right. She's out at the moment.'

'Only she did make a half-promise to come over yesterday, and when she didn't come and didn't phone, we rather wondered. There's usually someone here to answer the phone. I'm out at work, of course, but Barbara's been here with Christopher . . .'

Benet interrupted her. Her throat had dried and her voice sounded thin. 'I thought your grandson was called James.'

'No, dear. Christopher. Christopher John after his father.'

'My mother hasn't been over at all then?'

'We talked on the phone, that's all. But we should so like to see her so if you could ask her just to give us a ring when she has a moment . . .'

Benet murmured the necessary things. She felt curiously weak and enfeebled. She could see the boy busily drawing away in red felt-tip. Even from this distance you could recognize a woman, a dog, a tree. She said goodbye to Mrs Fenton, put the receiver down, sat there with closed eyes, pushing her fingers through her hair.

Presently she got up and went upstairs and searched Mopsa's room. The missing newspaper pages were probably with her in her handbag. Benet found the boy's red coat in his bedroom. Mopsa had evidently washed it. When she was halfway downstairs a curious idea came to her, not at all a rational idea, that he shouldn't wear it, that it marked him out, that it made him immediately recognizable. Whoever he was. She went all the way up to the top again and made herself open the cupboard door in James's room where all his clothes were. She had bought him a duffle coat in thick brown tweed for the winter but he had never worn it. It had been on the large side to allow for growth. She made herself not think, merely do. She took the coat off its hanger and carried it downstairs and dressed the boy in it. They were going out to buy a paper. She didn't know how it would be, walking out with a child in a pushchair, a boy the same age as James. It wouldn't kill her though, that was for sure, it wouldn't kill her and she had to know.

They came home simultaneously, she and the boy and Mopsa. Walking up the hill, she had already read the few paragraphs on an inside page of the newspaper. It wouldn't have been a few paragraphs last Thursday, she thought, it would have been the front-page lead.

Mopsa saw the paper under Benet's arm. She came warily up the path and the steps, picking her way, almost wincing, as if it were hot sand she walked on instead of cold concrete. Benet held the door open for her, closed it quickly. She hadn't yet tried calling the boy by his real name.

'Jason,' she said, 'let me take your coat off, Jason.'

Mopsa made a little sharp sound and covered her mouth. The boy gave Benet a radiant smile. He was Jason, the smile seemed to say, at last they had cottoned on, at last they knew.

Benet took him into the living room. She knew Mopsa would follow her. She opened the paper and read aloud,

'Six days after the disappearance of Jason Stratford, aged one year and eleven months, from a street in Tottenham, north London, a police spokesman said today that hopes of his being found alive are weakening. Jason was last seen in a street of houses scheduled for demolition near the North-eastern Canal at Winterside Down where he lived with his mother, Mrs Carol Stratford, 28, and Barry Mahon, 20, a carpenter.

Mrs Stratford made an appeal for Jason's return after the evening news on BBC1 yesterday. "Jason would never have gone willingly with anyone," she said. "He wasn't used to strangers."

'The street was Rudyard Gardens,' Benet said to Mopsa. It struck her sickeningly that it was she who had shown Mopsa the place. 'When you came back from the hospital last Wednesday I suppose you took my route. Where did you find him? In a garden? Outside a shop?'

'He was sitting on a wall,' said Mopsa. She made her voice throb with pathos. She thrust her face close to Benet's, the lips quivering. 'All by himself. Left on a wall. No one wanted him. Then a dog came along, one of those big black Dobermanns, and it sniffed him and he was frightened. He was so frightened, he fell off the wall and I picked him up. No one was looking, no one saw me.'

'Evidently not.'

Mopsa put her hands on Benet. She laid trembling hands on her arms.

'I did it for you, Brigitte. I said I'd do anything in the world for you. You lost your boy so I got you another one. I got you another boy to make up for losing James.'

# 8

Jason had been gone for twenty-four hours, more than that, before they knew he was missing. That was almost the worst thing about it for Barry, that he could have been lost like that because one set of people thought he was with another set and the other set thought he was home with Carol. It was the hardest thing to explain to the police. Barry had just explained it for the umpteenth time. He sat in a room in the police station watching Detective Superintendent Treddick and Detective Inspector Leatham gather up their papers and get up from the table and leave him alone for yet another half-hour 'to think things over, to think if there's anything you want to add to what you've said'.

There were things he wanted to add but he knew better than that. He knew what sort of construction they would put on it.

'Get on all right with the boy, do you?' they had asked him in an artless way, almost a light and casual way, only nothing they said was casual.

'Of course I do. Fine,' he had said.

And that was true. But it was also true that he had wanted to be rid of him. Not for ever, not in *that* way, but just so that he could be alone with Carol. He recalled now what a relief it had been when Iris said to leave Jason with her overnight and how he had welcomed Beatie Isadoro's laconic acceptance of another child in the house, provided the money was there. To have Carol to himself with no one shouting out or crying in the next room, that had made him go along with Carol in all her complex baby-minding arrangements. Sometimes his conscience had given him a twinge, though not enough of one to make him do anything about it. That day, for instance, when Karen Isadoro or her mother or Iris or whoever it had been lost Jason, his conscience had been awake and active then, telling him to do something. He had bludgeoned it asleep. Did that mean it was really he who was responsible for Jason's disappearance? He hoped not, he didn't want to think like that. He remembered the day very clearly. Last Wednesday.

Ken Thompson and he were putting fitted furniture into the bedroom of a flat near Page Green. Considering the neighbourhood and the dilapidated state of the house, it didn't seem worthwhile, but who were they to question it? The money was good. These days, jobs like that were getting fewer and farther between. Too many do-it-yourself shops flourished and there were too many do-it-yourself magazines about. Soon after one o'clock, they were finished but for the mirror which was still in the shop at Crouch End being cut to this fancy shape. Ken said they might as well knock off and he'd come back himself and do the mirror around four.

Foreseeing they had no more than a morning's work there, Barry had made up his mind, while doing a final bit of glasspapering, that he would take Jason out somewhere for the afternoon. He got on to the Isadoros from a phone box. It was Dylan, the second or third boy, who answered. Jason was just going out with Mum and Karen in the pushchair. Barry said OK, thanks, they'd pick him up around six. He had that familiar feeling, a mixture of guilt and relief, we all experience when prevented from doing a tedious duty. Of course he could have insised, he could have said he was coming straightaway to take Jason to the park or to the swings or whatever, but he didn't say that. He told himself Jason was better off playing with kids than trailing about in the cold with him. It *was* cold. It was a gloomy grey November day with leaves blowing about everywhere and wet leaves underfoot.

Barry's free afternoon stretched before him. Carol didn't

go to the wine bar on Wednesdays. She worked all day for Mrs Fylemon and knocked off at five. He decided he would go and pick her up, not exactly call at the house but wait for her at the top of Fitzroy Park. That was more than three hours off. He crossed Green Lanes into Delphi Road and made his way to Lordship Avenue by way of the passage between Rudyard Gardens and Zimber Road, coming out at the big junction where the ABC Cinema was. The ABC were showing *The Dark Crystal* and the first programme was about to start. Barry liked films that frightened him, horror films that made the audience gasp and jump. He considered for a moment, then went in, buying himself twenty Marlboro on the way and being shown to the smokers' side of the auditorium.

While he was in there, Karen Isadoro, sent by her mother to buy a large loaf, must have been pushing Jason in the pushchair over the pedestrian crossing in Lordship Avenue towards Rudyard Gardens, towards the only baker's open around there on a Wednesday afternoon. And when Barry had been in there half an hour, Karen had wheeled Jason back again, the loaf in a plastic carrier over the pushchair handles, and in Brownswood Common Lane rung Iris's doorbell in Griffin Villas and found no one at home. Karen had revealed all this later, too many hours later, when with Leatham and the sergeant they had gone round to her school. Barry had known nothing of it at the time, it hadn't cross his mind to think of it while watching *The Dark Crystal*.

By the time the film was halfway through, Karen had encountered her friend Debbie in Lordship Avenue. That Wednesday was the last day of their half-term holiday. Debbie wanted Karen to go round the shops with her and buy a funny card for her mum's birthday. They didn't want Jason. Besides, Karen's mother had said Mrs Knapwell would have him, Mrs Knapwell had promised to take over, she'd got enough on her plate without Carol Stratford's kid day in and day out. They phoned Iris. Or rather they phoned the lady upstairs at Griffin Villas, a Mrs Love, because Iris hadn't got a phone. Iris was still out.

They took Jason into a newsagent's. At this time, Barry calculated he must have been lighting his fourth cigarette. They took Jason into a sweetshop that also sold cards and he started to cry, wanting sweets, bawling when they said they had no money for sweets. Debbie said she was going to try down Halepike Lane, there was a shop down there that sold funny cards, and she was going *now*. Karen could come if she wanted but she was to get shot of Jason first.

Barry wasn't clear quite what happened next. Who was? Everyone told conflicting stories, saving their own faces, trying to present themselves in the best possible light. Karen said she took Jason out of his pushchair and sat him on a wall in Rudyard Gardens while she went into the phone box there to phone Iris. She took him out of the pushchair because the greengrocer's Dobermann dog was sniffing around and Jason was frightened of the dog which couldn't reach him up on the wall. The trouble was, kids had broken the phone box inside and it didn't work. So she'd left Jason on the wall and run round the corner, just a little way round the corner, and phoned Iris from the call box outside the greengrocer's. She'd only got 10p – well, two 5p pieces – and Mrs Love took so long about the message . . .

Iris had never got it. She'd got a message from Mrs Love, yes. Oh, there was no doubt about that. It was that Karen Isadoro had got Jason. She'd gone up with Mrs Love to talk to Karen on the phone and Karen had gone, the line was making a dialling tone.

'I left a message,' Karen said to the inspector. 'I said to the lady upstairs to tell Jason's nan Jason was sitting on the wall in Rudyard and to pop down for him.'

'Did you really give that message?' said Leatham. 'You really and honestly told the lady that?'

Karen stuck to it for a moment or two and then she started crying. 'I meant to,' she mumbled.

'You meant to, but what did you really do?'

'I hadn't got no more money and the pips went . . .'

She was only eight. What did they expect? What had *he* expected? Barry hadn't thought much about it. He hadn't thought about it at all sitting in the cinema, watching extra-terrestrial reptilian creatures, smoking his sixth cigarette.

Soon after four, the programme was over. Barry got a bus to Muswell Hill and another down the Archway Road. By then it was five to five, so he walked as fast as he could, running part of the way, up the steep hill into Highgate Village and through Pond Square into the Georgian grandeur of the Grove. At the entrance to Fitzroy Park, in the gateway that marks the private road, he waited for Carol. He lit a cigarette. He knew that when she appeared – having turned the bend in the lane which stretched before him, walking towards him between the high hedges, under the overhanging branches of trees – he would experience that movement of the heart and constriction of the throat that was almost a feeling of sickness, though a pleasurable discomfort, that he had each time he went to meet her or saw her coming from a distance or even, coming over the Chinese bridge, saw the lights on in her house. It was new to him, he had never had it before he met her, but he recognized it as a symptom of being in love, just as a man who has never had a heart attack knows the pain in his left arm and the iron grip on his chest for what they are.

He had been there about ten minutes when she showed herself to him at the end of the tunnel of trees. His heart moved, seemed to turn over and then right itself with a small delicate lurch. She saw him and waved. He began to walk towards her. When they met, he put his arms on her shoulders and stood looking at her, her porcelain doll face sullen and rather tired, the gold coin curls clinging to a forehead on which the make-up had clogged and smeared. He took the holdall she carried from her. He didn't like to see her with it. His mother said you could always tell a woman who went out cleaning by her carrier bag with overall and rubber gloves inside.

'I'm knackered,' Carol said. 'The Prince of Wales'll be opening. I'm dying for a drink.'

'Have to make it a quick one then. We've got to fetch Jason. Beatie was a bit funny with me this morning about leaving him there so much.'

Carol always flared. She didn't like criticism. Well, she wasn't alone in that, Barry thought.

'She can get stuffed. She gets paid for it, doesn't she? And bloody good money too. Anyway you needn't worry about Jason. I phoned Madame Isadoro from Mrs F's and Mum's got him, had him since three, so we can have ourselves a ball, my dear.' She took his arm and snuggled up. 'Mrs F's off to Tunisia for three weeks and she gave me my money in advance, fifty quid and a bonus for keeping the houseplants watered. How about that?' She produced and waved at him a fifty-pound note, crisp, greenish-gold.

'I've got money,' Barry said stiffly. 'I don't want you spending your money.'

'We had a turn-out of some of her stuff. There was this Zandra Rhodes dress she said I could have. I've got it in that bag. It's something else again, I tell you. Fancy a woman her age thinking she could wear Zandra Rhodes.'

And no doubt Beatie Isadoro genuinely had thought Jason was with Iris, had been safe with Iris since three. Karen thought so too. It wasn't the first time she had left Jason in the street at an appointed place for his grandmother to find him. As for Iris, she had scarcely thought about it at all. Why should she? For all she knew she had been let off the hook for the afternoon. Jason was with Karen, with Karen's family, in the security of the two overcrowded houses, and she had an unexpected free afternoon to unsqueeze her feet out of her high-heeled sandals, get a fag on, watch the TV, wait in peace for Jerry to come home and take her down the Bulldog.

Barry and Carol had a drink in the Prince of Wales and then another and then they went over to the Flask. Carol said Dennis Gordon had said something about this new club at Camden Lock called the Tenerife, a drinking club with a disco; you just paid a two-pound membership fee at the door, and she wouldn't mind trying it. They had something to eat in a steak house first, and Carol went into the Ladies and changed into the dress which was yellow and red and gold with a short skirt and huge balloon sleeves and a gold sash. She had her red boots on so it looked good, it looked marvellous.

'You look great,' said Barry. 'I wish I'd thought to change, I feel a bit of a mess.'

'You're OK,' Carol said indifferently. With overt narcissism, she gazed into a mirror on the wall of the restaurant at her glittering image.

Barry had suggested they gave the lady upstairs at Iris's a ring and say where they were and they would be late back. He was glad now he'd suggested that, though sorry he hadn't pressed the point. Carol had dissuaded him and dissuaded him easily. He was already anticipating dancing with her, their bodies pressed close among the other hot young bodies, the blue and violet and red lights winking and spotting, the music a hot, throbbing, heavy sound.

If he had got through to Iris, talked to Iris, what good would it have done? Jason was gone by then, gone three hours and more. And Iris would probably have been out anyway, and he would have thought she was doing what he always suspected her of doing but had never probed into too deeply – putting Jason to bed with a drop of whisky in his bottle and leaving him to go down the pub with Jerry.

As it happened, it was nearly two before he and Carol got back. They had to have a taxi. Winterside Down was dead at that hour, though the yellow lamps on their stilts were still on, casting over the straight streets, the U-shaped streets, the single lonely tower and the sluggish strip of canal a phosphorescence that bleached everything to moon-scape brown. The taxi wound through the chilly, yellowish-brown, treeless place. They had attempted to grow trees on Winterside Down but somehow they had quickly died natural deaths or kids had destroyed them. Overhead the sky was a reddish smoky ochre, uniform and starless. There had been a moon when they had been down at Camden Lock but the moon had gone now. Two of the motorbike boys without their machines loitered on the corner of Summerskill and Dalton. Barry wondered if they ever went to bed, sometimes he wondered if they were real. The colours of their plumage were drained by the lamps but he could tell from the shape and stance of them that they were Blue Hair and Hoopoe. They stared at the taxi. Their stillness and their silence, their apparently purposeless biding of time, gave them an air at once threatening and sinister.

Carol had had a lot to drink. She didn't want to wait to get upstairs. In the half-dark, street-lamp-lighted living room, without drawing the curtains she pulled off the Zandra Rhodes dress and her tights and bra. Her body, which was very white, gleamed like marble. She lay on the settee and pulled Barry on to her and into her, her thighs and hips no longer marble-like but soft and moist as cream. There was sweat in pearls on her upper lip. Carol had a way of making little moans alternating with giggles when she made love. Barry held his mouth over hers to stop the rippling, gurgling laughter.

She fell asleep. He had lit cigarettes for them but she was asleep. He picked her up and carried her to bed and then he went down again to fetch the dress and put it on a hanger.

The first time the police really questioned him – the first time they had him down here at the station – they had wanted to know why, next morning, the Thursday morning, Barry hadn't gone straight round to Iris's to fetch Jason. Carol didn't work on Thursday mornings till she started at the wine bar at eleven. Why hadn't he fetched Jason – why, rather, hadn't he *tried* to fetch Jason – from Iris's and taken him home to his mother before he went to work? It was something he had often done in the past. The first time Inspector Leatham asked him, he simply said he didn't know why, he was late, he left it to Carol. This time, half an hour ago, he had admitted to having had the worst hangover of his life that Thursday morning. With hammering going on in his head, with a dry mouth, hardly able to walk upright, he had staggered downstairs, drunk water out of the cold tap. If he was going to make it to the house in Alaxandra Park where Ken and he were due by nine sharp to start fitting bookshelves, he had to be out of Winterside Down by eight-twenty and out he was, grimly walking with hunched shoulders, his aching eyes screwed up against the cold. The last thing that concerned him was where Jason was or who was going to look after him that day. He didn't think of Jason, he had forgotten him.

Coming home, he remembered. He remembered because, as a matter of course, he called in on Iris or Beatie's to collect him. On Thursdays Carol did a split shift at the wine bar, eleven-till-three and five-till-eleven – long awful hours that Barry hated to think of her having to work.

'You hadn't seen the boy,' Superintendent Treddick said to him, 'for what? A day and a night and half a day? You hadn't seen him since about eight on the Wednesday morning?'

'We knew where he was.' Barry realized what a stupid answer this was as soon as he had made it.

'That's just what you didn't know.'

Iris lived in the bottom third of a very down-at-heel yellow brick Victorian house. There were three rooms and a kitchen with a bath in it, concealed most of the time by a wooden cover that doubled as a counter. Carol and Maureen had been born and brought up there. There they had been punched and kicked and scarred with belt buckles, and Maureen, who cried a lot, had had her arm broken. Barry had occasionally wondered what Iris had been doing while all this went on. Watching TV probably, smoking, calculating that it couldn't go on for ever and thankful at least that it wasn't her taking the brunt of Knapwell's violence.

It was Jerry who had come to the door.

'Jason?' he said as if he had never heard the name before, as if it were a foreign name he might not be pronouncing properly.

Iris screeched from inside somewhere: 'Who's that at the door, Jerry?' She came out, wiping her hands on a dishcloth. 'Oh, no, Barry, you've made a mistake there. Come to the wrong shop. Those blackies have got him. I haven't had sight nor sound of him since – when was it? – Monday. Don't know ourselves, do we, Jerry, we've been so quiet.'

Before he got to the Isadoros, Barry remembered being up in Highgate the night before and Carol saying she had phoned Beatie and Beatie saying Jason was with Iris. But he went to the double house just the same. Carol could have made that up to keep him quiet. She wasn't untruthful but she wasn't above telling a white lie so as not to spoil his evening. He thought of her fondly, of those small human weaknesses that made her more lovable.

'Jason's with his nan, Barry.' Beatie herself had come heavily to the door herself, the baby Kelly settled on her flabby hip as in a beanbag chair. 'Karen handed him over to his nan like half-three yesterday.'

That was when Barry had his first sensation of alarm. 'She hasn't got him; I've just been there.'

'Then he'll be with his auntie Maureen. Maybe that's what Karen did say, that he went to his auntie Maureen.'

Jason had never stayed a night at Maureen's. Maureen didn't like children. She liked her home and presumably her husband Ivan to whom, though only twenty-six, she had been married for nine years. In those nine years, she had turned her three-storey terraced house in Winterside Road into a little palace. She and Carol didn't look alike but you could see they were sisters. There was something similar in the roundness of face and the way their hair grew at their temples. But Maureen's hair was straight mouse and she was dowdy and flat-chested. She reminded Barry of a gerbil he had once seen in a children's zoo while taking Tanya and Ryan out one weekend.

'Carol shouldn't bloody have kids if she can't keep tabs on where they are,' she said. She had been ironing and the place smelt of spray-on starch, breath-catching, too scented. 'It's kids like hers get murdered, you see it on TV all the time.'

'For God's sake . . .'

'Someone's got him, that's for sure. He's not taken a bedsit somewhere on his own.'

After that he had phoned Carol at the wine bar.

'I can't tell the fuzz I haven't seen him since yesterday morning. I can't do that, Barry. What'll they say to me? You know what a bunch of shits they are. I can't stick my neck out like that. What'll they do to me?'

'I don't know,' said Barry, feeling young and useless.

'Oh, Dave, Dave,' Carol shouted. 'What did you have to die for? Why did you leave me all alone? Why aren't you here to look after me?'

Barry put his arms round her. 'I'll look after you.'

Dennis Gordon, the man who drove trucks across Europe, had brought her home. When he wasn't in Turkey or Yugoslavia or somewhere or in the big house he had out Mill Hill way, he was generally to be found in the wine bar. Barry caught a glimpse of his car, a metallic-finish blue Rolls, an amazing car, but he hadn't come in. Carol had gone very pale. She kept licking her lips until most of the lipstick had come off. It took him a while to persuade her to go to the police – they *had* to go, what else? – but in the end she agreed, making a face, clenching her fists. She went upstairs to change and came down dressed in a grey flannel skirt and black sweater with a fawn-coloured mac Barry hadn't seen before. It made her look older and, at the same time, more like Maureen's sister.

He hoped she would tell the police he was her fiancé but instead she said what she said to the neighbours at Winterside Down, that he rented her spare room. Barry didn't let himself be hurt by it. It was natural that Carol who had had a hard life and a struggle should want to appear respectable. No one believed her anyway, Barry thought tenderly. What man, looking at Carol, would believe she hadn't got a lover?

The search for Jason had begun that night. He had gone out with the search party himself. The police had questioned them all – him, Carol, Iris, Beatie, Karen, and all the kids, everyone on the estate for all he knew. And sometime on the Friday morning, around eleven, Carol and he and Inspector Leatham and a young constable, a whole party of them, had stood in Rudyard Gardens at the Lordship Avenue end and been shown something lying among the rubble and rubbish and litter that filled a narrow strip of front garden behind a low wall. Barry recognized it at once. He had washed it himself the previous week after Maureen had said, looking at it in Jason's hand, 'It's a disgrace, Carol, that animal, whatever it is. I reckon you ought to have that painlessly destroyed.'

A woolly lamb but made of nylon. A Christmas present from Kostas's wife Alkmini. Carol looked at the grey shapeless object and started screaming.

'His lamb! That's Jason's lamb! He'd never have gone off on his own without his lamb!'

So they had known then, they had known for sure.

Superintendent Treddick didn't come back and nor did Inspector Leatham. They sent a sergeant in. The sergeant told Barry he could go now if he liked and Barry walked home. Neither he nor Carol had been back to work yet. They had hardly been alone either. Iris and Jerry had been there most of the weekend and then there had been Maureen and Ivan and one neighbour after another. Carol had never got on with the Spicers next door, the people who kept the Old English rabbits Jason liked to look at through the fence, but Kath Spicer had been in and Carol had cried on her shoulder.

When he turned into Summerskill Road, he saw Dennis

Gordon's Rolls parked outside the house, half-a-dozen children round it and one of them, a Kupar not an Isadoro, with a sharp-pointed nail at the ready. They looked at Barry in silence as if Barry might tell them off but he didn't say anything, it was no business of his if Dennis Gordon was daft enough to leave his flash car unattended on council estates.

Dennis Gordon was in the house with Carol, and Kostas with them. Gordon had brought Carol an armful of red roses tied up in cellophane and silver ribbon. Kostas had brought her two bottles of Riesling. Though no more than forty, Kostas had a face like an old brown leather bag. His hair was jet-black, he had a brigand-like moustache and he always wore very pale-coloured suits. Today he was wearing a pale yellow one with a black shirt. Dennis Gordon, whom Barry had often heard about but never seen before, was a big dark man with a very long chin and hooded eyes. He wore a signet ring that looked as if hewn out of a nugget of silver – though more probably a nugget of platinum or white gold. It was a knuckle-duster of a ring, an ever-ready weapon, and Barry remembered Carol talking admiringly of his violent ways. He had the look of a thug, a gangster. There was some story that he had shot his first wife, only luckily for him she hadn't died of it but just divorced him.

When he saw Barry, Kostas acknowledged him by raising his dirty-looking hand an inch or two off his knee. Dennis Gordon looked round and away again. He was asking Carol if there was anything he could do for her, anything that was in his power he'd do, she only had to name it. It broke his heart thinking of her all alone.

Carol had probably told him that tale about having a lodger. 'She's not alone,' Barry said. 'She's got me.'

Dennis Gordon put his fist up to his mouth and bit on the great platinum lump. He ground his teeth on it for a bit. 'I saw you on the TV,' he said to Carol. 'You were a real little cracker.'

'D'you reckon?' Carol said, looking pleased.

'You've got what it takes, you're photogenic. They ought to give you a job at the studios.'

Barry went out into the kitchen, looking for something to eat. He made himself a cup of tea but he didn't take it into the living room. Somehow you couldn't imagine those two drinking tea in a million years. Dennis Gordon looked the sort who'd subsist on undiluted brandy. When he went back in, they had gone and Iris had arrived. Iris never drank tea either. They opened the Riesling.

'They've started dragging the canal, I see,' said Iris.

Carol looked at her wide-eyed. She clapped a hand up over her mouth. Barry could have killed Iris.

'It's routine,' he said. 'They told me it was just routine.'

Iris lit a cigarette. Her fingers were yellow with nicotine, her eyebrows and the front bit of her hair were yellow with it. She showed her yellowed teeth when she stuck out her tongue to take a shred of tobacco off it. 'There's swans sometimes on that canal. He was a little monkey, he used to want to get down to them swans.'

She spoke as if Jason were dead. Barry sometimes wondered if she had any feelings, any affection or interest even, or sorrow or anxiety. Perhaps all that sort of thing had been wrung out of her years ago in her married life. Carol took one of her cigarettes and lit it, and a little colour came into her face. She hadn't bothered to put any make-up on and Barry knew that was a sign of how she must be feeling. Her anxiety for Jason had distanced her from him, he felt, and they hadn't made love since that Wednesday night. She sat hunched up in the armchair in jeans and the grey sweater he didn't like, her arms wrapped round her knees. She looked about fifteen. They hadn't had a single photograph of Jason for the police. Carol had looked Leatham straight in the eye and said, 'I haven't got money to spend on cameras,' but the newspapers had made up for that by printing pictures they took of her. She had been on the front page of a couple of papers, looking like she looked now, young and unhappy and beautiful. Barry had kept those two front pages for the sake of the photos; he thought he would keep them for ever.

Perhaps it would sound unfeeling. The truth was he was upset about Jason, but his anxiety was for Carol. He couldn't honestly say he *loved* Jason, he wasn't gut-worried like he would have been if he was Jason's own father. It was for Carol's sake he wanted him back. Looking from Iris to Carol and then at smiling Dave in his frame on the radiator shelf, Barry thought for the first time about Jason's father. He had to have a father, somebody had to be his father, he hadn't been made in a test tube by some anonymous donor and planted in Carol.

While Jason was with them, he had never thought about who his father might be, but now he was gone it had begun to weigh on his mind. Somehow the identity of his father mattered more now. Sooner or later, and probably sooner, that man, whoever he was, would re-enter Carol's life because Jason was lost and Jason was his son as well as Carol's.

Barry made up his mind that he would ask Carol straight out who Jason's father was. He longed for Iris to go so that he could be alone with her.

# 9

Mopsa was proud of herself. 'I took his pushchair too. I folded it up and put it in the boot of the car.'

'Where is it now?'

'My goodness, it must still be there!'

'You really thought any child would do for me. I'd lost mine so any child would do for a substitute. Just get a new one. Like when your dog dies and you go out and buy a puppy.'

'It wasn't any child,' Mopsa protested. 'I found you a little boy. I found you a fair-haired boy.'

Benet said in a stifled faint voice, 'A puppy of the same breed . . .'

Jason came over to her for her to take his coat off. James's coat. They were almost the same size as well as the same sex, the same type. Two Anglo-Saxon boys. She thought of Gregory's dictum – not Angles but angels. Mopsa, driving by, had found him on a wall . . .

She took Jason's hand and went downstairs. Mopsa crept down after them. She really did creep, treading stealthily, as if to make one false move, one jarring noise, would bring Benet's wrath down upon her. She tip-toed across the kitchen, watching Benet out of the corner of her eye. Her face had a lopsided look today as if she had Bell's palsy or were purposely holding the cheek nearest to Benet rigid. Jason found his drawing things and a clean sheet of paper. Police over the whole country are searching for him, Benet thought, they suspect the worst, they think he's been assaulted, injured, murdered. And all the time he's been quietly here, drawing pictures, going for walks, watching television – watching his own mother on television and trying desperately to make the set disgorge her!

A timid hand was laid on her arm. Mopsa twisted her head round until it was touching her shoulder and looked up into Benet's face. It was a grotesque parody of a small child's appealing attitude. Mopsa's eyes were blurred and absolutely out of focus.

'I did it for you, Brigitte.'

'I know. You said so.' Benet tried to keep her voice gentle and even. I must not hate my mother . . . 'The question is whether I ring up the police and ask them to come and fetch him or whether I put him in the car and drive him down to the police station in Rosslyn Hill. The latter, I suppose. Explaining on the phone will be difficult, to say the least.'

'You mustn't do that,' Mopsa said. 'You won't do that, will you?'

'Which? Not phone them or not take him?'

'You mustn't go to them at all. You know what they'll say, Brigitte.' A look of ineffable foxy cunning spread over Mopsa's face. When she strained her face into these expressions, the tensed nostrils went white. She made her way over to Jason who was sitting on the floor drawing and pounced on him. She snatched him up in her arms, drawing paper and pen and all. He flinched as if he expected a blow. Mopsa clutched him, sitting him on her knee and holding him as if he were some sort of prop she needed for her act. 'You know what they'll say, don't you? They'll say you stole him to make up for losing your own boy. It's a well-known thing, it's what bereaved women do. I've often seen about it in the papers. And you're famous – well, you're well known, people have heard of you. It'll be all over the papers that you kidnapped him.'

Jason struggled off her lap. He made his escape, first to the door and then he started up the stairs. Back to make another attempt on the television, Benet guessed.

'Yes, but I didn't,' she said. 'You did.'

'They won't believe that.'

'Of course they will. I shall tell them. I'm sorry but I haven't any choice. I shall have to tell them you have a – a history of mental illness and you took him.'

What happened next made Benet glad Jason wasn't in the room to see it. Though he must have heard Mopsa's screams, he wasn't present. Mopsa simply opened her mouth as wide as it would go and let out screams of terrific volume. She stood there screaming into Benet's face. Benet had never seen or heard anything like it and for a moment, beyond putting her hands up ineffectually to cover her ears, she couldn't move. She knew the prescribed thing was to strike a hysterical person in the face but she couldn't bring herself to do this; her arm felt as weak as when one attempts to strike a blow in a dream.

'Mother, stop. Please stop . . .'

Mopsa went on screaming. She fell on her knees and put her arms round Benet's legs, hugging her legs and screaming, breathily and hoarsely now as she exhausted herself. She crouched on the floor, scrabbling at Benet's shoes.

'Mother, I can't stand this. Please stop.'

For a moment she had been afraid. The skin on the back of her neck had crept and she had felt the hairs standing erect on gooseflesh. She had been frightened of pathetic, crazed Mopsa. She bent down and got hold of Mopsa's shoulders and shook her, though without much result. Mopsa slithered out of her grasp and drummed her fists on the floor and shouted: 'They'll commit me, they'll make you commit me, I'll be certified, I'll never come out, I'll die in there!'

'Of course they won't. I won't let them.'

'You can't stop them if you tell. The court will do it. I'll be up in court and the court will make an order to put me away and I'll never come out again!'

Her voice rose once more to a scream. It was true too. She knew all about it. What fool was it had said the mad don't know they're mad? She knew all right and she knew what could happen. If she were convicted of abducting

105

Jason Stratford, the court might well make a hospital order that she be detained for treatment and then restrict her later discharge.

'Please stop shouting, Mother.'

Benet again tried to lift her up. Jason opened the door and stood there, looking in warily. It suddenly seemed to her unforgivable that they should detain him here and then subject him to this sort of thing. She picked him up and told him it was all right, there was nothing to be frightened of, though she was by no means sure if this were true. She wasn't sure if locking Mopsa up where she couldn't do any more damage and cause any more chaos might not be the best thing for everyone. Mopsa was sobbing now, crawling and groping to hoist herself up on a chair. She's my *mother*, Benet thought, I can't send my own mother into a madhouse. A feeling of helplessness took hold of her, a sense that she was inadequate to handle the situation Mopsa had got her into. And holding Jason like this, snuggled up against her, the way she had been used to holding her own child, was suddenly so repugnant she could have opened her arms with a violent rejecting gesture and dropped him.

Of course she didn't do that. She set him down as gently as she could. The urge that had come to her when Mopsa first brought him home now returned. Why shouldn't she leave, go off to a hotel somewhere, go abroad even, and leave them here together to sort out Mopsa's mess? Phone the police from an airport and tell them where Jason Stratford was?

Sitting on an upright chair, Mopsa wound her feet round its legs. She wrung her hands, pulling at her thumbs with her fingers.

'I haven't got a driving licence.'

'What does that mean?'

'It ran out before we went to live in Spain. I never got another one. Your father said it wasn't safe to let me drive.' Mopsa's manner had become a spiteful little girl's. 'They'll know I haven't got a licence. I'll tell them I can't drive. They can see I'm not strong enough to lift a big boy like that.' Because Benet wasn't answering she began to drum with her heels. 'Why would I take him? I don't like children. I didn't take him, I didn't and you can't make me say I did! How dare you say I took him!'

Now, too late, Benet saw she should have said nothing to Mopsa about going to the police. She should simply have gone. Put Jason in the pushchair, said she was going shopping and gone. Speaking firmly to Mopsa, speaking one firm sentence to her, had this terrible effect. She had been told it had, though she had never actually seen it happen before.

'I didn't take him, Brigitte. I didn't.'

'No, you didn't take him.'

'You took him and tried to put the blame on me.'

'All right,' Benet said. 'As you like, anything you say.'

I must not hate my mother . . .

She fetched two Valium for Mopsa and made her a cup of coffee. Jason would be hungry even if she and Mopsa were not, he would want his lunch. She opened the oven door. There was a cake tin inside. A tide of hysteria welled up inside her when she saw it. Mopsa had put that cake in the oven last week but she had never turned the oven on. Little circles of pale green mould grew on the uncooked but dry crust of the cake mixture. Benet ran the cold tap and threw water over her face. It kept the hysteria down, it left her with a slight headache. She had no idea what she was going to do and she pushed it out of her mind, concentrating on lunch, on keeping Mopsa calm and the boy contented.

Jason had a sleep and then they all went out for a walk on the Heath. Benet realized that ever since she had known who Jason was she had been hourly expecting the police to phone or call, that while she was out she expected policemen to come out from behind bushes. The doorbell rang after they had been back about ten minutes and she knew it was going to be two policemen in plain clothes, an older one and a young one, one of whom would produce a warrant card and put a foot in the door. She braced herself, hesitating for a second before she opened the door. It was a Jehovah's Witness, an ingratiating young woman with a child not much older than Jason.

Mopsa's day had exhausted her. She fell asleep on the settee watching television. The last item on the news was of police dragging the canal at Winterside Down. In the background Benet recognized the rears of the houses in Winterside Road where she and Mary and Antonia had lived and where Tom Woodhouse had lived next door. It seemed to mean nothing to Jason. If he recognized the Chinese bridge and the green lawns and the tower he gave no sign of it. He seemed more interested in Mopsa's sleep behaviour. Her mouth was slightly open and every so often she gave a tiny light snore. Jason was listening for the next snore, and when it came, he turned to Benet and laughed.

It was his bedtime. She supposed she would have to bath him. Why not? Tomorrow morning she would take him to the police without telling Mopsa. She would take him to the police and explain about Mopsa as sensibly and rationally as she could, and whatever the consequences might be, they must both face them. As it was, she had probably done a dreadful thing in keeping Jason from his mother a day longer than was necessary. She thought of James and of how she would have felt.

Jason sat on her lap in the bathroom and she took off his clothes. He was impatient to get into the water. She stripped off his vest. She caught her breath and made a little sharp sound.

Old bruises, yellowish now, covered the left side of his back, the side of his body and the underside of his left arm. There was also on the arm an abraded area which had scabbed. Besides this, on his back, a little to the right of the spine, was a big scar not yet whitened, that looked as if made by some metal object with sharp edges, and above it, almost at the shoulder, reachable if the collar of a shirt or jumper were pulled down, the deep scar of a small circular burn. Once while living in the Winterside Road attic, Benet had seen a man, reputed to be on hard drugs, unaware of what he was doing, stub out a cigarette on the back of his own hand. It had made a mark like that.

She lifted him into the water. Unable to bear the sight of his back, she turned her face away. To her own astonishment, because what she had seen first shocked her, then filled her with undirected anger, tears came into her eyes and began to fall. A violent emotion of quite a different kind from grief had triggered off the crying that had to come. At last she was crying for James. She laid her arms on the edge of the washbasin and her head on her arms and cried.

Jason stood up, banging the water and shouting, 'No, no, no, no!'

He hated her crying. She rubbed her face with a towel and took deep breaths. Watching her carefully, he waited until she was done with all that, until she was calm again, and then he picked the soap out of the soapdish and handed it gravely to her, indicating she was to wash him. His very mature face was intensely serious.

Up in the other bathroom were all James's bath toys. Washing Jason, going carefully over the bruised places, she supposed he would have enjoyed playing with them. But she would not have enjoyed seeing him play with them, to say the least, the very least. In spite of the bruises, the scarred back, her dislike of him returned. He had caused her so much trouble, it would be a relief to be rid of him, whatever the consequences of handing him over.

Early in the morning, before Jason and Mopsa were even awake for all she knew, she was down at Hampstead station buying a newspaper. The missing boy story rated three paragraphs on an inside page. Jason's mother was mentioned as having two other children, both in the care of the local authority. She had been a widow for nearly four years and for the past six months had been living with a man eight years her junior. There was nothing in the story about the possibility of murder or anyone being charged or even that it was expected someone would be charged.

She found a café open and sat in there drinking coffee and reading the paper and trying to eat toast. It reminded her of those distant days when she had lived in Winterside Road, had been trying to make it as a freelance journalist, before she met Edward, before James was dreamt of. Dropping into cafés had been a feature of her routineless life then, of her days in which time and its pressures were of minor significance. Yet she was not back in that time, she could not by any effort of the imagination unmake James.

When the High Hill Bookshop opened, she went in, found the sociology section and bought two paperbacks called *The Battered Child Syndrome* and *The Endless Chain: Some Aspects of Child Abuse*. The feeling that the police were waiting for her, watching her, tailing here even, had gone. She felt quite different from the way she had yesterday, the world looked different. She had had a hideous dream she wanted to forget of Mopsa being made to confess by sadistic policemen who were torturing her with lighted cigarettes.

Back in the Vale of Peace, Jason was sitting on the floor of the basement room drawing something that might have been a woman with curly hair. Mopsa was working over the room with spray polish and a cloth, humming to herself Herbert's hymn about who sweeps a room but for Thy laws makes it and the action fine. She broke off to say, though quite calmly, that she and Jason had wondered where Benet was, they had been worried, they hadn't been able to think where she had got to.

What am I going to do? Benet thought. I need time to think. Am I going to see my mother in court – and incidentally the fact that she is *my* mother all over the papers? Am I going to see her *committed*? I don't think I can face the beginning of it, let alone see it through. She sat in the chair by the window and started reading *The Battered Child Syndrome*. The case histories were painful to read about and ultimately depressing. One of the longest and most detailed was one of a boy to whom the author, to conceal his true identity, had given the after all common name of

James. Mopsa put her blue raincoat on and tied her head up in a scarf and took Jason out for a walk.

The phone rang twice but Benet didn't answer it. It was impossible to imagine at the moment speaking to anyone in that world outside, to anyone not involved with Mopsa and Jason. Or to anyone – and that was everyone – who did not know about James.

'When were you thinking of going home?'

Mopsa looked injured. 'I suppose you want to get rid of me.'

'Do you have to go to the hospital again?'

'On Friday morning.'

'Then if you went home on Saturday it might be the best thing. I don't want to be unkind, Mother, it isn't that I want to be rid of you. But we have to do something about this child. I thought, for your sake, I'd wait till you were on the plane and then I'd hand him over to the police. I'll wait until you've gone. And if it's any comfort to you, I'm pretty sure we don't have an extradition treaty with Spain. They couldn't get you back.'

'But I've got a return ticket and it's for next Wednesday week.'

'I'll buy you a seat on a plane for Saturday.'

'Fancy having so much money you can just buy plane tickets like other people go on a bus,' said Mopsa.

Benet made no answer to this. She was already marvelling at her own behaviour. How had it come about that yesterday morning there had been no doubt in her mind that Jason must immediately be returned to his family, while now she was calmly resolved on keeping him for a further four days? For Mopsa's sake? Yes, partly. To expose Mopsa to the humiliation, the terrors and indignities of appearing in court would serve no useful purpose, social or moral. All it could ensure – and there was a good deal of doubt about this – was that Mopsa would receive treatment. But she was receiving treatment already, or plans were afoot for her to receive treatment. That was what those tests at the Royal Eastern were about. But there was another reason for not handing Jason back in haste.

All day yesterday, while reasoning with Mopsa, while trying to keep Mopsa calm and on an even keel, she had been thinking about Jason's mother, about that woman of precisely her own age who had appealed on television for the return of her son. It was wrong of her, monstrously cruel, to keep that woman in suspense an hour, a moment, longer. And then she had bathed Jason and seen his scars. Since then she had read those books. Was she going to send him back to that?

It was not so much Carol Stratford she had in mind when she thought along these lines as the twenty-year-old boyfriend. Barry Mahon. There were young stepfathers or mothers' young boyfriends in a good many of those case histories. Benet had a picture in her mind of Barry Mahon, a big, good-looking probably illiterate hulk. Impatient with children. Given to violence. Maybe a drinker. She told herself she had no grounds for thinking this way – but didn't she have? Hadn't she seen the scar of a cigarette burn and the scar made by some metal tool?

She needed time to think. Those four days she had would give her time to think how she would handle Jason's return. Someone was going to have to be alerted about the violence that was being meted out to Jason. She wouldn't be in a very strong position to press this home, but somehow she was going to have to, so that he was never sent back to that.

Against Carol Stratford she hardened her heart. Mopsa was her concern and she herself was her concern and Jason who had been a defenceless victim, but not Carol Stratford whose other two children had already been taken away from her legally and justly . . .

# 10

Jason had been missing for a week. Wednesday had come round again and he had been gone a whole week. Barry had to go back to work. It might have been different if Jason had been his own child or if he had been married to Carol. As it was, he had no real excuse for leaving Ken to carry on on his own. Jobs were hard to come by too. It wasn't that he thought Ken would replace him but rather that he might just decide he didn't need a partner at all.

He asked Carol to marry him. It wasn't the first time, more like the fourth or fifth. They weren't as close as they had been, he felt that, he felt as if she had slipped a little away from him since Jason went. For one thing, they hadn't made love. He didn't like to touch her, it seemed wrong unless she made it plain she wanted him. The doctor had given her sleeping pills and she was asleep sometimes before he got into bed. Often he just sat there looking at her while she slept, for a whole hour he sat watching her and wondering what experiences were chronicled inside that sleeping brain under the soft blond baby curls. Thinking like that made him feel distanced from her, a stranger, as if she might wake up and ask him who he was and what he was doing in her bedroom.

That first evening he got home, he found her dressed up again and with make-up on. She looked like the Carol he had always known. There was nothing now to stop them going out in the evening. He thought that but he didn't say it aloud, he was shocked that he might have said it. They had the Turkish takeaway he had brought in with him and the wine he had bought on the way.

113

'Let's get married, Carol,' he said. 'If we make up our minds now we could be married in three weeks.'

She didn't answer him. Slowly she lifted her shoulders in a shrug.

'If I was your husband, I could look after you better. I could shoulder some of this.'

'I don't see what difference it makes,' she said.

He tried to persuade her. After a bit she said illogically, unfairly, 'It's not your kid that's missing, that's probably got himself murdered.'

She had hurt him. She could hurt him more easily than anyone. But he stood up to it. 'As good as,' he said. 'It'd be as good as mine if we were married.'

She made him a devastating reply that silenced him.

'A baby's part his mother and part his father and that's all there is to it. You can't alter that.'

He quoted that back to her next day. It was early evening and they were on their way back from the doctor's. The doctor had said to come back and see him next week and Carol had and got tranquillizers. She held on to his arm as they came into Winterside Down. It was the first time for a week she had touched him of her own volition and he was ashamed of feeling so happy.

'Do you really feel that, what you said, about the kids being part of their father? I mean, I expect you feel that about Dave, I can understand that. You'd sort of *see* Dave in Ryan and Tanya . . .

'I could see Jason's father in him then, couldn't I?'

Why had he asked? Why had he mentioned it? Until he met Carol, Barry had not known how serenity and contentment and peace can be cut off by a dozen indifferently uttered words. But I've no right to be happy, he thought, and it's only fair she's punishing me for it. He felt her hand tighten on his arm and he thought she was reassuring him, even saying she was sorry. He turned his face to hers. She was looking ahead of her at Beatie Isadoro walking towards them with Kelly in the pram and Karen and Dylan walking alongside.

114

Carol hadn't seen Beatie since Jason's disappearance. Beatie's vast shape in a pink mac over a green smock over a brown striped dress or skirt took up most of the pavement.

'Get out of my way, you fat cow,' said Carol.

Beatie stared at her. 'The police come up to me today,' she said. 'I told them a thing or two about the marks I seen on that poor little baby you neglected.'

Barry didn't know what she meant. His parents had almost pulled themselves up into the middle class, and among the middle-class attitudes he had grown up with was dread of a scene in public. But before he could get Carol away, she had thrown herself on Beatie, punching and scratching. Karen screamed. Barry got hold of Carol and pulled her away but not before she had drawn blood on one of Beatie's slab-like cheeks and Beatie had kicked her on the shin. Carol sobbed in Barry's arms. People in front gardens and on doorsteps watched them, silent, impassive, curious. Most of them had not been born in England, but they had absorbed, sponge-like and as unconsciously as sponges, English ways of reacting. They watched with vague cold curiosity. Barry took Carol home, holding his arm round her as if she had been taken ill. On the corner of Shinwell Close, the motorbike boys stood, Hoopoe, Blue Hair and the Jamaican that Barry had heard someone call Black Beauty. He felt their eyes following him and Carol, though he wouldn't look back.

It was lucky they had the tranquillizers. They calmed Carol down. She was talking on the phone to Alkmini at the wine bar when Iris called in with Maureen. They had brought the evening paper with an article in it about all the children in the London area who had gone missing and never been found in the past five years. Jason's disappearance had sparked it off. Jason's name was the first to be mentioned.

Maureen was only comfortable in her own home. She always looked uneasy in other people's houses. She didn't take off her coat. It was the same straight, up-and-down fawn raincoat she nearly always wore. She had flat brown shoes on and the hem of the raincoat came halfway down her thin calves. Her hair looked, Barry thought, as if she put her head under the tap, dragged the hair back as tight as it would go with a rubber band and let it dry that way. Although she wasn't a speedy person but rather slow and deliberate in her movements, she seemed unable to relax and wandered about the room picking things up as if looking for dust under them. She picked up Dave's photograph and studied it. You would have thought she had never seen it before.

Her voice had no rise and fall in it. It was low and lifeless.

'Why didn't you have an abortion?' she said to Carol.

Carol looked at her and asked her what she meant, her tone the slow dangerous one Barry knew he would hate if it were ever directed against himself.

'You told me when Dave was alive you didn't want any more kids. You could have had an abortion.'

'She was scared,' said Iris with the air of someone giving what seems the most reasonable explanation while knowing it is not the true one. 'You don't want to have those anaesthetics if you can avoid it.'

It was the tranquillizers, Barry thought, that stopped Carol flaring at Maureen. She had been looking at the paper in a listless way and now she laid it down.

'I'm going back to work tomorrow,' she said. 'I've got to go back sometime. It's no good hanging about here moping.'

'That's true,' Iris said. 'That won't bring Jason back.' Barry, in the recesses of his mind, feared Jason was dead and he knew Carol felt the same but Iris spoke as if he were dead beyond a doubt. She even looked cheerfully matter-of-fact about it. She lit a cigarette.

'Work will take my mind off things,' said Carol.

It came as a shock to Barry. Somehow he had thought of her never going back. They would find Jason, dead or alive, and she would either have to stay home getting over it or stay home to look after him. An awful, groundless, quite irrational thought came to him that perhaps they would never find Jason at all.

He didn't want Carol back in that wine bar with those men. But he wasn't her husband, he had no rights, he hadn't even a right to an opinion. How did those other, older, men deal with this kind of thing, how did they handle jealousy? How had Dave handled it? He liked her better made up and with her nails painted and wearing the stolen black and white dress but so would those others like her better. She was safer, more securely his, in the old grey jumper.

They watched television after Iris and Maureen had gone, sitting side by side on the settee. He took her hand and she let him hold it. The programme wasn't very compelling and his thoughts drifted away to Jason. He thought a lot about Jason, where he might be and what could have happened to him. Maureen's question had shocked him, though it was one he had sometimes dared to think about himself. Why hadn't Carol had an abortion? Was it because she had *loved* Jason's father?

He and Ken were working in the new office block just off Finchley High Road. It was a piece of luck they wanted the managing director's office panelled out in sapele wood and an even greater piece of luck that Ken had got the job. It was no more than half an hour after they started that the police came for him. Not Treddick this time but Detective Inspector Leatham and another man called Sergeant Dowson. Ken didn't say anything when they said they'd come to take Barry away for a bit to help them with a line of investigation but he looked incredulous.

In the car, no one said anything. Barry noticed that the driver took a route to the police station by way of Delphi Road and Rudyard Gardens, though it would have been easier and quicker to go straight down Lordship Avenue. Barry never used Rudyard Gardens. It was a depressing place, row after row of houses with their windows and doors sealed off under corrugated metal – a quite reasonable method of ensuring that squatters and meths drinkers and glue sniffers didn't get in but sinister to look at for all that. And there was no chance of Jason or Jason's body being inside one of them. The previous weekend each one had been opened, the metal removed from back doors like lids from cans and the squat, damp, mould-smelling rooms searched. The street had been cordoned off section by section for the search to be carried out, and Barry, who had been shopping in Lordship Avenue for Carol, joined the crowd that was watching.

'What would you say, Barry,' Dowson said when they were in one of the interview rooms, 'if I told you a young chap answering your description was seen in Rudyard Gardens last Wednesday afternoon?'

It was the first time they had called him by his first name. It was possible though that this was just Dowson's technique. Barry was astonished by the question. Who had seen him?

'It wasn't me. I never go down Rudyard Gardens. In the car just now was the first time since I started living here.'

Leatham pounced on that.

'You know where it is all right then?'

Of course he did. Didn't it turn out of Lordship Avenue directly opposite Winterside Down? Hadn't he been there with Carol and the police and found Jason's lamb?

'What's wrong with it then that you don't use it? Rudyard Gardens would be your shortest way through to Green Lanes.'

Barry knew why he didn't use it, because those boarded-up houses depressed him. Delphi Road or the canal bank, even though that passed nothing much but factories and warehouses and dumps, were more cheerful, but he didn't know how you explained that to men like Leatham and Dowson. They were both looking at him with impassive interested eyes. How to tell them Rudyard Gardens was a dead street, lined with the corpses of houses, all with blinded eyes? They'll think I've been watching too many horror films, thought Barry, too much TV.

'It's depressing,' he said. 'No one about, nothing to look at. I like a bit of life.'

'A bit of life?' Leatham made the phrase sound extreme and distasteful. Barry shrank awkwardly under his gaze, though he had nothing to feel awkward or guilty about.

'A bit of excitement then,' he said and had the feeling he had made matters worse.

They wouldn't leave it. They refused to understand. Barry's mother had labelled him 'too sensitive' years ago and he knew he had a lot of imagination, a lot of sensitivity to atmosphere. He knew too that an ordinary working man isn't supposed to be sensitive. That was for the middle class or for women. They kept on asking him about Rudyard Gardens. How did he know it was depressing if he never went down it? Had he ever tried? Just once or twice maybe? It got to lunchtime, and he thought they would let him go but they only took him into another interview room where they left him with another detective constable who didn't speak a word to him but sat behind a desk filling in forms. After about half an hour, someone came in with lunch for him on a tray – a Cornish pasty, some biscuits and a bit of cheese in a packet and a plastic cup of coffee.

Leatham returned with Dowson just when Barry was plucking up courage to tell the DC he was going, he couldn't hang about there all day.

'You were saying how you liked a bit of excitement,' Leatham said as if there had been no break in the talk; as if a couple of hours hadn't passed by. 'There can't have been much excitement living with Mrs Stratford with a little kid about.'

'He's a good kid,' Barry said. They had been on this tack before. 'He wasn't much trouble.'

'Come on, Barry. A kid of under two not much trouble? I've got one of my own that age and I know just what trouble they are. And I'm used to it.'

Barry said, 'We couldn't have gone out in the evenings anyway. My – Carol – Mrs Stratford works evenings.'

'Thought she'd got herself a nice little unpaid nursemaid when she picked you, didn't she?'

Barry felt his face colour. It was one of those blushes you feel rising in a tide, turning your face brick red. He touched his burning cheek. Leatham didn't seem to expect an answer. He was satisfied with Barry's blush. He sat back and folded his arms.

Dowson said, 'I'll put my cards on the table, Barry. We're not trying to trick you. Honesty is the best policy, don't you think?'

It was at this point, Barry always remembered, that the penny dropped. At this moment, for the first time, he understood that they thought he had murdered Jason. All these questions, these and the questions they had asked him on previous occasions, were not to establish Jason's movements or learn where he might have gone or what he might have done, but to make him, Barry Mahon, confess to the murder of Carol's child. A sweat broke out on his body and turned cold on his skin. He was not afraid, only horribly shaken and indignant. He found he was gripping the table edge in front of him in the way a man might when he intends to overturn it.

They thought he had murdered Jason. He stared at the policemen in dazed silence.

'We haven't found Jason's body,' Dowson was saying. 'Maybe we never shall. Maybe when we do find it it'll be too – well, let's just say it'll be too late in the day for us to see what we know is on that body. Marks, Barry, bruises, scars.'

Beatie Isadoro. Was that what she had meant when he and Carol met her in the street?

'Now Mr Leatham just called you a nursemaid and I'm not going to press that, I'm not in this game to make you look a fool, but just for the convenience of the word, let's say you were a nurse to young Jason over the past five or six months. Nurses get aggravated sometimes, don't they?

It gets too much for them like it does for anyone else and that's when they have to lash out.'

'I never laid a finger on him,' said Barry. 'I never touched him.' And nor had anyone else. He thought of Carol's sufferings at the hands of Knapwell. As if, after that, she would dream . . . 'He used to fall about and hurt himself,' he said. 'He was always falling over and he fell off things. He gave himself a black eye back in the summer walking into a key sticking out of a door lock.' Carol had told him that. He could remember the circumstances clearly, a heatwave it had been and he and Carol going swimming up the council pool. He'd gone up the road to get milk and beefburgers and baps to make their lunch and when he'd got back Jason had had this swollen eye starting to go black even by then.

'Funny how some kids are accident-prone and some aren't,' said Leatham. 'Very funny. It's always the kids that get taken into care, they're the accident-prone ones, they're the ones that are a mess of cuts and bruises, not to mention broken limbs. Now I don't think either of my boys has ever had even a minor accident. Funny, isn't it. It makes you think.'

It didn't make Barry think. He hadn't the faintest idea what Leatham was on about. He was smarting, burning, at the unspoken accusation against him. Dowson began asking again about his movements on the Wednesday afternoon and, truculently now, Barry told him all over again how he had been to the cinema to see *The Dark Crystal*. He was prepared to tell them the plot of *The Dark Crystal* but they didn't want to know, they said he could have got that from seeing it the day before or the day after. Had he kept the half of his ticket?

'I didn't keep it. Why would I?'

'You tell us, Barry. It'd make a difference if you'd kept it.'

Barry didn't answer.

'The way things are,' said Leatham, 'it looks a lot more likely you never went near the cinema. You walked home down Rudyard Gardens and found Jason sitting on that wall. It wasn't the first time he'd been dumped in the street, was it? Dumped in the street waiting for some hit-or-miss arrangement for picking him up. It looks like you found him and put him in that chariot of his and wheeled him off somewhere. Home maybe. Or maybe you took him into Lordship Park or out on the Marshes. What did he do, Barry? Go too far? Rile you too far? Start screaming and wouldn't stop? Did you stop him, Barry, and did you go too far?'

He hadn't been afraid of them – ever. In his total innocence, he knew they couldn't touch him. But he was insulted. He felt himself withdraw into a bitter offended silence they perhaps interpreted as guilt. At five-thirty, they let him go. By that time, no doubt they too had had enough and wanted to get home themselves. He would have liked to have walked back to Winterside Down but they insisted on taking him by car. Hoopoe and Black Beauty and the boy with the nose ring were in Bevan Square, bikes at rest round the *Advance of Man* sculpture. They watched the police car go by with Barry in it. Spicer was going in at his gate with a sack of rabbit food, weeds he'd pulled up out on the Marshes. In her widow-white sari, Lila Kupar, who no one ever spoke to and who never spoke to anyone, looked up from washing window sills and stared. It was never dark at Winterside Down; the overhead lamps brought it an endless unearthly daylight.

They could have put two and two together from the next day's papers anyway. There was a bit on the front page about a man being all day with the police helping them with their inquiries. That in itself wouldn't have been sufficient, but those reporters had made it follow quite a long account of how Mrs Carol Stratford waited in suspense day after day in the home she shared with twenty-year-old Barry Mahon. Then it said the man helping with inquiries was twenty and local and in the building trade. Barry winced. He bought the paper at the newsagent's in Bevan

Square and he sensed Mr Mahmud, the newsagent, and his pretty daughter with her long black pigtail looking at him with more than usual interest.

The police came for him again next day. It was Saturday so he was at home. Down at the station they hammered at him again. Had the cinema been crowded? Half-empty? Fewer people than that? How many people? Had he smoked? Which side of the cinema had he sat on to smoke? Barry answered calmly, he didn't have to invent anything, and when he couldn't remember, he said he couldn't.

They asked him if he had a bad temper. What did he think about corporal punishment? Did he think it possible to discipline a child without smacking it? Barry answered mechanically. He was wondering why he should be the only man to suffer this inquisition. Perhaps he wasn't. Perhaps they had had Ivan, Maureen's husband, down here for questioning. Perhaps they had questioned Jerry and Louis Isadoro. They hadn't got into the papers, though, as helping police with their inquiries . . .

There was another man in Jason's life. Had they asked about him? Had *they* asked Carol who he was? Barry wanted to shout at them: Jason's got a father! He nearly did. In the end he couldn't bring himself to do it. Loyalty to Carol, respect for her, stopped him. He suffered their questions, answering yes or no, sometimes not answering at all. In a curious way he had lost interest, just as on the previous day he had lost fear.

This time he walked home. Carol had gone out. There was a note from her though, with two crosses on it for kisses, so he had not to mind. He tried to watch the Ipswich–Arsenal match on television but he couldn't concentrate, he could only think of one thing. A fellow-feeling for Dave – something he had never experienced before – made him pick up the framed photograph and study it closely. Dave looked so happy, smiling and care-free. Within a month of that picture being taken, he was dead, his body mashed in the wreckage of his truck on a Croatian mountainside. Barry found it hard to imagine him and Carol and Tanya and Ryan as one happy ordinary family. He didn't know why but he couldn't imagine it, he couldn't see Carol as part of it. Yet Carol said that was how it had been. And afterwards? How had she handled her life afterwards?

The children had been taken into care and she had been on her own. Only Carol was too beautiful ever to be on her own for long. Who had taken Dave's place? Barry hardly knew what he would prefer, a hundred or just one. He found himself wondering what went on in her mind when she was alone, what thoughts were passing through her head now, for instance, as she walked somewhere window-shopping or sat in the pub having a drink with Iris and Jerry. If he thought of Jason so much, her mind must dwell on him all the time, on Jason himself as he had been last week and also on how he had been as a baby, at his birth, and in the months before his birth. It must be so. Barry knew that if he were a woman, if he were Carol, he would think like that. And how could he judge others' ways of thinking except from his own way? She must think of when she first knew she was going to have Jason and about the love-making that had led to that. Perhaps it was because she thought of those things that they were less close than they had been.

On an impulse, he wanted to make a good evening for them. He wanted to get her thoughts back for himself. Wine, he decided, and a chicken to roast, he could do that all right, he could make them a real meal for a change. Going out of Winterside Down by the main exit he saw no one he knew. It started to get dark very early, especially when the sky was overcast as it had been all day. People were coming back from the last shopping of the week, laden with heavy bags. By the time he came back with his own bags, the yellow lights had started to come on.

A half-formed idea of going to talk to Maureen brought him back this way, along Winterside Road to the canal and the Chinese bridge. He passed Maureen's house, he didn't even pause at the gate. She wouldn't tell him, she probably didn't know, and anyway it was Saturday and Ivan would be home. On the bridge a fresh sample of graffiti had appeared – *Chicken Rules* – done in red aerosol. Barry thought he ought to know what it meant, he was young enough, but for all that, he had grown too old to know. The canal water was very clear today. You could see the pebbles on the bottom, the cans and broken bottles.

The motorbike boys had assembled on the Winterside Down side of the bridge. They weren't supposed to take bikes on to the path, still less across the lawns, but who was going to stop them? There were deep tyre marks in the green turf. Hoopoe was wearing new leathers of kingfisher blue.

One of them – he thought it was Nose Ring – called out something as he passed by. That was all. He came over the bridge and they didn't try to stop him, they didn't molest him in any way, but as he passed, Nose Ring called out something he couldn't catch. It was the first time that had happened. He knew they called out dirty things to girls and others sorts of things to pensioners. He had heard Blue Hair say to Mrs Spicer when she wore her tight trousers, 'For an old woman you've got some good arse.'

But that they should pick on him who was of their own sex and generation – that narked him almost as much as the police getting at him. He hadn't caught what Nose Ring had said and he didn't want to know. But he felt their eyes on him as he walked the path between the green lawns. Their eyes, that in the past had glanced indifferently at him or even with tolerance, with acceptance, he now felt gazing with the same contempt he had noticed they had for others. Hard words and hard looks did you no harm, he thought. There were lights showing in the backs of the houses in Summerskill Road. He counted the houses from the end and in the eighth house, Carol's house, he saw the lights were on. She was home. He began to hurry.

The bikes revved up behind him and then, one by one, they coasted slowly past him, six of them, heavy powerful bikes, all gliding with deliberate slowness past him along the path.

There were a lot of mirrors in the house. Carol was standing in front of the one in the hall doing something to her hair with what Barry thought of as a 'kind of hairdresser's thing' she had plugged into the point above the skirting board.

'What's that?' said Barry, standing behind her with his hands on her waist.

'A hot brush. It's for styling hair. I nicked it from one of those rip-off places up Brent Cross.'

She smiled at him in the mirror. She was back to normal, she was as she used to be. From the feel of her, a softness yet somehow also a return to electric springiness, he knew they would make love that night, perhaps before tonight. Curling her hair, smiling, she let her body rest in his hands.

'I got a chicken,' he said. 'I got a couple of bottles of wine. You didn't want to go out, did you?'

She spoke dreamily, 'Whatever you say, lover.'

He took his bag of groceries into the kitchen. It made him smile to see how she hadn't been able to wait to try out her new gadget, all the more precious because she hadn't paid for it. That was typical of Carol, the old Carol, to rush in and drop her coat on the floor because she couldn't wait. He picked up the coat and her handbag and her gloves and a carrier the hot brush had been in and took them upstairs. Out of the bundle of Carol's things, whether from coat pocket or half-open bag or carrier he didn't know, had fallen a slip of paper. It was a receipt for purchases from Boots and on the back of it was written: Terry, 5 Spring Close, Hampstead. The writing wasn't Carol's, it was a man's. While she was out, she had met a man she used to know and he had changed his address since last they saw one another. It was all quite clear to Barry. He knew now why she seemed excited and loving and the way she used to be.

This man wouldn't have written down his address and Carol wouldn't have accepted it if she didn't intend to see him again. Barry made up his mind to ask her about it, just as he would ask her who Jason's father was. An idea that was very unpleasant came to him – that they might be the same person.

He would ask her all this later, after they had made love. He put the slip of paper into her bag and closed the clasp.

# Book Two

Book Two

# 11

Up until the last moment he hadn't believed Freda would go without him. All the odds and his own experience were against it. A woman of fifty-four lucky enough to get hold of a man of thirty-two doesn't go off on her own for an indefinite time to the Caribbean when she could easily afford to take him with her. She wasn't even a well-preserved fifty-four and she could never have been much to look at. It was humiliating to remember it now, but that last day, the day before she went, he had been waiting for her to surprise him with an air ticket.

They had been out to eat and were back in the house in Spring Close and Freda was packing her hand case.

'I suppose I'd better pack,' he had said. He had never quite got used to taking and using things in this house as if they were his own. 'Can I have one of the brown cases?'

She had smiled. Something was making her happy. 'Lambkins, we had all that out last week. I'm going alone and you're going to stay here and look after the house for me. I know you think I like surprising you and I've fixed a few surprises in the past but not this time. I'm sorry, lambkins.'

'Don't call me that.'

'I'm sorry, Terence. A month ago I said I was going to Martinique and would you stay here and look after the house for me and you said you would. Did you really think I was playing games?'

'You needn't look so bloody happy about it.'

'I'm looking forward to the sun and the sea, Terence. I'm looking forward to seeing old friends. Why shouldn't I be happy?'

The prospect of staying here on his own, a sort of caretaker, depressed him already. When she came downstairs, he had another go at persuading her. She wouldn't listen. It was as if she had gone already. Her body might be here but her heart and soul were up there in that Boeing 747, heading west.

They slept in different rooms that night, he on the futon on the lower level of the first floor. The house was an architect's extravaganza of split levels, teak wood, slate floors, Italian ceramics, smoked glass. The windows had blinds instead of curtains, the carpets were shaggy black and the furniture purple leather and chrome. The two baths were the sunken kind, one in a marble grotto. A black marble woman with a hole instead of a head stood on the pillar at the foot of the stairs, and a man with one leg throwing a sort of plate was poised on the edge of the stone houseplant garden in the hall.

Five more houses, the work of the same architect, were set at angles to each other in this enclave off Christchurch Hill. The only pleasing thing about it as far as Terence (whose taste ran to eighteenth-century cottages) could see was the view from the penthouse 'games room'. Much of Hampstead Village could be seen from there and all the East Heath, the ponds and the woods and the Vale of Peace.

In the view, Terence saw not its beauty nor the wonder that so many ancient buildings and so much open space had been preserved, but the affluence it evinced. He saw it as a 'rich' view, possibly the richest in the British Isles. Looking down on it, he could tell himself not that he had arrived but that he was well on his way to going places. It was all a far cry from his mother's council flat in Brownswood Common Lane, his room in Holloway, the furnished frame house he had shared with four other guys in Rockhampton working for the Queensland railways. It spoke of money, it was full of money.

'You're salivating,' Freda had said to him not long ago. '*What?*'

'You know what salivating means, lambkins. Your mouth waters. Whenever I talk about money, a little bead of saliva pops out of the corner of your mouth, Truly. I'm not kidding.'

Was that why she had refused to marry him? Because he couldn't conceal his fondness for money? He couldn't help it, he'd been deprived all his life. What did she know, a widow who had never had to work, whose husband had given her every little thing she wanted?

In the morning when she left for Heathrow, he had gone down into the street with her, as far as Heath Street actually, to get her a taxi. There was no point in quarrelling at this stage of the game. He had that horrible house to live in and he'd have to make the best of it. He even kissed her, not quite on the mouth though, because she had painted her lips very glossily a fuchsia colour to match her suit.

Just as last night, up till the last moment, he'd expected the presentation of that air ticket, so now, up till the last moment, he had awaited the wherewithal to carry him through till she came back. It couldn't be a power of attorney, he'd have had to sign something for that, gone with her to her bank maybe. But an open cheque or cash in notes . . .

'Are you still on the dole, lambkins?'

'Don't call me that, Freda. Dole's stopped. I get the SS. Twenty-three pounds fifty a week if you want to know.'

'Really?' she said. 'As much as that? Benefit for the unemployed is really wonderful in this country, isn't it? I don't think people appreciate it.'

He looked at her, at her puce-pink lips flapping. It was incredible, that sort of talk. It floored you.

'I asked about the dole,' she said, 'because I'm not going to give you any money. The rates are paid six months in advance, and the gas and electricity and phone I've fixed to get paid on a banker's order. Use the phone all you like, Terence, and don't be cold, will you?'

Empty-handed he made his way back to the house. He had made a mistake in taking it for granted she would marry him just because he was twenty-two years younger. Hangdog about it because the prospect didn't thrill him though the money did, he had said something, when next year came under discussion, about supposing they would be married by then. She had given him such a strange, long look and he could have sworn he saw tears come into her eyes. He had expected her to throw herself into his arms. And when she didn't but slowly shook her head, he anticipated one of those wisecracks of hers he always found hard to take. But all she said was: 'No, lambkins, I don't think so. I don't think that's ever going to be possible.'

He felt ditched. Landed like a foolish fish and left gasping. Stuck with the house but without the means to make anything of it. He couldn't even afford to have a party. She was punishing him, he was well aware of that, punishing him in that light, half-laughing way of hers for the way he had enjoyed it when people took her for his mother, for the times he had left her to give some girl the runaround, for his impatience when she couldn't stand the pace of staying up till three, for his raised eyebrows when she had a hot flush.

Alone in the house, he resolved to waste no time. Whatever she had left around in the house he was going to have, whatever money there might be and whatever objects were saleable. He began by making off across the black carpet – it was shiny and curly like the coat of a cocker spaniel – towards the bookshelves that filled the wall at the end of the upper level bit. Here a picture window gave on to a paved court with raised flowerbeds and urns round which the six houses were built. Terence twisted the acorn-shaped knob on the bottom of the blind cord, dimmed the room and made it impossible to see in.

Freda bought every new novel that made any sort of stir. Between *The Marriage Knot* by Benet Archdale and the latest Dick Francis was a Morris West in a striking cover. Terence knew that inside that cover was, in fact, a French dictionary with a cuboid hole cut out of the centre of its pages, roughly from *devoir* to *mille*. Freda kept it as a spare cash store. Once when she didn't know he was watching her, he had seen her abstract a fifty-pound note. But now when he opened the book the cache was empty. He shook the pages in vain.

He went down the step and over the carpet and up the other side into the bit where there were red-painted girders in the peaked ceiling, three thin windows like the slits they shot arrows through in castles and an indoor flowerbed built up with red bricks and full of castor oil plants and maidenhair fern. Against the wall opposite the windows was Freda's writing desk.

It would be locked and the key hidden somewhere. He looked around for the key, inside shiny black rhomboid vases, in the earth round the castor oil plants, under the carpet where it stopped at the polished wood steps. For once in his life, while he was living with Freda's predecessor, rehearsing for Freda so to speak, he had possessed a credit card. It had probably expired by now. Freda wouldn't settle his accounts for him so it had never been renewed. He had kept it because he had read that you can make yourself a gadget for opening simple locks with a piece of credit card. Eventually it was an old one of Freda's he found in her bedroom.

He had a look through the wardrobe and dressing table and vanitory drawers before he went down again. There was no money and she had put her jewellery in safe deposit somewhere. Would he dare to sell those silver-and-tortoise-shell-backed brushes, the property no doubt of the late John Howard Phipps? That was something to be thought about after he had been through the writing desk.

It took some opening. Whatever you were supposed to do with the credit card, he couldn't do it. In the end he used a cold chisel and a hammer and banged away until he heard the lock split. The front of the writing desk flopped down with a rattle. From the first he was sure he wasn't going to find any money. He went through the four small drawers and the two pigeon-holes. All the cash he found was an envelope with coins in it, two American quarters and a nickel, three-hundred-and-fifty lire and ten Swiss francs. Also in the drawer was a building society passbook which has once shown five thousand pounds in credit. The account had been closed a year before he met Freda and while her husband was still alive.

Underneath it lay a green cardboard National Savings Certificate book, the holder's name being that of Freda's late husband. There were two certificates of a hundred units inside, each purchased five years before for £500 and now worth, according to the small print on them, a total of £1400. The holder's name was on the back, along with the holder's card that bore his signature.

Terence had never in his life done anything really criminal. He wouldn't have had the nerve to try shop-lifting, for instance. Watching Carol Stratford nick that Pifco brush thing up at Brent Cross the other day, he had marvelled at her courage, her cool confidence. She had slipped it off the shelf and into her carrier and tripped jauntily out of the shop to the corridor where he had preceded her. He was tempted to put his hand on her shoulder and say, 'Excuse me, madam, but . . .' only he hadn't the heart. He had always been fond of Carol and she was having her share of trouble anyway with that business of her kid Jason.

So they had only had a bit of a natter over a coffee because the pubs weren't due to open for an hour. He had written down his address for her, though he didn't think he'd be there much longer. That was when he still thought Freda would take him with her. Carol was quite cheerful. She said she had been down at first but now she had a feeling Jason was all right and would come back.

'He'll turn up like a bad penny,' she said.

It was Carol who, two or three years before, had suggested the Golders Green beat to him. She was a widow herself, though only about twenty-five. Her husband had been killed in a road accident a few weeks before Terence had met her and had left her with two children.

Carol had done quite a lot of mildly criminal things. She

was a good shoplifter and had never been caught. At one point she had somehow managed to collect dole in her maiden name while having two jobs in her married one. She was always full of ideas for making money without working or for getting things on the fiddle and most of them were too fantastic to be taken seriously. But this one was different. She said she would do it herself, only she was the wrong sex.

What he was to do was hang around Golders Green Crematorium every day and keep an eye on the funeral parties that came in. It would be best to have a dark suit on and then no one would know he wasn't just another mourner. He was to look out for the widows until he spotted a likely one. She must be well-off – well-left, in fact – not too old, preferably childless. He would soon get the hang of it, Carol said, and she was right. Terence hung around ten funerals, all men's, and then he found his prey. Again Carol had been right when she had said all the younger ones that died would be men. He was a chance bystander at two women's funerals but in each case the woman had been over eighty.

Quite skilful by this time at diagnosing wealth and a measure of solitude, Terence latched on to Jessica Mason. She attended her husband's funeral in a sable coat. Terence introduced himself to her afterwards while they were admiring the floral tributes. He said her husband and his father had once been close friends. There were only four other people there, the late Roy Mason not having apparently been a popular man. Terence found out where Jessica lived, was impressed by the address and phoned her a week later. By the time Roy Mason had been dead a month Terence was living with her in her neo-Tudor detached house on the Cricklewood–Golders Green borders.

There was nothing wrong with Jessica. She was only forty-five. She had no children. She had even more money than he had guessed at – but she was the most possessive demanding perso. he had ever known. When she found out he was still sometimes seeing Carol, she threatened him with a kitchen knife. She was going to kill him and then herself. Terence stopped seeing Carol and stayed on for a few months more, spending freely on the Barclaycard Jessica had got for him and practising forging her signature. He became expert at this but just the same never quite got up the courage to use it as a means, for instance, of drawing a cheque on Jessica's account.

One afternoon while she was out visiting a friend's mother in hospital, Terence left. He simply walked out, taking with him all the clothes she had bought him in one of her suitcases. On the doorstep he hesitated and thought of going back and helping himself to some pieces of her jewellery and a knick-knack or two. Again his nerve failed him. He wasn't very brave and he knew it. Whenever he did anything of that sort – such as the time he took Jessica's wallet out of her handbag and persuaded her that the loss had occurred in the crowds at Oxford Circus tube station – he was liable to feel deathly sick and wake in the night in a cold sweat. Terence knew all about the native hue of resolution being sicklied o'er by the pale cast of thought. He left the jewellery and the knick-knacks behind and went off to his new home in Spring Close. By that time, as a result of further reconnaissance at Golders Green, he had met, ingratiated himself with, and already made love to, Freda Phipps.

Looking now at her late husband's National Savings book, Terence reflected that Freda could have cashed those certificates as soon as John Howard's will was proved. Sooner, probably. She had been his sole heir. She just hadn't bothered, she had enough without that £1400. Terence still couldn't help feeling bitter about things like that.

He thought he might as well have a look through the stack of papers on the two shelves of the writing desk. Nothing but reports of company meetings on the top one. What had she kept that lot for? Underneath was a copy of John Howard's will, and one each of his birth certificate and death certificate. Freda's birth certificate and her marriage

138

certificate were there too, along with some car and house insurance stuff and other documents. Useless. About as much use to him as those company meeting reports.

Terence found himself a sheet of writing paper and began to practise copying John Howard Phipps's signature. He wrote John H. Phipps a dozen times and then tried doing it faster and with a fine flourish. The trouble would be when he had to do it under the eye of some post office clerk.

Much later in the day, when he had been up to the King of Bohemia for a drink and had cooked himself baked beans and a fried egg for lunch and thought about trying the Golders Green circuit again, he sat down once more at the desk, pen in hand. After all, cashing those fourteen hundred pounds' worth of savings certificates was his only hope, any idea of ringing up and returning to Jessica not being realistic.

How old had John Phipps been? Her late husband's age was not a subject Freda had ever brought up. There was nothing as far as he could see on or in the green book to indicate the holder's age, unless there was some coded mark somewhere. It wouldn't do to present this in the post office and then find out the holder was supposed to be sixty-five. He knew he was experiencing one of his failures of nerve.

'The trouble with you, Terence Wand,' Carol had once said to him, 'is that you've got a well-known stomach complaint. No guts.'

Anyway the man's birth certificate was in among that lot somewhere. He pulled out the brown envelope in which he thought the certificates were contained and saw he had got the wrong one. This one was labelled: *Title Deeds of 5 Spring Close, Hampstead.*

Terence looked at the envelope. He slid the documents out. The deeds, on thick, lined, parchment-like paper, listed only one owner of this house which had been purchased five years previously. Ownership might have been in the joint names of John Howard Phipps and Freda Phipps or Freda might have had the title altered when she inherited, but neither of these contingencies were so. John Howard, though deceased, still appeared as the sole owner.

The magnitude of the idea which came into Terence's mind and exploded there, the sheer daring criminality of it, made him feel sick with fear. He felt the sweat start in pinhead drops on his forehead. Cashing someone else's National Savings would be nothing to this. It was impossible, he couldn't dream of doing it – or could he?

# 12

Jason sat in James's seat in the back of the car holding the white rabbit Mopsa had bought him. Benet put Mopsa's suitcases in the boot along with Jason's old pushchair that had been there ever since Mopsa stole him. He was looking fit and well, she thought, his colour less high, his expression more alert. Is it my imagination, she thought, or is he actually a bit better-looking? When Mopsa was gone, when in an hour or two Mopsa was gone and she had to face the music, or at least seriously contemplate and plan facing the music, nobody was going to be able to say Jason had suffered in her care. They could only congratulate her on the improvement in him.

'This is going to be a red letter day for Daddy,' said Mopsa. 'Do you know we've never been separated so long in all our married life?'

She had forgotten the long periods spent in psychiatric wards. This morning she was the epitome of sanity in her grey suit, a red chiffon scarf round her neck and lipstick to match but carefully blotted and powdered so as not to look too bold. As to her father's reaction to this home-coming, Benet doubted if he faced the day with the enthusiasm Mopsa predicted. On the phone the other night he had been reproachful.

'Surely you could have kept your mother with you for the month we planned on?'

And Mopsa herself had not helped when she took the receiver and said in a plaintive voice that there was nothing really to keep her in London now all the tests had proved negative. She didn't want to outstay her welcome.

John Archdale's voice was pregnant with unspoken

miseries. You had her for three weeks, it implied, I have her for life. I don't complain, I shoulder it, but all I asked was for four short weeks. It wouldn't have hurt Mopsa in the circumstances, Benet thought, to tell the poor man that she was looking forward to coming home.

Now of course, in the car, it was evident she was. The climate for one thing. The temperature would be twenty degrees higher than in England. And there would be the sunshine and her own cosy little home that Benet had only seen once and showed no sign of wanting to see again. She chattered on about the amenities of southern Spain in the winter when most of the tourists were gone, the expatriate couple from High Wycombe they played bridge with, the beach. Jason, it seemed, she had forgotten. For days she had virtually ignored him, leaving him to Benet's care. Once she had referred to him as James.

'Isn't it time James was in bed?'

The knife that was always poised, ready to rend Benet with reminders, struck home. But Mopsa had spoken unconsciously. She had never been much interested in James, still less in Jason, as a person. It seemed that, to her, they had blended and become one, little boys who were no more than tribal creatures sharing a group soul. Once only had Benet made another attempt to explain to Mopsa what she intended to do about Jason but Mopsa had merely shrugged.

'I shan't be here. Why tell me?'

At Heathrow, at the newsagent's within the check-in area, a pyramid of *The Marriage Knot* was on display. The sight of that familiar glossy cream paperback with the drawing of a woman in a jewelled headdress reminded Benet of what she was going to have to face when she handed Jason over. Mopsa was nobody; for Mopsa there would have been only a brief blaze of publicity, a day of notoriety. But she was Benet Archdale, a best-selling author, a famous name if not a famous face, already a personality. And she would never live it down. Whatever she might write, do, achieve, that she had once kidnapped a child would be forever remembered. If someone one day wrote her biography, it would be there. A chapter would be devoted to it. Her mother's mental instability would be brought up, the fact that she had had a child and he had died. There was no need to wait for some biography in the distant future. All that would be in the newspapers at the end of the week.

She bought a paper. The Jason affair was back on the front page, down near the bottom across two columns, another interview with Carol Stratford . . .

'It's your birthday!' she exclaimed to Jason. 'Oh, Jay, it's your second birthday!'

Jay was what she had taken to calling him. It was what he called himself. She picked him up and looked into his face.

'How awful that it's your birthday and we aren't doing anything about it.'

'He doesn't know, does he?' said Mopsa. 'He's too young to know what birthday means.'

'Many, many happy returns of the day, Jay!'

'It's *my* birthday next week. I don't notice you making a song and dance about that.'

Mopsa had become cross and sulky. She was apprehensive about her flight now, swallowing Valium with black coffee. Jason had ice cream because it was his birthday. Watching him, Benet marvelled how her dislike of him had faded. How could she have disliked a little child anyway, scarcely more than a baby? If she could make them understand, if they didn't deal too harshly with her, was it conceivable she might occasionally be allowed to visit him, to see how he was getting on?

The flight to Malaga was called. Reluctant as Mopsa might be to get into an aircraft, she was nevertheless raring to go at the first call. The plane might leave without her. She might get into trouble for being late. After all, her ticket had only been purchased four days ago.

Benet went as far with her as she could. They made their farewells at passport control. Mopsa who had been cold

143

and carping these past days, flung her arms round Benet's neck, kissing her fervently.

'You don't know how I miss you, Brigitte. I only had the one and it's a bitter fate to be separated by so many hundreds of miles.'

Benet said she would phone, she would write. She didn't remind Mopsa that it was she who had created the separation, who had chosen to live in Spain. Mopsa didn't say goodbye to Jason. She took notice of him. Benet was surprised how much she resented this, how deeply it embittered their parting. It's because I know she would have been the same with James, she thought.

I must not hate my mother . . .

Mopsa went through the doorway. The last Benet saw of her, she was dropping her handbag on to the conveyor belt of the baggage scrutiny.

Now she knew it was Jason's birthday – the newspaper had quoted Carol Stratford as saying so and lamenting the party she wouldn't be able to give him – Benet felt bound to buy him a present. Even though this might be his last day with her, he should have a birthday present. They would let him keep it afterwards. Why not?

Jason didn't make a choice. He would have chosen everything in the toyshop. The place recalled to Benet forcefully the playroom at the hospital. You could see where some of the toys in that playroom had come from. She remembered now how she had sat in that room, waiting for the phone to be free so that she could ring Mopsa, and how she had looked at the tree of hands. James had still been alive then. All the upraised hands had seemed to be pleading, but for what? For what?

A rocking horse was what she bought. It was big and beautiful and dappled grey. The shop would deliver it to the Vale of Peace first thing in the morning but Benet didn't want Jason to have to wait so long for it. The car was parked only a short way away. They took it with them, and set off to cross the road, Benet with her arms full of brown-paper-wrapped rocking horse. They were halfway over the pedestrian crossing when she saw Ian Raeburn on the other side.

Benet had a curious feeling when she saw him. It was as if she had always known him – no, more than that, as if he were a close friend or member of her family whom to see here unexpectedly was a delightful surprise. She felt as if he belonged to that small group of persons who loved her, so that in a moment he would turn his head and see her and his whole face would light up with the pleasure of it. This feeling lasted no more than a few seconds. It came over her in a vivid spontaneous flash: an instant of pure happiness, the first she had had since James's death. And it was immediately succeeded, or even overlapped, by apprehensiveness. The only thing was to hurry on past, to hope he hadn't seen her. An appalled regret took hold of her. She stepped on to the kerb, the hand that held Jason's tightening.

Ian Raeburn was buying fruit, two kiwi fruit and a bag of small loose-skinned oranges. He took his change and turned to meet her eyes, to smile with instant recognition. He must wonder at me, she thought, standing here holding a child's hand, I who lost my child. The explanation that had been Mopsa's, that had been believable for a while, was ready and waiting.

'I'm looking after him for a friend. I said I'd look after him while she went away.'

'Let me carry that for you,' he said.

He took the rocking horse from her. Its painted hoofs were breaking through the paper.

'Do you find it a help?' he asked gently.

He meant having Jason to care for, he meant having a child of the same sex and comparable age to James.

'I don't know.' She surprised herself with this entirely truthful reply. 'I honestly don't know.' A week ago she could only have shouted, No, no, never!

'I phoned you a couple of times. Just to see how you were. I expect your mother told you.'

Mopsa hadn't. But what difference would it have made if she had?

'My mother's gone home now.'

'Are you going to be all right alone?'

She nodded. He lifted the boot lid and put the rocking horse inside beside the stolen pushchair. In a moment he would suggest they meet, he would ask to see her again, she knew that, she could sense it in the charged air between them. But that was impossible, she had no future, nothing after she had given Jason up. Ian Raeburn wouldn't want to know her. She would be a lost woman, many would think her mad, mad as Mopsa.

She bent down and picked up Jason. He enjoyed farewells and had begun to wave his hand and say goodbye.

'A generous present for a friend's child.' Ian closed the boot lid. 'Is he your godchild?'

'It's not for Christmas. Today's his birthday.'

Saying that was something she immediately regretted. It had slipped out. But suppose he too had read those paragraphs on the front page?

His eyes were on her, gentle with understanding. And yet he didn't understand at all. How could he? He only thought he did. We despise those who claim to understand us when in fact their comprehension is wide of the mark. She didn't despise Ian but she wanted to get away from him. She said goodbye abruptly and got into the car.

The phone was ringing as she came into the house. It was Antonia, inviting her to dinner. Did she find it easy getting babysitters for James in the new place?

For a moment she couldn't speak. Because of Mopsa's lies, people were going to speak to her as if James were alive. Yet she found herself unable to tell Antonia the truth. Her voice sounded in her own ears remote, bemused, as she said no, she couldn't go out, she knew no one here yet, had no idea what sitters might be available. Jason came to her and pulled at her sleeve, asking for the horse to be unwrapped. She rang off.

He climbed on to the horse and rocked back and forth.

The expression on his face made her smile, there was so much in it of delight, of wonder, of a sort of glee. She began to imagine the conversation that would take place between her and a policeman or policemen when she took him back. Any explanation she might give of Mopsa's behaviour and then of her own subsequent behaviour now sounded insane to her, unreal – above all, unbelievable. Why hadn't she brought Jason back as soon as she knew who he was? They would ask that. That would be one of the questions they would hammer over and over at her. And she would only be able to say it had been to stop Mopsa screaming. Looking back now, she couldn't understand herself. Perhaps it was not only Mopsa whose mind had been unbalanced . . .

There was no dialogue she could construct between herslf and the police that did not end in their charging her with abducting Jason. The facts, the evidence, were all against her. The Winterside area was known to her, she had once lived there. The car used was her car. She had recently lost her own child. And more than that. She had concealed – or so it would seem – her child's death from all her friends.

Benet gave Jason his tea, a rather special one because it was his birthday. She set him on her lap and read Beatrix Potter to him, *The Tale of the Pie and the Patty-pan*, although it was too old for him. He liked the pictures. He seemed to like them more and with a more intense enthusiasm than she thought most children of his age would. If I were his mother, she found herself thinking, I should imagine him growing up to be a painter.

His mother . . . That pretty little blonde woman, that living doll. And the thuggish boy just out of his teens she lived with. They had to have him to back. There was no doubt about that. It was not for her, Benet, to judge them and pronounce sentence. All she could do was try to ensure that once the relief of having him back was past, they didn't begin beating him again.

The bruises were almost gone, she noticed as she lifted Jason into the bath. Only a faint yellowish staining remained at the base of his firm-fleshed rib cage. The burn hole would always be there, of course. It would be there when he was an old man. But she couldn't prove it had been made by a cigarette. And the police wouldn't want to believe it, she thought, they would rather not have the additional trouble of believing it.

She put Jason to bed and tucked him in. The white rabbit had disappeared. They had both hunted all over the house for it and now Benet began to wonder if Mopsa had inadvertently taken it back to Spain with her. She thought, she braced herself, and then she opened the toy cupboard and got James's tiger cub out and gave it to Jason. Seeing him with it hurt but not agonizingly. He accepted it happily as a substitute for the rabbit and fell asleep with one of its round golden ears stuffed in his mouth.

By this time she should have handed Jason back. Yesterday she had made a firm decision to take him to the police station by three o'clock this afternoon. She had even told herself she was *looking forward* to it. It was going to be a relief getting it over, being free of him, being alone again and responsible only for herself. She must have convinced herself then that they would accept her story of Mopsa's part in it, of Mopsa's almost total guilt. Another night must now pass before she could return him and that in itself, the fact that she had not handed him back immediately after Mopsa's departure, must further militate against her innocence.

Wandering downstairs again, walking about the base-ment room, alone for the first time since James had died, she knew quite suddenly that she was not going to take Jason to the police. The idea of it – realistically faced, fair and square – made her feel sick and horribly frightened. It was no good imagining conversations, anticipating ways of bringing the police round to her point of view. They weren't like that, it wouldn't be like that. Two minutes inside that police station and she would be turned into an insane criminal. And next day the newspapers would have everything. She would have to see in print the fact of James's death.

She wouldn't do it.

It was a relief to have decided. She felt quite limp and weak with relief. Jason would not be taken to the police, there would be no excuses, confessions, explanations, for her to make. Poor mad Mopsa would not be implicated.

That did not mean Jason wasn't to be returned. Of course he must be returned to his mother, his family, his home, and as soon as possible. Benet did something rare with her. She went upstairs to the drinks cupboard and poured herself a stiff double measure of whisky. Not since the days with Edward had she drunk whisky. She sat down in the window chair with her drink and began to think out ways of returning Jason, foolproof ways that were both safe and secret.

# 13

The photographs in the estate agents' windows were of all kinds of houses, from listed Grade One Georgian to 1980s studio open-plan. Terence looked at the pictures and the specifications underneath them, noting prices. He hadn't known quite how costly houses in Hampstead were and his investigation was starting to make him feel slightly, though not disagreeably, sick.

One more agent in Heath Street remained to be examined. Terence made his way down as far as the corner of Church Row and stood with his face close up to the glass. He didn't intend to go in. It was better to do these things by phone. It had been an educational morning, but as he walked back up the winding hill, he wondered if he hadn't undertaken these researches less because they were necessary than to put off still further the first fateful step.

Nearly a week had passed since he had found the deeds for 5 Spring Close. Since then he had thought of very little else but his plan, and short of Freda coming home suddenly or some agent or soliticor personally knowing John Phipps (or knowing he was dead) or the neighbours getting wise (how could they?), he didn't see how it could go wrong. But he was scared stiff. What scared him was that it seemed so simple, a real walkover once things got moving, that it couldn't happen, there must be a flaw somewhere. It couldn't be that easy to get hold of – what? A hundred thousand pounds? A hundred and fifty?

Both Jessica and Freda were regular users of Valium. Jessica took one every morning to start the day. Terence had removed a hundred in a container when he left.

'It's cheaper than drink,' frugal Freda used to say. She

had left him nearly two hundred. He was amply supplied and they didn't seem to go off, in spite of what doctors and chemists said. He took two with half a glass of water and on second thoughts added some of Freda's Chivas Regal. It made him shudder, he had never been much of a drinker.

The estate agent he had chosen answered the phone promptly. He was put on to a Mr Sawyer. Mr Sawyer's accent was very much like his own, north London born and schooled, overlaid (when the speaker remembered) with some mimicry of television announcers' diction. Terence had rehearsed his opening line over and over. He had found himself muttering it in his sleep. Now he uttered it aloud into the phone:

'I should like to put my house on the market.'

The sum Sawyer named as the asking price was a hundred and forty thousand pounds or, in estate agent's parlance, a hundred and thirty-nine thousand, nine hundred and ninety-five.

'When would it be convenient to come and measure up, Mr Phipps?'

'Measure up?'

'We like to take measurements of the rooms for our specifications. And perhaps a photograph. Of course I'm familiar with the property. A very nice property indeed.'

'How about this afternoon?'

'Wonderful. Three? Three-thirty?'

Three o'clock was fixed. Get it over with, thought Terence. He had never thought much about the neighbours before. When, for instance, he used to bring Freda's car in at two in the morning, give the accelerator a final flip, get out and bang the door, the neighbours might not have existed for him. He looked out of the middle one of the three narrow windows. A thin worn-looking woman with white hair was planting something, bulbs probably, round the trunk of the catalpa tree which grew in the middle of the courtyard. She looked the nosy kind but there was nothing he could do about her. Suppose she or any of them saw Sawyer taking a photograph? Even if they knew who Sawyer was, they would only think Freda was selling her house. They might not even know she had gone away.

The only danger would be in someone hearing Sawyer call him Phipps. Terence made up his mind not to let this happen. Now he had taken the first step, he felt less nervous. What had he done, after all? He had committed himself to nothing, he could always withdraw, change his mind. As for being called Phipps, he might easily be a cousin of the late John Howard. A young cousin. John Howard had died at the age of fifty-one, Terence had noted from his death certificate.

Sawyer turned up on time, in fact two minutes early. Before he could make too much of a song and dance on the doorstep about how lovely and tasteful this little enclave was, Terence got him inside by saying to shut the front door, he thought he had a cold coming.

'The market,' said Sawyer, on his knees with the tape measure, 'is, so to speak, moribund.'

It sounded like a word he had just learned. Terence supposed it meant 'improving' or some such thing. The afternoon's proceedings had an unreal feel to them.

'Townhouses,' said Sawyer, 'are by no means easy to sell at this moment in time, but these, of course, are in a class of their own. Describing this as a townhouse at all might give a false impression. Careful handling will be in order. I shall have to put my thinking cap on. May I ask if you've found somewhere else?'

'Pardon?'

'I mean are you in the process of purchasing a new property?'

'You needn't worry about that. I'm going abroad. And I want a quick sale. I don't want to hang about.'

He asked Sawyer if he'd mind seeing himself out and then he ran upstairs and watched the photograph being taken. As far as he could tell, no one else was watching. Sawyer put his camera away and strolled off under the archway that led into older, cobbled regions of Hampstead.

Terence didn't expect any developments for a week or two, but two days later, as he was plucking up courage to go up to Heath Street and see if the photograph was in Steiner & Wildwood's window and how he felt about that if it was, Sawyer phoned to say a Mr and Mrs Pym would like to see over the house. Would in an hour's time suit him?

Freda had done her own housework. She said it gave her something to occupy herself and she didn't like cleaners in the place. In a way Terence was glad of that. A cleaner would have taken a keen interest in everything he was doing, would have gossiped, might even have written letters to Martinique. But he had also rather taken it for granted that the house was clean and stayed that way by magic. No one had laid a duster on it for nearly a fortnight and it wasn't looking its best. Still it was too late to worry about that. He took two Valium and was feeling quite serene by the time the Pyms arrived.

They didn't stay long. When they found the garden was approximately the same size as the smallest bedroom, they lost interest. But it was a start. Terence got out the vacuum cleaner, found some dusters and cleaned up. He hooked a cobweb off one of the red girders and polished the discus thrower. It was the first time in his life he had attempted house cleaning but he didn't find it difficult. It would even be a way of making a living if all else failed, he thought.

The photograph Sawyer had taken wasn't in Steiner & Wildwood's window. They must have used it only to stick on the forms with measurements and whatnot that they gave prospective buyers. This comforted him. He would have felt very exposed if that photograph had been there staring at everyone who went past.

Ever since Freda went away, he had been living a hermit's existence, so that evening he broke out and went to an old haunt of his, Smithy's in Maida Vale, where he had sometimes gone with Jessica and where you could drink all night. In Smithy's he picked up a girl called Teresa and told her his name was John Phipps. She went home with him in a taxi and was deeply impressed by the house. In fact she was overwhelmed and kept on saying he hadn't seemed that sort of fella. They were still in bed next morning when Sawyer phoned. A Mrs Goldschmidt would like to come and see the house at 2.00 p.m.

That gave him time to get rid of Teresa. He caught her taking a note of Freda's phone number from the disc in the middle of the dial, but it didn't seem important. He swallowed two Valium once she was out of the way and another at one-thirty. Mrs Goldschmidt was late, and by the time the doorbell rang, he had almost given her up. He made himself go slowly to the door, keep her waiting for a change.

She was an extremely good-looking woman, of the same type as Carol Stratford, but there was as much difference in class and style between her and Carol as Sawyer had said there was between 5 Spring Close and your average townhouse. She had very short, back-swept blond hair, a pale, gleaming tan and her mouth was like a cross-section of a ripe strawberry. She wore a pale grey suede coat, primrose leather boots and a long primrose scarf. Such as she, Terence thought, were never to be found being assisted out of Daimlers at crematorium steps.

He had no experience of buying or selling houses but he knew by instinct or telepathy that she would want to buy this one. It wasn't that she said much as he led her from room to room, she hardly spoke at all, but she took a long time, she was thorough, sometimes she nodded to herself in a satisfied way. It was three-thirty by the time she had finished, the worst time of day to offer anyone a drink and he didn't feel like making her a cup of tea. Tea-making hardly fitted in with his 5 Spring Close image. In a way it was a pity she so obviously liked the house. It put paid to any ideas he had about using that image to get to know her better.

She had a monotonous zombie-like voice which Terence found rather attractive. 'I'd like my husband to see it.'

'Fine. Any time.'

'I'll fix it through Steiner's'.

Terence's nerves needed calming, in spite of the Valium. He got out the vacuum cleaner and did a bit more to the spaniel-fur carpets so that he wouldn't have to worry when Goldschmidt came. After that he put in an hour's practice on John Howard's signature. His hand was steady, he breathed deeply. He went through the desk again and found two old books of cheque stubs, one with a single unused cheque remaining in it. John Howard had died suddenly of an unforeseen heart attack. Funny to think he couldn't have had a clue that cheque no. 655399 would never be used or that 655398 (to North Thames Gas for £95.43) would be the last he would ever draw. Six days later he had an appointment at Golders Green . . .

Such fatalistic musings were not really Terence's style and he soon dismissed them. Freda's husband's bank account had been with Barclay's in Hampstead High Street which was what he wanted to know. He wanted to know which branch of which bank to avoid.

Goldschmidt himself came along next day and again on the following day. He was fat and dark and bald with thick-lensed, thick-rimmed glasses. His wife was in a black leather suit with a kind of scarf thing made of mink wound round her.

'It's my dream house,' she said in the voice of one coming out of a coma.

'Would you be open to an offer?'

Terence said what Sawyer had instructed him to say. 'You'll have to do anything like that through Steiner & Wildwood.'

Within the hour Sawyer was on the phone. Terence found himself nearly voiceless, a common enough symptom of nerves with him.

'Still got that cold of yours, Mr Phipps?'

Terence croaked out some sort of assent.

'Mr Goldschmidt would like to make you an offer of one hundred and thirty thousand pounds.'

That would have been acceptable. He wouldn't have argued. It was Sawyer who suggested haggling. Twenty-four hours went by during which Terence was afraid to go out in case Sawyer phoned. Besides he felt continually nauseous and he had an idea that the cold – it had turned bitterly cold – would attack him and make him actually throw up. He was in Freda's *en suite* bath when the phone went and he jumped out and rushed for it, not even waiting to grab a towel. The receiver slithered in his wet hand.

'That seems to be a compromise satisfactory to both parties, don't you think, Mr Phipps?'

Terence nodded. Realizing Sawyer couldn't see him, he translated the nod into a staccato fusillade of 'Yes. Sure. Fine. Right. Yes.'

It looked as if he had sold, or was well on the way to selling, Freda Phipps's house for one hundred and thirty-two thousand, nine hundred and fifty pounds.

# 14

It was rain falling, though it was cold enough for snow. An icy wind blowing down the side street caught you at the corners. Barry, doing the Saturday shopping, saw Maureen coming down the steps of the public library with a thin flat book under her arm. Maureen had black wellies on and her long mud-coloured mac. She stopped on the steps to put up a big black umbrella that was probably Ivan's.

He had wanted to catch her alone. He followed her into the International. She had laid her umbrella and the library book (*Advanced DIY for the Home Expert*) in her shopping trolley. Her face showed no more reaction at the sight of Barry than it did when confronted by a pyramid of dog food in cans.

'I heard about you helping the police with their inquiries,' she said, and in the same tone, 'Pass me one of them packets of Flash. I can't reach.'

'Have you got time for a coffee, Maureen, or a drink?'

She scratched the side of her nose. 'What for?'

'I want to ask you something. I mean I thought if we were sitting down somewhere . . .'

'I'm washing the paint in our lounge. I only came out for a sponge.'

'It doesn't matter,' said Barry.

They walked side by side towards the check-out. Like a couple with prams going to the baby clinic, thought Barry. He remembered what Carol had said about Maureen not being human. In a way that made it easier to talk to her of things that were only too human. He brought it out quickly.

'Maureen, do you know who Jason's father is?'

'Is what?'

He said it again, he explained, and had to stop because the check-out girl could hear. Maureen trudged along the pavement reading the print on the Flash packet. She let him hold the umbrella over both of them. He tried again.

'It made me think, you see. I mean she might still be fond of Jason's father. She might have a sort of special feeling for him on account of that.'

Maureen didn't lift her eyes from the green print. 'There was a lot of fellas. There was a fella that drove about in a beach buggy and that garage fella three or four doors down from me and there was a black bloke. Me and Ivan were disgusted. There was a fella called something Wand, Terry Wand. Mum used to know his mum down Brownswood Common.' She looked at Barry for the first time since they had left the shop. Talking about herself aroused a small spark of interest in her. 'I've never been with any fella except Ivan,' she said. 'I wouldn't. I don't see what people want to for. It just goes to show the difference between sisters. Can I have that bag you've got your butter in? If this stuff gets wet, it'll be a right old mess.'

He left her at the bridge. It struck him that she was very happy. She had got what she wanted. She and Ivan hardly ever spoke to each other. All the time he wasn't at work or she wasn't doing things to the house they sat in front of the TV holding hands. They would never have children, split up, move, go away on holiday, make a friend, feel jealousy, suffer. One day they'd wake up and find they were sixty and things were just the same. He could almost envy them.

Terence Wand's name had been the only one Maureen could remember. It sounded from what she said as if he and Carol had been friends since childhood. The other men – well, Maureen hadn't any *proof*, she and Ivan had just been guessing. No doubt they had been after Carol. Men would always be after Carol. Terence Wand was different – somehow Barry intuited he was Jason's father. Being a father gave you a sort of dignity, a sort of *weight*. It made you memorable. It was Jason's father's name that Maureen had remembered.

Carol had started working Saturdays. All across the lunchtime and throughout the evening. She had never done that before, but as soon as she went back, Kostas had asked her if she would work Saturdays and she had agreed. The house smelt of the perfume she had taken to wearing, a musky French cologne Barry knew – because he had priced it in the chemist's – cost twelve pounds a bottle. It was her money, she worked for it, she had a right to spend it as she liked. Barry wouldn't even have thought about it if only he could have been sure it was Carol herself who had bought that perfume.

Unpacking the shopping, putting things in the fridge, he began to think along lines he often did when he was alone in the house. He would fancy then that Jason was still there, that the events of the past weeks had never happened, and that he would turn round and see him standing in the doorway. The little boy's face he could easily conjure up, he had no difficulty in remembering what he looked like. Jason had an *unusual* face, not babyish at all, not in the least like Carol's. It was a funny thing, an ironical thing, that Carol who had a baby face at twenty-eight had produced a boy who at two had, if not a grown-up's face, at least a mature one for his age.

That meant he must look like his father. He bore no resemblance to any Knapwell Barry knew, nor was he like his half-brother and sister. Barry was suddenly absolutely sure he would recognize Jason's father if he saw him, just from having known Jason. This wouldn't be a case for blood tests but something you could see at a glance. Barry imagined a tall biggish man, fair haired and sharp featured with white skin that got sunburned red, and eyes darker than Carol's and with more green in them.

He wandered into the living room, wondering what he was going to do with himself for the rest of the day. He could go down to Kostas's himself for the evening of course. An evening spent with Dennis Gordon who had two topics of conversation, money and his own aggressive exploits, wasn't an attractive prospect. Dennis Gordon treated Barry as if he really believed he was Carol's lodger or a boy she let stay with her in exchange for doing odd jobs. He was crazy about Carol, you could see that, but he wasn't jealous of Barry. He didn't take him seriously enough for that, Barry thought.

A police car had stopped outside. The Spicers were coming in with two bags of washing from the laundrette just as Leatham got out of the car. Barry closed his eyes momentarily. He realized he need not have wondered about how he was going to pass the rest of the day.

They had found Jason's body. They told him that as if it were true, positive, beyond a doubt. But all the same they wanted him to identify the thing that had been dug up in a garden in Finchley.

First he was taken to the police station. Chief Superintendent Treddick was there, talking in knowing tones as if to say Barry was being very clever and he understood all about that and even rather admired it, only Barry must realize the police were cleverer still. He talked as if Barry were a murderer beyond a doubt and insinuated that if he would only admit everything – take his time and admit every single thing – the police would be very kind and lenient with him. Leatham was more brusque and offhand. His beefy red face and hooked nose and corrugated yellow hair brought to Barry's mind what he had been thinking of earlier. Leatham was the Jason's father type, though not handsome enough.

The Finchley householder had been digging a hole to plant a tree. Two to three feet down he had unearthed a rotting bundle. He had been living in the house just a week, which before that had been empty for six months. The house and garden were about a hundred yards – a stone's throw, Treddick said – from where Barry and Ken Thompson were panelling the office.

'We've only been working there a week,' Barry said.

'It was six weeks ago you went over there to have a look at the place for an estimate,' said Treddick.

But Barry hadn't been there. It was always Ken who did the estimates. He tried to explain this but it seemed to have no effect on them. The fact that he had some little hearsay knowledge of the area was enough for them.

'I'd never been there,' he protested. 'I never talked about it with Ken. You might as well say because I've got a street plan I might have looked it up.'

'Maybe you did,' said Leatham.

They were illogical, they didn't reason things out. This made him much more uneasy than any evidence they might fancy they had against him. They asked him about the street in which the dead child had been found, about where he and Ken went for their lunches, about how he got to Finchley, by what method of transport, and then they took him to the mortuary.

Until then he hadn't known this building was the mortuary. He had known it all his life as a red brick wall with windows high up through which you could see white tiles. They took him in through a door that had a very highly polished brass handle. The image of that shiny brass sphere remained in Barry's mind, making him flinch whenever he saw well-polished brass. There was a very powerful smell – not of death or decay but of disinfectant, yet ever afterwards when Barry smelt it or had a whiff of something like it, he associated it at once with death.

In the mortuary he behaved, he thought, as he might have done if he had really murdered Jason. They uncovered the face. Barry's throat rose up, closed, strangled him. He covered his face and staggered back. Someone must have caught him. He didn't remember any more till he was sitting in a chair with his head down on his knees.

If they had tried to get Carol there to identify the awful thing under the cover, he thought he would have fought them all, killed them all. That would have made a murderer of him. But they didn't attempt that. They got Maureen. He saw her brought in, blank-faced, head tied up in a

161

scarf, and come out again, no less steady and calm. They drove him back to Summerskill Road where two reporters were with Carol who had been fetched from the wine bar. But before that, they put him through the gruelling process again. How well did he know that part of Finchley? How many times had he been there? For several months an estate agent's board had stood in the front garden of the house where the child's body had been found. The side gate had been off its hinges and had stood propped against a fence. On the day of Jason's disappearance Barry had been working in Wood Green, hadn't he? It was easy to get by bus from Wood Green to Finchley. He could have picked up Jason in Rudyard Gardens, taken him to Finchley, killed him and buried his body and still been in Highgate by five . . .

He and Carol slept that night because they were both drunk. They didn't bother with wine. They had a bottle of gin between them. He woke up with a cracking headache and a mouth that felt as if it were filled with dry fur. Carol's face on the pillow was young, china pink and white, beaded with sweat. He left her sleeping and went off to buy the Sunday papers. He wanted to see what they said about him and if they had yet established who the dead child was.

Mr Mahmud at the paper shop was always a bit distant and his daughter off somewhere in a world of her own, so Barry hardly noticed that he didn't get a thank-you for producing the right money for the *Sunday Mirror* and the *Express*. This Pakistani family were known for conducting a lot of their business in silence. But as he came out of the shop and into Bevan Square, he encountered two girls who hadn't that reputation at all. Stephanie Isadoro and a girl Barry thought was called Diane Fowler, Blue Hair's sister, were coming across the square, mackintoshed, wearing high-heeled sandals, arm-in-arm. He had been reading headlines, so relieved that there was nothing new that he could even distract his mind enough to admire the big beautiful photograph of Carol on the *Mirror*'s front page, but now he looked up to say hallo to them.

These girls were usually giggling, usually pleased with themselves. Karen had once told him that Stephanie fancied him. If it had ever been true, she had got over it now, for she pointedly turned her head the other way and so did Diana. It was a funny thing, he'd often thought most of this lot couldn't read but they had read the papers all right, they had read the bits about him helping the police with their inquiries.

Carol didn't get up till lunchtime. The phone rang a couple of times before that but they must have been wrong numbers, for each time Barry picked up the receiver, he got silence and then the dialling tone. Unless, he thought, it was someone trying to get Carol who didn't want to speak to him, who didn't even want him to know they wanted to speak to Carol – 'they' being a man of course. He cleared up in the kitchen, washed their glasses from the night before and the cups and saucers the reporters had used when Iris had made tea for them, and carried the rubbish bag out from the waste bin to the dustbin that stood by the back door.

It was cold today but dry, colder than it had been when he went out for the papers. He noticed how green Winterside Down was, all the little rectangles of garden, all the lawns and banks and slopes, a brilliant, hard, acid, treeless green. It was a green to hurt the eyes. Mrs Spicer was putting bowls of some sort of steaming mash stuff into her rabbits' hutches. She turned round and smiled at Barry and said good morning to him and it was better today, wasn't it, at least it was dry. He felt unreasoningly grateful to her for speaking to him, for greeting him with warmth. He could have kissed her.

Carol said she couldn't stand another evening on their own, she'd go off her rocker. She had a long leisurely bath with avocado and peachnut essence in the water and a herbal pack on her face. In the black and white dress with, over it, Mrs Fylemon's cast-off, beauty-without-cruelty synthetic fox coat, she was the old Carol again, his love, his child-mother of three children. They hadn't seen Tanya and Ryan since before Jason went. Barry didn't want to think about that, he pushed it away, he had enough without that. He and Carol were going to meet Iris and Jerry in the Bulldog, but just as they were leaving, the phone rang again. Carol answered it this time. Barry was already in the hall, waiting for her by the front door. She had gone back into the living room to answer the phone, and when she'd said, 'Hallo,' and a less impersonal 'Oh, hi,' he saw the door pulled shut. She had shut herself in with the phone, leaving him alone in the hall. He felt the sudden swift descent of the worst loneliness he had ever known in his life. It made him cold. He shivered with the cold. She was only on the phone a few minutes, three at most. She came out and took his arm and said it had been Alkmini.

Iris and Jerry were sitting at a corner table with a couple Iris said lived down the road from them. Barry immediately thought of Terence Wand's mother. Could this possibly be her? Iris never introduced anyone to anyone. You were supposed to know who people were without being told. Carol knew all right. She called the woman Dorothy. Barry found himself studying the sixty-year-old, raddled, sagging face, the bravely painted mouth, the henna'ed grey hair, looking for a likeness to Jason. In the nose perhaps, in the eyes which were faded now but once might have been as blue as cornflowers. He was working out ways of finding out what he wanted to know when the Dorothy woman and her husband or boyfriend or whatever he was got up quite abruptly and said they must be going. Barry was rather disappointed. It was only afterwards that he realized that, just before they left, just before a glance passed between them and they got up, Iris had spoken to him and had called him for the first time that evening by his Christian name.

Carol looked rovingly round the saloon bar, twining a curl round one of her fingers. A great cavernous place it was, of Edwardian etched glass and red plush and a ceiling whose scrollwork was chestnut-brown with nicotine. Jerry sat silent, dumb with gin, his face a dull blue. Her claw of a hand on Barry's arm, Iris cocked her head in the direction of the departing neighbours.

'Don't take no notice, Barry. There's some get very funny about folks what have contact with the police.'

Her habitual placid half-smile lay on her mouth. It was a fat woman's smile on a thin woman's face. Iris pushed two cigarettes into the smile, lit them and handed one to Carol.

On the way home with Carol, taking her arm and putting it into his, he asked her if Dorothy's surname was Wand. She was preoccupied. He didn't wonder at that. He asked her again, looking into her face this time, though he never much liked doing that after dark in Winterside Down. The khaki, colour-draining light was unkind to even the prettiest face. It made skulls out of faces and gave them empty eye sockets.

'You what?' she said.

'I thought she might be a Mrs Wand.'

'Well, she's not, she's a Mrs Bailey. What's made you so nosy all of a sudden?'

The tall single tower block dominated the estate, lights on all over it. It was like a chimney full of holes which the fire inside showed through. They went across Bevan Square where Hoopoe and Black Beauty and Nose Ring and a couple of girls with black lips and fingernails – or lips and fingernails that looked black in this light – stood outside the Turkish takeaway, eating chips. Hoopoe said something as they passed but he didn't say it loudly and all Barry caught was the word 'woman'.

'They're just ignorant,' said Carol loud enough for them to hear. 'That's what you have to put up with living round here, ignorant scum and scrubbers like those two.' Her body trembled against his side and he was filled with a fierce pride that she should be angry for him. Then she said, speaking softly, to him alone, 'I'd do anything to get away from here. I hate this dump. Sometimes I think I'll be in this dump till I'm old, till I die.'

'Carol,' he said. 'Carol – a year or two, just give me a

year or two. I'll make money. I'll get the down payment on a house for us.'

She looked away from him. Her words were rough but she didn't speak them unkindly. 'It'll just be piddling little bits of money, won't it? I want real money, I'm sick of struggling. I had a chance of that with my husband and he had to go and die.'

'I'm young. I can make as much as Dave ever could. Let's get married, Carol. I want it to be me you mean when you say "my husband".'

'How can I get married?' she said. 'I can't get married when we don't know if Jason's alive or dead.'

Her voice sounded sincere yet he had a feeling it was something entirely different she was saying, some far more genuine excuse she was really making.

The police came in the morning and told Carol they had established beyond a doubt that the dead child wasn't Jason. Carol didn't say anything; she lifted her shoulders in an indifferent little shrug. They had caught her as she was leaving for Mrs Fylemon's, her first day back since Mrs Fylemon's return from Tunisia. The detective sergeant told her that the boy whose body they found had been nearer three than two and, from the shape of his skull, was shown not to have been Caucasian. In any case he had been dead for at least six seeks, a fact which didn't surprise Barry, remembering that face.

He had an unreasonable urge – unreasonable only because he knew they wouldn't dream of doing it – to ask the police to put posters and banners up all over Winterside Down saying, *Barry Mahon Is Innocent*, or something like that. Maybe have a car going round and a man with a loudspeaker like they did before elections, shouting that he hadn't done it, that he was in the clear. His imagination was running wild, he knew that. He watched the sergeant go, having said not a word.

What did it matter anyway? Sticks and stones may break my bones but hard words cannot hurt me. His mother had

166

taught him that when he was a little kid and had been subjected to verbal bullying in the school playground. He had always remembered. It wasn't important that an old bag with dyed hair didn't want to sit in a pub with him or that Hoopoe called after him that some folks wouldn't dare show their faces outside – for he was certain now that this was what had been said – without a woman to protect them.

But it was in the forefront of his mind as he and Carol walked together to the bus stop. Not that there was anyone for her to 'protect' him from this morning. Going along the path to the Chinese bridge, they met no one but the old boy in the Sherlock Holmes hat who sat there fishing in the canal most wet mornings under a green umbrella. Barry's bus came first. He didn't want to go to Finchley, he never wanted to go there again. He was hours late anyway.

One bus to Wood Green and then change on to another. What curious trick of chance brought that double decker bus with an L plate rather slowly and steadily past the stop? No buses to Hampstead or through Hampstead came this way but this bus, out on a practice run, had Hampstead on its front. The address on the paper that had fallen from Carol's coat came back to him. 5 Spring Close, Hampstead. Terence Wand. It had said Terry on the paper but Barry didn't want to think of him like that, it sounded too close to his own name, it put it in the same *class* of name. Terence. Terence Wand, who lived in Hampstead at a classy address that was a far cry from what Carol called 'this dump', from Winterside Down.

Getting on the next bus that came, climbing up to the top deck, Barry found himself looking at all the men about, looking for the kind of man he sought. He sat in the front, looking at the men in the street. It seemed to him that there were more of them about at this time of day than there had used to be a few years back. That was all the unemployment, of course. Barry didn't want to think about unemployment, it made him go cold down his back.

A lot of the men were black or Indians or men he instinctively knew to be of Irish descent like himself, dark and wild of face with a light in their eyes. Some were fair and sharp-nosed but none he could see really looked like Jason grown-up. The idea formed and grew solid in Barry's mind that for his own peace of mind – or if not for peace, for the easing of his mind – he would have to go up to Hampstead and find Spring Close and take a look at Terence Wand.

# 15

It gave Benet a curious feeling when she read in the newspaper about the discovery of the child's body in Finchley. If they decided it was Jason she wouldn't have to give Jason back. There were two major faults in this hypothesis: one that the child's body couldn't be Jason's since Jason himself was standing a yard or two from her feeding his rocking horse with sugar lumps, and secondly, that nothing could be more disastrous for her, nothing so militate against her work and her life as feeling herself obliged to hang on to Jason. Yet the discovery of the body had strangely pleased her. For that she castigated herself. It was dreadful and wrong to feel that way, for whoever this wretched little corpse might have been, it had once been a child, some child, murdered or killed by a violence that went too far, and buried in squalid suburban earth.

Just as she had been almost pleased by the unearthing of the corpse so she was vaguely and irrationally disappointed when it was identified as that of Martin M'Boa, a Nigerian child who had been missing for more than three months. It brought her back to something she had shelved or suspended while there was doubt about the child's identity, it brought her back to decision-making. She still had to fix on a way of returning Jason, though it was a week now since she had decided to return him clandestinely. Jason had taken to waking up in the night, waking just once and calling for her. The first time he called 'Mummy' she felt a sort of horror because, momentarily, as she woke to that cry, he had been James. She hadn't wanted to go in to him, to see him instead of James, but she had gone. It wasn't his fault, he was responsible for none of it, and he

169

called her what he would have called any young woman who had the care of him. After she had quietened him, she lay awake for a long time wondering at herself and what had happened to her. Mopsa, of course, was mad. But hadn't she too been a little mad from shock and grief in that she had kept Jason so long after she knew who he was? She wasn't mad now. She was sane and level-headed – she was even writing again, working well in the study room after Jason had been put to bed – but it was *too late now*. A rational mind had been recovered too late. That mind looked askance at Mopsa-type ideas for taking Jason back, restoring him to the wall where he had been when Mopsa found him, taking him into a store crowded with Christmas shoppers and giving him into the care of the management as a lost child, placing him in the arms of a policeman in the street and then running like a hare. Mopsa ideas all of them, if Mopsa could ever have been persuaded Jason must be returned home.

She hadn't spoken to Benet since her return to Marbella. It was Benet's father who had phoned to say her mother had arrived safely, had a good journey, been in good spirits and talking constantly of her visit. It made Benet wonder what story she had told to account for Jason's presence. If she had told any. She must have said something for John Archdale asked just before he rang off, 'How's the boy?'

It wasn't until an hour or two afterwards that Benet understood he had meant James.

She needed someone to confide in. Curiously enough, in an unsatisfactory and inadequate sort of way, Mopsa had filled that role. In the middle of this populous place, Benet was aware of her isolation, a solitude she had created for herself and must maintain until Jason was gone. Since Antonia's, there had been only one phone call and that had been from Ian Raeburn. He asked her to come out for a meal with him.

Benet longed to go. Her abruptness to him, her coldness, when she met him in the street with Jason and the rocking horse had troubled and nagged at her ever since. Without

Jason, in some restaurant and later on their own, she could get to know him better. It surprised her how very much she wanted to do this. But Jason couldn't be left and there was no one she could ask to sit with him. All the people she could think of as possibilities had, in the past, sat for her with James. This was an excuse she couldn't make to Ian. She had to tell him she was busy every evening.

'Some other time?' he said. 'How about next week?'

She found herself saying, 'Yes, *please*,' like a child promised a treat, a way she had never before spoken to a man.

Now next week had come and she was waiting for him to phone. If he would phone, that would make her do something about Jason. Lying in bed thinking like that at three in the morning seemed perfectly rational, to arrange to have dinner with Ian on, say, Thursday night and therefore be impelled to get rid of Jason by Wednesday. Dressing Jason next morning, giving him his breakfast, talking to him about the day ahead, she felt quite different. Her sense of responsibility returned, her care for Jason's welfare and for his status as a human being worthy of respect. But she waited for Ian's phone call like a teenager with a first boyfriend. She kept on thinking she heard the phone when it hadn't rung. And when one day she found the receiver had been off for hours because Jason had been playing with it, she had to make an effort not to show her anger.

It was that afternoon when, to divert him from the phone, she broke down another barrier and unlocked James's toy cupboard.

He fetched the toys out in a methodical adult manner, examining each one. A paintbox James had never used, had been far too young to use, interested him deeply. He couldn't possibly have known what the paints in their small square troughs were or what they were for. Perhaps he simply liked the colours. It brought Benet enormous entertainment to observe how manually dextrous he was. He hardly ever dropped anything. He was a clean and tidy eater. Now he took out a paintbrush and tested the soft camel hair on the pad of his left forefinger. The feel of it made him look up at her and give her one of his broad, radiant smiles. After a while he found the xylophone with its rainbow octave. It was the colours, the spectrum and the gold, that held his attention. James, she remembered with a catch of pain, had wanted the notes of the scale, that was what had pleased him. But Jason, after a time, did pick up the wooden mallet and slowly and speculatively produce a *do-re-mi-fa-so-la-ti-do*. . .

Up above them the front doorbell rang. She heard the gate close, footsteps on the short paved path, then the bell. She jumped up and went to the window. No one ever came to the door, no one ever had. The police would come, she thought, and her mouth went dry.

At six o'clock it was dark, the Vale of Peace lamplit in its cosy, antique Hampstead sort of way. She looked out through the slats of the blind. No police car, no stranger's car at all. What cars there were were her own and those of her neighbours habitually parked in this corner of the Vale of Peace. The thought came then that her caller might be Ian. Perhaps he didn't live far away. That the Vale was not exactly on the way to anything except the dark uninhabited Heath itself did occur to her. And wouldn't he have phoned first? Well, Jason had had the phone off the hook for hours.

The bell rang again, a long insistent peal this time. She ran upstairs. All the time she was thinking, let it be him, let it. To sit and talk to him over a cup of tea down here in the warm basement with Jason was the nicest thing she could think of doing. Yes, please let it be him . . .

She put on the hall light and opened the front door. It wasn't the police and it wasn't Ian.

It was Edward.

The firm of solicitors Terence found to act for him was in Cricklewood. He saw the name in gilt letters on a row of windows over the premises of a building society. Cricklewood was safer than Hampstead. He took the deeds with him. By now he was getting used to being addressed as Mr

Phipps and he felt fairly confident about signing as Phipps, having practised John Howard's signature every day.

Terence expected a lot of questions but the solicitor wanted nothing more than the name of the estate agents. He seemed surprised to be offered the deeds of the house.

'We'll press for an early exchange of contracts and ten per cent of the purchase price on that date,' he said.

Going down the stairs, Terence worked that one out. Thirteen thousand, two hundred and ninety-five pounds. If he lost his nerve, if the strain of it all got too much for him, he could pull out once he got that money. He could simply walk out and go. The thought comforted him and his churning stomach quietened. When he got home he found a letter waiting for him on the mat. It was one of the few letters he had ever received while living in Spring Close, the first since Freda went away.

He recognized Freda's writing on the envelope.

'Dear Terry' – he would have expected 'Dearest lambkins', though he had never had a letter from her before. The opening seemed ominous. He read quickly, fearful she might be coming back. There was no risk of that though. Not much was said about what she was doing, yet somehow the two sheets reeked of happiness, and all through them were references to someone called Anthony. A brief explanation of who Anthony was – 'an old friend I knew before I was married, we lost touch over the years. He has a house here . . .' – came near the end. Terence saw it all. That was why she had gone: she had had a letter from, perhaps even been invited by, this Anthony. Some old rich man. Money calls to money, he thought. Very likely she would marry Anthony.

The letter annoyed him. She was obviously indifferent to his welfare. The tone was rather as if she were writing to a caretaker. 'The heating system should be overhauled before Christmas. Would you like to ring them and arrange a date? It is on contract so there is no need for you to worry about payment . . .' It also pleased him. She wasn't coming back, she wouldn't poke her nose in where she wasn't wanted. If he could only hold on to his nerve, keep cool, why do a moonlight flit with thirteen thousand when he had only to wait in perfect safety for ten times that?

He phoned Steiner & Wildwood to give Sawyer the name of his solicitor. In the course of conversation it came out that they would be taking three per cent commission. Terence had been told this when he first put the house in their hands but it was irritating to be reminded of it. A pleasanter piece of news was that Mr and Mrs Goldschmidt were not dependent on the sale of their own house to buy 5 Spring Close.

'There won't be any question of a chain,' said Sawyer.

'A chain?'

'I mean there won't be any question of Mr and Mrs Goldschmidt waiting to sell their property to a purchaser who is waiting for someone to buy his property. And so on.'

'I see. Great. That's fine.'

There seemed cause for celebration. Terence seriously contemplated selling those National Savings certificates of John Howard's. He was confident of his ability to forge the signature perfectly. And he would only have to forge the signature on a withdrawal form. He had found out there would be no need to present himself for scrutiny at a post office. But was it worth even that small risk for £1400? How would he feel forever afterwards if he threw up his chances of £130,000 for not much more than a hundredth of that?

For the time being, he had to be content with the benefit he got from the DHSS. He phoned Teresa and took her to the cinema. They went to the Screen on the Hill so they were back at Spring Close soon after ten. For the first time Terence had used Freda's car, noting it was high time it had some exercise. The battery needed a good deal of stirring into life. Because he put the car away in the garage again, they entered the house by the back way.

Teresa said could she have a bath? Freda's *en suite* bathroom reminded her of a photograph of one she had seen in *Homes and Gardens* while waiting to have her teeth scaled. Terence went to the bedroom window to pull down the blind which was made of black silk with a Chinese painting on it. It was not modesty or prudishness that stopped him putting the light on before doing this but rather an unwillingness to draw any sort of attention to himself on the part of the neighbours. Seeing a naked man and a girl in Freda's bedroom wouldn't, of course, have the effect of making a neighbour ring up Steiner & Wildwood and spill the beans, but it would make him conspicuous and even talked about in a way he felt – at this moment in time, to quote Sawyer – undesirable.

A man was standing under the archway that was the entrance to Spring Close. Terence could see him quite clearly in the light from the fancy carriage lamps that were secured on each side to the uprights of the arch. He was a young man, very young, perhaps no more than what newspapers and television called a youth. The lamplight showed Terence that he was dark, handsome in an Irish sort of way, very lanky and narrow-hipped. He had jeans on and a leather jacket, a sweater with a high polo neck. Exactly the way a young detective constable would dress getting himself up to be taken for a yobbo.

Terence's heart thudded as if it were kicking him. There was no doubt the man was watching this house. A non-confronter and one who could readily convince himself black was white and things almost anything but what they seemed, Terence nevertheless couldn't be persuaded that the man under the arch was interested in any other house or was there for any other purpose but to keep his eye on 5 Spring Close. Their eyes met, only Terence knew the man couldn't actually see him, having sometimes himself looked back at this window from the arch after dark.

What was he doing there? Had the police somehow got wise to what he was doing? That solicitor, he thought, and he broke out into a sweat. Probably the solicitor had been a personal friend of John Phipps. Terence padded over to the bedside table and swallowed two Valium. He could hear Teresa splashing about in the bath. Why would the police watch the house? Why wouldn't they just come and arrest him?

It occurred to him that the man might be waiting to do just that, only he thought he was still out. He'd soon know, he *had* to know. What had he done, anyway? Nothing. He had signed nothing. He would say that he was Freda's cousin and that she'd asked him to sell her house for her in her absence. And if they asked her at this stage, she wouldn't betray him. She might hate him, never speak to him again, but she wouldn't betray him to the police. He took a deep breath, snapped on the overhead light and immediately pulled down the blind.

Teresa came dancing out of the bathroom in wafts of Freda's *Opium* bath essence. Her scented nakedness had not the slightest effect on Terence who hoped to God things would improve later. It was his turn for the bathroom. He cleaned his teeth. Then he stood on the rim of Freda's bidet and looked out of the window.

The close was empty but for a white cat sitting under the catalpa tree. The man had gone.

In the light of her porch he looked pale and rather thinner than three years before. He walked in without a word as if he were expected. And suddenly, as he was unwinding his long scarf and hanging up his jacket, she understood that he *was* expected. At least as far as he knew. He had been among those anonymous phone callers, one of the many Mopsa alone had spoken to and given God knows what replies. Of course Mopsa had invited him. It would be one of Mopsa's dearest wishes to see her and Edward married, irrespective of their feelings for each other, for the sake of a weird, specious propriety, for the sake of James who was dead.

'I suppose my mother asked you?'

'Your mother said *you* asked me.'

'Edward, what on earth do you mean?'

'You were ill in bed when I phoned. She said she knew

you'd like to see me, you were always saying so, but to leave it a week or two till you were better. She said you'd call me back if Wednesday turned out not to be convenient.'

Had his tone always been so sulky? It was a voice, she thought; full of paranoia.

'I didn't invite you. It's the first I've heard of any of this.'

'I had an extraordinary feeling as I was coming along this dank enclave,' said Edward, 'that when I got here I wouldn't be greeted with open arms.'

He hadn't changed in his ways or his appearance. He was dressed as he always had been, with all the eccentricity of an athletic teenager: jeans, open-necked thin white shirt, leather jacket and striped scarf that hung to his knees. The boyish look was still there, the lock of yellow hair dipping over the forehead, the chiselled mouth with its tilted corners, but it was growing strained, the process of desiccation was beginning. Edward's nose looked sharper and more aquiline. The wonderful blue of his eyes was as intense as ever.

'Come and have a drink,' she said.

She had been going to take him into the living room where the drinks were but she remembered Jason. Jason was down in the basement on his own and the kitchen was full of dangerous gadgets, the electric kettle, the gas taps, knives. She went towards the basement stairs, Edward following. He always walked softly and springily, in a cat-like way, as if on his toes. He is like a cat, she thought. We always think, when we make that comparison, of dark people, dark-haired people, and Edward is fair. Yet he is like a cat, a long, lean ginger tomcat . . .

The same explanation of Jason's presence must be given to him as had been given to Ian Raeburn. Why not? He wouldn't be interested anyway. In the past he had often said he disliked children.

'I read your book,' he said. 'I liked it. It's a great book, it deserved to win that prize.'

She was astonished and touched. She turned her head to him. 'Why, Edward, how very nice of you!'

'One of the things that gratified me was how much of it you owed to me.'

There was nothing to say. He had taken her breath away.

'The fact that you went to India at all, for one thing. That you had the entry to places you'd never have set foot in but for me. Not to mention what you learned about writing from me. You might have given me a credit, a single line of acknowledgement would have been less ungracious – "For Edward Greenwood without whose help et cetera".'

'The gratification you felt wasn't an adequate recompense then? You'd have liked a fee?'

She ran down the last half dozen stairs, her heart pounding with anger. Jason, who had abandoned the xylophone for the time being and was filling James's wheelbarrow with James's bricks, looked up and smiled when he saw her. His pleasure at her return lit up his whole face. He had waited, he hadn't cried, but he was relieved to the point of delight that she had come back. He came to her and put up his arms. She picked him up, calmed by him, her anger cooling.

Edward was looking at them both. A flush had come up into his face. He said in his sullen way, 'So that's my son?'

She hadn't expected that. Bringing Edward down here she hadn't foreseen it, though obviously she should have. It would be easy to say yes, the easiest way out. After all she would seldom see Edward again, she was going to make sure of that. In no possible way were they going to become 'friends'. If James had lived, if this were James he was looking at in Benet's arms, that would still be true. There was nothing to make a link between them now that James was dead.

She had only to nod. A shrug, simple silence, would do it. To put an end to questions, inquiries, suspicions, she had only to nod her head, take a step forward and present this handsome, fair-haired, blue-eyed child to this handsome, fair-haired, blue-eyed man. She couldn't. It seemed an outrage. So Edward did mean something to her still? Or what there had been between herself and Edward meant something? Enough anyway to make it impossible for her to look him in the face and tell him this was his child.

'No. He's a friend's child I'm looking after.'

He didn't believe her. 'Don't give me that, Benet. You've kept yourself from me and your book and your success, you must be the meanest-spirited woman living. And now you'd even deny me the identity of my son.'

'I'm not denying anything, Edward. This isn't James.'

She set Jason on the rocking horse and set it swinging. But Jason had had enough of rocking horses and xylophones and wheelbarrows. He rubbed his fists into his eyes.

'Jay wants juice.'

It was what he always said when he was tired. She carried him with her to the fridge, took out the feeding bottle of apple juice, held it under the hot tap to take the chill off, Jason seated on her hip. Edward followed her. He was standing very close to them.

'If it's not James, where *is* James?'

To gain courage, to have the strength to say the words, she found herself doing a curious thing. She tightened her grasp on Jason and held him close to her, feeling his warmth.

'James is dead, Edward.'

'*What?*'

'I did say that. You did hear me. James is dead. He died in hospital about six weeks ago.'

'Children don't die these days,' he said. 'Children don't die.'

'That's what I thought. I was wrong. They do.'

Jason liked best to feed himself with the juice. She sat him in the big Windsor chair, propped with cushions. Edward was staring at him.

'I don't believe you, Benet. It would be typical of you to invent some stratagem to keep me totally from my son. I've no legal claim anyway but the fact that he's my son and you know it and I know it would be enough to bother you. You'd even cut that.'

She lifted her shoulders. She said stonily, 'I'll show you the death certificate.'

When Mopsa had come home in the late afternoon of that first day Benet left the hospital, she had seen her tuck a long buff-coloured envelope into one of the pigeonholes of the desk. They had not talked about it but she knew what was inside. She took out the certificate, and, without looking at it, handed it to Edward. He read it and looked up at her with haggard eyes.

'How did you let that happen to him? How could you allow him to – to asphyxiate?'

So that was what it said. She didn't want to see. She felt a cold, contemptuous anger against Edward. What did he know? What did he *care*? He put his head into his hands and covered his face. Jason leaned against her, then climbed into her lap. She hoped and prayed Edward would go now, that he would have his little show of a grief he couldn't possibly feel for a child he had never known and then – doubtless uttering threats, abusing and accusing her – he would go. He took away his hands and looked at her, red-eyed.

'You offered me a drink about half an hour ago. I should have thought the least you could have done was fetch it when you went upstairs just now. After what you've told me, I rather *need* a drink.'

She knew who he reminded her of. Of Mopsa. Had it always been so? Was there something in her own personality that needed a Mopsa, a parasite creature to batten on her and insult her and amaze her with its own gross selfishness? It made her laugh, not ironically but with pure amusement.

'Three years ago,' he said, 'I thought you couldn't be harder but I was wrong. I hoped you'd changed. Don't you want to know why I came here? I thought we might get together again. I even thought we might marry.'

'But now you're disillusioned?' Jason had fallen asleep.

She took the bottle gently from him. 'If you want that drink, Edward, you'll have to fetch it yourself. Room above this one, cupboard by the window. I have to put this boy to bed.'

Barry went down the hill towards Hampstead tube station. He felt shaken. There had been very little warning of what had happened. All evening the house had been in darkness and then, just as he was giving up hope of seeing Terence Wand that evening, a faint light had come on, not in one of the front rooms but a light somewhere in the back of the house seen from where he stood through an arch or an open doorway. Terence Wand had come in the back way. It hadn't occurred to Barry that there *was* a back way, but after he moved away from the arch and before he left for the station, he had investigated and found the garages, the one numbered five with the small blue Volvo tucked inside.

But after that light came on, he had for a while been given new hope of seeing and identifying Terence Wand. He counted on him showing himself at a window and this was what had eventually happened but in a shocking and almost horrible way. Barry wondered how long Terence Wand had known he was there and, come to that, known who he was and where he stood in relation to Carol. For that Terence Wand must have known this, his subsequent behaviour clearly showed.

If Barry had had any doubts about Terence Wand, they were gone now. About who Wand was to Jason and had been to Carol and would be again if he could. Wand had mocked him with it in a single moment's *macho* display. The house had been dark but for that glimmer of light in the back regions. Somehow its darkness seemed permanent, still, enduring. He had let his attention wander and watched a white cat jump one of the low walls and stroll towards the tree in the centre of the courtyard. What had made him look up again towards the blank, black, shiny windows? Certainly not any change in the unchanging aspect of the house. A sixth sense perhaps, a spark of electricity transmitted from this man to him with whom he had something strong in common.

He lifted his head and looked up. The light came on in an explosive flood and a naked man stood there for an instant of mocking exposure. The light made a gold gleam on his hair, he looked tall as a statue. Then the blind went down in a black cascade and shut him out.

Barry came home over the Chinese bridge. He counted the houses from where the footpath met Summerskill Road but there were no lights on in Carol's. It was only just gone eleven, the winebar didn't close till eleven.

Winterside Down seemed unusually empty. Even the motorbike boys weren't about. Lila Kupar, who never drew her curtains, whose curtains were perhaps not ample enough to draw, could be seen in her scarcely furnished front room ironing a white sari. A naked light bulb, rather too powerful, hung just above her head. Barry let himself into the house. The Spicers had their television on loudly and you could hear the meaningless prompted laughter in Carol's hall. In the dark, Barry saw Terence Wand's face. In reality he had glimpsed it for no more than five seconds but he was sure it had imprinted itself on his mind. It was Jason's face thirty years on that he conjured up.

Barry didn't possess a pair of gloves. He put Carol's rubber ones on that hung over the rim of the kitchen sink. Wearing the gloves, he found himself the ballpoint pen he and Carol used for writing messages to each other and the milkman and the notebook Tanya had for school and had once left behind in the house. He would have to buy an envelope tomorrow. He began to write his letter, carefully printing the words.

# 16

The anonymous letter came into the hands of Detective Inspector Tony Leatham by way of Chief Superintendent Treddick and those forensics experts who had examined it in vain for fingerprints and other possible giveaways. By this time the lined paper, exercise book paper, was crumpled and rather limp. Leatham already knew what it said. A conference had been held solely for the purpose of discussing this letter.

*Jason Stratford's father is Terence Wand, 5 Spring Close, Hampstead.*

The writer evidently wanted them to believe this Wand had snatched his son and was keeping him hidden somewhere. The aim was probably no more than the vindictive one of wanting to cause trouble for Wand. Treddick, of course, believed Jason was dead and had been dead since the day he disappeared, had almost certainly been dead even before his disappearance was reported. He had been murdered and buried somewhere like the African child in Finchley, and one day, like that child's, his body would be unearthed.

For his part, Leatham wasn't so sure. He still thought it possible Jason had been abducted. Tough, hard, with little faith left in human nature, he nevertheless hoped for Jason. He was fond of children. Since Jason had gone, he sometimes found himself looking at his own sons with fiercely protective paternal feelings, something he hadn't consciously experienced before.

Treddick was gunning for Barry Mahon. He thought it

was only a matter of time before he got him. One day Barry would betray himself, probably lead them to Jason's grave, and Treddick was patient, he could wait. Tony Leatham couldn't see they had a scrap of real evidence against Barry. The only offence he had committed, Leatham thought, was to write this letter. He was nearly sure Barry had written it. Treddick was too. He said it was an attempt on Barry's part to turn the heat off himself.

Leatham didn't care much, he was losing interest in all of it. What he would have liked was to find Jason alive and in good shape – preferably for *him* to find him – and then let bygones be bygones. Another case he had been involved in back in the summer affected him more. The man in question, a bank robber, had broken prison while on remand, escaped and made his way halfway across the world. They had recaptured Monty Driscoll in Melbourne, and when the Australian government agreed to give him up, Leatham hoped to be the officer sent out to bring him back. It would be the kind of excitement that seldom came his way. He was pulling strings to get himself to Melbourne.

In the meantime this Terence Wand business had to be attended to. They couldn't just leave it.

Mrs Goldschmidt rang up early in the morning. Could she come and have another look at the house, take a few measurements? Terence didn't want her there but he didn't know how to refuse. There were all sorts of risks attached to having anyone in the house except his own personal invitees. He took two Valium.

She arrived at ten-thirty, dressed this time in a pink leather coat with a fur collar. Each time Terence had seen her, she had been wearing animal skins. Today her short blond hair was swept forward in wispy curls round her face, her make-up mauvish with damson lips. She had the manner of someone on depressant drugs, downers, and her first remark therefore sounded sarcastic.

'I'm thrilled we're going to have your house.'

184

She spoke in the grey monotone of someone commenting on continual bad weather or chronic illness. Terence walked about the house with her. In the bedroom where the futon was, she took off her coat and dropped it over one of the low Japanese tables. Under it she wore a very short, pink, knitted dress with a bulky polo collar.

'That's better.'

She stood on a stool to measure the window for curtains. 'Blinds are so cold on their own, don't you think?'

She put out a hand for Terence to help her down, even though the stool stood no more than a foot off the floor. Now in stockinged feet, she climbed on to the ottoman which filled the window embrasure in the master bedroom. She stretched up with her tape measure, lost her balance and would have fallen had Terence not caught and steadied her. He caught her round the waist and, instead of a stiff nervous body, found himself clasping a relaxed, even yielding, one. He asked himself what was going on. Something certainly was. Terence knew he was attractive to women – it had made a living for him as having a flair for design or management might – but he didn't know why. He was a little below medium height, nothing to much to look at and with the sort of colouring that in a woman is called 'mousy'. Carol Stratford had once asked him if he was a man or a mouse and it was true he often felt mouselike, smallish and brown and nervous. Perhaps that was what the women liked.

He took his hands away from Mrs Goldschmidt's waist, giving her a light pat on the flank. He was wondering what to do, what response to make if things hotted up – would refusal jeopardize the sale of the house or, on the other hand, would acquiescence? – when, glancing out of the window, he saw two men come into the court from under the arch and stand just this side of it, looking at the five houses.

Terence had not been able to make up his mind about the watcher of a few nights ago but he knew these two were policemen. He was one of those people who have a nose for policemen. No one else had quite those tired bleary eyes, rubber-mask faces, clothes that looked as if their wearers had lost weight, black shoes that needed polishing. They stood there looking at the five houses. Then they began to move across the courtyard towards number one. Terence let out his held breath. Mrs Goldschmidt put out her hand to him to be helped down as if she expected him to kiss it first.

As they were on their way down, he took a look out of one of the slit windows that lit the staircase. The policemen had gone inside number one but the front door still stood open. Terence didn't like it. He wanted Mrs Goldschmidt to go. She moved slowly and languidly ahead of him, trailing her hand down the banisters, once looking back over her shoulder to give him a vague wistful smile. In the hall, by the statue with a hole for a head, she stood making notes on a pad in large backward-sloping writing.

'Oh, I forgot my coat. I left it upstairs.'

She would go up to fetch it, he thought, and then call him and then . . .

'I'll get it for you.'

He leaped for the stairs. The bedroom window showed him the two policemen on the narrow stone terrace outside the front door of number three in conversation with the woman who lived there. He grabbed the pink leather coat. Downstairs again, he held the coat for her, actually took hold of her right arm and pushed it into the sleeve opening. It took all the meagre courage he had to open the front door. The policemen were outside, about three yards away, staring at the door and now at him.

His throat closed up and his heart took a painful leap towards the middle of his chest. Somehow they had got on to him. Someone, one of those neighbours perhaps, had seen the house was up for sale, was a friend of Sawyer's, had had a letter from Freda . . . Mrs Goldschmidt went slowly out of the door, down the steps, extending her swan neck, vaguely smiling. He realized the police weren't going to move or speak until she was out of the way. That was their brand of tact. As if he cared! It could have been her who put them on to him for all he knew.

She turned back once. 'Well, goodbye for now and thank you so much.'

Don't call me Phipps, he screamed silently, don't call me Phipps!

'I may be in touch. I may want to come back.'

It sounded inexorable, it sounded like a dour threat. He had nothing to say and couldn't have spoken if he had wanted to. His voice would have been a reedy pipe. She walked past the policemen as if they weren't there or were mere furnishings of the courtyard, additional trees or urns, and backed with tiny slow steps across the paving to gaze at the house she had just left. It was only when she turned away once more, smiling with unparted lips in Terence's direction, began on her measured stroll towards the arch, that the policemen moved. They walked up the steps and the older one, ruddy and fair-haired in a flapping raincoat with dangling belt, said in a low conversational tone to Terence: 'Mr Wand? Mr Terence Wand?'

Terence nodded. He felt as limp as a leaf. The front door closed with a soft dainty little click. They were looking round Freda's hall, at the statues, the Modigliani copy, the black spaniel carpet, the way policemen always do look as if they themselves were condemned by an ungrateful society forever to live in pre-war council houses. Terence opened the double glass doors into the living room. He wished he hadn't eaten those cornflakes, that boiled egg and that croissant for breakfast because he was sure that any moment now he was going to have to make an excuse and go away to be sick.

They walked in. They stood looking curiously about them as if they too had come with a view to buying the house. Just as Terence was trying to frame the words that would get him out of there and into the bathroom, the younger one said, 'Jason Stratford, Mr Wand. Young Jason Stratford. That's why we've come to see you.'

For a moment the name meant nothing to Terence. It

was shock only insofar as it was utterly distant from what he had expected.

'May we sit down?'

Again Terence nodded. He didn't sit down. He was holding himself still and tense because he was afraid he might retch if he moved.

'You'll be aware of course that young Jason is missing. I don't reckon there's many people unaware of that now. Am I right in thinking you're a personal friend of his mother, Mrs Carol Stratford?'

Relief hit Terence like a soft warm pillow pushed into his face. He could hardly breathe for it. Whatever this might be about it was nothing to do with fraudulent schemes to sell Freda Phipps's house. He wondered if he could speak but was still afraid to try.

'According to our information there's a possibility you're Jason Stratford's father.'

If anything could have fetched a voice out of Terence it was this. It came very shrilly.

'Me?'

They didn't say anything. They went on looking at him, though not in an unfriendly way.

'Did she tell you that?' said Terence, articulate again and gruff-voiced with indignation.

'Well, no, Mr Wand. We're not able to divulge our source of information but I think I can tell you who it wasn't and it wasn't Mrs Stratford.'

Terence didn't believe him. It would be just like Carol to tell them that. No doubt she was shielding Jason's true father because the guy was up to something shady or really had got the boy. It could be almost anything with Carol, she was very devious. He could see what they were up to. They'd called on the neighbours to find out if any of them had seen a strange child about.

'I didn't know the kid existed,' he said. 'That is, not until I saw on TV about him being missing.'

They continued to look polite, impassive. Terence could

tell that the bigger fair one was wondering why he had been so nervous if he had nothing to hide.

'I don't suppose you'd object if we had a look over the house, would you?'

What a way to put it! The younger one said it was a nice place he'd got here. Terence didn't object, he knew that would be very unwise, but he went upstairs behind them. In the bathroom off the master bedroom they found Teresa's eyeliner pencil lying on the glass top of the vanitory unit.

'Married, now, are you, Mr Wand?'

Terence shook his head. He didn't explain. The younger one's eyes shifted as if this only confirmed the likelihood of Terence's having bastards he didn't know about all over the place. Terence felt an increasing grievance against Carol Stratford. He'd make it his business to have a word with Carol over this.

The policemen didn't exactly search. They just looked into all the rooms. They asked to see his passport which gave him a dreadful pang for a moment in case they had powers to confiscate it. But they handed it back without a word and soon after that they went. Terence took two Valium and poured himself a very stiff whisky. He sat down with his drink and asked himself seriously if he was going to have the stamina to carry things through. Not was it worth it. He knew very well it was worth almost anything to get his hands on £130,000. Not was it worth it, but could he stand the pace?

Terence knew himself. He had the rare quality of knowing himself quite well. The agony of the morning had brought him fresh self-knowledge. His fear had been so great and also so prolonged that he wondered now why he hadn't had a heart attack or fallen down in a fit. If he reacted like that because two policemen called on him, how would his body and his nerves behave when he had to sign that contract, receive that huge sum of money, draw it from the bank and escape with it? How would he stand up to things while, with the money in a bag in his hand, he had to get to an airport and board a plane?

Suppose he dropped dead of fear?

Might it not be wiser, after all, to opt for the thirteen thousand odd of the deposit money and call it a day? Take Goldschmidt's cheque and vanish? Goldschmidt's cheque . . . A chilly tremor ran through Terence. He set his glass down.

This was something he hadn't though of, something he had entirely neglected to think of. Goldschmidt's – or his firm of solicitors' – cheque would be drawn to John H. Phipps and would certainly be a crossed cheque. He, Terence, would therefore have to pay it into John Phipps's bank account. But he didn't have a bank account, he didn't exist.

There was nothing to stop Terence going to, say, the Midland in West End Lane and opening an account in the name of John Howard Phipps except that they would want a reference. They would want someone else, preferably an account holder with the same bank, if not the same branch, to vouch for him that he was a suitable, respectable and credit-worthy person. As John Phipps. He knew all about it. Jessica had opened an account for him at the Anglian-Victoria in the Market Place in Hampstead Garden Suburb and had of course herself been his referee.

Who was there in the world prepared to say that Terence Wand, posing as John Phipps, was respectable and trust-worthy? Come to that, who was there prepared to tell a bank Terence Wand was John Phipps?

No one. There was no one he could take on as an accomplice. To do so would necessarily mean sharing the £132,000, splitting it down the middle in fact. He would rather forgo it all than do that, he thought, far rather.

A little snow had fallen during the night. It lay like a thin patchy sheet of gauze on roofs and the tops of cars but where commuters and the postman had already trodden were wet brown footprints. A steady *drip-drip-drip* came from the house eaves. Over the Heath a grey mist hung.

When he had finished his breakfast, Jason sat on the floor drawing. He drew a picture of the xylophone and crayoned all the notes in in appropriate colours. It was a very good drawing indeed for a two-year-old, Benet thought; you could easily see what it was supposed to be.

She had dressed Jason in clothes she had bought for him, not James's. She picked the labels out in case they were clues. Jason wore blue velvet-corded dungarees with a blue-and-white striped tee shirt and a sweater in natural undyed wool. He had fawn socks and brown leather lace-up half-boots. Benet sat him on her lap to put his coat on, a brown tweed coat with hood and toggle buttons, lined in Black Watch tartan. She was rather worried about that coat. She had bought it in Hampstead, in an exclusive expensive shop, and she and Jason had been in there for a long time while he tried coats on. Would the woman remember her? The point was, she really did want him to have that coat. He had to leave the rocking horse and the xylophone and the drawing things behind but she wanted him to keep that warm winter coat.

He liked riding in the car so much he was never any trouble. She wondered how he would react when they came to Lordship Avenue, if he would remember. And would he remember this house in the Vale of Peace? Not to tell people now, of course, that was not what she meant. He had nowhere near the required command of speech. But one day when he was grown-up, would he, if he came to Hampstead and perhaps walked up from South End Green or down from Heath Street, have a sense of *déjà vu*? Would he think, I have been here before? And if they had told him of that six-week-long lacuna in his life, would he then ask himself if he had spent it here?

She had very little real apprehension that she herself was in danger. She was not the kind of person the police would suspect. If they had questioned women known to have lost a child, they would already have come to her. There could not be so many. No, they had either neglected to take this step or else considered her so unlikely – the well-known, well-off young writer who probably didn't know where Lordship Avenue was – as to be beyond suspicion. So if she had been beyond suspicion while Jason was missing surely she would continue to be so once he was found.

At red traffic lights she looked over her shoulder as she always did to speak to him.

'All right, Jay?'

'White,' he said. 'Snow.'

'It's going fast but there'll be some more and you can make a snowman.'

'Snowman,' said Jason, liking the word. 'Snowman, snowman.'

She began to speak her thoughts aloud to him.

'I'm going to take you into the public library in Lordship Avenue, Jay, the branch called Winterside. You may have been in there before with your mother or – or Barry? I remember the library. I used to go in there a lot when I lived in Winterside Road. There's a children's section with chairs set round a table. I'm going to sit you on one of those chairs and get you a book to look at from the shelf and then I'm going to leave you there. But first I'm going to pin a label on your coat that says who you are. I've done a label with "This is Jason Stratford" on it.'

'Coat,' said Jason. 'Jay's coat.'

'That's right, pinned on to Jay's coat. And when they see you're on your own, the people in the library will read the label and know who you are and fetch your mother.'

And the police, she thought. She tried to imagine it all, the hue and cry, but somehow she couldn't. With Jason's return the world ended.

'Mummy,' said Jason in a pleasant conversational tone. 'Mummy.'

She drove eastwards along Rudyard Gardens, looking for a place to park. Parking had got a lot worse since the days when she had lived there. There were double yellow lines all the way along Lordship Avenue now. She didn't want to be too far away from the library. Winterside Road itself might do, only there was no entry to Winterside from Lordship Avenue. She had to make a long detour, coming into Winterside Road from Canal Street, passing Woodhouse's garage and the house where they had had the attic flat. There was a parking space almost outside the garage but suppose Tom Woodhouse were there and were to come out and see her?

The pollarded plane trees were a hideous sight at this time of the year, their trunks like old bones. The heavy grey sky looked full of snow. She had first met Edward during a snowy winter, and it had been a cold hard winter, spring rather, when she had parted from him. They had been living in Tufnell Park and it was he who had left and found himself a flat or room somewhere round here. Brownswood Common Lane? Brownswood Dale? She couldn't remember and he wasn't there now anyway. The address he had left her was Kentish Town. He had told her he hated her, she was hard as nails, that they had never been suited to each other, and then had done one of his about-faces, tried to get her into his arms and make her promise to go back to him, to marry him.

There was a slot to park the car in on the Winterside Down side of the street just by the footpath that led to the Chinese bridge over the canal. She put Edward out of her mind. He lived here no longer, he was the last person she was likely to see.

The lawns of Winterside Down were a bright December green. In the branches of a Norway spruce someone had put a network of Christmas lights. Benet took Jason's pushchair, the original one, out of the boot of the car and debated whether to return it with him. It was old and battered but it was Carol Stratford's and she, Benet, had no right to keep it. On the other hand, they might stop her taking it into the library or suggest she fold it and that would draw unwanted attention to herself. She decided to replace it and leave it in the boot. The clothes Jason was wearing more than compensated for the cost of a new one.

She lifted Jason down out of the car. He looked towards Winterside Down, the rows of redbrick houses, the white roadways, the single tall tower. His cheeks went bright pink in the cold air. As they walked along he kept his head turned towards the estate, his eyes fixed on it, his hand in hers dragging a little. Then he pointed. He looked at her inquiringly, putting the question in the form all his questions took.

'What's this?' he said. 'What's this?'

'It's where you used to live, Jay. It's where you're going to live.' She picked him up. He sat firmly on her hip. 'I'm sorry, Jay,' she said, for now was her last chance to say it. 'I'm sorry about it all. It wasn't my fault in the beginning. You and I, we were victims of circumstance. Well, we were victims of poor Mopsa who's ill. And later on – I couldn't do that to Mopsa, could I? I've no excuse for keeping you so long after she went home. I don't really know why I did. I'm a coward, I suppose, or else I'd take you boldly into a police station. I'd take you to your mother over there. But I can't. I haven't the nerve, I'm a coward. So I'm sorry about it, Jay, and I hope you haven't been unhappy, I hope there's been no harm done.' He wasn't looking at her. He was frowning and his lower lip stuck out. 'Go on,' she said, 'say something. One kindly word will do.'

'Dog,' said Jason, pointing at the Dobermann sniffing packing cases outside a fishmonger. And then, shrinking up against her, 'Mummy!'

The Winterside library was a Victorian building with a Dutch façade and the words PUBLIC LIBRARY carved in recess on a red sandstone plaque over the doors. Benet walked up the steps, carrying Jason. An elderly man, a pensioner with an armful of books, held the door open for her.

Two librarians, both women, stood in the area between the IN and OUT counters, one in the act of stamping a book, the other studying a catalogue. Benet saw that the book which the borrower put out his hand for was her own *The Marriage Knot* in its large, handsome hardcover edition.

Her photograph was on the back of the jacket, a young, heart-shaped, half-smiling face, unrecognizable surely as the gaunt woman who had just come in carrying a child, her head tied up in a scarf to hide the mass of dark shiny hair.

The children's section of the library was still there, though changed, brightened up, the little chairs now painted a variety of colours, and pinned up on the wall a collage poster to make her stare and smile. Was this a recurring motif in current teacher training courses? Or had one of those librarians a child who had been in the hospital where James had been? The poster, though less ambitious in its execution, though small, sparser and less adventurous, was a tree of hands.

Finding it here seemed an omen. But of what? She didn't believe in omens. She sat Jason down on a turquoise-blue chair and found a picture book from the shelves for him. The library was silent now but for the faint footfalls of two borrowers moving between the bookcases and the sound of a man reading today's paper at a table clearing his throat. There was no one in the children's section but themselves. Jason turned the thick cardboard pages of his book, looking at pictures of a dog, a cat, a pair of shire horses.

'What's this?'

She laid a finger on her lips, then on his, the way she had of telling him to be very quiet. The hands on the tree were all like her own, thin, brown, ringless hands, all the same, all pointing downwards. Her own hands were like those as they dipped into her bag for the label and the pin.

Jason pointed at the book. He whispered because she had asked him to.

'What's this?'

'You know what that is, that's a dog.'

He spoke the first real sentence he had yet uttered. It was slowly and perfectly articulated, and he must have been aware of his triumph, for his proud smile began as he spoke.

'I don't like dogs,' said Jason and, in spite of the sentiment, gave a pleased giggle.

She held the label in her left hand, the pin in her right. She felt sick, almost faint. It had struck her, what she was about to do, the realization. And she saw what lay beyond, this afternoon, tonight, the desert, the loneliness. She looked as if for the first time, yet with eyes which saw very differently from that first time, at the fair-haired, sturdy, small boy whose legs as he sat there were not quite long enough to reach the ground, who laughed with delight at his own cleverness, whose scars would never fade. Of course she wasn't going to label him like some sort of parcel and leave him here. She wasn't going to leave him at all. How could she have imagined it? How was it she hadn't understood what had been happening to her as the days with him became weeks and dislike became toleration, toleration acceptance, acceptance camaraderie and at last . . .

Why, I couldn't live without him now, she thought. Jason was getting down off the chair. He handed her the book and put up his arms. He had had enough of the library, he wanted to go home.

# 17

Last Christmas, Carol had had Tanya and Ryan home. Barry wondered who else had been there with Carol, apart from Iris and Jerry and the children. Terence Wand perhaps or one of those others Maureen had mentioned. Carol didn't even want to talk about Christmas, she said she'd work right through the holiday, she hadn't anything to celebrate. What was the good of saying they'd have Tanya and Ryan home when most of the time she wouldn't even be there?

If his own job had been a bit more secure, he might have been able to persuade her not to put in so many hours for Kostas. But he wouldn't have liked to bet on his having a job at all this time next year. Ken Thompson hadn't any more work lined up once the Finchley job was over. And it almost was over. They were dragging their feet really, Barry knew, because after that, unless someone came in with an order in the next couple of days, there'd be nothing. Ordinarily, of course, Ken couldn't get rid of him, couldn't sack him without very good cause, but it would be another thing if he could prove there wasn't the work about to justify employing him. He couldn't say to Carol to slacken off when any time he might be on the dole himself.

Ken was acting differently towards him anyway. It was hard to put your finger on it, but Barry noticed he had stopped calling him by his first name. It used to be Barry this and Barry that but now he didn't use any name to him at all. And sometimes, while they were putting the finishing touches to the managing director's office, Barry looked round and caught Ken looking at him. Not in any sort of vindictive or disgusted way, it wasn't like that. Barry thought Ken looked at him as one might steal a glance at something not quite included in humanity, a variety of ape perhaps or a picture of prehistoric man.

At least the police hadn't been back. Was his letter responsible for that? It seemed likely. He imagined Terence Wand being put through those long gruelling sessions with Treddick or Leatham, Terence Wand asked if he saw himself as a nursemaid or if he beat up kids. It would shake him up a bit being fetched away from that fancy house of his in a police car. Barry tried to imagine how anyone with Terence Wand's background could ever have come to own such a house. He must have started himself off in some business when he was very young. Barry knew that was the way it was done and longed to do the same himself, to have a house like that for Carol, a car, only the times weren't right for it; things were different, he'd heard, ten years ago. There was no use in him starting up on his own now when even Ken who was a businessman and known couldn't get the jobs.

Winterside Down was giving him the cold shoulder. The Spicers next door weren't acting the way the Isadoros did or the people in the Bevan Square shops, they weren't staring and then turning ostentatiously away, they were just pretending they hadn't seen him when they had. Barry had to do something in the evenings, he couldn't sit at home all the time on his own watching television. He took to going to the Bulldog for a drink round about seven. The Bulldog was far enough away from Winterside Down for the people in there not to know who he was.

He met Iris and Jerry, coming from the opposite direction, bound for the same destination. That is, he saw them coming a long way off. They were arm in arm, Iris taller than Jerry in her wobbly stilt-heeled sandals. Barry had never thought the day would come when he would be glad to have even Iris and Jerry to talk to. He didn't wave, he didn't feel they had ever reached waving terms, but he quickened his pace a bit. The Bulldog was on this side, only a few yards away now. The brewery had put up a new sign, a bulldog with a cigar in its mouth and a sailor hat on. Barry saw Iris tug at Jerry's sleeve and whisper something. They weren't anywhere near a pedestrian crossing but they crossed the road, getting halfway and having to wait on the white line, they were that desperate to avoid him.

Barry could hardly believe it. Carol's own mother! She couldn't think he'd murdered Jason. She was as much responsible as anyone for his disappearance, more than anyone really. He was in the Bulldog's doorway now but he stopped, he didn't go in. He could see them on the other side of Lordship Avenue, pretending to look in a shop window, no doubt watching the Bulldog's entrance reflected in the glass.

Obviously Iris was thinking along the same lines as the rest of them. He could hear her state her reason, if reason it could be called, in that placid indifferent whine of hers.

'There's no smoke without fire when all's said and done, is there, Barry?'

Only she wouldn't call him by his Christian name again, any more than Ken did. He began to walk rapidly on down Lordship Avenue. Put a mile between himself and Winterside Down and he wouldn't feel everyone he passed was thinking child-killer, child-killer. He'd go and have a drink in the wine bar, he thought. Carol would have something to say about Iris avoiding him like that. He imagined her anger on his behalf and her calling him 'lover' in front of all those people.

It wasn't worth getting a bus now he'd come so far. You could see the wine bar's neon sign a long way off because it was on a curve where the road bent round to the right. It was funny, he thought, how he always saw her lights in the distance and was pulled by fast magnetism towards them.

The wine bar was on the corner of a little side street called Java Mews. Down at the bottom was a pub called the Java Head that was Ken Thompson's local. Barry didn't want to run into Ken now. The awkwardness and the constraint would be worse than at work. He didn't want to see Dennis Gordon either but there was no avoiding it. The silvery-blue Rolls, a diamond on a rubbish heap, was parked a little way down the mews and directly under a street lamp as if the lamp were there specially to highlight it. Dennis Gordon was getting into the car, was in the driving seat, though the hand with that great gleaming lump of a ring on it still held the door open.

He got out again and waved to Barry. There seemed no reason for his getting out unless it was to show himself off and the cream leather trench coat he wore. He raised his hand with a backward flip at Barry and then he bent over the windscreen to scratch a grain or tiny smear off the glass.

Barry didn't nod at him or acknowledge the wave. It didn't occur to him to be grateful to Dennis Gordon for deigning to notice him. The Rolls moved off quietly, with smooth elegance, like a lovely ship leaving a port that is necessarily squalid with docks and wharfs. Barry thought what a lot of people there were about who had money: Ken, Mrs Fylemon, Kostas, Terence Wand, Dennis Gordon. Sometimes his longing for money or for the opportunity to make it was as great as his longing for Carol. He sensed somehow that if he had it he could keep her for ever.

The wine bar was full of trailing plants, pictures of the sea, posters of ruined temples, very Greek. Alkmini, round, dark, heavy-browed, dressed in unrelieved black, was serving behind the bar on her own. Barry was glad afterwards – insofar as he was glad of anything – that he hadn't betrayed himself by asking for Carol. He hadn't got as far as speaking a word. At the sight of him, Kostas, unsmiling, lifted a brown hand an inch or two off his knee. It was Alkmini who told him.

'You forget it's Wednesday, Barry?'

He said nothing for a moment. He felt something move involuntarily inside his chest. His face grew hot. He knew at once with the intuitiveness of the lover what Alkmini was implying. Carol still worked at the wine bar, had even taken on Saturdays, but she had given up Wednesday evenings. She had given up working Wednesday evenings and she hadn't told him.

'It went right out of my head,' he said.

He hardly cared whether they guessed or not. Or even, when he looked back over his shoulder and saw Alkmini whispering to a customer, whether it was him she was whispering about – 'That's Carol Stratford's boyfriend, that's the *one*.'

If Carol hadn't told him, it was because she must be going somewhere on Wednesday evenings she didn't want him to know about. Of course he could guess where that was. He got on a bus, the first that came along, hardly knowing where it was going, anywhere to put distance between himself and Winterside Down. A curious idea came to him – but one he quickly pushed away – that she must love him, she must care for what he thought and felt, if she bothered to deceive him. She must still care about hurting him.

He tried to remember what she had worn that day. Even if he could have remembered, it would mean nothing. For going out with Terence Wand, she would have come home and changed after being at Mrs Fylemon's. The Zandra Rhodes dress perhaps or the black and white zig-zag with the fake fur over it, it was cold enough for that tonight. He got off the bus in Camden Town and went into the tube station. At Hampstead, when he came out into Heath Street, it was snowing a little, the odd occasional flake of snow falling out of the black smoky sky.

Hampstead was like a museum full of old things, beautiful, preserved, unreal. The richness of it, even on this mid-winter night, the money-breathing walls, depressed him. He made his way through winding lanes and little alleys to the walls that enclosed Spring Close as if it were a castle. Which, of course, it was, a rich man's castle guarded from the rough world. Barry stood under the arch. The lamplight in there was of quite a different kind from that which glared upon and bleached Winterside Down. It seemed to *stroke* the brownish-red bricks, the pale smooth stonework, the dark shiny wood, the glass. There was enough of it to throw a shadow of the tree on to the paving stones, a shadow like a piece of branched coral. The snow had stopped.

Terence Wand's house was in total darkness. They were out somewhere together, of course they were, though they might intend to come back here later. What could he have done anyway if they had been there? He couldn't march in, fight the man, seize Carol. He wasn't her husband. She hadn't even promised he might be her husband one day.

He walked round the perimeter of Spring Walk. Number five's garage was empty, the door standing open. They had gome out in the car. He went back into Hampstead, into Heath Street, down to the High Street for a drink in the King of Bohemia. It was warm in there and crowded. Carol would have to be home by eleven-thirty, he thought, if she wanted him to go on thinking she had been at the wine bar. It was getting on for ten now. The cold hit him, coming out of that warm bar. It was stupid going back to Spring Close but he went back.

The arrival of a police car put an end to his vigil. It slid in under the arch, a little sleek blue and white car with the orange-coloured illuminated sign on its roof. Barry was caught in its headlights like a wild animal on a country road. His first thought was that they wanted him again for another half-dozen hours of questioning, that they had followed him here observing all his movements, the transport he had used, and now were going to carry him off to the fresh humiliation of some interview room.

But the young uniformed officer who got out and came up to him only asked him quietly and politely what he was doing there. Barry didn't know what to say. He didn't know what he was doing there himself.

'I was just looking,' he said and he heard a stammer in his voice. 'I didn't know there were any modern houses down here so I came in to get a closer look.'

'You're taking your time about it.'

One of the neighbours had been on to them, Barry guessed. Somebody in one of the lighted houses must have phoned them to report a loiterer.

'I should get off home if I were you,' the policeman said. 'It's getting a bit late to be hanging about looking at other people's houses. Let's see you on your way. Know where the station is, do you?'

No question of their mistaking him for a Hampsteadite! They made sure he went to the station. They watched him from the car, and when he was at the top of Christchurch Hill, he heard the car crawl up behind him, felt her lights flood his back. The time was after eleven-thirty. If he didn't make haste he could miss the last Piccadilly Line train out of King's Cross. He'd be late anyway. For once Carol would wonder where *he* was. The police car followed him down Heath Street and, when he had been seen to go into the tube station, went off down Fitzjohn's Avenue.

It was possibly the last train he got and it brought him to Turnpike Lane at nearly half-past midnight. He had a long walk from there. The only people about were young men of his own sort of age, walking alone like he was, or in groups. There wasn't a woman to be seen. The traffic was light. It had snowed a lot while he was in the train and the snow had melted into puddles. A young black man passed him, carrying a transistor playing very loud rock.

Barry turned into Winterside Road and went down the path to the Chinese bridge. He counted the houses from the corner, but with no joy in his heart this time. Her lights would draw him to her but not happily, not at a run.

They were on, upstairs and down. He began to think what he would say to her. He couldn't just let it go. The green lawns were khaki-brown in the sodium lamplight and the sky held its reddish London sheen, but the lights at each end of the footpath ahead were timed to go out at midnight. The passage itself was dark though light at the end, as the mouth of a cave is when looked at from the inside. Barry thought suddenly, suppose he'd been wrong all the time, suppose she'd given up Wednesday evenings only this week and she'd forgotten to tell him? Alkmini hadn't said anything that didn't fit in with that. And then after leaving Mrs Fylemon she'd gone shopping somewhere, to one of the centres that stayed open till eight. It was something she often did. He had gone out himself at seven. She was in now. She might have been home waiting for him for hours, he thought.

Barry very much wanted to believe this. He thought that, if Carol told him the story he had just told himself, he would believe her, he would be happy. He entered the passage between the high fences and as he did so two men came in at the other end. Their bodies blocked out the light and he could see the shape of them only, not their faces. For a moment he thought nothing of it. Two men had come into the passage and were walking towards him, that was all.

He went on walking, slowing down when he realized there was something odd. The odd thing was that they were still walking abreast. One hadn't stepped behind the other to let him pass. They still walked side by side, the pair of them coming towards him as if they hadn't seen him – no, not that, as if they meant to come smack into him.

Barry was aware of a danger that raised prickles on the back of his neck. He turned round. Another man, thin, lanky, his black clothes glistening in the little light that showed in the mouth of the passage, had come from the path across the grass and entered the footpath on purposefully silent feet. He stood there, waiting, his arms folded.

Not men, of course. Boys. He recognized the one with folded arms, he could see him. It was Blue Hair. They had been watching for him, they must have been. Waiting for him to be out late on his own. He turned again in the way a cornered animal does and his face met Hoopoe's hot breath, kebab-stinking. Black Beauty with him had pock-marks under his cheekbones as if his face had once been peppered with shot.

204

'Let me pass,' said Barry.

'Fucking baby killer.'

Barry knew he was for it. It wouldn't make any difference what he did, cringe, plead or what, so he wouldn't cringe. He wouldn't argue. That this lot should set themselves up as keepers of a social conscience was a bitter irony. He lifted his right arm and elbowed Hoopoe out of the way. He used both his arms, elbowing. He did it so fast that it nearly worked with Hoopoe. Not with the black boy. The black boy grabbed his shoulder and wheeled him round and struck him in the face with the flat of his hand. Barry punched back. He punched hard at Black Beauty and kicked out at Hoopoe and the adrenalin streamed into his blood and, for a moment, a split second, it was good, he was kicking and lashing out and winning. But only for a moment.

Blue Hair, who had been waiting, took a leap down the passage like someone doing the long jump and then he ran and landed on Barry with both arms flailing down hard. He had leather gauntlets studded with shallow metal spikes. Black Beauty, who Barry had kneed in the groin, grabbed his arms and pinned them behind him while Blue Hair punched hard, mostly at his head and face.

Black Beauty held him long after he would have fallen. He held him for Hoopoe and Blue Hair to use as a punching bag. Darkness came down in a sagging curtain and Barry felt his mouth fill with blood as a tooth went. Black Beauty dropped him, perhaps to keep himself clean of the blood which was spilling down Barry's chin. Barry fell, hitting the fence, making the fence shake and vibrate. Hoopoe's pointed boot went hard into his side. But this was his right foot and Hoopoe was left-footed. He drew back his left foot and kicked Barry's ribs as hard as he could.

The last thing Barry knew was a window opening upstairs in the house behind the fence and a voice calling something he never heard.

# Book Three

Book Three

# 18

This agreement is made the _____ day of _____ nineteen
eighty _____ between John Howard Phipps of 5 Spring Close,
Hampstead, London NW 3 (hereinafter called 'The Vendor')
of the one part and Morris Goldschmidt and Rosemary Catalina
Goldschmidt his wife, both of 102 The Dale, Cricklewood,
London NW2 (hereinafter called 'The Purchaser') of the other
part.

Terence's eyes wandered down past the first two clauses to
the vital point three:

The price shall be £132,950 and the Purchaser shall on the
signing hereof pay a Deposit of £13,295 to Lewis & Plummer,
Solicitors for the Vendor, by Solicitors' Client Account
Cheque, Building Society Cheque or Banker's Draft.

Did that perhaps mean that this solicitor would hang on to
Goldschmidt's cheque, investing it perhaps, until the whole
transaction was complete? Terence wouldn't have been at
all surprised, it was typical of people like that, sharks and
money grubbers. In any case it would make a difference of
no more than a month or so. If he didn't manage to get
himself a bank account by the end of the month, he must
by completion date.

No date had been entered. But the solicitor's covering
letter which had arrived with the contract suggested 15
February and would Mr Phipps indicate in his reply if this
suited him? Terence phoned. The man himself wasn't there
but he spoke to a secretary.

'It would be usual practice for such a deposit to be

held by the vendor's solicitors until completion date, Mr Phipps.'

Terence didn't want to arouse any suspicions by hinting he was in need of funds, though he was. He rang off. It had occurred to him that it would be wise to buy a plane ticket a week or so before completion to be used on completion day. What sort of a day was 15 February? Hanging up behind the kitchen door was a calendar for this year but nowhere in the house was there one for next year. He had to work it out on his fingers. February 15, thank God, was a Tuesday. Imagine if it had been a Friday with Goldschmidt paying the money in in the afternoon and him not being able to get at it till the Monday.

Would he dare wait to buy a ticket for a flight to, say, South America until that Tuesday? It was cutting it fine. Terence, whose anxiety neurosis derived rather from the anticipation of frightful fear than from fear itself, could picture the jelly-like tongue-tied abjectness of his condition as, with a suitcase full of cash, he went from airline to airline attempting to buy a ticket. His tremulous glance would hardly dare to take in anything but that which lay straight ahead, for fear of the encroaching law. His throat would be too dry to speak, his hands shaking as he fumbled with the catches on the case. No, he must secure his seat in advance. His self-knowledge told him he would sail more or less serenely through such a purchase because at that point he would scarcely have done anything illegal. At any rate he wouldn't have laid hands on a penny of Goldschmidt's money.

But without Goldschmidt's money, how was he even going to buy a plane ticket? A one-way ticket to anywhere as distant as he intended to go to would hardly be less than £500. He wasn't going to mess about with charter flights you had to pick up in Amsterdam. The sum of £500, which he had randomly seized on as likely, suggested to him the credit limit allowed him on his Barclaycard. He hadn't used the card since moving out of Jessica's house. Barclaycard didn't know of his change of address and the card would no longer be valid anyway.

Or was there a chance it was? Terence hadn't the faintest idea where the card might be except that he was sure he wouldn't have thrown away anything that might, however remotely, be a source of money. He went upstairs and hunted about. In the cupboard of the room where the futon was he had hung most of the clothes he brought with him after flitting from Jessica's. He went through all his pockets. Nothing but a few valueless copper coins, a dirty tissue and a piece of chewing gum. Books had never been much in his line and he possessed none. What had become of the suitcase he had 'borrowed' from Jessica to bring his things in?

No doubt it was with the rest of the luggage in the big store cupboard next to the guest bathroom. He looked in there and found it, a brown Revelation suitcase with a zip-up compartment inside the lining of the lid which he could feel was full of papers . . . He undid the zip and took out a copy of *Knave* magazine, a letter from Freda, indiscreetly sent to him at Jessica's, a bill from Brian of Brook Street for two shirts, a bank statement – and the Barclaycard. The expiry date was February of next year. He remembered now. Jessica had got him the card in the early spring nearly two years ago and three or four months later he had left her. He could hardly believe his luck. What he must do was write at once to Barclaycard and inform them of his change of address so that they could send him a new card in time for the expiry date of this one.

Once he had the new card things would be easy. The fact that his credit limit was only £550 mattered not at all. He could buy a one-way ticket through a travel agent, paying the deposit on the ticket out of one month's credit and the balance out of the next month's – Barclaycard's accounting always taking place, he remembered, round about the twentieth of the month. And this way he wouldn't even have to make the requisite percentage repayment of ten or twelve pounds, for this percentage instalment would not be demanded before the eighteenth of the month following the first credit and on the fifteenth he would be away.

Terence went back to the writing desk and wrote to Barclaycard, giving his change of address and requesting a new card. Only just in time he stopped himself signing the letter John Howard Phipps. He wrote to his solicitor, confirming 15 February as completion date, and then he braced himself for the signing of the contract. Thank God a witness wasn't needed.

A drink would be a good idea. Just one though. One to steady his hand and calm the ravening anxiety that gripped him whenever he contemplated taking this step which would commit him to selling Freda's house. One and a half inches of whisky and the same of water. The Valium he had taken after lunch had more or less worn off by now. He sometimes thought he had taken so much of it that it didn't really work well any longer. It was starting to get dark, though still afternoon. He put on some of the lamps with black shades and some with white shades and paced up and down on the black spaniel carpet, drinking his drink.

Outside in the courtyard the fairy lights someone had put in the catalpa tree winked and sparkled. First of all the green and yellow lights came on, then the blue and red, then the white, then the lot together. Terence walked purposefully to the desk, sat down and signed the contract. He took two or three deep breaths, grasped the pen firmly and signed the document with the signature of John Howard Phipps. It was the best signature he had ever done, almost better than the genuine article if that were possible.

The post wouldn't go out till morning now but he might as well take his letters to the box and have a drink in the White Bear on the way back. He had a couple of quid left. It was while he was in the pub, minding his own business in a corner over a half of Foster's lager, that he remembered the bank statement he had found in the zip-up compartment of Jessica's suitcase. So excited had he been over the discovery of the credit card and finding it still valid that he hadn't even bothered to look at that statement. Suppose there was some money still in the account? Suppose there was as much as twenty pounds? There might be. He had never drawn anything out after leaving Jessica. Some kind of wariness had stopped him. At any rate he must check up on it. The last thing he wanted was to leave the country, having made the Anglian-Victoria bank in Golders Green a substantial money present.

First thing in the morning he would go there and ask his discreet question. Equally discreetly the girl would let him know what the account contained by writing the sum on a scrap of paper and passing it face-downwards to him under the grille. Not tomorrow, though. Tomorrow, he remembered, would be Christmas Day.

Next week, then. He still had to think how he was going to establish somewhere or other a bank account for John Howard Phipps. The mean underhandedness of the solicitors had staved off the need for an account for a while but only a while. The banker's draft for the balance of the £132,000 Goldschmidt would produce on 15 February had to be paid in somewhere. Terence couldn't ask his solicitors to convert it into cash for him. Or, rather, he *could* but he knew he wouldn't dare, he wouldn't take the risk.

And then suddenly he saw. He saw how it could be done. He was gazing into the clear golden liquid in his glass with its light swirl of foam, as if into a crystal. It became the elixir of life or a fount of wisdom. He drank it down and asked for another.

'Merry Christmas,' he said to the girl behind the bar, though he didn't go so far as to buy her a drink.

The dream of a Christmas Party for Jason had come to no more in the end than three infant guests and their mothers confronted by more food than twice as many could have eaten and a bewildering display of decorations and presents. But it had been a success too. They had enjoyed themselves, and Chloe and her two-year-old daughter Kate who

213

hadn't seen James for six months were in no doubt Jason was him. The others, a boy and girl and their mothers living in the Vale of Peace, had of course no idea there was any doubt about it. They all called him Jay, though Chloe raised an eyebrow at the diminutive.

When they had all gone home and Jason was in bed, Benet sat in the basement room among the dirty plates and cups, the present wrappings and the glittering litter and looked at the two trees, the Christmas tree hung with lights and the tree she had painted on the wall and adorned with green and yellow and scarlet hands. Each hand had held – or had had cunningly hooked on to it – a tiny present for Jason: a toy car, an orange, a marble, a magnet, a packet of nuts. She knew she had gone overboard with excess. A more temperate climate must prevail in future. She mustn't spoil him just because they had so blissfully found each other. But this first Christmas with him, she had been unable to help herself. It had been a celebration of her own joy as much as for his pleasure. Pleasure for him there had been, enormous delight. She thought for the rest of her life she would remember his slowly dawning gleeful smile, his advance upon the tree and his last-minute glance up at her for permission to help himself to what the hands held. Nevertheless it was for herself she had done it, to see that look on his face, to exult. Since that day in the library she had been warm with joy – literally warm. It was as if she couldn't feel the cold of dark sleety December. Often she found herself going out wearing only a light jacket, she was so heated by inner happiness.

For the rest of that day when she had taken him to and snatched him from the Winterside library and for a day or two afterwards, she had been beset by fear amounting sometimes to terror that she had betrayed them both, had been detected, and that the police would come. And her fear had no longer been for publicity or disgrace or retribution but solely that Jason would be taken from her. But when no one came and when at the same time all references to Jason seemed to disappear from the newspapers, a happy

214

calm succeeded the fear. She moved into a lovely never-never land which had no past and no future beyond next week and which allowed for no thought about the impossibility of continuing like this or the inevitability of eventual discovery. She was happy, she was serene and she was working. She knew that no rebuff and no rejection could hurt her and it was in this frame of mind that she rang the hospital and asked for Ian Raeburn to invite him to the Vale of Peace.

He came that same evening. Jason had been in bed about an hour. It was curious what happened. Benet had never had such an experience before. It was as if they both knew what they must do, as if this was the way they had greeted one another for a long time now. They went into each other's arms and kissed passionately. What they were doing surprised them equally. They hadn't expected this, it had seemingly been involuntary, and they looked into each other's faces and smiled. But the smiles were brief because passion, until it is old and customary, is not amused. They held each other and kissed and Benet knew they wouldn't speak or explain or excuse but go up, still holding each other, to her bedroom up that long staircase. Only Jason cried. He screamed out in his frightened nightmare voice:

'Mummy! Mummy!'

It broke what had existed between her and Ian. Running up the stairs to Jason, she knew it had broken it only for a while, that one day soon what they had begun would proceed to consummation, but not this evening, not now. She picked up Jason and held him against breasts that ached, a body where half-forgotten little pulses beat. But when she came downstairs and found Ian in the basement room, it was only to take his hands and sit beside him. And it was better so, better to go forward with caution into what she began to feel might be for a lifetime.

He asked her if she were fostering the boy called Jay with a view to adopting him and she clutched at this straw and said yes. Yes, she was.

'He isn't a replacement for James. It isn't that at all. I don't know if you can understand.'

'I'll try.'

'It's as if I had two sons and one of them died. I'll never forget him and there'll always be an empty space in life where he used to be. An empty chair at the table, if that doesn't sound too sentimental.'

'Not to me.'

'I suppose the truth is you can't replace someone. You can just have other people. I won't say my feeling for Jay is greater or less than my feeling was for James. It's not even different. It's the same kind of love but for a different person.'

'I'm glad for you,' Ian said. 'You've done something very wise and clever for yourself, haven't you?'

She had a momentary shivery feeling of what would he think if he knew the real facts? It passed, swallowed by her happiness.

'We're going to see each other all the time now, aren't we, Benet?'

'All the time,' she said.

'And this is *it*?'

'Oh, yes, I think this is it, don't you?'

They laughed at each other. Benet said, 'Every evening?'

'Every lunchtime and every afternoon,' he said. 'Just for the next fortnight anyway. I'm on nights.'

'And I was forgetting I'm writing a novel.'

'Could I make you forget *that*?' he said.

Since then they had met every day – with Jason. Ian had had to go home for Christmas to his parents in Inverness. At nine he would phone her. She began clearing up the basement room with the radio playing light country music. The new novel was going well. She wrote contentedly at night after Jason was asleep, sometimes until midnight. Of course there would have to be some changes there when Ian came back and went on day duty . . . In the glass, pausing with a tray of crockery in her hands, she saw a fuller and younger-looking face, though there were a few white hairs among the dark, about an inch long they were or two months' growth, and she knew they had come when James died.

She picked up the phone and dialled her parents' number in Spain to wish them a happy New Year. Mopsa answered.

'It's unlucky before the Eve itself,' said Mopsa.

'Nonsense.' Benet astonished herself by speaking so robustly. 'I'll probably be out on the Eve enjoying myself.'

There was a silence. Then, 'I only wish I had it in me to be as selfish as that.' Mopsa paused for a reply and when none came said, 'How is James?'

Benet's heart turned over, and for a moment she couldn't speak. It was to her father only that she had spoken when last they had been in touch a week before Christmas and he, of course, couldn't be expected to know. But Mopsa! I must not hate my mother . . .

But the explanation was simply that Mopsa had forgotten. Her actions in the matter of kidnapping Jason had not been well-received, still less applauded, so in the way she always reacted to any censure or criticism she had blocked the whole experience off with whatever mechanism of her curious mentality handled these things. She had forgotten. Memory for her had always been like the writing on a blackboard, which any kind of unease would wipe away at a single stroke.

'He's well,' Benet managed to say. 'We've had a party.'

'I don't remember getting an invitation.'

'Well, of course not. You'd hardly come eight hundred miles to a children's party.'

'When your father's managing director's daughter got married in Santiago, she sent us an invitation and that was more like eight *thousand* miles.'

Benet knew the uselessness of pursuing this. She spoke to her father who sounded tired and subdued. Mopsa refused to come back to the phone. She said the line was so bad it hurt her ears.

I must not hate my mother . . .

And suddenly, at last, Benet understood that she didn't

hate Mopsa any more. That she would never have to adjure herself with those words any more. She would be eternally grateful to her and that was only a step from love. For without Mopsa she would never have had Jason. Mopsa had stolen him for her, knowing with a wisdom unsuspected in her that given long enough Benet would come to love him. And to this end she had risked what was most frightful to her, incarceration – indeed, forced imprisonment – in a mental hospital. She had stolen Jason and given him to Benet and, rather than be the only witness to this abduction, had with her methodical madness forgotten all about it.

'It doesn't matter,' Benet said to her father. 'Say goodbye to her for me. And give her my best love.'

The chill damp limbo that occupies the spaces between the high holidays of Christmas was making itself felt in Finchley High Road. On this the twenty-ninth of December, half the shops were still closed but not of course the banks. Buoyed up by a small whisky and two Valiums, Terence found ample parking space in Regent's Park Road for Freda Phipps's car. The few people about with shopping bags looked bemused, stunned by recent festivities.

Terence walked along rather slowly. He had passed the Westminster Bank and Lloyds and the Midland and Barclays and was beginning to fear (also in a way to hope) that there was no branch of the Anglian-Victoria here, that the phone book had been wrong or the branch had moved, when he saw it ahead of him, its A and V monogram on the orange signboard sticking out between the post office and a building society. He hesitated. He stood gazing into the darkened and barred window of a men's boutique as if the dimly discerned yellow pullover and beige cords in its shadowy depths held an obsessive fascination for him. There was no help for it, he had to go into the bank. It was either going in there or else giving up the whole thing, abandoning the project.

Eleven-thirty and the pubs were open. He was rather

well-off for actual cash, having, since the discovery in Jessica's suitcase, bought a good deal of his food, meals out and drinks on the still-valid Barclaycard. He could easily have run to a couple of Scotches. But he was scared of slurring his speech or of making a mess of John Howard Phipps's signature should he be asked to produce it.

What could they do to him in the bank after all but refuse him? They weren't going to send for the police because he asked for a bank account in the name of Phipps. It wasn't a crime to call yourself by a different name from your own, you could call yourself what you liked in this country. And he had found a foolproof way of getting round that reference business, hadn't he? They could do nothing but refuse him . . .

Terence had often tried these methods of combating paranoia, these recognized ways of reassuring oneself by repeating such handy aphorisms as 'Most of the things you've worried about have never happened' and 'There is nothing to fear but the fear itself' and 'They can't eat you' and so on. But they had never helped much, they had never seemed to get through. They were just things you said which sounded good. They didn't probe into the core of fear, still less start the process of breaking it up. There in Finchley High Road, in the grey gloom of a post-Christmas morning, a dreadful wave of depression flowed over Terence as he understood, staring unseeing at a pair of fawn trousers, that he was going to be beset by fear all his life, live in it and be paralysed by it, and there wasn't enough Valium and whisky in the world to keep it at bay. It wasn't worth it, he thought, there was no way it was worth it. But what did he mean by that? What was worth what? Did he mean that life itself wasn't worth the fear it took to live it?

Thinking along those lines wouldn't do at all. He had no alternative now anyway, he'd gone too far. He had signed the contract and committed himself. In for a penny, in for a pound, in for one hundred and thirty-two thousand pounds. He walked into the bank and in a hoarse sentence, split by a clearing of his throat, asked to see someone about opening an account.

'Phipps,' he said when they asked his name.

He was told to take a seat and did so in one of the orange leather chairs that stood about. After a minute or two someone came out and said the assistant manager would see him. Terence went into a very small office, also done up in orange, and shook hanks with a man who said his name was Fletcher.

'I want to open a bank account.' Terence's voice was back to normal though his body felt rather as if he were treading water. 'With fifty pounds,' he said, aware of what a small sum this sounded these days. It was the utmost he had been able to amass out of three weeks' Social Security.

Fletcher looked, if anything, relieved. It occurred to Terence that perhaps he had thought his visitor was a customer who had wanted an overdraft. 'That shouldn't present too many problems, Mr Phipps.'

He produced a form which Terence scanned quickly, his throat constricting afresh. There was nothing really to dismay him. A specimen signature was required and, under Fletcher's eye, Terence signed 'John Howard Phipps' with a hand that desperate concentration made steady.

Then came the bit about furnishing the name and address of a referee.

'You could apply for a reference,' said Terence, 'to someone who has an account at your Golders Green branch. Would that be all right?'

'I should think that would do very well, Mr Phipps.'

So Terence wrote in the space provided, 'Mr Terence C. Wand', and underneath it, '14 Gibbs House, Brownswood Common Lane, London N15', which was his mother's address.

# 19

The gun wasn't the kind of thing Barry had expected. A pistol of some sort, he had speculated vaguely, a revolver, the kind of thing Dennis Gordon must have shot his wife with. This looked more like a rifle someone had messed about with and made a botched job of at that. But the man called Paddy was prepared to take £40 for it and Barry knew that wasn't much for a real gun.

'You're sure it works?' he said.

'Sure,' said Paddy.

The room he lived in was one of the nastiest places Barry had ever been into. He hadn't known such places existed in the Hornsey where he had been brought up and where his parents still lived. It had no furniture but a mattress on the floor and an old meat safe with a wire front, and it smelt of unwashed clothes and hamburgers and urine. It was from this meat safe that Paddy had brought the gun.

'What sort is it?' Barry asked warily.

He wanted to be told one of those famous names familiar to all lovers of violent movies and fiction – Luger, Smith & Wesson, Beretta.

Paddy gave him a sidelong look.

'It's a sawn-off shotgun, isn't it?' he said.

He was a big burly fair man, not a bit Irish to look at and surnamed Jones. Or so he said. He hadn't much of an Irish accent either, Barry thought. His voice was a zombie drone. But he guessed that Paddy wouldn't have talked to him in the pub or brought him back here or be offering him the gun if he hadn't heard Barry's Irish name and noted in him the black hair and blue eyes and white skin of Connemara.

Barry thought of himself as English – well, British. And sawn-off shotguns he equated with terrorism. But he had to have the gun, he was never going to cross Winterside Down after dark again unarmed. A replica wouldn't satisfy him. His brother had said to get himself one of those replicas, they'd never know the difference, but Barry himself would know, he had thought. Besides, they cost nearly as much as the real thing.

'I don't suppose we could try it out?'

'Like where? In here? Down the High Street?'

Barry had thought of Alexandra Park but even that wasn't really big enough for experimenting with guns. When fired it would no doubt make a terrible noise.

'You have to trust me,' said Paddy.

He suddenly looked – well, *political* was the word. Like one of those Irish National Liberation Army people whose faces were always being shown on the news. Barry took the thin roll of notes out of his jacket pocket. They were practically all he had in the world, nearly all his last week's pay, and it *was* his last week now Ken Thompson had gone bust and been obliged to send him away.

Paddy wrapped the gun in a piece of rag, part of an old grey vest. He put it into Barry's hands as if he were making him a rare and delicate gift.

He said simply, in his dead voice, 'Kill English.'

That made Barry's blood run cold, those light eyes staring at him and that numb tone and the deadly hate in it. He couldn't get out of the house fast enough but he made himself move nonchalantly until he was beyond Paddy's sight. The last thing he saw of the vendor of weaponry was that chunky puffy face with the unblinking pig eyes watching him over the banisters as he went down all those flights of stairs.

It was too late now to go back to his parents' house. Carol would he home in half an hour. This was the first time he had been out in the evening since coming out of hospital. He had sworn he wouldn't go out until he had the means of protecting himself. Blue Hair and Hoopoe

222

and Black Beauty had taken a tooth from him and cracked two of his ribs and for a while the doctors thought they had ruptured his spleen. They weren't going to get the chance of that again. He fingered the gun in its grey rag wrapping inside the plastic carrier. It was cumbersome to carry but he would take it with him everywhere he went now. He smiled to himself, thinking how he would fire over their heads and see them run.

The day after he was taken into hospital, the police had come to see him, a sergeant and a constable he hadn't seen before. They asked him if he knew his attackers, and he hesitated for only a second or two before saying no. No, he couldn't identify them, he wouldn't recognize them again, he didn't know their names or where they came from. What was the use of telling? Blue Hair and the rest wouldn't go to jail. They'd be given suspended sentences or sent to psychiatrists and the first thing they'd do was revenge themselves on him.

'I never saw them,' he said. 'It was pitch dark. I never had sight nor sound of them till they were on me.'

He could tell from the look on the sergeant's face that he thought what had happened only rough justice. The police couldn't touch Barry, they hadn't the evidence, so where was the harm if a bunch of yobbos gave him the private treatment? A few more questions were put to him but their tone was half-hearted. Maybe the doctors also thought he had killed Jason. And if his spleen really had been ruptured, maybe they'd have let him die and seen it as the best thing.

He and Carol would have to get away, they'd have to move. Perhaps they could get an exchange with a council house in another area. Crouch End, he would like, or Palmer's Green, but no further west than that, nowhere remotely near Hampstead. Wherever they lived it would be as far as possible away from Terence Wand.

Had she seen him while Barry was in hospital? He didn't know and he hadn't asked. In spite of the pain – his body had felt as if on fire and racked with stabbings for days –

Carol's care for him, her shocked horror at his injuries, had brought him a blissful happiness. That first day she came in at visiting time, ran to him and threw herself on to the bed and into his arms with a little hysterical cry. The pressure on his bruised side and arm and thighs had been an intense agony but his joy had outweighed the pain. He hadn't uttered a sound of protest even though she lay on top of him clutching at him with her fingers, and he only whispered to her to get up when the sister was coming and he was embarrassed.

After that first day she hadn't been able to come in all that often. Visiting times were also the times she had to be at work. Naturally he understood that. He had lain there thinking about Terence Wand and wondering if the police had ever done anything about that letter he had sent them. It had been in some ways a silly letter to write. After all, it wasn't of taking away Jason that he suspected Terence Wand, was it?

Maureen came in one evening. He was surprised to see her. She wore her long raincoat and her hair was scraped back in an elastic band. She didn't ask him how he was. His right arm, with the pyjama sleeve rolled up, was lying outside the bedclothes and she lifted it up by the wrist as if it were some inanimate object, a branch, say, or a piece of piping, and examined impassively the by then brown and yellowish bruises.

'At any rate,' she said, 'you're still here.'

She meant he wasn't dead.

'They didn't murder me, if that's what you mean.'

'Mum says the trouble was he came between you.'

'Who did?' he said, though he knew. 'Who came between who?'

'Jason.'

He looked at her, at the plain round face that was still somehow Carol's face with a broadening here, a flattening there, just sufficient to deny it beauty. The vacant blue eyes met his. What she said took his breath away, a frequent effect of Maureen's utterances.

'Maybe it's just as well. Maybe it's all to the good. The fact is no one wanted him and he's best out of the way.'

He knew then that she also believed him a murderer. The difference was that she believed but didn't care. She continued to stare at his bruised arm and made as if to pick it up again. He had a creepy feeling that she was capable of taking it by elbow and wrist and snapping the forearm bone in two. Quickly he withdrew it under the sheet and after a while she got up and left, saying as she went, 'I wouldn't hurry to come out if I was you.'

He had sometimes wondered what that meant. Coming out of hospital, he knew. He was not welcome in the hostile world of Winterside. The revenge taken on him somehow confirmed his guilt. People still spoke to him but no one used his name and their eyes looked at him as if he were different from they, as if the unspeakable thing he was accused of doing set him apart from even the worst of them for ever. That Carol stuck to him, that he still lived in Carol's house, was a wonderful thing, something to be treasured. He was stupidly grateful. Stupidly, he thought now, because he had done nothing, had never laid a finger on Jason, had in fact been one of the few who were really fond of him. They were all wrong in their suspicions and he was right. Even if no one in the world believed in his innocence, he would still be innocent, he still would not have killed Jason. Yet he was learning how hard it is to stand alone, how hard to hold to the truth in isolation, so that one even begins to doubt if it is truth. Several times in hospital and back at home he had dreamed he was in the garden of one of those condemned houses in Rudyard Gardens, burying Jason's body.

Awake, it was a street he always avoided. Getting off the bus, he walked down Delphi Road, past lighted houses, some of which still had Christmas trees and decorations in their windows. Two or three boys in leathers were sitting on the seat outside the public library. The muscles of Barry's stomach tightened, there was a constriction in his throat. He took the gun out of the carrier and put it inside his zipper jacket. He thought he would slit the pocket lining so that he could keep the gun in there and easily reach for it.

But the boys on the seat were not Blue Hair or Hoopoe or any of them. They were strangers who scarcely looked at him, who hadn't yet learned to know by sight the murderer of Jason Stratford. He made himself enter Winterside Down by the Chinese bridge and the path across the grass, the way he had gone on the night they attacked him. Sooner or later it had to be faced and sooner was best. The gun made a difference.

The night was less dark than that other night and it was much earlier. The grass had a sheen on it in the moonlight and frost painted the tops of the fences phosphorescent. With a leap of the heart he saw that lights were on in Carol's house. Just to make certain he counted the houses as he came across the green to where the footpath ran between the houses, one, two, three, four – yes, eighth from the corner the lights were on.

And the passage between the fences was empty. He walked quickly through, keeping himself from actually running, passing the place where they had knocked him down, wondering if in daylight the stains of his own blood were still there on the concrete and the fence.

He didn't show Carol the gun or even tell her about it. She might have reproached him for spending the money when he was out of work. She was watching television with her feet up, a bottle of red wine from which she had drunk a couple of glasses beside her. He poured himself a glass of wine and sat down next to her. She let him kiss her and her mouth quivered a little under his.

The dress she was wearing was the black and white zig-zag one. Her black lacy tights he remembered her saying she had pinched from a stand in a fancy newsagent's up in Highgate. Had she also stolen the watch on her left wrist that looked as if it were made of diamonds?

There was a long angry bruise on her arm where the sleeve was rucked up. The watch covered the end of the bruise. Barry remembered with a kind of inner wince that time she had wanted him to strike and hurt her, how she had seemed to enjoy pain. She was laughing now at something on the television, reaching for her cigarettes. He knew he wasn't going to be able to ask her about the bruise and the watch any more than he had brought himself to ask her where she was that night the motorbike boys nearly killed him.

# 20

Terence lay in bed on the futon with Mrs Goldschmidt. Both of them had fallen asleep and she still was. Waking, he didn't know where he was and scarcely who he was, let alone who the naked blonde with her face buried in the pillow was. For a few seconds he guessed Carol Stratford but that was wishful thinking. This was Mrs Goldschmidt – or Rosemary as he knew from the contract and only from the contract – with whom he had gone to bed some hours before. She slept on, occasionally giving a light girlish snore. Terence now wished very deeply and passionately that he had not succumbed to her.

She had called unexpectedly. Terence was increasingly alarmed by these surprise callers. After a morning spent writing a reference for the bank for John Howard Phipps in the name of Terence Wand, he naturally expected when the doorbell rung that it was the police. His stomach squelched. He made himself go to the door and open it, clenching his teeth but unclenching them into a sickly smile when he saw who it was. She wore a pale green knitted dress with, over it, a fur coat made of innumerable tiny skins as if uncounted thousands of mouse-size creatures had given their lives to make it.

This time there was no ambiguity about the reason for her visit. She walked upstairs, Terence following. At the top she put her arms round him and kissed him with silent voracity. She proceeded to the room where the futon was, took off her coat and let it fall to the floor. It lay there like a slumbering bear. Terence had a feeling of being borne helplessly along on one of fate's tides. Sometimes he thought it was his timidity which attracted him to them, what Freda had called his 'feebleness', which made him theirs to do as they like with, to boss or mother or eat up.

Mrs Goldschmidt ate him up. But what choice did he have? If he had said no perhaps she would have gone home to her husband and told him not to sign the contract, she had changed her mind. He had had some experience of the fury of women scorned. On the other hand, he couldn't now help thinking, she might be one of those who confessed to their husbands, in which case Goldschmidt's own fury would stop him signing.

He looked at her despondently. Rosemary. The name didn't suit her. His gaze had its effect and she opened her eyes, got up and made her way to the *en suite* guest bathroom. Terence put on his underpants and went downstairs. He put the whisky bottle and a bottle of Perrier from the fridge and two glasses on to a tray. At the point where the stairs turned at a right angle, he paused and looked out of the window into the court. The lights on the catalpa had been taken down the week before. Someone had dropped a white plastic carrier on to the cobbles and the wind was blowing it about, in and out between the light and the dark, finally pasting it up against one of the low walls. The sky was a brownish-purple with a few smudged stars showing. Terence hadn't set foot out all day but it looked cruelly cold. Under the arch a young man was standing, looking up at the house and towards Terence so that it seemed to him as if their eyes met. He quickly turned his away. The watcher resembled the younger of the two policemen who had called on him but he couldn't be positive they were the same.

Mrs Goldschmidt was dressing, the lights on and the window blind up. Terence pulled down the blind.

'I thought you'd like a drink, Rosemary.'

'Katie.'

'Pardon?' said Terence.

'I'm called Katie.'

He nodded, remembering her second name was Catalina.

It didn't suit her any better than Rosemary. She slid her feet into bronze high-heeled shoes.

'Would you consider parting with any of the furniture?'

He was nonplussed. He lifted his shoulders helplessly.

'Only I'd take that futon off you if the price was OK.'

They had their drinks. Terence screwed his courage to the sticking place and asked her if she and her husband had yet signed their contract. It was waiting at home, she said. It had come by the second post that morning and they were going to sign it tonight. In fact she thought she had better get off home and sign it. Terence wasn't going to quarrel with that. She wrapped herself in the multi-mouse coat, remembered about the futon and wrote him a cheque. He was glad of the money, though it did rather give him the feeling he was being paid more directly than usual for his services.

The first time Jason picked up the phone to answer it himself the caller was Ian. It was Ian who heard him shouting, 'Mummy, Mummy, there's a man!' So that was all right. The next time it was John Archdale from Marbella, and when she came to the phone, Benet thought she heard wonder in her father's voice and a kind of relief. He would accept the fact of the child now, no longer think of him as some sort of monster or skeleton in the family cupboard.

The first night she spent with Ian, she felt guilty because Jason was in the house. Waking very early with Ian's arms still round her, still holding her close to him spoons-fashion, she thought at once of Jason, of how it would be if he were to walk in and see them there together. It was strange because she wouldn't have felt like that if James had lived and it had been he sleeping in the next room. When she had had a child, she had not planned on remaining celibate until he was old enough to leave home. She got up and went into Jason's room.

Immediately it struck her how he had changed. His own mother doubtless would know him still. No one else would. She had had his hair cut the day before and the trim symmetry of the cut changed him from a toddler into a little boy. Yet in an odd way, she thought, he looked *younger*. His body was thinner and taller but his face had become more soft and full. Except to a mother's knowing intuitive eye, Jason Stratford had disappeared as entirely as might a person who has had plastic surgery. In that moment she knew he would never be Jason to her again. Letting down the side of the cot, she bent over him and kissed his firm, round, pink cheek.

When she came back with the tea on a tray, the cot was empty and he was in bed with Ian. Her life seemed suddenly full to overflowing and she caught her breath. She hesitated only for a moment before getting into bed with them, Jay between them, snuggling up.

In the middle of the morning the phone rang. It stopped so she knew Jay had answered it. But when she came downstairs the receiver was back and Jay was playing the xylophone. She asked him who had phoned.

He smiled. He used a made-up word, a combination perhaps of 'ugly' and 'ghastly'. 'Gugly,' he said.

With a faint sinking of the heart, she guessed what he meant. 'Jay, do you put the phone back without telling Mummy if you don't like the person's voice?'

'Yes,' said Jay and he nodded vigorously to give more emphasis. 'Gugly man.'

That made Benet laugh though it left her uneasy. Probably she had been wrong in thinking he had answered the phone only twice before. There might have been many times when he hadn't liked the sound of the caller so had simply replaced the receiver. Any brusqueness or even embarrassment would do it, she thought. She took Jay on her knee and explained carefully to him that he must always tell her when someone phoned. If she were upstairs and the bell was switched off there, she might not hear it and then she wouldn't know who had called her. Did he understand?

Later in the day the publicity director from her publishers phoned. They wanted her to go on a promotional tour of the United States in May to coincide with the American paperback publication of *The Marriage Knot*. Benet asked if he had phoned before. Yes, once, he said in his rather sharp, abrupt voice, but her little boy had answered and then cut them off.

Benet was immediately relieved, though she didn't quite know why.

The woman whose shape he had seen at Terence Wand's window Barry was certain wasn't Carol. She was dressing, raising white arms above her head and her hair was short and blond. There were too many hours in the day for him and not enough to do with them. Or that was what he told himself was his reason for taking himself over to Hampstead.

He hadn't been able to get another job, though Carol had. An additional one to Mrs Fylemon and the wine bar. Part-time hotel receptionist. Barry was a little over-awed. It seemed such a middle-class thing, verging on a profession really. He scarcely knew anyone who had been trained for anything, who sat at a desk answering the phone and filling in forms.

'Did you answer an advert, love?' he said to her. 'You never told me.'

She was vague. 'This guy who runs it saw me in the wine bar. He told Alkmini he thought I was a model.'

Serving drinks on trays? Barry thought this but he didn't say it aloud.

She had her Diagem watch on and a ring with a red stone she said she'd got at Christmas at Iris's. It was like no ring Barry had ever seen come out of a cracker. 'He said he'd be willing to pay the earth to have someone like me at the Rosslyn Park.'

'I hope he is,' said Barry.

To look in and see her, he should have turned left out of the tube station, not right and up the hill towards the Heath. But he hadn't come to Hampstead to see Carol. Why would he do that? She'd think he was checking up on her. He turned right and went up the hill and into Spring Close instead. It was soon afterwards that he had seen the woman dressing. That was why he hadn't stopped there long. Once he had seen her, he left, a bit excited and a bit embarrassed. It wasn't Carol, he knew it wasn't Carol, and surely he ought to know, he had seen her dressing and undressing often enough. Yet when he was in the tube again and later when he was crossing Bevan Square, he couldn't help asking himself how he was so sure it wasn't Carol. What single thing was there about that woman he could positively say made her not Carol? Wasn't it just that he didn't want her to be Carol?

Hoopoe and Stephanie Isadoro and Black Beauty and a couple of other kids were sitting on the seats in the square eating Turkish takeaway out of waxed-paper cartons. Whenever Barry saw Hoopoe, he remembered the feel, like an electric pain, of that pointed boot kicking his ribs. None of them took any notice of him. He put his hand into his jacket pocket and through the split lining and felt the gun. He wasn't going to need it but it was a comfort feeling it there, just as a wad of money in one's pocket was a comfort or a word of love remembered.

Had it been Carol in Terence Wand's bedroom? He had been sure at the time it wasn't but he wasn't so sure now. Perhaps he had only been certain it wasn't because he knew Carol was at the reception desk at the Rosslyn Park Hotel. His eyes went to the phone on the shelf with the framed photograph of Dave beside it. He didn't know the number of the Rosslyn Park but he could ask Directory Inquiries. If she were there now, of course, that wouldn't do anything to prove she had or hadn't been in Spring Close an hour ago.

He dialled Inquiries and got the hotel number but that was as far as he went. It was a mystery why he should suddenly feel so enormously cheered up to be told the phone number of the Rosslyn Park, almost as if he hadn't really believed in its existence.

Barry changed the sheets and vacuumed the bedrooms and took the washing round to the laundrette.

When he had been told contracts were exchanged, the deposit in the hands of Goldschmidt's solicitor and the completion date confirmed for 15 February, Terence went into a travel agent near where his mother lived to book a flight to Singapore on that date. When it came to the point, Terence's courage, such as it was, failed him at the idea of being alone with a suitcase full of money in Central or South America. He would go to Singapore and there board plane or ship for Bali.

All this would depend, of course, on what time the Singapore flight left. Goldschmidt's banker's draft would come into John Howard Phipps's account at noon on the fifteenth and that gave Terence three and a half hours before the bank closed to draw it out again. He had to allow for that and for getting to Heathrow. The idea of spending the night of the fifteenth in London appalled him, his nerves wouldn't stand it. The Goldschmidts' removal van full of furniture would arrive at Spring Close soon after lunch. The house would be full of furniture too, Freda's furniture, and Freda's car in the garage. That would matter a good deal less if, when they made this discovery, he was already on his way to the airport.

It was therefore a relief to find that the Qantas flight, stopping at Bahrain and Singapore, left at nine forty-five in the evening. He booked himself a seat, economy class, and at a reduced rate owing to his paying for it a month in advance. His new Barclaycard which had arrived that morning took care of that. By the same post his solicitors had sent him a document called 'Transfer of Whole' which was something to do with land registration and required his signature. His and another's, for this time a witness was needed. Terence drove down the hill to the wine bar to have lunch there with Carol Stratford. He had given her a ring as soon as he saw that transfer.

'No news, I suppose?' said Terence.

'Not a sausage.' Carol was used to being asked, as a preamble to any sort of conversation, if she had had news of Jason.

'He wasn't mine, you know, Carol.'

'I never told the fuzz he was. I'm not saying I don't know who did but it wasn't me.'

Terence shrugged. He told Carol he had sold his house and would she mind witnessing his signature to a document. He reasoned that Carol was the only person he could possibly ask, the only person he knew who, if questioned about it – before 15 February that is, for after that who cared? – would lie stoutly for the mere sake of lying, the only person who wouldn't look too closely at the document itself, knowing by a sort of nose for that kind of thing that there was bound to be something fishy about it.

The fishiness was that Terence had photo-copied the document at an instant print place on his way over. He intended to sign it in his own name in her presence. What he wanted was a specimen of Carol's signature to copy on the real transfer when he signed it later on in the name of Phipps.

She signed in her round backward-sloping hand but not before she had proved him wrong and read it, pausing at and rereading the bit where the price was given.

'Three years ago,' said Carol, 'you were as skint as me.'

'I've had a bit of luck,' Terence said vaguely.

She asked him what he was going to do with the money and Terence told her he was going round the world. 'You fancy coming along?'

'You're kidding,' said Carol, all round doll's eyes and baby curls.

Terence admitted that he was. He was really. It would be more of a business trip than pleasure. But she'd come out and have a meal, wouldn't she, the night before he went? Barclaycard would pay, he thought.

# 21

Over dinner in the Villa Bianca, Ian told her about the job he had been offered in Canada. It was the first time Benet had been out in the evening since Jay came. She had phoned one of the babysitters from her Tufnell Park days, an eighteen-year-old who had last sat for her when James was fourteen or fifteen months old. Jay was in bed and asleep anyway by the time she came.

'It would be a great opportunity for me,' Ian said. He smiled. 'My big chance. The hospital is new. It's equipped as a matter of course in a way that would be just a dream here.'

'When would you go?'

'I don't have to let them know definitely for another month.' He hesitated and she found herself holding her breath. 'Would you consider living in Vancouver, Benet?'

Would she? When her parents had gone to Spain, she had categorically declared nothing would persuade her to live outside England. She hadn't known then that she would fall in love and that would change everything. Then, as always now when she contemplated any plan or change, she thought of Jay. The last risk of his being identified would be removed if she took him half across the world. But to commit herself utterly and so soon . . . ? She laid her hand over his on the table.

'Let me think about it. Give me a little time, will you, Ian?'

He said, 'I'll give you all the time I have. I was sure you'd say no. You've made me ridiculously happy by not just saying no.'

They were a little later getting back than they had told

Melanie they would be and she was ready to leave. Benet had time only to pay her and thank her before Ian drove her home. She found the note by the telephone in the basement room: *Edward Greenwood phoned 8.30*. Reading the words, Benet knew now why she had felt uneasy about Jay answering the phone and not always telling her. She was afraid there had been phone calls from Edward. It was a month now since she had seen him but thoughts of him had been niggling there under the surface of her mind. To go to Vancouver would be to escape him also . . .

She said nothing of any of this to Ian when he returned. It was their last night together before he went back on night duty. She tried to rid her mind of Edward and believed she had succeeded but she dreamed of him, a bad nightmare in which he threatened her with a knife and tried to persuade her to enter into a suicide pact with him. She awoke screaming, terrified, looking for Ian. The other half of the bed was empty. She put on bedlamps and called for him in a panic of fear. He came rushing in from Jay's room.

'He started yelling first and then you joined in.' He took her in his arms. 'What's got into the pair of you?'

'I don't know, I don't know. What would I do without you?'

'You don't have to do without me,' he said.

In the morning when Ian had gone and they had arranged to meet and have tea somewhere, Benet steeled her nerves and dialled the number Edward had given her. She thought she might finally get rid of Edward by telling him she was getting married and going to live in Canada. There was no reply. Very likely there wouldn't be at eleven in the morning. No doubt Edward had some sort of job and had to go to work. Had she phoned him at eleven because she knew he wouldn't be there? To quieten some pricking of alarm and disquiet, to be able to say to herself, I did phone him, I did try?

She was upstairs at the front door giving a pound to someone who had called collecting for charity when she heard the phone ringing. It rang twice and stopped. Jay must have answered it. No small shrill voice called, 'Mummy, Mummy!' Benet ran down the passage and the basement stairs. Jay was on the rocking horse, swinging vigorously.

'Phone ring,' he said and he gave her his widest, most radiant smile.

Edward wore his thin clothes and the thick long scarf wound twice round his neck. His face was red, with a bluishness about the lips. Jay's face would go like that, Benet thought, if he were really cold. He was behind her now as she opened the door, clutching on to her skirt.

'If you'd sent him to answer the door,' Edward said, 'I'd have had it slammed in my face.'

All day she had somehow known he would come and had been bracing herself for it. 'Come in,' she said. 'It's freezing.'

He took her to imply he was letting in the cold. 'Forgive me for making a draught.'

'Edward, you know I didn't mean that. Don't always make me out such a bitch. When you phoned, I'm afraid Jay was playing with the phone and didn't always tell me. I'm sorry.'

'You shouldn't let that little devil answer the phone.'

Benet said nothing, though she didn't like hearing Jay called a little devil. Jay himself, silent, was staring with fascinated wonderment at Edward in the way very young children stare at those they dislike. It was the middle of the afternoon. Having had lunch with Ian, Benet had been about to take Jay out for his walk in the pushchair and, on the way, make inquiries about the play group she wanted him to join two mornings a week. She wondered why Edward had come, and as they went down the stairs to the basement room, two answers to that came to her mind. He wanted money. He wanted to bring some sort of action against the hospital for negligence leading to James's death.

Well, she could handle that. She could handle either or both of those contingencies.

The tree of hands, denuded of course of the packages the hands had held, still hung on the wall. She saw Edward look at it and then, with the same mild reflective distaste, at the piles of toys which filled this end of the room. Ringed by a zoo of cuddly animals, lay the two drawing blocks she had bought Jay while they were out, the top sheets of which he had already covered with shapes of birds and flowers and trees in bright crayon colours. Having had his fill of gazing at Edward, he returned to his work, selecting with a smile a hitherto unused coloured pencil in a brilliant shade of veridian green.

'You shouldn't let him scribble on that,' Edward said in exactly the same tone as he had admonished her for letting Jay answer the phone.

Suddenly Benet remembered that, the last time Edward had been here, nearly two months ago, she had told him she was minding Jay for a friend. Eight weeks was a very long time, an unheard-of length of time, to mind someone else's child. She filled the kettle and plugged it in. She set cups on a tray and opened a jar of orange juice for Jay. Edward would say something about that any minute now, he would ask why Jay was still here, and she would have to have a reasonable anwer for him. He had seated himself in the rocking chair where he could watch Jay. After a moment or two he got up again and picked up, first, the drawing block Jay wasn't working on and then, murmuring something to him, the one on which Jay was filling in with his bright green pencil the outline of a tree.

Jay didn't cry out or scream. He simply stood up and stared in stupefaction. It was Benet who wanted to yell at Edward. She made a mammoth effort at self-control. She explained to Edward that she thought Jay had a real talent for drawing, that he should be encouraged in every possible way, knowing as she did so that the words she spoke made her role as a mere temporary minder of Jay less and less likely. His lips had begun to quiver now. He started to cry and, putting up his arms, threw himself against her skirts. Picking him up, holding him, she waited for Edward's inevitable comment: Who is this child? What is he to you?

It didn't come. Edward shrugged and put the drawing blocks back on the floor. The blood, drawn into the surface of his skin by the cold, had receded and he seemed paler than usual. His face had a concentrated look. Benet wiped Jay's tears and put him back on the floor.

'Gugly,' said Jay to Edward who fortunately had no idea of the significance of this word.

Benet made the tea, putting the single flat teaspoonful of sugar into Edward's cup.

'You remembered,' he said.

'Well, of course. You don't forget something like that.'

He was silent. Jay finished his tree and started drawing a strange bird with large feet and red legs. Benet found she had nothing to say. There was absolutely nothing she could think of to say to Edward to fill this silence. It became embarrassing, almost tangible. He filled it with an abruptness and with a subject that astounded her.

'Benet, I want us to get together again, be as we once were. I want to come back and live with you. It's the natural, obvious thing to do. There hasn't really been anyone else for either of us – at least there hasn't for me.' He added a kind of envoi that made her stand up and take a step or two away from him: 'We belong together, Benet.'

'It isn't possible,' she said. 'It's out of the question.'

'Why is it? We're older now. I'm older, if you like. I shouldn't resent your success and I've lost any ambition of my own. I'd be content to take any routine job I could get. There's a course going teaching English to foreign students. I could get in on that. I've got a degree. I'd be quite content for you to go on in your high-flying way and be a humble teacher myself.'

She nearly laughed but it would have been unkind. She was less in danger of uttering the base retort about relative incomes which came to her. He had said nothing yet to deserve that. And she was so enormously relieved that he hadn't come here to talk about Jay that something like real affection warmed her, moved her back to sit beside him and lay her hand gently on his.

'It really isn't possible, Edward. Dear Edward. It's not your fault any more than mine. Maybe it's more mine. I know I did you an injury.' She didn't want to name that injury, confident he would understand what she meant. 'But it's too long ago.' Should she mention Ian? There was no need, not yet. 'I've changed – and not in a way to bring me closer to you.'

'I can't see any change in you.' He hesitated. 'We could have more children, you know. I could put up with children for your sake.'

Her heart hardened again. Jay was watching them in silence, aware without understanding it of the emotion with which the room had become charged.

'I couldn't do it, Edward. I've already said it isn't possible.'

'Perhaps I didn't make myself clear, Benet. I was suggesting we get married. I'm asking you to marry me.'

He said it with the air of one conferring a great benefit. He said it pompously. An enormous compliment was being paid, a reward bestowed. This time she did laugh.

'A proposal isn't necessarily something women feel passionately grateful about these days, Edward. I can't think of any good reason for marrying you and I've one very good reason against. I don't want to.'

He bowed his head, looked down at his hands in his lap, then up at her, into her eyes.

'I'll tell you a good reason.' He cocked his thumb in Jay's direction. 'Do you think a judge would allow you as a single woman to adopt that child over there?'

Something clenched and chilled inside her. She felt muscles stiffen. Had she told him Jay was a child she was fostering and hoped to adopt? She was sure not. The last time she had seen or spoken to Edward she was still – incredible as it now seemed – bent on finding a way to return him to his family.

'That's what you want, isn't it?' he said. 'That's what you're planning on?'

She nodded, held still, mesmerized, by his eyes. What he said next made her feel faint. The room darkened and she thought she would fall as she had fallen in the hospital when they told her James was dead. But she stood still, she held her shoulders back, driving her nails into the palms of her hands.

'I know who he is, you know,' Edward said. 'I put two and two together. It wasn't difficult. He's Jason Stratford, the missing boy.'

# 22

Afterwards she wondered why she hadn't denied it. She could have bluffed it out. But she hadn't had the nerve or been cool enough. She hadn't been cool at all. By asking him how he knew – and that was the first thing she did – she admitted everything.

'How did you know?'

'You calling him Jay for one thing. You don't use shortened forms of people's names. You're the only person I know who's never called me Ted. Then his colouring. He's been described often enough in the papers as fair-haired and blue-eyed. Your situation – it's women who've lost a child that abduct a child. And then the place he comes from. You used to live round the corner.' Edward looked pleased with himself. 'Satisfied?' he said.

It was a strange word to have used. She felt dry and hollow inside. She thought of the true explanation of Jay's presence, but was there any point in relating all that to Edward? It was all the same now as if she had taken him herself, all the same as if she had set out deliberately to steal him. Besides, there was only one thing she was interested in and that was what he was going to do about it. Yet already she knew that his knowledge in itself was bad enough. He knew. He wouldn't forget as Mopsa had forgotten. His knowing was almost the end of the world.

'What are you going to do about it?'

'I imagine you've been living in some sort of fool's paradise but you must have known you weren't going to get away with it indefinitely. What did you think was going to happen in the future?'

She had never looked to the future beyond a day or two.

'I suppose I thought he would change as he grew older and no one would recognize him. I thought of taking him away, a long way away . . .' Had she? She realized she was thinking of it now. 'I don't think anyone but his mother would know him now.' She was trying to keep cool but her voice cracked. Her voice was hoarse with fear. Edward was looking at her like a judge, leaning forward, frowning.

'What steps were you going to take to protect yourself?'

'What do you mean, steps? I'd kidnapped him, abducted him. I haven't any rights at all, I know that.'

Jay chose that moment to put down his crayon and come to her, holding up his arms to be lifted on to her lap. The feel of him in her arms made her give a little sobbing cry which she stifled with her hand. Jay began to hug and squeeze her with a small child's surprising strength.

'Jay, you're choking me, no, darling . . .' She was determined not to cry in front of either of them. Her face and eyes felt burning and swollen. 'Please, Edward, tell me what you're going to do?'

He said rather scornfully, 'You make me sound like a blackmailer.'

Wasn't he one? She understood that was what she had been thinking. 'Edward . . .'

'I knew you'd taken against me but I didn't know you rated me as low as that.'

She held Jay. It was as if people had actually come to take him from her but she knew they wouldn't do it by main force, they wouldn't physically tear him away. At the same time she was aware of the picture of demented, misplaced maternity she must be presenting to Edward. Gently yet with a more gargantuan effort than she ever remembered giving to any task, she made herself lift Jay down and set him on the floor.

'I'm sorry,' she found herself saying, 'but you frightened me. You must mean to do something or you wouldn't have come here.'

'Don't you think he ought to have a father?'

'No doubt he has one somewhere. I've never thought much about it.'

Edward was looking at her with a curious emotional intensity. His face was sharpened with it.

'You see yourself as his mother. If I were your husband we could be his parents. We'd be highly suitable *adoptive* parents, Benet. You've got money and this house. We're the right sort of age. Neither of us has been married before. I'd say we'd quite easily get an adoption order made if we applied to the court.'

'You must want to marry me an awful lot,' she said dryly.

'That's right. I do.'

Her eyes rested reflectively on Jay. I wonder how long it would be before *you* started beating him up, she thought. You *hate* children.

'It's impossible anyway. He's not up for adoption, he's got parents. I *stole* him. I thought you understood that, that's what you've been telling me.'

Edward said, 'I spent the whole of yesterday in the newspaper library at Colindale reading up on the Jason Stratford case. It's obvious his mother doesn't give a damn for him. Her other two children are in care and Jason would have gone the same way in a year or two. She's a barmaid and her boyfriend's out of work. Don't you think there's a good chance she'd sell Jason to you?'

Hope came back, intruding itself, wriggling in like a small finger pushing through a crevice. She saw a clean innocent above-board world in which everyone knew the truth and everyone was happy, the death of James proclaimed and the existence of Jay announced, she and Edward having drunk perhaps some blinding love potion, living together and seeing each other as they once had with the eyes of illusion. The finger crept in and a door closed on it, not with a slam but with decisive firmness.

'I thought of offering her twenty thousand.'

'It doesn't seem much,' Benet said drearily. 'It seems

very little for him. I paid five times that for this house.'
She felt the warning signs of an hysteria she rigidly
suppressed. 'A house in Hampstead costs five times what a
child costs. There's something wrong with that somewhere,
Edward.'

'Could you go up to fifty thousand if I had to?'

Everything I have, she thought. This house, all the
money from all my sales, everything I have. Of course. It
goes without saying. Why doesn't he know that?

'Suppose she won't have anything to do with it? Suppose
she just goes to the police?'

'That's a risk you have to take.'

'Why do I, Edward? Why do I have to take any more
risks? You could walk out of here now and put it out of
your mind and we need never meet again.'

'To put it at its most basic, leaving out emotion, I'd
know, wouldn't I? All the time you'd know I knew. Why
don't you think about it, Benet? You can have three days.
I've made a date to meet Carol Stratford but she doesn't
know why, she only knows it's something to do with money
and she likes money.'

'You were very sure,' she said in a low voice.

'I was sure, yes.'

Three days to get away in, three days in which to escape
with Jay. She felt almost glad that he had given her a
chance. The police wouldn't have done that.

The night Carol didn't come home at all Barry phoned the
Rosslyn Park Hotel at midnight. He had drunk a whole
bottle of wine and was past caring what people thought of
him. There were always bottles of wine in the house these
days, brought home by Carol. The answering voice told
him Carol wasn't working late, they hadn't given her a bed
for the night because of the snow and the bad roads – a
straw clutched at by Barry – she hadn't been working that
evening and in fact she didn't work there at all. Barry fell
asleep at last on the sofa in the living room.

He didn't see her all next day. Late in the afternoon a

man with a posh voice phoned and asked for her. Barry was going to ask if he was Terence Wand but the man put the phone down before he had the chance. After he had been to the Job Centre to see if there was anything going, but of course there wasn't, he went for a long walk for something to do, the gun knocking lightly against his chest as he tramped the streets.

Carol was there when he woke up next morning. She was in bed with him – that is, they were in the same bed. She lay on the extreme edge of the mattress and it was only the way the bedclothes were tucked tightly in that kept her from falling out. It was late in the morning, ten or eleven, he thought. He went down to make tea.

The first things that caught his eye when he went back into the bedroom were the diamond watch and the ring with the red stone in it that she had taken off and laid on the bedside table. She was awake now, lying on her back, her blue eyes wide open.

'Hi,' she said and then, when she saw the tea tray, 'Are there any cigs in the house?'

He shrugged. He didn't know. Mysteriously he had given up smoking a week or two before without willing it or scarcely even noticing it had happened. One day he had been smoking twenty or thirty and next he hadn't smoked at all. He didn't miss it.

Carol said in Iris parlance, 'You've got a face like a wet week. What's got into you? If it's on account of me getting back late, we had an emergency at the Rosslyn Park. I missed the last bus and I had to wait for a lift.'

'You don't work there,' Barry said. 'You've never worked there.'

'OK, so I don't.' She was still in a good humour. He could smell stale brandy on her breath after all those hours but her face was a little girl's, dewy, satiny, pink and white and innocent. She sat up and he saw that she was quite naked, her breasts resting softly on top of the sheet. 'If you didn't ask questions,' she said, 'you wouldn't get lies. What's it to you anyway where I go? You're not my husband. You're as bad as bloody Dave, you are. Where were you? Who were you with? Where've you been?'

He felt he was on the brink of terrible revelations. Never before had she given him a hint that Dave had been anything but totally loving and beloved. An intense red colour showed in two spots on her cheekbones.

'I don't ask you to account for your movements,' she said in a higher voice. 'I don't follow you about, spying on you. I don't ask where you've been morning, noon and night, by Christ I don't!'

'Carol,' he said, 'you were with that fella that's Jason's father, weren't you? He's a rich man, I know that. You didn't nick that watch and you didn't get that ring out of a cracker at your mum's.'

She got out of bed. There was a bruise of loving teeth marks on the side of her neck. He thought for some reason of the bruises on Jason who had that same fine white skin.

'Run my bath, will you?' she said.

Her hard voice, both mocking and commanding, made him tremble. But he didn't move. He stared at her standing there naked with her mouth set and her fists clenched and for the first time he noticed imperfections in her, the droop of flesh on her inner thighs, the childbearing stretch marks. It was as if lengths of old grey elastic had been inserted in the white silk skin.

'He's Jason's father, isn't he?' he said.

As if she'd had a fuse and he'd lit it, Carol blew up. She was little and a woman and naked but she wasn't afraid of him. She came to him and put up her arms and clutched his shoulders and yelled into his face. She yelled into his face in Iris's raucous broken voice.

'You want to know? Is that what you want? You want to know who his father is? Well, I'll tell you. I don't know who his fucking father is. I don't know and nobody bloody knows. The week I reckon I fell for him, I had eight men in seven days and it could be any one of them. See? Any one of them or maybe one of the seven or eight I had the next week. I don't know and I don't fucking care.'

248

'Carol,' he said. 'Carol . . .' He got hold of her by the neck, squeezing the sore place where someone's teeth had bitten. 'That isn't true, say it isn't.'

'Of course it's true. Take your hands off me!'

He slackened his hold. He was aghast as if he had opened some forbidden door and seen carnage inside. She twisted out of his grasp and ran out of the room. He heard the surge and splash of the bath taps turned on too hard. Suddenly he was afraid she would lock herself away from him in the bathroom. He followed her and stood in the doorway, holding the door.

She was bending over the bath, pouring in a trickle of herbal essence. A smell that was like a mixture of rosemary and Dettol rose from the steaming water. As she turned round slowly, straightening up and standing up, to look at him, he was hit by a wave of powerful desire for her. In spite of what she had just told him, he wanted her. It was humiliating and in a way shocking but he wanted to take her in his arms and drop that warm, naked, white body among the tumbled towels on the floor, caring nothing for the sea-watery smell on it of another man.

'What happened to us?' he cried. 'What went wrong, Carol? Can't we make it right? It's not too late. I love you, I want to marry you, I still do.'

'You must be joking,' she said and she spat the words. ' "Still do",' she said. 'I like that. I should co-co. I expect you "still do". I expect you *still* think I'd marry the man who murdered my Jason.'

'What?' he said. It was as if she had struck him. 'What did you say?'

'You heard.'

If she had struck him, he could have handled it, but not this. Had his ears really sent that message to his brain?

He spoke like a child unjustly accused of some classroom crime. '*You* can't think that. Not *you*. You know I didn't, I couldn't have. Whatever the rest of them say, you know I couldn't have.'

'Of course you did,' she said, 'only I was too dumb to

see it.' She turned off the taps with a squeak. There was a jug standing on the bath rim she used for washing her hair. He was too stunned to realize what she was doing when she bent over and dipped the jug into the hot water.

She jumped up with a very swift twisting movement and flung the jugful of water into his face. He gasped. She pushed at him with both hands and slammed the bathroom door.

# 23

Every day she saw Ian, and each time they met, she meant to tell him. She intended to confess everything and throw herself on his mercy. A small voice inside her whispered that if she did that two people would know, not just Edward. Or by tomorrow Edward and Carol Stratford.

Besides, Ian would immediately advise her to give Jay up, hand him over to the police. He was that sort of man. He wouldn't connive at what she was doing. The irony was that she wouldn't want the sort of man who would connive at what she was doing. That was another reason why she didn't want Edward.

Ian was on night call and she was glad of it. Her nights were nearly sleepless but sometimes she slept, always started awake by a violent dream. Edward came back on Sunday evening. She found him in the study room reading a page of manuscript.

'How did you get in?'

He smiled and held up a bunch of keys. The smile wasn't triumphant or presumptuous, still less menacing. He had come home again, it said, he was taking it for granted he was accepted back.

'You don't look well, Benet.'

She shrugged. She said nothing.

'There's nothing to worry about.' He tried to put his arms round her. She stood stiffly in his arms. 'If she says yes, we're in business, and if she says no, you're no worse off than before.'

'If she says no, she'll also tell the police.'

'People like her are very loath to tell the police anything, Benet. I've read the newspaper stories, remember. It was a day and a night after he'd disappeared before she went to the police.'

'I don't want you to see her, Edward,' Benet said. 'I want you to go away and leave us alone. If I was prepared to give her money . . .'

He let her go. 'Don't turn me into a blackmailer.'

She went into the living room, took out two glasses and the whisky bottle. She poured one for him and one for herself. Her hands were shaking. Jay was upstairs asleep, two floors away at the top of the house, yet she sensed all around her his even, tranquil breathing.

I will take him away, she thought. I'll take him away where no one can find us. Edward's plan would never work, his reasoning was faulty, for if Carol said no, the police would trace Jay through Edward, and if Carol said yes, Jay would inevitably have to be produced and for a time returned to her. If for a time, why not for good, since the buying of a child was illegal? Edward would offer her a sum of money to agree to the adoption, and the balance when the adoption was completed. She would take the first payment, Benet thought, and then go to the police. I will take him away to avoid that happening, I will take him out of the country, a long long way, to the Far East perhaps. I'll use my money to hide him, not to buy him.

She handed Edward his glass. 'You must do as you please,' she said. 'Do whatever you like.'

After he had gone, she marvelled that she, who was a middle-class, law-abiding person, who until a few months ago had envisaged her only possible brushes with the police as being the outcome of traffic offences, should have become – and so easily and inevitably – a kidnapper, a felon and a fugitive. She went upstairs and into Jay's room and looked at him. He had tossed and turned in his sleep, thrown off the covers and slipped his pyjama top off one shoulder. Even in the half-dark she could see the burn hole the cigarette had made, an inch away from his spine. She overcame an hysterical need to pick him up and clutch him. Gently she covered him up. She began in a haphazard feverish sort of way to pack clothes into suitcases.

By the first post, next morning, Jay's passport came. She had forgotten about that, she had forgotten they couldn't leave the country without it. Still she hadn't decided where to go. The suitcases had been packed in a panic without thought as to whether their destination would have a hot or cold climate. Impossible, in the here and now, to imagine sunshine, warmth, clear skies! A light dry powdery snow had begun to fall. She found her own passport and put it in her handbag with Jay's new one. Jay woke up late. She dressed him and gave him his breakfast.

'Snow,' he said, pressing his face against the window. 'Make a snowman.'

'We're going a long way from the snow, Jay.'

She wrapped him up in his duffel coat, put his boots on, wool hat, warm scarf. While she loaded the car, he played with snow, throwing handfuls into the air. The cold reddened his cheeks and the tip of his nose and she remembered its similar effect on Edward's face. An idea came to her that was suddenly appalling and she thrust it away with a violent act of inhibition.

By Monday morning Carol still hadn't come back. It was St Valentine's Day. Buying a birthday card for Carol soon after they had first met, Barry had thought about this day, had looked forward to it and even made a mental note of the particular Valentine's card he would buy to send her. A card did come for her by the morning's post in a large pale pink envelope. Barry opened it, looking for Terence Wand's name, but it was signed only with a row of crosses.

Snow was falling in a steady fine mist. By midday Winterside Down was white once more and the house filled with pale, radiant, reflected light. Carol had been gone since Saturday. Round and round in his mind went the things she had said. That there had been a hundred, a thousand, men in her past no longer really mattered. He could bear that. But that she too could accuse him of being

253

Jason's killer, she who had met him on the afternoon Jason disappeared and run to him and kissed him and pirouetted in her new dress!

He hated her for that. Nothing mattered, not the men, not the lies, not her using him as if he were her servant, but that mattered. While she believed in him, he hadn't cared about the rest who didn't. He sat in the living room that glowed with snow light and thought of what she had said about not marrying the man who had murdered her Jason. An overwhelming desire took hold of him to be away from her, never to see her again, to be away for ever from Winterside Down and back in the comfort and caring of his parents' house. It was childish, it was immature, he knew that, but he didn't care, that was what he wanted.

But at the same time he didn't. At the same time he loved her. He was learning on St Valentine's Day something that had never hinted itself to him before, that it is possible to hate fiercely and love fiercely at the same time. When he made this discovery he made a sound. He heard himself groan aloud and at once, though there was no one to see or hear, he clapped his hand over his mouth.

What he had to do was see her, be with her again. He had to get her to retract what she had said, to admit she had said it in the heat of the moment, that it was false, false as hell. A snowball slapped against the window and he jumped up, sure it must have been vindictively thrown. But it was only little kids out there, Isadoros and Kupars and O'Haras, and their snowballs were simply handfuls of snow that contained no stones or pieces of glass.

The sun had come out and a thaw already begun, *drip-drip-drip* off the gutterings. She would come back if he waited long enough, she would have to, but he couldn't bear the inactivity. He was putting on his jacket and slipping the gun inside it when the phone began to ring.

Barry answered it. He thought it might be Carol and he held his breath. A man's voice asked cautiously if Carol was there.

'No, she's not.'

'Will she be at Bacchus?'

It was so long since Barry had heard it called this that he had almost forgotten the wine bar's proper name. 'Is your name Wand?' he said.

There was a silence, whispered into by the sound of indrawn breath. Then the receiver was replaced.

Carol would of course be at the wine bar on a Monday at lunchtime, Barry thought. She would be there until three.

The Channel had been icily calm. Benet wondered if Jay had ever seen the sea before. He stared at the sea with a long concentrated gaze, then turned his face to hers and laughed. It was only during those few early years, she thought, that we laugh with delight at what pleases us. After that, laughter is strictly for amusement only.

They were coming into the harbour at Calais, in a chill grey mist, when she understood where it was she was going. Down to the tip of Spain to Mopsa and her father. She was their daughter and she had a son. Their neighbours, their circle, would know that now. What could be more natural and acceptable than if she and their grandson came to stay with them?

Britain had no extradition treaty with Spain. Or from there she could easily go on to North Africa. She saw herself fleeing with Jay to infinite distances. He was too small for a piggy-back, he sat astride her shoulders, shouting, 'I like the sea, I like the sea!'

When she got to Paris, she would phone her parents and tell them she was coming. Or perhaps, when she got to Paris, she would abandon the car and take a flight to Malaga.

The house was in darkness. Coming in under the arch, Barry could have sworn he had seen a light in one of the narrow slit windows on the left-hand side but now he thought that what he had seen had probably been no more than the reflected image of one of the streetlamps.

255

He was going to ring boldly at Terence Wand's door. If she was there with him and they tried to beat him up between them, he didn't care. He had to find her and see her and have his confrontation. If need be, he would use the gun to threaten. For Terence Wand he no longer had any feelings. The man might be Jason's father and he might not. Barry wondered why he had ever cared who Jason's father was. He rang the doorbell, once, twice, then insistently. It might only be his imagination that there was someone in there lying low, refusing to answer. How could you tell? There was no sound, the silence was total. Trying to see into one of the windows showed him nothing but the filtered light from a lamp in the close striking silky dark carpet and the bronze limbs of a statue. He went round to the back and looked through the window of the garage. The car was there. He tried the garage doors but they were locked.

Piles of snow, yellowish or rimmed with grit, were stacked against fences. It had become very cold. Ice glittered where before there had been black wetness. Barry went down to the station. He would try Maureen, he thought, and, if he had to, Iris.

As he came off the Chinese bridge on to the crusty remains of snow that lay in islands on the sea of grass, he saw lights on in Carol's house. His heart jumped as it always did but heavily this time, with pain. Although he knew it was her house he counted from the end to make sure: two, four, six, eight . . .

He had the gun so he wasn't even apprehensive about going through the passage in the dark. Before he entered the black tunnel, slippery underfoot tonight and the fences on either side of it silvered, he got out the gun and held it clutched in both hands the way Paddy Jones had shown him. But he met no one and no one followed him in. He came out into the street at the other end and from there he could see the light from her living-room window shining on to the little bit of front garden. Then the light went out. He couldn't be sure if all the lights in the house went out, he couldn't see from there.

A woman came out of Carol's house. For a moment he thought it was Iris, the way she clutched her coat round her, the quick, almost scuttling walk. The light from a street lamp showed him her hair, the pale gleaming natural curls. It was Carol herself. She was wearing Mrs Fylemon's fake fur and sandals with very high heels. Sometimes, he remembered, she would come home with her feet blue with cold.

She darted quick glances about her as if she were afraid of something or someone, afraid perhaps that someone might be following her. He didn't flatter himself that she might ever be afraid of him, but he followed her. There seemed nothing else in the world to do, no other occupation for him. Looking about her but never directly behind her, she came into Bevan Square. Black Beauty and Blue Hair were up at the top end of the square, on the corner of the row of shops, draped negligently over their bikes as if the saddles were bar stools.

Barry had replaced the gun inside his jacket. He held on to the butt of it but he didn't get it out. One of them said something, a muttered, indistinct, probably obscene word he didn't catch. Carol thought it was directed at her. She turned, quick as a flash, and shouted at them to piss off. He admired her nerve. The two of them sniggered. Carol was heading for Lordship Avenue.

He slackened his pace, uncertain what to do. It occurred to him that she might merely be going to Iris's. But she too was walking less quickly, and at the corner where the entrance road ran in between the two blocks of flats, she stopped and waited. Or, rather, she paced on one spot, turning round and round on those nearly bare feet, her arms folded and wrapped round her. A little snow, fine as dust, stingingly cold, needled on to his face and the backs of his hands. He pushed his hands inside his jacket. The cold was biting yet the sky was the colour of smoke from a burning rubbish heap.

The car turned in from Lordship Avenue. It turned in, looped round and stopped at the left-hand kerb. Barry couldn't see the driver but he thought the car was the one he had seen an hour before in Terence Wand's garage.

Carol darted across the road as the passenger door swung open. She jumped in – she almost dived in to escape from the intense cold – and the door slammed. The car slid out into Lordship Avenue once more and moved off down the hill.

It had disappeared by the time Barry came out into the main road but he thought he knew where it had gone. There were people standing round something by the kerb, looking at something that lay there. A woman stepped back and began to walk away, leaving a gap in the crowd. Barry saw that a van had run over an animal and its driver was arguing with one of those bystanders who mysteriously spring out of the ground when an accident happens. The thing in the road, black, lean, sleek, apparently unmarked, dead, was the greengrocer's Dobermann. The sight of it made him feel slightly sick.

He meant to walk but a bus came as he reached the stop outside the pub. The gun was sticking out, pushing out the front of his jacket as if he had a deformed breastbone. The woman in the seat opposite stared. He pushed the gun down and held on to it.

They weren't in the bar. He could see that, he didn't have to ask. Alkmini was serving. Kostas sat at a table with a group of middle-aged Greeks like himself. Dennis Gordon, three parts drunk, his face dark and swollen, hung slouched against the black curvy counter. He looked at Barry and their eyes met but neither of them said a word. Then Barry saw the other man's eyes move. Glazed and bloodshot, they strayed back to where they had previously been fixed – on Kostas's black glass clock whose hands pointed to five minutes to nine.

Barry had the bare price of a drink on him but he didn't spend it. He went back outside. In Java Mews, Dennis Gordon's silver-blue Rolls was parked as it had been the other night. Barry heard the side door of the wine bar swing open and shut with a slam but he didn't look behind him. His instinct had been wrong and she wasn't there and he wondered where to look for her.

Probably, instead of coming here, they had gone down to the West End. Go home, the sensible voice inside him said, go back to where you were before you met her. Sooner or later you'll have to, so why not now? A solitary bus appeared over the crest of the hill, rounded the curve in the road with its lumbering galleon-like motion, a red double-decker bus going up to Hornsey that passed the end of his parents' street.

He let the bus go. They might be in a pub instead. They might be down there in the Java Head. Barry didn't approach it from the mews but from around the block, walking round the square formed by Lordship Avenue and the three small streets, looking into parked cars.

It was dark with lamps only at the corners. He wasn't in danger here, no one knew him here, but the two boys waiting under a corner lamp looked too much like Hoopoe, were too much in Hoopoe's style, for comfort. He held the gun and felt a quickening, strengthening surge into his blood. The boys didn't even look at him.

He was almost at the pub, he was entering the pool of light under the saloon bar window, when he heard the first shot. He was still grasping the gun through the lining of his jacket and for a wild moment he fancied it was he who had made the shot, fired the gun. Then there came a volley of shots and a scream that split the cold thick air. Barry began to run. The pub doors opened behind him and people poured out. He ran up the mews, not knowing whether he was running away from the shots or towards them.

There was one more shot. He saw Dennis Gordon on the pavement ahead of him, a blind, staggering, King Kong shape, a silhouette as black as a gorilla. The little gun half the size of Barry's was in his paw of a hand and he flung it in an arc away from him.

Barry didn't know where all the people had come from. The cold had kept them in and blood and screams and the heat of violence had brought them out as if melting their doors. The mews was full of people and their noise.

He saw the bullet hole in the wing of the car before it registered with him whose car it was. He pushed his way through, he elbowed the crowd out of his way. The passenger door he had seen opened for Carol stood open again, and thin threads of blood came out over the edge of the seat and in winding narrow rivulets over the rim of the door.

There was a lot of blood on the floor of the car, a lake of it forming. Barry had often wondered how he would feel, what he would do, if he saw Carol in another man's arms, in, say, Terence Wand's arms. He witnessed that sight now and knew the total negation of feeling shock brings. Impossible to say whether they had been embracing before they were shot or had fallen into each other's arms in death. There was no blood on Carol's golden baby curls. The shot that had killed her had made a round hole just below the lobe of her left ear where the clotting blood formed an earring like a cluster of dark jewels.

Barry turned away and elbowed through the people to the end of the mews. He walked up the hill like an automaton or a contestant in a walking race. Police cars with sirens blasting and a useless ambulance came past him through red traffic lights. The night was suddenly filled with the howls of sirens. Barry felt nothing, but all the time he could see Carol's face with that red jewel just below her ear and he fancied he could smell limes as he had smelled them in the mortuary. Mechanically he walked, the gun moving rhythmically like a fifth limb.

At the top of the hill he leaned over the bridge and dropped the gun over the parapet into the canal. The water rings from the splash were still widening when he got on to the Hornsey bus.

# 24

The taxi set him down in Golders Green. That was far enough, he could get a tube from there. He felt curiously carefree and light of heart. Light of body he was too. He had weighed himself before leaving and found he had lost eleven pounds since Christmas. All his troubles seemed left behind with his discarded past. He was so relaxed that he bought an evening paper in the station for something to read in the train.

Going down the steps to the platform, he glanced at the front-page lead. Glanced, then stopped and read. The shock gripped and twisted his insides. If he hadn't phoned Carol yesterday afternoon to say he couldn't make it, it might have been him with her in what the paper called the 'death car'. So his nerves had come in useful and saved his life. If his nerves hadn't told him that the only way he was going to get through his last night in Spring Close was alone and on a stupefying mixture of tranquillizers, alcohol and sedatives, it might have been him! He and she would certainly have spent part of their time together in the wine bar. One always did with Carol. He hardly took in the name of the murdered man, Edward Greenwood, whoever he might be. His hand was trembling so much that the one good clasp on the brown suitcase shook undone.

Rather late in the day, he spared a thought for Carol. Poor old Carol. Suppose he had taken her out last night as they had originally planned? Even if he hadn't got shot, he would doubtless have been involved in some unpleasant way in all the fracas that went on between her and this jealous guy with whom she'd apparently been living on and off. The one he'd spoken to on the phone yesterday perhaps. The result would have been all the business of Freda's house coming out and his getaway with the money prevented. Terence decided he must have a guardian angel after all.

He got out of the train at Euston and walked to the small hotel where he had booked a room for the night in order to have the use of it during this afternoon and evening. There he counted the money. Two thousand or so fifty-pound notes wouldn't have taken up all that much room, but the bank manager hadn't been able to let him have it all in fifties, and so at least half was in twenties and tens. In fact the case was hardly big enough to contain it. That was why the clasps kept coming undone.

He dared not leave the money in his room. He took the case with him and walked along Tottenham Court Road. There in a shop that sold leather goods and souvenirs, he bought a canvas strap to put round the suitcase and – as an afterthought when he was leaving the shop – a nylon fold-away bag.

Back at the hotel, he surprised himself by the amount of intense anxiety he seemed to find it necessary to devote to the packing of these bags and the disposal of the money. He had packed them both and re-packed them over and over and finally got all the money in the nylon bag and the few clothes he was taking and his toilet things in the other, when it occurred to him he might very likely be permitted only a single item of hand baggage. The nylon bag only, then. It was the kind on which the zip goes almost all the way round so that when empty the bag could be opened out flat, folded into its own pocket and reduced to handker-chief size. It weighed practically nothing and was more capacious than he had at first supposed.

He realized as he emptied both bags once more that his nerves were screwing up again. Carol, he thought, Carol, trying to feel sad and upset but succeeding only in thinking about 5 Spring Close and the Goldschmidts' removal van arriving to find it full of furniture and Freda's car in the garage. That would have happened by now. What would they do? Go to Steiner & Wildwood and get Mr Phipps's forwarding address from Sawyer. That would be care of Wand in Brownswood Common Lane, Tottenham, and Terence knew for a fact his mother would be out all day visiting her sister in Palmers Green as she always was on a Tuesday.

But even if the Goldschmidts were at this moment trying to trace him to get his furniture moved out, that wouldn't make them suspect him of never having owned the house in the first place. That and its implications would very likely not dawn on them for a week or more. Just the same, he was on tenterhooks as he re-packed the bag and watched the time creep very slowly towards seven-thirty, and it was an enormous relief to be in the tube at last with the nylon bag on his knee and a single ticket to Heathrow Central in his pocket.

Detective Inspector Tony Leatham had a rather smart over-night bag, not leather but as good as, a dark cream fake pigskin. He'd wangled it so that he'd be stopping two nights in Melbourne. Monty Driscoll had been there three months anyway so a couple more days wouldn't do him any harm, while a brief twenty-four-hour stopover would have been cruel on the jet lag, Leatham thought. Not that he knew anything about jet lag. He had never been further abroad before than the Costa Del Sol.

He was going to enjoy himself. No tube for him. They let him have a car to take him right up to Terminal Three. Like all tyro travellers, Leatham was early and one of the first to check in on the Qantas flight that went out at 21.45. He had a cup of coffee and bought a paperback. Not *The Marriage Knot* you saw on display everywhere, he didn't think that was quite his line, but a new collection of twelve horror stories. Then, because there seemed nothing left to do, he presented his passport, and went through the gate from which there was no returning this side of the air.

The girl was his type, with a little round face and blond

curls, though hers were permed. She was surrounded by stacks of luggage. He didn't know how on her own – for the little kid with her would have been more hindrance than help – she had managed to hump it into the train. She was wearing jeans and a brown fur jacket, coney probably, and at first he thought she must have an enormous bust, unnaturally huge on so small girl. It was only after he had been talking to her for a few minutes – or she had been talking to him, she had cottoned on to him fast the way they did – and told him her name was Jane that he realized it was a baby in a sling she was carrying strapped to her chest. She bent forward and he saw its round nearly bald head where he expected her cleavage to be.

Two kids and all that baggage! Terence didn't want to get involved but it was too late. She had already read the label on Jessica's suitcase that said Singapore and the name of the hotel he was going to. He could see in her eyes the greedy relief that she had found herself an escort and a porter for the next twenty hours. It would distract his mind, there was that to it. Talking to her would stop him dwelling on the Goldschmidts. And when they got to Singapore . . .

'Bill's going to be stuck in Penang till April,' she was saying, 'but he's got an ayah all lined up for me.'

Terence understood vaguely that she meant some sort of nurse for the kids. He thought he could do worse than enjoy her undivided companionship for a day or two if that was what fate had in store for him. The older child, sexless in velour dungarees and crew cut, though called Miranda, climbed on to his knee and began fiddling with the zip of the nylon bag. Terence hoped the ayah would be waiting at the airport, preferably on the tarmac.

He carried three cases, pushed one that was on wheels, the nylon bag hooked over his left wrist. Jane carried the baby and two more cases while Miranda hung on to the hem of her jacket, grizzling. There were no policemen loitering around the check-in desks – one of Terence's fears. Relief at getting rid of the cases was succeeded by anxiety at going through baggage scrutiny. And for Terence it was a literal scrutiny. He thought it was all up with him when they said they wanted the nylon bag opened and then opened it so that half the contents fell out. But no one said anything. They turned over the wads of notes with the same indifference as that with which they had handled Jane's package of disposable napkins. He saw Jane looking at the money but she didn't say anything.

They all went into the duty-free shop where Jane bought perfume. Terence didn't buy anything. One hour to go and he wouldn't need whisky any more, he had never really liked the taste. They had coffee and Miranda had a packet of crisps, and while they were sitting at the table wondering whether to have a sandwich or wait for food on the plane, Qantas announced that boarding was about to begin on their flight QF2 for Bahrain, Singapore and Sydney. It was only the first call, there was a long time to go yet.

Jane said she thought she ought to go to the loo, or rather to the mothers' room if they had one, and change the baby's napkin. She might not have another chance for hours. Everyone knew what it was like queuing up on those flights. Terence thought she would take Miranda with her but she didn't, and as soon as her mother was out of sight, Miranda knocked over a nearly full cup of coffee. The coffee flooded over Terence's nylon bag. He ripped open the bag through which coffee had begun to seep and as he did so, Miranda, contrite perhaps or merely frightened, jumped on to him and locked her arms round his neck.

Passengers were now getting up all round Terence and flocking towards the gates. He decided to go too and to hell with Jane and her kids and her bags and her ayah. He struggled to his feet, still holding or being held by Miranda, and as he tried to prise her off found himself looking into the face of Detective Inspector Leatham. Recognition was mutual, immediate. Terence experienced the same sick, dizzy feeling of faintness he had had when Leatham called on him in Spring Close.

Leatham had been sitting at a table three or four yards

away. He got up and came slowly towards Terence, looked at Terence and at Miranda and said:

'Jason Stratford, I presume?'

The words were audible to Terence but they didn't register as more than sounds, as an unknown foreign language might. His nerve burst and frayed open like a too tightly stretched string. He let out a low inarticulate cry. He thrust Miranda off him, grabbed the open bag and ran. The bag peeled itself inside out and the contents tumbled out behind him like the laying of a paper chase: razor, newspaper, underclothes, toothpaste, tranquillizers, a hundred and thirty-two thousand pounds . . .

# 25

They were taking the book back. Holding Jay's hand, Benet went into the Winterside library on a March morning, handed the book across the counter and tried to explain how she happened to have it. Though not a member, she had happened to be in the library some months before, her little boy had picked it up and inadvertently . . .

The animal picture book was large and gaudily coloured, hardly an unconsidered trifle. But the librarian seemed glad to get any missing book back, on any terms. Benet could have returned it by post. She had made herself come here to this corner of Tottenham, to Lordship Avenue and Winterside, because she felt that if she didn't do it now she might never have the courage again, she might avoid it for ever, making elaborate detours whenever it was necessary to cross this part of London. The book was only an excuse to fetch her for a painful but cathartic look at the neighbourhood where Edward had died and Carol Stratford with him.

As on their previous visit she had left the car parked in Winterside Road. It was a sparkling icy day, daffodils out but not a leaf bud showing, not a breath of spring in the air. Jay was growing out of his duffel coat. He might need a new one before the warm weather came. She strapped him into his seat and drove the car into Woodhouse's garage to fill up with petrol.

A young girl served her. Benet went into the office with her to pay with a credit card. Tom Woodhouse was sitting at a desk, talking into the phone. She looked at him, in two minds whether to declare herself when he put the receiver back or to let it go, and then she looked harder. A curious feeling that was a mixture of wonder and of intense embarrassment washed over her. It was almost like an unexpected and unwelcome encounter with an old lover. Yet, of course, Tom Woodhouse had never been her lover. He had been Carol Stratford's. There was no doubt of that.

The resemblance was uncanny, something to send a shiver down the spine. The man on the phone had a high forehead, sea-blue eyes, a hook of a nose and a long chin. His eyebrows were blond thatch eaves and his hair a sandy fair. The first time she had seen Jay, hadn't he forcibly reminded her of someone she had once known? She signed the chit mechanically. Tom Woodhouse said goodbye into the phone, put the receiver down, wrote something on a pad, slowly raised his head.

Benet took her receipt and, keeping her head turned, walked quickly out of the office. The last thing she wanted was to renew her acquaintance with this man who was Jay's undoubted father.

It was a week since she had seen Ian and the departure for Canada was less than a fortnight away. He rang the doorbell at seven, just after Jay had gone to bed.

'I'm not coming with you,' she said, moving out of his embrace. 'But you know that, you've guessed, haven't you?'

His face wore the same heavy look of sadness that had been there when she told him that it hadn't occurred to her to tell him she was going to Spain, that she had forgotten him. She had been three days with Mopsa and her father, the news of Edward's death had reached her, before she remembered to phone Ian. And yet it hadn't been a lack of love, only that fear drives out all other emotion.

'I know you're not but I don't know why,' he said.

She was going to tell him a lie in order to avoid all the lie-telling of a future. Any future for them without those lies would be impossible for he would never connive at what she had done. On the other hand, a future of lies in which she passed on to him one invention and prevarication after another to account for Jay's presence, legal status, continued situation as her son, was equally unthinkable. The relationship would be destroyed even if he believed her – and she didn't think he would believe her for long.

Some future lover, some man in time to come – if such a man ever appeared – would know nothing of her history, would be content with a word or two of explanation. But Ian was the only living person who knew Jay could not be the James Archdale of his passport, the only person who had known James and knew that he was dead. So she had to make a choice and she had made it. Ian or Jay – she had chosen. And first she had to tell that lie.

'I'm sorry, Ian. I just don't care enough for you to follow you half across the world. I thought I loved you and I do, but not enough.'

He wouldn't accept it. 'We could try six months' separation. You could see how you felt after that.'

'I shall feel the same.'

She knew she would never see him again after that evening. 'I'll buy your books,' he said. 'If I can't be anything else to you, I'll be your constant reader.'

She cried after he had gone. She poured herself a drink and sat in the study room and took cold comfort from the fact that her last obstacle was gone. It was she herself who had chosen it, who had deliberately mapped out her life on these lines. Cold comfort in a lonely midnight house.

Jay woke up and cried for a drink of water. She might as well go to bed, she thought, and not come down again. She sat him on her lap and gave him the cup of water to drink. He went back into the cot willingly, closing his eyes even before she had covered him up. A little ruefully and with a lot of hope she looked at him. Some words of Edward's came back to her.

'Well, Jay,' she said, 'it looks as if we're in business.'

# A Demon In
# My View

For Margaret Rabbs, with love

From childhood's hour I have not been
As others were; I have not seen
As others saw; I could not bring
My passions from a common spring.
From the same source I have not taken
My sorrow; I could not awaken
My heart to joy at the same tone;
And all I loved, I loved alone.
Then – in my childhood, in the dawn
Of a most stormy life – was drawn
From every depth of good and ill
The mystery which binds me still ...
And the cloud that took the form
(When the rest of Heaven was blue)
Of a demon in my view.

EDGAR ALLAN POE

The cellar was divided into rooms. Each of these caverns except the last of them was cluttered with the rubbish which usually encumbers the cellars of old houses: broken bicycles, old mould-grown leather cases, wooden crates, legless or armless chairs, cracked china vessels, yellowing newspapers bundled up with string, and in heaps, the nameless unidentifiable cylinders and tubes and rods and rings and spirals of metal which once, long ago, bolted or screwed or linked something on to something else. All this rubbish was coated with the thick black grime that is always present in cellars. The place smelt of soot and fungus.

Between the junk heaps a passage had been cleared from the steps to the first doorless doorway, on to the second doorway and thence to the bare room beyond. And in this room, unseen as yet in the pitch blackness, the figure of a woman leaned against the wall.

He came down the steps with a torch in his hand. He switched on the torch only when he had closed and bolted the door behind him. Then, led by its beam, he picked his way softly along the path that was hedged by rubbish. There was no sound but the shuffle of his slippers on the sooty stone, yet as he entered the second room he told himself he had heard ahead of him an indrawn breath, a small gasp

1

of fear. He smiled, though he was trembling, and the hand which held the torch shook a little.

At the second doorway he raised the beam and let it play from the lower left-hand corner of the room upwards and then downwards, moving it languidly towards the right. It showed him pocked walls, a cracked ceiling hung with cobwebs. It showed him old broken long-disused electric wires, a trickle of viscous water running from the fissure in a split brick, and then playing in a downward arc, it showed him the woman's figure.

Her white face, beautiful, unmarked by any flaw of skin or feature, stared blankly back at him. But he fancied, as the torch shivered in his hand, that she had cringed, her slim body in its short black dress pressing further into the wall which supported it. A handbag was hooked over one of her arms and she wore scuffed black shoes. He didn't speak. He had never known how to talk to women. There was only one thing he had ever been able to do to women and, advancing now, smiling, he did it.

First he rested the torch on a brick ledge at the level of his knees so that she was in shadow, so that the room took on the aspect of an alley into which a street lamp filters dimly. Then he approached her, paralysed as she was, and meeting no resistance – he would have preferred resistance – he closed his hands on her throat.

Still there was no resistance, but what happened next was almost as satisfactory. His hands squeezed till the fingers met, and as forefinger pressed against thumb, the beautiful white face changed, crumpled, twisted in agony and caved in. He gave a grunting gasp as her body fell sideways. He released his hold, swaying at the earthquake inside him, and he let her fall, prone and stiff into the footmarked soot.

2

It took him a few minutes to recover. He wiped his hands and the corners of his mouth on a clean white handkerchief. He closed his eyes, opened them, sighed. Then he picked up the plastic shop window model and set her once more against the wall. Her face remained caved-in. He wiped the dust from it with his handkerchief and, inserting his fingers through the split in her neck, a split which grew wider each time he murdered her, pushed out sunken nose and crumpled eyes and depressed chin, until she was blank and beautiful again.

He straightened her dress and replaced the handbag, which had come unhooked, once more on her arm. She was ready to die for him again. A week, a fortnight, might go by but she would wait for him. It was good, the best thing in his life, just knowing she was there, waiting till next time ...

# Chapter 1

The houses were warrens for people, little anthills of discomfort. Almost each one, built to accommodate a single family, had been segmented into four or five separate units. Ungracious living was evinced by a row of doorbells, seven in an eight-roomed house, by the dustbins that had replaced rose bushes in the front gardens, by the slow decay that showed in a boarded window, a balcony rail patched with chicken wire, a latchless gate that tapped ceaselessly, monotonously, against its post.

On the odd-numbered side of Trinity Road the houses were tall and with high basements so that the flights of steps mounting to their front doors seemed to assault the very hearts of these houses like engines of siege. They faced terraces of brown brick, humbler-looking and only three floors high. Outside number 142 was parked a large shiny car, a green Jaguar. A toy dog that nodded its head at the slightest vibration rested inside the rear window, and hanging from the centre of the windscreen was a blonde doll in a two-piece bathing suit.

The car looked incongruous in Trinity Road, along which such vehicles generally passed without stopping. Just inside the low wall that bounded the front garden of number 142 grew two lopped-off lime trees, stumps bearing on their summits excrescences of leathery leaves that gave them the look of pre-

4

historic vegetation. Behind them was a small patch of brown turf. On the ground floor was a bay window, curtained in orange; above that two windows curtained in floral green – frayed curtains these, with a rent in one of them; on the top floor brown velvet curtains which, parted, disclosed a white frilly drapery like the bodice of a woman's nightgown.

A shallow flight of steps, of pink granite but grazed instead of polished, led to a front door whose woodwork might have been of any colour, green, brown, grey, it was so long since it had been painted. But the glass panels in it kept the dim glow they had always had, rubber plant green and the dull maroon of sour wine, the kind of stained glass found in chapel windows of the last century.

There were five bells, each one but the lowest labelled. A psychologist would have learned much from the varied and distinctive labelling of these bells. The topmost bore below it a typewritten slip, framed in a plastic container clearly designed for this purpose, which stated: Flat 2, Mr A. Johnson. Beneath this and the next bell, on a scrap of card secured with adhesive tape, was scrawled in a bold reckless hand: Jonathan Dean. While under the third bell two labels seemed to quarrel with each other for pre-eminence. One was of brown plastic with the letters on it in relief: Flat 1, B. Kotowsky. Its rival, jostling it, stuck to the corner of it with a gob of glue, announced in felt-tipped pen: Ms V. Kotowsky. Last came a frivolous oval of orange cardboard on which, under a pair of Chinese characters done with a brush, the caller might read: Room 1, Li-li Chan.

The space beneath the lowest bell was vacant, as was Room 2 with which it communicated.

Between the door of the vacant room and the long diagonal sweep which was the underside of the staircase, a shabby windowless space, Stanley Caspian, the landlord, had his office. It was furnished with a desk and two bentwood chairs. On top of the shelves, bristling with papers, which lined the rear wall, stood an electric kettle and a couple of cups and saucers. There was no other furniture in the hall but a rectangular mahogany table set against the banisters and facing the ground floor bathroom.

Stanley Caspian sat at the desk, as he always did when he came to a hundred and forty-two for his Saturday morning conference with Arthur Johnson. Arthur sat in the other chair. On the desk were spread the rent books and cheques of the tenants. Each rent book had its own brown envelope with the tenant's name printed on it. This had been an innovation of Arthur's and he had done the printing. Stanley wrote laboriously in the rent books, pressing his pen in hard and making unnecessary full stops after every word and figure.

'I'll be glad to see the back of that Dean,' he said when he had inked in the last fifty pence and made the last full-stop. 'Middle of next month and he'll be gone.'

'And his gramophone,' said Arthur, 'and his wine bottles filling up our little dustbin. I'm sure we'll all be devoutly thankful.'

'Not Kotowsky. He won't have anyone to go boozing with. Still, thank God he's going off his own bat, is what I say. I'd never have been able to get rid of him, not with this poxy new Rent Act. Put the kettle on, me old Arthur. I fancy a spot of elevenses.'

And tenses and twelveses, Arthur thought. He plugged in the electric kettle and set out the cups. He wouldn't have dreamed of eating anything at this

6

hour, but Stanley, who was enormously fat, whose belly almost burst open the front of his size seventeen collar shirt, opened one of the packages he had brought with him and began devouring sandwiches of bread rolls and processed cheese. Stanley spluttered crumbs all over his shirt, eating uninhibitedly like some gross superannuated baby. Arthur watched him inscrutably. He neither liked nor disliked Stanley. For him, as for everyone, he had no particular feeling most of the time. He wished only to be esteemed, to keep in with the right people, to know where he stood. Inclining his head towards the door behind him, he said:

'A little bird told me you'd let that room.'

'Right,' said Stanley, his mouth full. 'A little Chinese bird, was it?'

'I must confess I was a bit put out you told Miss Chan before telling me. You know me, I always believe in speaking out. And I was a little hurt. After all, I am your oldest tenant. I *have* been here twenty years, and I think I can say I've never caused you a moment's unease.'

'Right. I only wish they were all like you.'

Arthur filled the cups with instant coffee, boiling water and a dribble of cold milk. 'No doubt, you had your reasons.' He lifted cold eyes, of so pale a blue as to be almost white. 'I mustn't be so sensitive.'

'The fact is,' said Stanley, shovelling spoonfuls of sugar into his cup, 'that I wondered how you'd take it. You see, this new chap, the one that's taking Room 2, he's got the same name as you.' He gave Arthur a sidelong look and then he chortled. 'You have to laugh. Coincidence, eh? I wondered how you'd take it.'

'You mean he's also called *Arthur Johnson*?'

'Not so bad as that. Dear, oh, dear, you have to

7

laugh. He's called Anthony Johnson. You'll have to take care your post doesn't get mixed up. Don't want him reading your love letters, eh?'

Arthur's eyes seemed to grow even paler, and the muscles of his face tightened, tensed, drawing it into a mask. When he spoke his accent smoothed into an exquisite, slightly affected, English. 'I've nothing to hide. My life is an open book.'

'Maybe his isn't. If I wasn't in a responsible position I'd say you could have a bit of fun there, me old Arthur.' Stanley finished his sandwiches and fetched a doughnut from the second bag. '*The Sexual Behaviour of the Human Male*, that's the sort of open book his life'll be. Good-looking young devil, he is. Real flypaper for the girls, I shouldn't wonder.'

Arthur couldn't bear that sort of talk. It made him feel sick. 'I only hope he's got a good bank reference and a decent job.'

'Right. He's paid two months' rent in advance and that's better than all your poxy bank references to me. He's moving in Monday.' Stanley got heavily to his feet. Crumbs cascaded on to desk, envelopes and rent books. 'We'll just have a look in, Arthur. Mrs Caspian says there's a fruit bowl in there she wants and young Anthony'll only smash it.'

Arthur nodded sagely. If he and his landlord were in agreement about anything, it was the generally destructive behaviour of the other tenants. Besides, he enjoyed penetrating the rooms, usually closed to him. And in this one he had a special interest.

It was small and furnished with junk. Arthur accepted this as proper in a furnished room, noting only that it was far from clean. He picked his way over to the window. Stanley, having secured his fruit bowl, of red and white Venetian glass, from hetero-geneous stacks of crockery and cutlery on the draining board, was admiring the only object in the place less than twenty years old.

'That's a bloody good washbasin, that is,' he remarked, tapping this article of primrose-coloured porcelain. 'Cost me all of fifteen quid to have that put in. Your people did it, as I remember.'

'It was a reject,' said Arthur absently. 'There's a flaw in the soap dish.' He was staring out of the window which overlooked a narrow brick-walled court. Above an angle of wall you could see the topmost branches of a tree. The court was concreted and the concrete was green with lichen, for into the two drains on either side of it flowed – and sometimes overflowed – the waste water from the two upstairs flats and Jonathan Dean's room. In the wall which faced the window was a door.

'What are you looking at?' said Stanley none too pleasantly, for Arthur's remark about the washbasin had perhaps rankled.

'Nothing,' said Arthur. 'I was just thinking he won't have much of an outlook.'

'What d'you expect for seven quid a week? You want to remember *you* pay seven for a whole flat because the poxy government won't let me charge more for unfurnished accommodation. You're lucky, getting your hooks on that when I didn't know any better. Oh, yes. But times have changed, thank God, and for seven quid a week now you look out on a cellar door and lump it. Right?'

'It's no concern of mine,' said Arthur. 'I imagine my namesake will be out a lot, won't he?'

'If he's got any sense,' said Stanley, for at that moment there crashed through the ceiling the triumphant chords of the third movement from Beethoven's Eighth. 'Tschaikowsky,' he said learnedly.

9

'Dean's at it again. I like something a bit more modern myself.'

'I was never musical.' Arthur gravitated into the hall. 'I must get on with things. Shopping day, you know. If I might just have my little envelope?'

His shopping basket in one hand and an orange plastic carrier containing his laundry in the other, Arthur made his way along Trinity Road towards the launderette in Brasenose Avenue. He could have used the Coinerama in Magdalen Hill, but he went to Magdalen Hill every weekday to work and at the weekends he liked to vary his itinerary. After all, for good reason, he didn't go out much and never after dark.

So instead of cutting through Oriel Mews, past the Waterlily pub and making for the crossroads, he went down past All Souls' Church, where as a child he had passed two hours each Sabbath Day, his text carefully committed to memory. And at four o'clock Auntie Gracie had always been waiting for him, always, it seemed to him, under an umbrella. Had it invariably rained on Sundays, the granite terrace opposite veiled in misty grey? That terrace was now gone, replaced by barrack-like blocks of council flats.

He followed the route he and Auntie Gracie had taken towards home, but only for a little way. Taking some pleasure in making the K.12 bus stop for him alone, Arthur went over the pedestrian crossing in Balliol Street, holding up his hand in an admonitory way. Down St John's Road where the old houses still remained, turn-of-the-century houses some enterprising but misguided builder had designed with Dutch façades, and where plane trees alternated with concrete lamp standards.

The launderette attendant said good morning and

Arthur rejoined with a cool nod. He used his own soap in the machine. He didn't trust the blue stuff in the little packet you got for five pence. Nor did he trust the attendant to put his linen in the drier nor the other customers not to steal it. So he sat patiently on one of the benches, talking to no one, until the thirty-five minute cycle was completed.

It afforded him considerable satisfaction to note how superior were his pale blue sheets, snowy towels, underwear and shirts, to the gaudy jumble sale laundry in the adjacent machines. While they were safely rotating in the drier, he went next-door to the butchers and then to the greengrocers. Arthur never shopped in the supermarkets run by Indians, in which this area of Kenbourne Vale abounded. He selected his lamb chops, his small Sunday joint of Scotch topside, with care. Three slices off the roast for Sunday, the rest to be minced and made into Monday's cottage pie. A pound of runner beans, and pick out the small ones, if you please, he didn't want a mouthful of strings.

A different way back. The linen so precisely folded that it wouldn't really need ironing – though Arthur always ironed it – he trotted up Merton Street. More council flats, tower blocks here like pillars supporting the heavy overcast sky. The lawns which separated them, Arthur had often noticed with satisfaction, were prohibited to children. The children played in the street or sat disconsolately on top of bits of sculpture. Arthur disapproved of the sculptures, which in his view resembled chunks cut out of prehistoric monsters for all they were entitled *Spring* or *Social Conscience* or *Man and Woman*, but he didn't think the children ought to sit on them or play in the street for that matter. Auntie Gracie had never allowed him to play in the street.

11

Stanley Caspian's Jaguar had gone, and so had the Kotowskys' fourth-hand Ford. A fistful of vouchers, entitling their possessor to three pence off toothpaste or free soap when you bought a giant size shampoo, had been pushed through the letter box. Arthur helped himself to those which might come in handy, and mounted the stairs. There was a half-landing after the ten steps of the first flight where a pay phone box was attached to the wall. Four steps went on to the first floor. The door of the Kotowskys' flat was on his left, that to Jonathan Dean's room facing him, and the door to the bathroom they shared between the other two. Dean's door was open, Shostakovich's Fifth Symphony on loud enough to be heard in Kenbourne Town Hall. The intention apparently was that it should be loud enough merely to be audible in the bathroom from which Dean, a tall red-haired, red-faced man, now emerged. He wore nothing but a small mauve towel fastened round him loincloth-fashion.

'The body is more than raiment,' he remarked when he saw Arthur.

Arthur flushed slightly. It was his belief that Dean was mad, a conviction which rested partly on the fact that everything the man said sounded as if it had come out of a book. He turned his head in the direction of the open door.

'Would you be good enough to reduce the volume a little, Mr Dean?'

Dean said something about music having charms to soothe the savage breast, and beat his own which was hairy and covered with freckles. But, having slammed his door with violence but no animosity, he subdued Shostakovitch and only vague Slavic murmurs reached Arthur as he ascended the second flight.

And now he was in his own exclusive domain. He occupied the whole second floor. With a sigh of contentment, resting his laundry bag and his shopping basket on the mat, he unlocked the door and let himself in.

# Chapter 2

Arthur prepared his lunch, two lamb cutlets, creamed potatoes, runner beans. None of your frozen or canned rubbish for him. Auntie Gracie had brought him up to appreciate fresh food, well-cooked. He ended the meal with a slice from the plum pie he had baked on Thursday night, and then, without delay, he washed the dishes. One of Auntie Gracie's maxims had been that only slatternly house-keepers leave dirty dishes in the sink. Arthur always washed his the moment he finished eating.

He went into the bedroom. The bed was stripped. He put on clean sheets, rose pink, and rose pink pillow cases. Arthur couldn't sleep in a soiled bed. Once, when collecting their rent, he had caught a glimpse of the Kotowskys' bed and it had put him off his supper.

Meticulously he dusted the bedroom furniture and polished the silver stoppers on Auntie Gracie's cut-glass scent bottles. All his furniture was late-Victorian, pretty though a little heavy. It came up well under an application of polish. Arthur still felt guilty about using spray-on polish instead of the old-fashioned wax kind. Auntie Gracie had never approved of short cuts. He gave the frilly nets, with which every window in the flat was curtained, a critical stare. They were too fragile to be risked at the launderette, so he washed them himself once a

14

month, and they weren't due for a wash for another week. But this was such a grimy district, and there was nothing like white net for collecting every bit of flying dust. He began to take them down. For the second time that day he found himself facing the cellar door.

The Kotowskys had no window which overlooked it. It could be seen only from this one of his and from the one in Room 2. This had long been known to Arthur, he had known it for nearly as long as the duration of his tenancy. Very little in his own life had changed in those twenty years. The cellar door had never been painted, though the bricks had darkened perhaps and the concrete grown more green and damp. No one had ever seen him cross that yard, he thought as he laid the net curtains carefully over a chair, no one had ever seen him enter the cellar. He continued to stare down, considering, remembering.

He had been at school with Stanley Caspian – Merton Street Junior – and Stanley had been fat and gross and coarse even then. A bully always.

'Auntie's baby! Auntie's baby! Where's your dad, Arthur Johnson?' And with an inventiveness no one would have suspected from the standard of Stanley's school work: 'Cowardy, cowardy custard, Johnson is a bastard!'

The years civilize, at least inhibit. When they met by chance in Trinity Road, each aged thirty-two, Stanley was affable, even considerate.

'Sorry to hear you lost your aunt, Arthur. More like a mother to you, she was.'

'Yes.'

'You'll be wanting a place of your own now. Bachelor flat, eh? How about taking the top of a hundred and forty-two?'

'I've no objection to giving it the once over,' said

15

Arthur primly. He knew old Mrs Caspian had left her son a lot of property in West Kenbourne.

The house was in a mess in those days and the top flat was horrible. But Arthur saw its potential – and for two pounds ten a week? So he took Stanley's offer, and a couple of days later when he had started the re-decorating he went down into the cellar to see if, by chance, it housed a stepladder.

She was lying on the floor of the furthest room on a heap of sacks and black-out curtains left over from the war. She was naked and her white plastic flesh was cold and shiny. He never found out who had brought her there and left her entombed. At first he had been embarrassed, taken aback as he was when he glimpsed likenesses of her standing in shop windows and waiting to be dressed. But then, because he was alone with her and there was no one to see them, he approached more closely. So that was how they looked? With awe, with fear, at last with distaste, he looked at the two hemispheres on her chest, the soft swollen triangle between her closed thighs. An impulse came to him to dress her. He had done so many secret things in his life – almost everything he had done that he had wanted to do had been covert, clandestine – that no inhibition intervened to stop him fetching from the flat a black dress, a handbag, shoes. These had belonged to Auntie Gracie and he had brought them with him from the house in Magdalen Hill. People had suggested he give them to the W.V.S. for distribution, but how could he? How could he have borne to see some West Kenbourne slattern queening it in her clothes?

His white lady had attenuated limbs and was as tall as he. Auntie Gracie's dress came above her knees. She had yellow nylon hair that curled over her cheekbones. He put the shoes on her feet and hooked the handbag over her arm. In order to see what he was doing, he had put a hundred-watt bulb in the light socket. But another of those impulses led him to take it out. By the light of the torch she looked real, the cellar room with its raw brick walls an alley in the hinterland of city streets. It was sacrilege to dress her in Auntie Gracie's clothes, and yet that very sacrilege had an indefinable rightness about it, was a spur . . .

He had strangled her before he knew what he was doing. With his bare hands on her cold smooth throat. The release had been almost as good as the real thing. He set her up against the wall once more, dusted her beautiful white face. You do not have to hide or fear or sweat for such a killing; the law permits you to kill anything not made of flesh and blood . . . He left her and came out into the yard. The room that was now Room 2 had been untenanted then as had the whole house but for his flat. And when a tenant had come he had been, as had his successor, on night work that took him out five evenings a week at six. But before that Arthur had decided. She should save him, she should be – as those who would like to get hold of him would call it – his therapy. The woman who waited in the dark streets, asking for trouble, he cared nothing for them, their pain, their terror. He cared, though, for his own fate. To defy it, he would kill a thousand women in her person, she should be his salvation. And then no threat could disturb him, provided he was careful never to go out after dark, never to have a drink.

After a time he had come to be rather proud of his solution. It seemed to set down as nonsense the theories of those experts – he had, in the days of his distress, studied their works – that men with his problem had no self-control, no discipline over their own compulsions. He had always known they talked rubbish. Why shouldn't he have the recourse of the members of Alcoholics Anonymous, of the rehabilitated drug addict?

But now? Anthony Johnson. Arthur, who made it his business to know the routines and life-styles of his fellow-tenants, hoped he would soon acquire a thorough-going knowledge of the new man's movements. Anthony Johnson would surely go out two or three evenings a week? He must. The alternative was something Arthur didn't at all want to face.

There was nothing for it but to wait and see. The possibility of bringing the white lady up into the flat, installing her here, killing her here, occurred to him only for him to dismiss the idea. He disliked the notion of his encounters with her taking on the air of a game. It was the squalor of the cellar, the dimness, his stealthy approach that gave to it its reality. No, she must remain there, he thought, and he must wait and see. He turned from the window and at the same time turned his mind, for he didn't much care to dwell upon her and what she truly was, preferring her to stand down there forgotten and unacknowledged until he needed her again. This, in fact, he thought as he took away the curtains to put them in soak, was the first time he had thought of her in those terms for many years.

Dismissing her as a man dismisses a compliant and always available mistress, Arthur went into the living room. The sofa and the two armchairs had been re-upholstered since Auntie Gracie's death, only six months after, but Arthur had taken such good care of them that the covers still looked new. Carefully he worked on the blue moquette with a stiff brush. The cream drawn-thread antimacassars might as well go into the water with the nets. He polished the oval mahogany table, the mahogany tallboy, the legs and arms of the dining chairs; plumped up the blue and brown satin cushions, flicked his feather duster over the two hand-painted parchment lamp-shades, the knobs on the television set, the Chelsea china in the cabinet. Now for the vacuum cleaner. Having the flat entirely covered with wall-to-wall carpet in a deep fawn shade had made a hole in his savings, but it had been worth it. He ran the cleaner slowly and thoroughly over every inch of the carpet, taking his time so that its droning zoom-zoom wouldn't be lost on Jonathan Dean, though he had little hope of its setting him an example. Finally, he rinsed the nets and the chair backs and hung them over the drying rack in the bathroom. There was no need to clean the bathroom or the kitchen. They were cleaned every morning as a matter of course, the former when he had dried himself after his bath, the latter as soon as breakfast was over.

At this point he sat down in the chair by the front window and, having left all his doors open, surveyed the flat along its spotless length. It smelt of polish, silver cleaner, soap and elbow grease. Arthur recalled how, when he was about eleven and had neglected to wash his bedroom window as thoroughly as Auntie Gracie demanded, she had sent him round to Winter's with threepence.

'You ask the man for a pound of elbow grease, Arthur. Go on. It won't take you five minutes.'

The man in the shop had laughed himself almost into a fit. But he hadn't explained why he had no elbow grease, and Arthur had to take the threepenny bit – a threepenny joey, they called them then – back home again.

19

'I expect he did laugh,' said Auntie Gracie. 'And I hope you've been taught a lesson.' She rubbed Arthur's arm through the grey flannel shirt. 'This is where your elbow grease comes from. You can't buy it, you have to make it yourself.'

Arthur hadn't borne her any malice. He knew she had acted for the best. He would do exactly the same by any child in his charge. Children had to be taught the hard way, and it had set him on the right path. Would she be pleased with him if she could see him now? If she could see how well he kept his own place, his bank balance, how he ordered his life, how he hadn't missed a day at Grainger's in twenty years? Perhaps. But she had never been very pleased with him, had she? He had never reached those heights of perfection she had laid before him as fitting for one who needed to cleanse himself of the taint of his birth and background.

Arthur sighed. He should have washed the Chelsea china. It was no good telling himself a flick with that duster would serve as well as a wash. Tired now but determined to soldier on, he put the shepherdesses and frock-coated gentlemen and dogs and little flower baskets on to a tray and carried them into the kitchen.

# Chapter 3

Arthur was a sound sleeper. He fell asleep within five minutes of laying his head on the pillow and hardly ever awoke before the alarm went off at seven-thirty. This ability to sleep was something to confound those silent critics, that invisible army of psychiatrists whose words he had read but never yet heard, and who would, he suspected, categorize him disagreeably. Which was absurd. Neurotic people don't sleep well, nor do hysterics. Arthur knew he was a perfectly normal man who happened (like all normal men) to have a small peculiarity he was well able to keep under control.

He was always the last to leave for work and the first to get home. This was because the others all worked further afield than he. Jonathan Dean went first. He left at five past eight while Arthur was still in his bath. This Monday morning his room door was slammed so loudly that the bath water actually rocked about like tea in a joggled cup. The front door also crashed shut. Arthur dried himself and, for decency's sake, put on his towelling robe before washing down bath, basin and floor. As soon as he was dressed, he opened his own front door and left it on the latch.

The Kotowskys burst out of their flat while he was pouring out his cornflakes. As usual, they were quarrelling.

21

'All right, I get the message,' he heard Brian Kotowsky say. 'You've told me three times you won't be in tonight.'

'I just don't want you ringing up all my friends, asking where I am.'

'You can settle that one, Vesta, by telling me where you'll be.'

They clumped down the stairs, still arguing, but Arthur couldn't catch Vesta Kotowsky's reply. The front door closed fairly quietly which meant Vesta must have shut it. Arthur went to his living room window and watched them get into their car which was left day in and day out, rain, shine or snow, parked in the street. He was sincerely glad he had never taken the step of getting married, had, in fact, taken such a serious step to avoid it.

As he was returning to his kitchen he heard Li-li Chan come upstairs to the half-landing and the phone. Li-li spoke quite good English but rather as a talking bird might have spoken it. Her voice was high and clipped. She was always giggling, mostly about nothing.

She giggled now, into the receiver. 'You pick me up soon? Quarter to nine? Oh, you are nice, nice man. Do I love you? I don't know. Yes, yes, I love you. I love lots, lots of people. Good-bye now.' Li-li giggled prettily all the way back down the stairs.

Arthur snorted, but not loudly enough for her to hear. London Transport wouldn't get rich out of her. Don't suppose she ever spends a penny on a train or bus fare, Arthur thought, and darkly, I wonder what she has to do to make it worth their while? But he didn't care to pursue that one, it was too distasteful.

He heard her go out on the dot of a quarter to. She always closed the doors very softly as if she had something to hide. A well set-up, clean-looking young Englishman had come for her in a red sports car. A wicked shame, Arthur thought, but boys like that had only themselves to blame, they didn't know the meaning of self-discipline.

Alone in the house now, he finished his breakfast, washed the dishes and wiped down all the surfaces. The post was due at nine. While he was brushing the jacket of his second-best suit and selecting a tie, he heard the dull thump of the letter box. Arthur always took the post in and arranged the letters on the hall table.

But first there was his rubbish to deal with. He lifted the liner from the wastebin, secured the top of it with a wire fastener and went downstairs, first making sure, with a quick glance into the mirror, that his tie was neatly knotted and that there was a clean white handkerchief in his breast pocket. Whether there was anyone in the house or not, Arthur would never have gone downstairs improperly dressed. Nor would he set foot outside the house without locking the doors behind him, not even to go to the dustbin. Once more, the bin was choked with yellowish decaying bean sprouts, not even wrapped up. That wasteful Li-li again! He would have to make it clear to Stanley Caspian that one dustbin was inadequate for five people – six when this new man came today.

Unlocking the door and re-entering the house, he picked up the post. The usual weekly letter, post-marked Taiwan, from Li-li's father who hadn't adopted Western ways and wrote the sender's name as Chan Ah Feng. Poor trusting man, thought Arthur, little did he know. Yet another bill for Jonathan Dean. The next thing they'd have debt collectors round, and a fine thing that would be for the house's reputation. Two letters for the Kotow-skys, one for her and one for both of them. That was the way it always was.

He tidied up the circulars and vouchers – who messed them about like that out of sheer wantonness he didn't know – and then he arranged the letters, their envelope edges aligned to each other and the edge of the table. Ten past nine. Sighing a little, because it was so pleasant having the house to himself, Arthur went back upstairs and collected his briefcase. He had no real need of a briefcase for he never brought work home, but Auntie Gracie had given him his first one for his twenty-first birthday and since then he had replaced it three times. Besides, it looked well. Auntie Gracie had always said that a man going to business without a briefcase is as ill-dressed as a lady without gloves.

He closed his door and tested it with his hand to make sure it was fast shut. Down the stairs once more and out into Trinity Road. A fine bright day, though somewhat autumnal. What else could you expect in late September?

Grainger's, Contractors and Builders' Merchants, weren't due to open until nine-thirty and Arthur was early. He lingered to look at the house where he had lived with Auntie Gracie. It was on the corner of Balliol Street and Magdalen Hill, at the point where the hill became Kenbourne Lane, a tall narrow house, condemned to demolition but still waiting along with its neighbours to be demolished. The front door and the downstairs bay were sealed up with gleaming silvery corrugated iron to stop squatters and other vagrants getting in. Arthur often wondered what Auntie Gracie would say if she could see it now, but he approved of the sealing up. He paused at the gate and looked up to the boarded rectangle on the brick façade which had once been his bedroom window.

Auntie Gracie had been very good to him. He could never make up to her for what she had done for him if he struggled till the day of his death. He knew well what she had done, for, apart from the concrete evidence of it all around him, she had never missed an opportunity of telling him.

'After all I've done for you, Arthur!'

She had bought him from his mother, her own sister, when he was two months old.

'Had to give her a hundred pounds, Arthur, and a hundred was a lot of money in those days. We never saw her again. She was off like greased lightning.'

How fond Auntie Gracie had been of grease! Elbow grease, greased lightning – 'You need a bit of grease under your heels, Arthur.'

She had told him the facts of his birth as soon as she thought him old enough to understand. Unfortunately, Stanley Caspian and others of his ilk had thought him old enough some months before, but that was no fault of hers. And she had never mentioned his mother or his father, whoever he may have been, at all. But in that bedroom – with the door open, of course. She insisted on his always leaving the door open – he had spent many childhood hours, wondering. How foolish children were and how ungrateful ...

Arthur shook himself and gave a slight cough. People would be looking at him in a moment. He deplored anything that might attract attention to oneself. And why on earth had he been mooning away like this when he passed the house every day, when there had been no unusual circumstance to give rise to such a reverie? But, of course, there was an unusual circumstance. The new man was coming to Room 2. It was only natural that today he should dwell a little on his past life. Natural, but governable too. He turned briskly away from the gate as All Souls' clock struck the half-hour. Grainger's yard was next door but one to the sealed-up house, next to that a half-acre or so of waste ground where houses had been demolished but not yet replaced; beyond that Kenbourne Lane tube station.

Arthur unlocked the double gates and let himself into the glass and cedarwood hut which was his office. The boy who made tea and swept up and ran errands and whose duty it was to open the place, hadn't yet arrived. Typical. He wouldn't be late like this morning after morning if he had had an Auntie Gracie to put a spot of grease under his heels.

Raising the venetian blinds to let sunshine into the small neat room, Arthur took the cover off his Adler standard. Plenty of post had come since Friday, mostly returned bills with cheques enclosed. There was one irate letter from a customer who said that a pastel blue sink unit had been installed by Grainger's in his kitchen instead of the stainless steel variety he had ordered. Arthur read it carefully, planning what diplomatic words he would write in reply.

He called himself, when required to state his occupation, a surveyor. In fact, he had never surveyed anything and wouldn't have known how to go about it. His work consisted simply in sitting at this desk from nine-thirty till five, answering the phone, sending out bills and keeping the books. He knew his work back to front, inside out, but it still caused him anxiety, for Auntie Gracie's standards were always before him.

'Never put off till tomorrow what you can do today, Arthur. Remember if a job's worth doing, it's worth doing well. Your employer has reposed his trust in you. He has put you in a responsible position and it's up to you not to let him down.'

Those, or words like them, had been the words with which she had sent him off to be Grainger's boy a week after his fourteenth birthday. So he had swept up better than anyone else and made tea better than anyone else. When he was twenty-one he had attained his present responsibility, that of seeing to it that every customer of Grainger's got his roof mended better than anyone else's roof and his kitchen floor laid better than anyone else's kitchen floor. And he had seen to it. He was invaluable.

*Dear Sir*, Arthur typed, *I note with regret that the Rosebud de Luxe sink unit (type E/4283, pastel blue) was not, in fact*

Barry Hopkins slouched into the office, chewing bubble gum.

'Hi.'

'Good morning, Barry. A little late, aren't you? Do you know what time it is?'

'Round half nine,' said Barry.

'I see. Round half nine. Of all the lackadaisical, feckless . . .' Arthur would have liked to advise him to go over to the works and ask for a pound of elbow grease, but the young were so sophisticated these days. Instead he snapped, 'Take that filthy stuff out of your mouth.'

Barry took no notice. He blew an enormous bubble, like a balloon and of a pale shade of aquamarine. Leaning idly on the window sill, he said:

'Old Grainger's comin' across the yard.'

Arthur was galvanized. He composed his face into an expression suggestive of a mixture of devotion to duty, self-esteem and simpering sycophancy, and applied his hands to the typewriter.

27

# Chapter 4

Anthony Johnson had no furniture. He possessed nothing but a few clothes and a lot of books. These he had brought with him to 142 Trinity Road in a large old suitcase and a canvas bag. There were works on sociology, psychology, his dictionary of psychology, and that essential textbook for any student of the subject, *The Psychopath* by William and Joan McCord. Whatever else he needed for reference he would obtain from the British Museum, and from that excellent library of criminology – the best, it was said, in London – housed in Radclyffe College, Kenbourne Vale. In that library too he would write the thesis whose subject was *Some Aspects of the Psychopathic Personality*, and which he hoped would secure him from the University of London his doctorate of philosophy.

Part of it, he thought, surveying Room 2, would have to be written here. In that fireside chair, presumably, which seemed to be patched with bits from a woman's tweed skirt. On that crippled gate-leg table. Under that hanging lamp that looked like a monstrous, joke shop, plastic jellyfish. Well, he wanted his Ph.D and this was the price he must pay for it. Dr Johnson. Not, of course, that he would call himself doctor. It was Helen who had pointed out that in this country, the land of such anomalies, the bachelor of medicine is called doctor and the doctor of philosophy mister. She too had seen the funny side of being Dr Johnson and had quoted epigrams and talked about Boswell until he, at last, had seen the point. But it was always so. Sometimes he thought that for all his Cambridge First, his Home Office Social Science diploma, his wide experience of working with the poor, the sick and the deprived, he had never woken up to awareness and insight until he met Helen. She it was who had turned his soul's eye towards the light.

But as he thought this, he turned his physical eye towards Stanley Caspian's green-spotted finger-marked mirror and surveyed his own reflection. He wasn't a vain man. He hardly ever thought about the way he looked. That he was tall and slim and strongly-made with straight features and thick fair hair had never meant much to him except in that they denoted health. But lately he had come to wonder. He wondered what he lacked that Roger had; he who was good-looking and vigorous and – well, good company, wasn't he? – hyper-educated with a good salary potential, and Roger who was stupid and dull and possessive and couldn't do anything but win pistol shooting contests. Only he knew it wasn't that at all. It was just that Helen, for all her awareness, didn't know her own mind.

To give her a chance to know it, to choose between them, he had come here. The library, of course, was an advantage. But he could easily have written his thesis in Bristol. The theory was that absence made the heart grow fonder. If he had gone to his parents in York she could have phoned him every night. He wasn't going to let her know the phone number here – he didn't know it himself yet – or communicate with her at all except on the last Wednesday in the month when Roger would be out at his gun club.

29

And he couldn't write to her at all in case Roger intercepted the letter. She'd write to him once a week. He wondered, as he unpacked his books, how that would work out, if he had been wise to let her call the tune, make all the arrangements. Well, he'd given her a deadline. By November she must know. Stay in prison or come out with him into the free air.

He opened the window because the room smelt stale. Outside was a narrow yard. What light it received came from a bit of sky just flicked at its edges by leaves from a distant tree. The sky was a triangular patch because most of it was cut off by brick wall meeting brick wall diagonally about four yards up. In one of these walls – they were festooned with pipes betwigged with smaller pipes like lianas – was a door. Since there was no window beside it or anywhere near it, Anthony decided it must lead down to a cellar.

Five o'clock. He had better go out and get himself something to cook on that very old and inefficient-looking Baby Belling stove. The hall smelt vaguely of cloves, less vaguely of old unwashed fabrics. That would be the bathroom, that door between his and Room I, and that other one to the right of old Caspian's table, the loo. Wondering what sort of a woman or girl Miss Chan was and whether she would get possession of the bathroom just when he wanted to use it, he went out into the street.

Trinity Road. It led him via Oriel Mews into Balliol Street. The street names of London, he thought, require an historical treatise of their own. Someone must know why this group in Hampstead are called after Devon towns and that cluster in Cricklewood after Hebridean islands. Were the Barbara, the Dorinda and the Lesley, after whom roads are named just north of the City, once the belles of

30

Barnsbury? Did a sorcerer live in Warlock Road, Kilburn Park, and who was the Sylvia of Sylvia Gardens, Wembley, what is she, that all our maps commend her? In that corner of Kenbourne Vale, to which his destiny had drawn Anthony Johnson, someone had christened the squalid groves and terraces after Oxford colleges.

A cruel joke cannot have been intended. The councillor or town planner or builder must have thought himself inspired when he named Trinity Road, All Souls' Grove, Magdalen Hill, Brasenose Avenue and Wadham Street. What was certain, Anthony thought, was that he hadn't been an Oxford man, had never walked in the enclosed quadrangles of that city or even seen its dreaming spires.

Such a fanciful reverie would once have been alien to him. Helen had taught him to think like this, to see through her eyes, to associate, to compare, and to dream. She was all imagination, he all practical. Practical again, he noted mundane things. The Vale Café for quick cheap snacks; Kemal's Kebab House, smelling of cumin and sesame and fenugreek, for when he wanted to splash a bit; a pub – the Waterlily, it was called. Just opening now. Anthony saw red plush settees, a brown-painted moulded ceiling, etched glass screens beside and behind the bar.

The pavements everywhere were cluttered with garbage in black plastic sacks. A dustmen's strike, perhaps. The kids were out of school. He wondered where they played. Always on these dusty pavements of Portland stone? Or on that bit of waste ground, fenced in with broken and rusty tennis court wire, between Grainger's, the builders, and the tube station?

Houses marked here for demolition. The sooner

they came down the better and made way for flats
with big windows and green spaces to surround
them. Not many truly English people about. Brown
women pushing prams with black babies in them,
gypsy-looking women with hard worn faces, Indian
women with Marks and Spencers woolly cardigans
over lilac and gold and turquoise saris. Cars parked
everywhere, and vans double-parked on a street that
was littered with torn paper and bruised vegetables
and silvery fish scales where a market had just
packed up and gone. Half-past five. But very likely
that corner shop, Winter's, stayed open till all hours.
He went in, bought a packet of ham, a can of beans,
some bread, eggs, tea, margarine and frozen peas.
Carried along by a tide of homegoing commuters, he
returned to 142 Trinity Road. The house was no
longer empty.

A man of about fifty was standing by the hall table,
holding in his hand a bundle of cheap offer vouchers.
He was tallish, thin, with a thin, reddish and coarse-
skinned face. His thin, greyish-fair hair had been
carefully combed to conceal a bald patch and was
flattened with Brylcreem. He wore an immaculate
dark grey suit, a white shirt and a maroon tie dotted
with tiny silver spots. On his rather long, straight
and quite fleshless nose, were a pair of gold-rimmed
glasses. When he saw Anthony he jumped.

'These were on the mat,' he said. 'They come every
day. You wouldn't think there was a world paper
shortage, would you? I tidy them up. No one else
seems to be interested. But I hardly feel it's my place
to throw them away.'

Anthony wondered why he bothered to explain.

'I'm Anthony Johnson,' he said. 'I moved in today.'

The man said, 'Ah,' and held out his hand. He had

a rather donnish look as if he perhaps had been responsible for the naming of those streets. But his voice was uneducated, underlying the pedantic preciseness of Kenbourne Vale's particular brand of cockney. 'Moved into the little room at the back, have you? We keep ourselves very much to ourselves here. You won't use the phone after eleven, will you?'

Anthony asked where the phone was.

'On the first landing. My flat is on the second landing. I have a *flat*, you see, not a room.'

Light dawned. 'Are you by any chance the other Johnson?'

The man gave a severe, almost reproving, laugh. 'I think you must mean *you* are the other Johnson. I have been here for twenty years.'

Anthony could think of no answer to make to that one. He went into Room 2 and closed the door behind him. On this mild, still summery day the room with its pipe-hung brick ramparts was already growing dark at six. He switched on the jellyfish lamp and saw how the light radiated the whole of that small courtyard. Leaning out of the window, he looked upwards. In the towering expanse of brick above him there was only one other window, and that on the top floor. The frilly net curtains behind its panes twitched. Someone had looked down at him and at the light, but Anthony's knowledge of the geography of the house was as yet insufficient to tell him who that someone might be.

Every morning for the rest of that week, Arthur listened carefully for Anthony Johnson to go off to work. But Jonathan Dean and the Kotowskys always made so much noise over their own departures that it was difficult to tell. Certain it was, though, that Anthony Johnson remained at home in the evenings.

33

Peering downwards out of his bedroom window, Arthur saw the light in Room 2 come on each evening at about six, and could tell by the pattern of two yellow rectangles divided by a dark bar, which the light made on the concrete, that Anthony Johnson didn't draw his curtains. It was a little early for him to feel an urge to visit the cellar again, and yet he was already growing restless. He thought this restlessness had something to do with frustration, with knowing that he couldn't go down there however much he might want to.

On the Friday morning, while fetching in the post, he saw Anthony Johnson come out of Room 2 and go into the bathroom, wearing nothing but a pair of jeans. Didn't the man *go* to work? Was he going to stop in there all day and all night?

Among that particular batch of letters was the first one to come for Anthony Johnson. Arthur knew it was for him as it was postmarked York and written on the flap was the sender's name and address: Mrs R. L. Johnson, 22 West Highamgate, York. But the front of the envelope was addressed, quite ambiguously, to A. Johnson Esq., 2/142 Trinity Road, London W15 6HD. Arthur sucked in his lips with an expression of exasperation. And when, a minute or so later, Anthony Johnson re-emerged, smelling of toothpaste, Arthur pointed out to him the possible consequences of such impreciseness.

The young man took it very casually. 'It's from my mother. I'll tell her to put Room 2, if I think of it.'

'I hope you will think of it, Mr Johnson. This sort of thing could lead to a great deal of awkwardness and embarrassment.'

Anthony Johnson smiled, showing beautiful teeth. He radiated health and vigour and a kind of modest virility to an extent that made Arthur uncomfortable.

34

Besides, he didn't want to look at bare brown chests at ten past nine in the morning, thank you very much.

'A great deal of awkwardness,' he repeated.

'Oh, I don't think so. Let's not meet trouble half-way. I don't suppose I'll get many letters, and the ones I do get will either be postmarked York or Bristol.'

'Very well. I thought I should mention it and I have. Now you can't blame me if there is a Mix Up.'

'I shan't blame you.'

Arthur said no more. The man's manner floored him. It was so casual, so calm, so poised. He could have coped with defensiveness or a proper apology. This cool acceptance – no, it wasn't really cool, but warm and pleasant – of his approach was like nothing he had ever come across. It was almost as if Anthony Johnson were the older, wiser man, who could afford to treat such small local difficulties with indulgence.

Arthur was more than a little irritated by it. It would have served Anthony Johnson right if, when Arthur took the post in on the following Tuesday, he had torn open the letter from Bristol without a second thought. Of course he didn't do so, although the postmark was so faint as to be almost illegible and there was no sender's name on the flap. But this one, too, was addressed to A. Johnson Esq., 2/142 Trinity Road, London W15 6HD. The envelope was made of thick mauve-grey paper with a rough expensive-looking surface.

Arthur set it on the table on the extreme right-hand side, the position he had allotted to Anthony Johnson's correspondence, and then he went into the front garden to tidy up the mess inside, on top of and around the dustbin. The dustmen had now been on strike for two weeks. In the close sunless air the rubbish smelt sour and fetid. When he went back into the house the mauve-grey envelope had gone.

He didn't speculate about its contents or the identity of its sender. His concern with Anthony Johnson was simply to get some idea of the man's movements. But on the following evening, the last Wednesday of the month, he was to learn simultaneously partial answers to all these questions.

It was eight o'clock and dusk. Arthur had long finished his evening meal, washed the dishes, and was about to settle in front of his television. But he remembered leaving his bedroom window open. Auntie Gracie had always been most eloquent on the subject of night air and its evil effects. As he was pulling down the sash, taking care not to catch up the fragile border of the net curtain, he saw the light, shed on the court below, go out. Quickly he went to his front door, opened it and listened. But instead of leaving the house, Anthony Johnson was coming upstairs.

Arthur heard quite clearly the sound of the phone dial being spun. A lot of digits, not just the seven for London. And presently a lot of coins inserted ...

Anthony Johnson's voice: 'I'm taking it that the coast is clear, he's not listening on this extension and he won't come up here and shoot me in the morning.' A pause. Then, 'Of course I'm teasing you, my love. The whole business is sick.' Arthur listened intently. 'I had your letter. Darling, I need footnotes. You must be the only married lady who's ever quoted *The Pilgrim's Progress* in a letter to her lover. It was *Grace Abounding*? Then I do need footnotes.' A long, long pause. Anthony Johnson cursed, obviously because he had to put more money in.

'Shall I transfer the charges? No, of course I won't.

36

Roger would see it on the bill and so on and so on.'
Silence. Laughter. Another silence. Then: 'Term starts
a week today, but I'll only be going to a few lectures
that touch on my subject. I'm here most of the time,
working and – well, thinking, I suppose. Go out in
the evenings? Lovey, where would I go and who
would I go with?'

Arthur closed his door, doing this in the totally
silent way he had cultivated by long practice.

# Chapter 5

The air of West Kenbourne, never sweet, stank of rubbish. Sacks and bags and crates of rubbish made a wall along the pavement edge between the Water-lily and Kemal's Kebab House. Factory refuse and kitchen waste, leaking from broken cardboard boxes, cluttered Oriel Mews, and in Trinity Road the household garbage simmered, reeking, in the sultry sunlight.

'And we've only got one little dustbin,' Arthur said peevishly to Stanley Caspian.

'Wouldn't make any difference if we'd got ten, they'd be full up now. Can't you put your muck in one of those black bags the council send round?'

Arthur changed his tack. 'It's the principle of the thing. If these men insist on striking, other arrangements should be made. I pay my rates, I've got a right to have my waste disposed of. I shall write to the local authority. They might take notice of a strongly-worded letter from a ratepayer.'

'Pigs might fly if they'd got wings and then we shouldn't have any more pork.' Stanley roared with laughter. 'Which reminds me, I'm starving. Put the kettle on, me old Arthur.' He opened a bag of peanuts and another of hamburger-flavoured potato crisps. 'How's the new chap settling in?'

'Don't ask me,' said Arthur. 'You know I keep myself to myself.'

He made Stanley's coffee, asked for his envelope and went back upstairs. The idea of discussing Anthony Johnson was distasteful to him, and this was partly because any conversation in the hall might easily be overheard in Room 2. Stanley Caspian, of course, would be indifferent to that. Arthur wished he too could be indifferent, but there had crept upon him in the past few days a feeling that he must ingratiate himself with Anthony Johnson, not on any account offend him or win his displeasure. He now rather regretted his sharp words about the imprecise addressing of letters. Vague notions of having to become *friendly* – the very word distressed him – with Anthony Johnson were forming in his mind. For in this way he might perhaps persuade Anthony Johnson to draw his curtains when his light was on, or provide himself with a Venetian blind as an ostensible heat-retaining measure (Stanley Caspian would never provide one) or even succeed – and this would take much subtle and weary work – in convincing him that he, Arthur, had some legitimate occupation in the cellar, developing photographs, for instance, or doing carpentry.

But as he gathered up his laundry and stuffed it into the orange plastic carrier, he felt a fretful dismay. He didn't want to get involved with the man, he didn't want to get involved with anyone. How upsetting it was to have to *know* people, and how unnecessary it had been for twenty years!

*The psychopath is asocial – more than that, he is in positive conflict with society. Atavistic desires and a craving for excitement drive him. Self-centred, impulsive, he disregards society's taboos* ... Anthony had been making notes all the morning, but now as he heard Stanley Caspian leave the house, he laid down his

39

pen. Was there any point in beginning on his thesis before he had attended that particular lecture on criminology? On the other hand, there was so little else to do. The music from upstairs, which had been hindering his concentration for the past half-hour, now ceased and two doors slammed. So far he had met none of the other tenants but Arthur Johnson and, as fresh sound broke out, he went into the hall.

Two men were sitting on the stairs, presumably so that one of them, smallish with wild black hair, could do up his shoelaces. The other was chanting:

'Then trust me, there's nothing like drinking,
So pleasant on this side the grave.
It keeps the unhappy from thinking,
And makes e'en the valiant more brave!'

Anthony said hallo.

His shoelaces tied, the small dark man came down the stairs, extended his hand and said in a facetious way, 'Mr Johnson, I presume?'

'That's right. Anthony. The "other" Johnson.'

This remark provoked laughter out of all proportion to its wit. 'Put that on your doorbell, why don't you? Brian Kotowsky at your service, and this is Jonathan Dean, the best pal a man ever had.'

Another hand, large, red and hairy, was thrust out. 'We are about to give our right arms some exercise in a hostelry known to its habituates as the Lily, and were you to . . .'

'He means, come and have a drink.'

Anthony grinned and accepted, although he was already wondering if he would regret this encounter. Jonathan Dean slammed the front door behind them and remarked that this would shake old Caspian's ceilings up a bit. They crossed Trinity Road and

40

entered Oriel Mews, a cobbled passage whose cottages had all been converted into small factories and warehouses. The cobbles were coated with a smelly patina of potato peelings and coffee grounds, spilt from piled rubbish bags.

Anthony wrinkled his nose. 'Have you lived here long?'

'For ever and a day, but I'm soon to depart.'

'Leaving me alone with that she-devil,' said Brian. 'Without your moderating influence she'll kill me, she'll tear me to pieces.'

'Very right and proper. All the best marriages are like that. Not beds of roses but fields of battle. Look at Tolstoy, look at Lawrence.'

They were still looking at, and hotly discussing, Tolstoy and Lawrence, when they entered the Waterlily. It was crowded, smoky and hot. Anthony bought the first round, the wisest measure if one wants to make an early escape. His tentative question had been intended as a preamble to another and now, in the first brief pause, he asked it.

'What is there to do in this place?'

'Drink,' said Jonathan simply.

'I don't mean in here. I mean Kenbourne Vale.'

'Drink, dispute, make love.'

'There's the Taj Mahal,' said Brian. 'It used to be called the Odeon but now it only shows Indian films. Or there's Radclyffe Park. They have concerts in Radclyffe Hall.'

'Christ,' said Jonathan. 'Better make up your mind to it, Tony, there's nothing to do but drink. This place, the Dalmatian, the Hospital Arms, the Grand Duke. What more do you want?'

But before Anthony could answer him, a woman had flung into the pub and was leaning over them,

41

her fingers whose nails were very dirty, pressed on the table top. She addressed Brian.

'What the hell are you doing, coming here without me?'

'You were asleep,' said Brian. 'You were dead to the world.'

'In the rank sweat,' remarked Jonathan, 'of an enseamed bed.'

'Shut up and don't be so disgusting.' She levelled at him a look of scorn, such as women often reserve for those friends of their husbands who may be thought to exercise a corrupting influence. For that Brian was her husband Anthony was sure even before he waved a feeble hand and said, 'My wife, Vesta.'

She sat down. 'Your wife, Vesta, wants a drink, G. and T., a big one.' She took a cigarette from her own packet and Dean one from his, but instead of holding out his lighter to her, he lit his own cigarette and put the lighter away. Turning her back on him, she struck a match and inhaled noisily. Anthony regarded her with interest. She seemed to be in her mid-thirties and she looked as if she had come out without attempting to remove the 'rank sweat' of Jonathan Dean's too graphic description. Her naturally dark hair was hennaed and strands of the Medusa locks – it was as wild and unkempt as her husband's but much longer – had a vermilion metallic glint. A greasy-skinned, rather battered-looking face. Thin lips. Large red-brown angry eyes. A smell of patchouli oil. Her dress was long and of dark dirty Indian cotton, hung with beads and chains and partly obscured by a fringed red shawl. When Brian brought her gin, she clasped both her hands round the glass and stared intensely into the liquid like a clairvoyant looking into a crystal.

42

Three more beers had also arrived. Jonathan, having directed several more insulting but this time ineffectual remarks at Vesta – remarks which seemed to gratify rather than annoy her husband – began to talk of Li-li Chan. What a 'dish' she was. How he could understand those Empire builders who had deserted their pallid dehydrated wives for Oriental mistresses. Like little flowers they were. He hoped Anthony appreciated his luck in sharing a bathroom with Li-li. And so on. Anthony decided he had had enough of it for the time being. Years of living in halls and rooming houses and hostels had taught him the folly of making friends for the sake of making friends. Sooner or later the one or two you really want for your friends will turn up, and then you have the problem of ridding yourself of these stopgaps.

So when Brian began making plans for the evening, a mammoth pub crawl, he declined firmly. To his surprise, Jonathan also declined, he had some mysterious engagement, and Vesta too, suddenly becoming less zombie-like, said she was going out. Brian needn't start asking why or who with and all that. She was free, wasn't she? She hadn't got married to be harassed all the time and in public.

Anthony felt a little sorry for Brian whose spaniel face easily became forlorn. 'Some other time,' he said, and he meant it.

The sun was shining and the whole afternoon lay ahead of him. Radclyffe Park, he thought, and when the K.12 bus came along he got on it. The park was large and hardly any of it was formally laid-out. In a green space where the grass was dappled with the shadows of plane leaves, he sat down and re-read Helen's letter.

*Darling Tony, I knew I'd miss you but I didn't know how
bad it would be. I feel like asking, whose idea was this? But
I know we both came to it simultaneously and it's the only
way. Besides, neither of us is the sort of person who can be
happy in a clandestine thing, an intrigue. Being discreet
seems pointless to you, doesn't it, a squalid bore, and as for
me, I always hated lying to Roger. When you said – or was
it I who said it? – that it must be all or nothing, I, you,
we, were right.*

*But I can't be very good at lying because I know Roger
has sensed my defection. He has always been causelessly
jealous but he never actually did things about it. Now he's
started phoning me at work two or three times a day and
last week he opened two letters that came for me. One of
them was from my mother and the other was an invitation
to a dress show, but I couldn't get all upstage and
affronted virtue with him. How could I? After all, I do
have a lover, I have deceived him . . .*

A child, playing some distance off, gave his ball a
massive kick so that it landed at Anthony's feet. He
bowled it back. Funny, how people thought it was
only women who wanted to marry and have children of their own.

*I remember all the things you taught me, principles on
which to conduct one's life. Applied Existentialism. I tell
myself I am not responsible for any other adult person and
that I am not in this world to live up to Roger's
expectations. But I married him, Tony. Didn't I, in
marrying him, go a long way towards promising to be
responsible for his happiness? Didn't I more or less say
that he had a right to expect much from me? And he has
had so little, poor Roger. I never even pretended to love
him. I haven't slept with him for six months. I only*

*married him because he pressed me and pressed me and
wouldn't take my no ...*

Anthony frowned when he came to that bit. He
hated her weakness, her vacillations. There were
whole areas of her soft sensitive personality he didn't
begin to understand. But here was the Bunyan
passage – that made sense.

*So why don't I just tell him and walk out? – Leap off the
ladder even blindfold into eternity, sink or swim, come
heaven, come hell ... Fear, I suppose, and compassion.* But
sense that was too short-lived. *It's because at the
moment compassion is stronger than passion that I'm here
and you're alone in London ...* He folded the letter and
put it back in his pocket. He wasn't downcast, only
rather lonely, more than rather bored. In the end she
could come to him, her own feelings for him were
too strong to be denied. There had been things
between them she would remember in his absence,
and that memory, that hope of renewal, would be
stronger than any pity. In the meantime? He threw
back the child's ball once more, rolled over on his
side on the warm dry grass and slept.

The tube took Anthony one stop back to Kenbourne
Lane. At the station entrance a boy of about ten came
up to him and asked him for a penny for the guy.

'In *September*? A bit premature, aren't you?'

'Got to make an early start, mister,' said the boy,
'or someone else'll get my patch.'

Anthony laughed and gave him ten pence. 'I don't
see any guy.'

'That's what me and my friend are collecting for.
To get one.'

The children, those in the park, and the two at the

45

station, gave him an idea. A job for the evenings and
the occasional weekend afternoon, a job for which he
was admirably and thoroughly trained . . . It was six
o'clock. He let himself into Room 2, wrote his letter,
addressed an envelope and affixed a stamp to it. The
whole operation took no more than ten minutes, but
by the time it was done the room was so dark that he
had to put the jellyfish light on. Emerging, he
encountered Arthur Johnson in the hall, and Arthur
Johnson was also holding a letter in his hand.
Anthony would have passed him with no more than
a smile and a 'good evening', but the 'other' Johnson
– or was that he? – turned, almost barring his
passage, and fixed him with an intense, anxious and
almost hungry look.

'May I enquire if you are going out for the
evening, Mr Johnson, or merely to the post?'

'Just to the post,' Anthony said, surprised.

The hopeful light in the other man's eyes seemed
to die. And yet why should he care one way or the
other? Perhaps, on the other hand, that was the
answer he had wanted, for now he held out his hand,
smiling with a kind of forced bonhomie, and said
ingratiatingly:

'Then, since I am going there myself, let me have
the pleasure of taking your letter.'

'Thanks,' Anthony said. 'That's nice of you.'

Arthur Johnson took the letter and, without
another word, left the house, closing the front door
silently and with painstaking care behind him.

46

# Chapter 6

The dustmen's strike had ended, Arthur read in his paper, on the last Monday of September. Two days later, on the first Wednesday of October, he heard the crashing of lids, the creak of machinery and the (to his way of thinking) lunatic ripostes of the men, that told him Trinity Road was at last being cleared of refuse. He might have saved himself the trouble of writing to the local authority. Still, such complaints kept them on their toes; they had replied promptly enough. The brown envelope was marked: London Borough of Kenbourne and addressed to A. Johnson Esq., 2/142 Trinity Road, London W15 6HD. Arthur put it in his pocket. The rest of the post, a shoe shop advertising circular for Li-li Chan and a mauve-grey envelope, postmarked Bristol, for Anthony Johnson, he arranged in their appropriate positions on the hall table.

They were all out but for himself. From the phone call he had overheard, Arthur knew Anthony Johnson would be going off to college or whatever it was today, but he was relieved to have had assurance made doubly sure by the sight of the 'other' Johnson, viewed from his living room window, departing at five past nine for the tube station. Not that it was of much practical assistance to him, as he too must go to work in ten minutes; it was simply comforting to know the man went out sometimes. It was a beginning.

He went back upstairs and slit the letter open with one of Auntie Gracie's silver fruit knives. *London Borough of Kenbourne, Department of Social Services.* Well, he'd have expected to hear from the sanitary inspector but you never could tell these days.

*Dear Sir, in reply to your letter of the 28th inst., requesting information as to the availability of work in children's play centres within the Borough, we have to inform you that such centres would come under the auspices of the Inner London Education Authority and are not our ...*

Arthur realized what had happened and he was appalled. That he – he out of the two of them – should be the one to open a letter in error! It would have mattered so much less if it had been someone else's letter, that giggly little Chinese piece, for instance, or that drunk, Dean. Obviously the letter must be returned. Arthur was so shaken by what he had done that he couldn't bring himself to write the necessary note of apology on the spot. Besides, it would make him late for work. It was nearly a quarter past nine. He put the envelope and its contents into his empty briefcase and set off.

The demolition men were at work and Auntie Gracie's living room – brown lincrusta, marble fireplace, pink linoleum – all exposed to the public view. There on the ochre-coloured wallpaper was the paler rectangle marking where the sideboard had stood, the sideboard into whose drawer he had shut the mouse. His first killing. Auntie Gracie had died in that room, and from it he had gone out to make death ... Why think of all that now? He felt sick. He unlocked the gates and let himself into his office, wishing there was some way of insulating the place from the sounds of hammer blows and falling masonry, but by the time Barry lounged in at a quarter to ten, he was already composing the first draft of a note to Anthony Johnson.

Fortunately, there was very little correspondence for Grainger's that day, the books were in apple pie order and well up to date. Arthur found the task before him exacting, and one draft after another went into the wastepaper basket. But by one o'clock the letter – handwritten, as typewritten notes were discourteous – was as perfect a specimen of its kind as he could achieve.

*Dear Mr Johnson, please accept my heartfelt apologies for having opened your letter in error. Considering the gravity of this intrusion into your private affairs, I think it only proper to give you a full explanation. I was myself expecting a letter from the council of the London Borough of Kenbourne in reply to one of my own requesting action to be taken with regard to the disgraceful situation concerning the cessation of a regular refuse collection. Reading the Borough's name on the envelope, I opened it without more ado only to find that the communication was intended for your good self. Needless to say, I did not read more than was strictly necessary to inform me that I was not the proper recipient. In hopes that you will be kind enough to overlook what was, in fact, a genuine mistake, I am, Yours sincerely, Arthur Johnson.*

Who could tell what time Anthony Johnson would return? Arthur let himself into a hundred and forty-two at 1.15. The house was silent, empty, and the mauve-grey envelope was still on the hall table. Beside it, neatly aligned to it, Arthur placed the

Kenbourne council letter and his own note, the two fastened together with a paper clip. When he returned from work just before five-thirty all the letters were still there and the house was still empty.

Alone in his flat, he began to speculate as to Anthony Johnson's reaction. Perhaps the whole incident would turn out to be a blessing in disguise. Anthony Johnson would read his note, be moved by its earnest rectitude, and come immediately upstairs to tell Arthur he quite understood and not to give it another thought. This would be his chance. He put the kettle on, set a tray with the best china, and left his front door on the latch so that Anthony Johnson would know he was expected and welcomed. For, irksome as it was to entertain someone and make conversation, it was now of paramount importance. And how wonderful if, in the course of that conversation, Anthony Johnson should announce his intention of securing an evening job – as the letter had intimated he might.

He sat by the window, looking down. Li-li Chan was the first to get home. She arrived with a different young man in a green sports car, and ten minutes after they got into the house Arthur heard her on the phone.

'No, no, I tell you I very sorry.' Li-li almost, but not quite, said 'velly'. 'You give theatre ticket some other nice girl. I wash my hair, stay in all night. Oh, but you are so silly. I don't love you because I wash my hair? I say I do love you, I love lots, lots of people, so good-bye now!'

Arthur craned his neck to see her and her escort leap into the car and roar off in the direction of Kenbourne Lane. He waited. Vesta Kotowsky came in alone, looking sulky. There was one, Arthur thought, who could do with an evening at home to get that draggled greasy hair washed. At five past six Anthony Johnson emerged from under the arched entrance to Oriel Mews. And as Arthur watched him approach, the tall well-proportioned figure, the firm-featured handsome face, the mane of hair crowning a shapely head, he felt a stirring of something that was part envy, part resentment. Yet this wasn't evoked by the 'other' Johnson's good looks – hadn't he, Arthur, had just as great a share of those himself? – or by his occupancy of Room 2. Rather it was that there, in the process of its mysterious unfair work-ings, fate had been kinder. Fate hadn't saddled this man with a propensity that placed his life and liberty at constant risk . . .

The front door of the house closed with a thud mid-way between Arthur's pernickety click and Jonathan Dean's ceiling-splitting crash. Ten minutes went by, a quarter of an hour, half an hour. Arthur was on tenterhooks. It was getting almost too late for tea. Time he started cooking his meal. The idea of anyone even tapping at the door, let alone coming in, while he was eating was unthinkable. Should he go down himself? Perhaps. Perhaps he should reinforce his note with a personal appearance and a personal apology.

A car door slammed. He rushed back to the window. It was the Kotowsky car, and Brian Kotow-sky and Jonathan Dean got out of it. There followed a resounding crash of the front door. A long pause of silence and then a single set of footsteps mounted the stairs. Could it be at last . . . ? But, no. Dean's door banged beneath him.

Very uneasy now, Arthur stood at the window. And again Brian Kotowsky appeared. Arthur caught his breath in sharply as he saw Anthony Johnson also emerge from the house. He looked reluctant, even irritable.

'All right,' Arthur heard him say, 'but it'll have to be a quick one. I've got work to do.'

They crossed the road, bound for the Waterlily. Arthur crept down the first flight. A low murmur of voices could be heard from Jonathan Dean's room and then a soft throaty laugh. He went on down. From over the banisters he saw that the hall table was bare but for the inevitable cheap offer vouchers. Li-li Chan's shoe shop circular and the two envelopes for Anthony Johnson had gone. Arthur stood by the table, nonplussed. Then some screws of paper lying in Stanley Caspian's wastepaper basket caught his eye. He picked them out. They were the note he had written with such care and anxiety to Anthony Johnson and the envelope in which the council's letter had been contained.

The Inner London Education Authority told Anthony that they couldn't possibly say over the phone whether they had a vacancy for him or not. Would he write in? He wrote and got a very belated reply full of delaying tactics which amounted to telling him that he had better apply again at Christmas. At least the Kenbourne authority had replied promptly. Anthony smiled ruefully to himself when he recalled the evening on which he had received their reply. It had been fraught with annoyance.

Firstly had come that letter from Helen, a letter which was more like an essay on Roger's miseries. *I sit reading escapist literature and every time I look up I find his eyes on me, staring accusingly, and every little innocent remark I make he takes me up on ('What's that supposed to mean?' 'What are you getting at?') so that I feel like some wretched shoplifter being interrogated by the great detective. I started to cry last night and – Oh, it was awful – he began to cry too. He knelt at my feet and begged me to love him* ... Anthony had been so exasperated by this letter which, in his delight at receiving it, he had stood reading out in the hall by the table, that it was some minutes before he had even noticed that there was another one for him. And when he did, when he opened and read that ridiculous note from Arthur Johnson, his impatience had reached such a pitch that he had screwed it up and tossed it into the wastepaper basket. It was at this point that Brian Kotowsky had arrived and, deserted by the best pal a man ever had, had pressed him to accompany him to the Waterlily. There Anthony had been obliged to listen to a dissertation on the horrors of matrimony, the undesirable independence having a job of her own gave to a wife, and what Brian would do after Jonathan's departure he honestly didn't know. Obliged to listen, but not for more than half an hour.

Returning alone to a hundred and forty-two Anthony considered going upstairs to reassure Arthur Johnson. The man obviously had an acute anxiety neurosis. A better-adjusted person would simply have scribbled *Sorry I opened your letter* and left it at that. The circumlocutions, the polysyllabic words were pathetic. They breathed a tense need for the preservation of an immaculate ego, they smelt of paranoia, fear of retribution, a desire to be thought well of by all men, even strangers. But men like that, he thought, cannot be reassured, their deep-seated belief in their own worthlessness is too great and too long-established at fifty for self-confidence ever to be implanted in them. Besides, Arthur Johnson liked to keep himself to himself, and would probably only be further perturbed by an invasion of his privacy.

Much better wait until they happened to meet in the hall.

In the week which followed he didn't encounter Arthur Johnson but he was again accosted by the children at Kenbourne Lane station.

'Penny for the guy, mister?'

'Where are you going to have your bonfire?' asked Anthony. 'In Radclyffe Park?' He handed over another ten pence.

'We asked. The park keeper won't let us, rotten old bastard. We could have it in our back yard if my dad lets us.'

'Old Mother Winter,' said the other boy, 'got the cops last time your dad had a bonfire.'

Anthony went off down Magdalen Hill. The kids and their parents called it Mag-da-lene, just as they called Balliol Street Bawlial. How stupid these pseudo-intellectuals were – Jonathan Dean was one of them – to sneer at mispronunciations. If the people who lived here hadn't the right to call their streets what they wanted, who had? His eye was caught by the piece of waste ground, enclosed by its rusty tennis court netting. The authorities wouldn't let him do official social work, but why shouldn't he do some privately and off his own bat? Why not, in fact, think about organizing November 5th celebrations on that bit of ground? The idea was suddenly appealing. He gazed through the wire at the hillocky weed-grown wilderness. On one side of it was the cutting through which the tube ran down to London, on the other the mountains of brown brick, broken woodwork and yellow crumbled plaster which was all that remained now of the demolished houses. Backing on to the ground rose the grey-brown rears of Brasenose Avenue terraces, tall tenements hung

54

with Piranesi-like iron stairways. A man seen building a bonfire there would soon attract all the juvenile society in the neighbourhood. And he could rope in the parents, mothers especially, to organize a supper. The great Kenbourne Vale Guy Fawkes Rave-up, he thought. Why, he might set a precedent and they'd start having one there every year.

It was six o'clock on a Friday evening, Friday, October 10th. If he was going to do it he'd better start on the organization tomorrow. Work tonight, though. Seated at the table in Room 2, its gateleg propped up with Arieti's *The Intrapsychic Self*, Anthony assembled and read his notes.

*Not to be classified as schizophrenic, manic-depressive or paranoid. Condition cannot strictly be allied to any of these. Psychopath characteristically unable to form emotional relationships. If these are formed – fleetingly and sporadically – purpose is direct satisfaction of own desires. Guiltless and loveless. Psychopath has learned few socialized ways of coping with frustrations. Those he has learned (e.g. a preoccupation with 'hard' pornography) may be themselves at best grotesque. For his actions . . .*

With a sudden fizzle, the light bulb in the jellyfish shade went out.

Anthony cursed. For a few moments he sat there in the dark, wondering whether to appeal for help from Jonathan or the Kotowskys. But that would only involve him in another drinking session. The gentle closing of the front door a minute or two before had told him of Li-li's departure. He'd have to go out and buy another light bulb. Just as well Winter's didn't close till eight.

Making for the front door, he was aware of footsteps on the landing above him. Arthur Johnson. But as he hesitated, glancing up the stairs – now might be an opportunity for that belated reassurance

– he saw the figure of which he had only caught a glimpse retreat. Anthony shrugged and went off in search of his light bulb.

# Chapter 7

Arthur was certain he had given mortal offence to Anthony Johnson and thus had wrecked his own hopes. Now there was nothing for it but to watch and wait. Sooner or later the 'other' Johnson must go out in the evening. He went out by day on Saturdays and Sundays all right, but what was the use of that? It was darkness that Arthur needed, darkness to give the illusion that the side passage, the courtyard, the cellar, were the alley, the mews, the deserted shadowed space that met his desires. Darkness and the absence of noisy people, car doors slamming, interference . . .

He could remember quite precisely when this need had first come upon him. The need to use darkness. He was twelve. Auntie Gracie had had two friends to tea and they were sitting in the back round the fire, drinking from and eating off that very china he had set out in vain for Anthony Johnson. Talking about him. He would have liked, as he would often have liked, to retreat to his own bedroom. But this was never allowed except at bedtime when, as soon as he was in bed, Auntie Gracie would turn off the light at the switch just inside the door and forbid him on pain of punishment to turn it on again. The landing light was always left on, so Arthur wasn't afraid. He would have preferred, in fact longed for, enough light to read by or else total darkness.

57

Mrs Goodwin and Mrs Courthope, those were the friends' names. Arthur had to sit being good, being a credit to Auntie Gracie. They talked a lot about some unnamed boy he supposed must be himself from the mysterious veiled way they spoke and the heavy meaningful glances exchanged.

'Of course it puts a stigma on a child he can never shake off,' Mrs Goodwin said.

Instead of answering, Auntie Gracie said, 'Go into the other room, Arthur, and get me another teaspoon out of the sideboard. One of the best ones, mind, with the initial on.'

Arthur went. He didn't close the door after him but one of them closed it. The hall light was on so he didn't put on the front room light, and as a result he opened the wrong drawer by mistake. As he did so a mouse scuttered like a flash across the sideboard top and slithered into the open drawer. Arthur slammed it shut. He took an initialled spoon out of the other drawer and stood there, holding the spoon, his heart pounding. The mouse rushed around inside the drawer, running in desperate circles, striking its head and body against the wooden walls of its prison. It began to squeak. The cheep-cheep sounds were like those made by a baby bird, but they were sounds of pain and distress. Arthur felt a tremendous deep satisfaction that was almost happiness. It was dark and he was alone and he had enough power over something to make it die.

Strangely enough, the women didn't seem to have missed him, although he had been gone for quite five minutes. They stopped talking abruptly when he came in. After Mrs Goodwin and Mrs Courthope had gone, Auntie Gracie washed up and Arthur dried. She sent him to put the silver away which was just as well, because if she had gone she would have heard the mouse. It had stopped squeaking and was making vague brushing, scratching sounds, feeble and faint. Arthur didn't open the drawer. He listened to the sounds with pleasure. When he did at last open it on the following evening, the mouse was dead and the drawer, which contained a few napkin rings and a spare cruet, spattered all over with its blood. Arthur had no interest in the corpse. He let Auntie Gracie find it a week or so later, which she did with many shrieks and shudders.

Darkness. He thought often in those days of the mouse afraid and trapped in the dark and of himself powerful in it. How he longed to be allowed out in the streets after dark! But even when he was at work and earning Auntie Gracie wanted him to come straight home. And he had to please her, he had to be worthy of her. Besides, defiance of her was too enormous an enterprise even to consider. So he went out in the evenings only when she went with him, and once a week they went together to the Odeon that was now Indian and called the Taj Mahal. Until one night when old Mr Grainger, catching him in the yard as he was sweeping up at five-thirty, sent him over to the other side of Kenbourne to pick up an electric drill some workman had been careless enough to leave behind in a house where he was doing a re-wiring job. He'd tell Miss Johnson on his way home, he told Arthur, and he was to cut along as fast as he could.

Arthur collected the drill. The darkness – it was midwinter – was even lovelier than he thought it would be. And how very dark it was then, how much darker than nowadays! The blackout. The pitch darkness of wartime. In the dark he brushed against people, some of whom carried muffled torches. And in a winding little lane, now destroyed and lost, replaced by a mammoth housing complex, he came up against a girl hurrying. What had made him touch her? Ah, if he knew that he would know the answer to many things. But he had touched her, putting out his hand, for he was already as tall as a man, to run one finger down the side of her warm neck. Her scream as she fled was more beautiful in his ears than the squeaking of the mouse. He stared after her, into the darkness after her, emotion surging within him like thick scented liquid boiling. He knew what he wanted to do, but thought intervened to stay him. He had read the newspapers, listened to the wireless, and he knew what happened to people who wanted what he wanted. No doubt, it was better not to go out after dark. Auntie Gracie knew best. It was almost as if she had known why, though that was nonsense, for she had never dreamed ...

His own dreams had been troubling him this past fortnight, the consequence of frustration. Each evening at eleven, before going to bed, he had taken a last look out of his bedroom window to see the courtyard below aglow with light from Room 2. It seemed a personal affront and, in a way, a desecration of the place. Moreover, Anthony Johnson hadn't been near him, had avoided all contact with him. Arthur wouldn't have known he was in the house but for the arrival, and the subsequent removal from the hall table, of another of those Bristol letters, and of course that ever-burning light.

Then, on a Friday evening just before eight, it went out. Carrying his torch, Arthur let himself out of his flat and came softly down the top flight. He had heard the front door close, but that might have been Li-li Chan going out. Both she and Anthony Johnson closed it with the same degree of moderate care. And it must have been she, for as Arthur hesitated on the landing he saw Anthony Johnson appear in the hall below him. Arthur stepped back and immediately the front door closed. Through its red and green glass panels the shape of Anthony Johnson could be seen as a blur vanishing down the marble steps. No one, Arthur reasoned, went out at this hour if he didn't intend to stay out for some time. He descended the stairs and, delaying for a moment or two to let the occupant of Room 2 get clear, left the house, crossed the lawn and entered the side passage.

There was no moon. The darkness wasn't total but faintly lit by the far-reaching radiance of street lamps and house lights, and the sky above, a narrow corridor of it, was a gloomy greyish-red; the darkness, in fact, of any slum backwater. And this passage resembled, with the colouring of Arthur's imagination, some alleyway, leading perhaps from a high road to a network of shabby streets. The muted roar of traffic was audible, but this only heightened his illusion. He crossed the little court, all the muscles of his body tense and tingling, and opened the cellar door.

It was three weeks since he had been here, and being here at last after so much dread and anguish brought him a more than usually voluptuous pleasure. Even more than usual, it was nearly as good as the real thing, as Maureen Cowan and Bridget O'Neill. So he walked slowly between the jumbled metal rubbish, the stacks of wood and newspapers, his torch making a quivering light which snaked ahead of him. And there, in the third room, she was waiting.

His reactions to her varied according to his mood and his tensions. Sometimes she was no more than the instrument of his therapy, a quick assuagement.

But there were times, and this was one of them, when strain and memory had so oppressed him and anticipation been so urgent that the whole scene and she in it were altered and aggrandized by enormous fantasy. So it was now. This was no cellar in Trinity Road but the deserted, seldom-frequented yard between a warehouse, say, and a cemetery wall; she no lifesize doll but a real woman waiting perhaps for her lover. The light of his torch fell on her. It lit her blank eyes, then, deflecting, allowed shadows to play like fear on her face. He stood still, but he could have sworn she moved. There was no sanctuary for her, no escape, nothing but the brick wall rising behind her to a cracked cobweb-hung sky. His torch became a street lamp, shining palely now from a corner. On an impulse he put it out. Absolute silence, absolute darkness. She was trying to get away from him. She must be, for as he felt his way towards the wall he couldn't find her.

He touched the damp brickwork, and a trickle of water fell between his fingers. He moved them along the wall, feeling for her, grunting now, making strong gruff exhalations. Then his hand touched her dress, moved up to her cold neck. But it felt warm to him and soft, like Bridget O'Neill's. Was it he or she who gave that choking stifled cry? This time he used his tie to strangle her, twisting it until his hands were sore.

It took Arthur a long time to recover – about ten minutes, which was much longer than usual. But the deed had been more exciting and more satisfying than usual, so that was only to be expected. He restored her to her position against the wall, picked up the torch and made his way back to the cellar door. Cautiously he opened it. The window of Room 2 was still dark. Good. Excellent.

He stepped out into the yard, turned to close the door behind him. As he did so the whole court was suddenly flooded with light. And this light was as terrifying to him as the beam of a policeman's torch is to a burglar. He wanted to wheel round, but he forced himself to turn slowly, expecting to meet the eyes of Anthony Johnson.

At first he saw only the interior of Room 2, the pale green flecked walls, the gateleg table propped by and piled with books, the primrose washbasin and that light glowing inside the pink and green polythene shade which, for some reason, was swinging like a pendulum. Then Anthony Johnson appeared under the swinging lamp, crossing the room; now, at last, staring straight back at him. Arthur didn't wait. He hastened across the court, his head bent, a burning flush mounting across his head and neck. He scuttled through the passage, let himself into the house and went swiftly upstairs.

There, in his own flat, he sat down heavily. Vesta Kotowsky had come up in his absence and pushed her rent under his door, but he was so upset he let the envelope lie there on the doormat. His hands were trembling. Anthony Johnson had returned within less than half an hour of going out. It almost looked as if the whole exercise had been a plot to catch Arthur. But how could he know? He would know now or know something. Probably he was looking for some way of getting back at him for opening that letter. On the face of it, that letter hadn't seemed very private, not like the ones postmarked Bristol would be, but you never could tell. It might be that this college of his had some sort of rule about students not taking jobs – Arthur admitted to himself that he knew very little about these things – and that he would be expelled or sent down or whatever they

63

called it for attempting to do so. After all, what else could explain Anthony Johnson's enraged rejection of his note, his deliberate shunning of him, his sneaking out like that followed by his purposeful illumination of the courtyard just as Arthur was emerging from the cellar?

The euphoria he felt after one of his killings totally ruined, Arthur passed a bad night. He sweated profusely so that he fancied the pink sheets smelt bad, and he stripped them off in a frenzy of disgust. Li-li had put her rent envelope under his door at some time in the small hours. By half-past nine he had assembled hers, the two envelopes of the Kotowskys' – Vesta insisted on paying her half-share separately from that of her husband – and his own and was seated downstairs waiting for Stanley Caspian. No more rent from Jonathan Dean who would be leaving today, thank God, and none to collect (thank God again) from Anthony Johnson who had paid two months in advance.

The hall was cold and damp. It was a foggy morning, an early harbinger of the winter to come. Stanley stumped in at ten past ten, wearing a checked windcheater that looked as if it was made from a car rug, and carrying a huge cellophane bag containing cheese puff cocktail snacks. Arthur began to feel queasy because the cheese puffs, orangey-brown, fat and curvy, reminded him of overfed maggots.

Stanley split the bag open before he had even sat down, and some of the cheese larvae spilt out on to the desk.

'Put the kettle on, me old Arthur. Have a Wiggly-Woggly?'

'No, thank you,' said Arthur quietly. He cleared his throat. 'I was down the cellar last night.' Forcing the carefully planned lie out with all the casualness he could muster, he said, 'Looking for a screwdriver, as a matter of fact. The wires had come out of one of my little electric plugs.'

Stanley looked at him truculently. 'You're always grumbling these days, Arthur. First it was the dustbin, now it's the electricity. I suppose that's your way of saying I ought to have the place re-wired.'

'Not at all. I was simply explaining how I happened to be in the cellar. In case – well, in case anyone might think I was snooping.'

Stanley picked cheese puff crumbs off the bulge of his belly whose ridges seemed as if they had been artfully designed to catch everything their possessor spilt. 'I couldn't care less if you go down the cellar, me old Arthur. Have yourself a ball. Ask some girls round. If you like spending your evenings in cellars that's your business. Right?'

Somehow, though he had intended wit, Stanley had got very near the truth. Arthur blushed. He was almost trembling. It was all he could do to control himself while Stanley filled in his rent book, banging in the full stops until it looked as if he would break his pen. Arthur put it back in its envelope himself and, muttering his usual excuse about Saturday being a busy day, made for the stairs. Half-way up them, he heard Anthony Johnson come out of Room 2 and use to Stanley – in mockery? He must have been listening behind the door – his own words of a few moments before:

'I was down your cellar last night.'

# Chapter 8

Winter's being out of stock of all but forty watt light bulbs, Anthony had been obliged to go as far as the open-till-midnight supermarket at the northern end of Kenbourne Lane. This unsettled him for work, and when he saw Arthur Johnson coming out of the cellar its possibilities intrigued him. He had penetrated no further than the first room, but that was enough.

Stanley Caspian burst into gales of laughter. 'I suppose you were looking for a screw?'

Anthony shrugged. Bawdy talk from a man of Caspian's age and girth disgusted him. 'You've got a lot of wood and cardboard and stuff down there,' he said. 'If you don't want it, can I have it? It's for a Guy Fawkes bonfire.'

'Help yourself,' said Stanley Caspian. 'Everyone's got very interested in my cellar all of a sudden, I must say. You weren't planning to have this here bonfire on my premises, I hope?'

Anthony said no, thanks, it wasn't suitable, which didn't seem the reply to gratify Caspian, and left him to his rents. He walked over to the station where the little boys were once more at their post, and with them this time a black child. The white children knew him by now. Instead of asking for money, they said hallo.

'Why don't we have a bonfire on that bit of waste ground?' But even as he spoke he checked himself.

Wasn't that the insinuating approach a child molestor would use? 'If you like the idea,' he said quickly, 'we'll go and talk to your parents about it.'

Leroy, the coloured boy, lived with his mother in a ground floor flat in Brasenose Avenue. Linthea Carville turned out to be a part-time social worker, which gave her an immediate affinity with Anthony, though he would in any case have been drawn to her. He couldn't help staring at her, this tall daughter of African gods, with her pearly-bloomed dark face, and her black hair, oiled and satiny, worn in a heavy knot on the crown of her head. But he remembered his plan, explained it, and within ten minutes they had been joined by white neighbours, the chairman of the Brasenose Tenants' Association, and by the mother of Leroy's taller friend, Steve.

The chairman was enthusiastic about Anthony's idea. For months his association had been campaigning for the council to convert the waste ground into a children's playground. This would be a feather in its cap. They could have a big party on 5th November and maybe invite a council representative to be present. Linthea said she would make hot dogs and enlist the help of another friend, the mother of David, the third boy. And when Anthony told them about the wood, Steve said his elder brother had a box barrow which he could bring over to a hundred and forty-two on the following Saturday.

Then they discussed the guy Steve's mother said she would dress in a discarded suit of her husband's. Linthea made lots of strong delicious coffee, and it was nearly lunchtime before Anthony went back to Trinity Road. He had forgotten that this was the day of Jonathan Dean's departure. The move, he now saw, was well under way. Jonathan and Brian were carrying crates down the stairs and packing them into Brian's rather inadequate car. Vesta was nowhere to be seen.

'I'll give you a hand,' Anthony said, and regretted the offer when Brian slapped him on the back and remarked that after Jonathan had deserted him he would know where to turn for a pal.

Jonathan, like Anthony, possessed no furniture of his own but he had hundreds of records and quite a few books, the heaviest and most thumbed of which was the *Oxford Dictionary of Quotations*. While they worked and ate the fish and chips Brian had been sent out to buy, the record player remained on, and the laughter sequence from Strauss's *Elektra* roared out so maniacally that Anthony expected Arthur Johnson to appear at any moment and complain. But he didn't appear even when Jonathan dropped a crate of groceries on the stairs and collapsed in fits of mirth at the sight of egg yolk and H.P. Sauce and extended life milk dripping from the treads.

They had to make several journeys. Jonathan's new home was a much smaller room that the one he had occupied at a hundred and forty-two, in a squalid run-down house in the worst part of South Kenbourne. And this alternative to Trinity Road seemed to perplex Brian as much as it did Anthony. What had possessed Jonathan? he kept asking. Why not change his mind even at this late stage? Caspian would surely let him keep his old room if he asked.

'No, he wouldn't,' said Jonathan. 'He's let it to some Spade.' And he added, like Cicero but less appositely, *'O tempora! O mores!'*

The record player was the last thing to be shifted. A container was needed in which to transport it so Brian and Anthony went down to Anthony's room where Anthony said he had found a cardboard box in the wardrobe. The books impressed Brian and soon he had found out all about Anthony's thesis, taking up much the same attitude to it as he would have done had he learned Anthony was writing a thriller.

'There's a study for you,' he said as they drove past the cemetery. 'You could use that in your writing. Twenty-five years ago last month that's where the Kenbourne Killer strangled his first victim. Maureen Cowan, she was called.'

'What, in the cemetery?'

'No, in the path that runs along the back of it. A lot of people use that path as a short cut from the Hospital Arms to Elm Green station. She was a tart, soliciting down there. Mind you, I was only a kid at the time but I remember it all right.'

'Kid?' said Jonathan. 'You mean you're *kidding*. You were thirteen.'

Brian looked hurt but he made no response. 'They never caught the chap. He struck again' – he employed the journalese quite unconsciously as if it were standard usage – 'five years later. That time it was a student nurse called Bridget Something. Irish girl. He strangled her on a bit of open ground between the hospital and the railway bridge. Now would he be a psychopath, Tony?'

'I suppose so. Was it the same man both times?'

'The cops thought so. But there were never any more murders – not unsolved ones, I mean. Now why, Tony, would you say that was?'

'Moved out of the district,' said Anthony who was getting bored. 'Or died,' he added, for he had been less than a year old when that first murder was committed.

'Could have been in prison for something else,' said Brian. 'Could have been in a mental home. I've often wondered about that and whether he'll ever come back and strike again.' He parked the car outside Jonathan's new home. 'What a dump! You could still change your mind, Jon old man. Move in with Vesta and me for a bit. Have our couch.'

'Christ,' said Jonathan. 'There's one born every minute.' He delivered this platitude as if it were a quotation, as, perhaps, Anthony thought, it was.

They invited him to accompany them to the Grand Duke for an evening's drinking, but Anthony refused. It was nearly five. He went home and read J. G. Miller's doctoral dissertation: *Eyeblink Conditioning of Primary and Neurotic Psychopaths*, remembering at ten to put his clock and his watch back. It was the end of British Summertime.

Watching from his eyrie, his living room window, Arthur saw the new tenant of Room 3 arrive on Sunday afternoon. At first he thought this must be some visitor, a disreputable friend perhaps of Li-li or Anthony Johnson, for he couldn't recollect any previous tenant having arrived in such style. The man was as black as the taxi from which he alighted, and not only black of skin and hair. He wore a black leather coat which, even from that distance, Arthur could see had cost a lot of money, and he carried two huge black leather suitcases. To Arthur's horrified eyes, he resembled some Haitian gangster-cum-political bigwig. He had seen such characters on television and he wouldn't have been surprised to learn that a couple of revolvers and a knife were concealed under that flashy coat.

Staying here obviously, but as whose guest? Arthur put his own front door on the latch and listened. The house door closed quietly, footsteps crossed the hall, mounted the stairs. He peeped out in time to see a sepia-coloured hand adorned with a plain gold signet ring insert a key in the lock of Room 3. He was incensed. Once again Stanley Caspian hadn't bothered to tell him he'd let a room. Once again he had been slighted. For two pins he'd write a strongly-worded letter to Stanley, complaining of ill-usage. But what would be the use? Stanley would only say Arthur hadn't given him the chance to tell him, and it was vain to grumble about the new man's colour with this Race Relations Act restricting landlords the way it did.

On Tuesday Arthur learned his name. He took in the letters, a whole heap of them this morning. One for Li-li from Taiwan, sender Chan Ah Feng; two for Anthony Johnson, one postmarked York, the other, in a mauve-grey envelope, Bristol. *Her* letters, Arthur had noted, always came on a Tuesday or a Wednesday, and were still addressed to A. Johnson Esq., 2/142 Trinity Road. Mrs R. L. Johnson, however, had learned sense and put Room 2. All the other correspondence, five official-looking envelopes, was for Winston Mervyn Esq., 3/142 Trinity Road. Winston! The cheek of it, some West Indian grandchildren of slaves christening their son after the greatest Englishman of the century! It seemed to Arthur an added effrontery that this presumptuous black should receive letters so soon after his arrival – five letters to fill up the table and make him look important.

But he didn't see the new tenant or hear a sound from him, though nightly he listened for voodoo drums.

As Anthony had expected, the departure of Jonathan Dean was the signal for Brian to put on the pressure. He was marked to succeed Jonathan, and evening after evening there came a knock on the door of

71

Room 2 and a plaintive invitation to go drinking in the Lily.

'I do have to work,' Anthony said after the fourth time of asking. 'Sorry, but that's the way it is.'

Brian gave him his beaten spaniel look. 'I suppose the fact is you don't like me. I bore you. Go on, you may as well admit it. I *am* a bore. I ought to know it by now, Vesta's told me often enough.'

'Since you ask,' said Anthony, 'yes, it'd bore me going out and getting pissed every night. And I can't afford it.' He relented a little. 'Come in here for a while tomorrow night, if you like. I'll get some beer in.'

Brightening, Brian said he was a pal, and turned up at seven sharp on the Friday with a bottle of vodka and one of French vermouth which made Anthony's six cans of beer look pathetic. He talked dolefully about his job – he sold antiques in a shop owned by Vesta's brother – about the horrors of living always in furnished rooms, Vesta's refusal to have children even if they got a house, her perpetual absences in the evenings – worse than ever this week – his drink problem, and did Anthony think he was an alcoholic?

Anthony let him talk, replying occasionally in monosyllables. He was thinking about Helen's latest letter. It was all very well to talk of absence making the heart grow fonder, but 'out of sight, out of mind' may be just as true a truism. He hadn't expected her letters to concentrate quite so much on Roger's woes. Roger had scarcely been mentioned during that summer of snatched meetings, that clandestine fortnight of love when a shadowy husband had been away somewhere on a business trip. Now it was Roger, Roger, Roger. *I ask myself if it wouldn't be better for both of us to try and forget each other. We could, Tony.*

*Even I, whom you have called hyper-romantic, know that people don't go on loving hopelessly for years. The Troilus and Cressida story may be beautiful but you and I know it isn't real. We should get over it. You'd marry someone who is free and trouble-free and I'd settle down with Roger. I just don't think I can face Roger's misery and violence, and not just for a while but for months, years. I'd know for years that I'd ruined his life ...* Stupid, Anthony thought. Illogical. He and she wouldn't go on loving hopelessly for years, but Roger would. Of all the irrational nonsense ...

He said 'Yes' and 'I see' and 'That's bad' for about the fiftieth time to Brian and then, because he couldn't take any more, he bundled him out with his two half-empty bottles under his arm. Having drunk no more than a pint of beer himself, he set to work and was still writing at two in the morning. The coarse talking-with-his-mouth-full voice of Stanley Caspian woke him at ten, and he waited until he and Arthur Johnson had gone before going to the bathroom. It was lucky he happened to be in the hall when Linthea Carville, her son and Steve and David arrived, for it was Arthur Johnson's bell they rang. Anthony saw them silhouetted behind the red and green glass and, making a mental note that sometime he must put his own name under his own bell, he went outside and took them round the back to the cellar. Linthea had brought a torch and two candles, and the boys had the box barrow. They didn't take the barrow down but carried the wood up in armfuls.

He was impressed by Linthea's strength. She had a perfect body, muscular, but curvy and lithe as well, and the jeans and sweater she wore did nothing to impede those graceful movements which he found himself watching with a slightly guilty pleasure.

73

'There's more wood here than I thought,' he said hastily when he realized she was aware of his gaze. 'We'll have to make a second journey,' and he pushed the door as if to shut it.

'Don't forget my boy's still down there,' said Linthea. 'They all are. And they've got your torch.'

The training they had in common had prevented them from falling into the adult trap of doing all the work themselves on the grounds that they could do it faster and more efficiently than the children. But once the barrow was filled, they had left the boys to explore the rest of the cellar. Linthea called out, 'Leroy, where are you?' and there came back a muffled excited call of 'Mum!' which held in it a note of thrill and mischief.

David and Steve were sitting on an upturned box, the torch between them, in the first room of the cellar. They giggled when they saw Linthea. Carrying a candle, she went on through the second room, walking rather fastidiously between the banks of rubbish. Anthony was just behind her and when, at the entrance to the last and final room, her candle making the one tiny puddle of light in all that gloom, she stopped and let out a shriek of pure terror, he caught her shoulders in his hands.

Her fear was momentary. The shriek died away into a cascade of West Indian merriment, and she ran forward, shaking off Anthony's hands, to catch hold of the boy who was hiding in a corner. Then and only then did he see what she had seen and which had sent that frightened thrill through her. As the candlelight danced, as the woman caught the laughing boy, the torch beam levelled from behind him by Steve, showed him the pale figure leaning against the wall, a black handbag hooked over one stiff arm.

'You wanted to give your poor mother a heart

attack, I know you,' Linthea was saying, and the boy: 'You were scared, you were really scared.'

'They were all in it,' said Anthony. 'I wonder how on earth that thing came to be down here.'

He went up to the model, staring curiously at the battered face and the great rent in its neck. Then, hardly knowing why, he touched its cold smooth shoulders. Immediately his fingertips seemed again to remember the feel of Linthea's fine warm flesh, and he realized how hungry he had been to touch a woman. There was something obscene about the figure in front of him, that dead mockery of femaleness with its pallid hard carapace as cold as the shell of a reptile and its attenuated unreal limbs. He wanted to knock it down and leave it to lie on the sooty floor, but he restrained himself and turned quickly away. The others were waiting for him, candles and torch accounted for, at the head of the steps.

# Chapter 9

November was the deadline Anthony had given Helen for making up her mind. It was nearly November now and he was due to make his phone call to her on Wednesday, 30 October. The letter he had received from her on the previous Tuesday had dwelt less on Roger's feelings and more on her own and his. In it she had written of her love for him and of their lovemaking so that, reading it, he had experienced that curious pit-of-the-stomach *frisson* that comes exclusively when nostalgia is evoked for a particular and well-remembered act of sex. With this in mind, he knew he would want to refer to it in their telephone conversation, would use it to reinforce his pressures on her, and he didn't want that conversation overheard by the Kotowskys, Li-li Chan or the new tenant of whom he had once or twice caught a glimpse.

Why not ask Linthea Carville if he could make the call from her flat? This seemed to have a twofold advantage. He would have complete privacy and, at the same time, the very making of such a request, involving as it would an explanation of his situation with Helen, would reinforce the friendship that was growing between Linthea and himself.

But by Tuesday, 29 October, that situation had changed again. He retrieved Helen's letter from under the huge pile of correspondence for Winston

Mervyn which had fallen on top of it, and tore open the envelope only to be bitterly disappointed. *On Wednesday when you phone I know you will ask me if I've come to a decision. Tony, I haven't, I can't. We have had a terrible weekend, Roger and I. First of all he started questioning me about my movements during that fortnight he was away in the States in June. I'd told him before that I'd spent one weekend with my sister and apparently he's now found out from my brother-in-law that I was never there. He made a lot of threats and raved and sulked but in the evening he became terribly pathetic, came into my room after I'd gone to bed and began pouring out all his miseries, how he'd longed for years to marry me, served seven years like Jacob (of course he didn't, I'm not old enough) and now he couldn't bear to be frozen out of my life. This went on for hours, Tony. I know it's blackmail but most people give in to blackmail, don't they?*

He was glad now he hadn't made that request to Linthea. Hedging his bets? Maybe. But the West Indian girl had seemed more attractive to him than ever when he had had lunch with her and Leroy after they had collected the wood and when they had met again at the Tenants' Association last Saturday afternoon. And if, as it would seem, he was going to lose Helen, be dismissed in favour of that sharp-shooting oaf ...? Was it so base not to want to jeopardize his chances with Linthea – her husband, at any rate, was nowhere in evidence – by making her thinking herself a second choice, a substitute?

Rather bitterly he thought that he didn't now much care who overheard his phone call, for there would be no reminiscing over past love passages. One who wouldn't overhear it, anyway, was Vesta Kotowsky who rushed past him in a floor-length black hooded cloak as he was coming up the station steps. He went to the kiosk and bought a box of matches with a pound note, thus ensuring a supply of tenpence pieces for his phone call. He was going to need them, all of them.

Her voice sounded nervous when she answered, but it was *her* voice, not heard for a month, and its effect on him was temporarily to take away his anger. That voice was so soft, so sweet, so civilized and gentle. He thought of the mouth from which it proceeded, heart-shaped with its full lower lip, and he let her talk, thinking of her mouth.

Then he remembered how crucial this talk was and what he must say. 'I got your letter.'

'Are you very angry?'

'Of course I'm angry, Helen. I'm fed up. I think I could take it even if you decided against me. It's probably true what you said in your other letter, that we'd forget each other in time. What I can't take is being strung along and ...' He broke off. The Kotowskys' door opened and Brian came out. Brian started making signals to him, ridiculous mimes of raising an invisible glass to his lips. 'Can't,' Anthony snapped. 'Some other night.'

Helen whispered, 'What did you say, Tony?'

'I was talking to someone else. This phone's in a very public place.' He shouted, 'Oh, Goddamnit!' as the pips sounded. He shovelled in more money. 'Helen, couldn't you call me on this number? I'll give it to you, it's ...'

She interrupted him with real fear in her voice. 'No, please! I'll have to explain it when the bill comes.'

He was silent. Then he said, 'So you're still going to be there when the bill comes?'

'Tony, I don't *know*. I thought if you could come here at Christmas, stay in an hotel here, and we could see each other again and talk properly and I could make you understand how difficult . . .'

'Oh, no!' he exploded. 'Come for a week, I suppose, and see you for half an hour a day and maybe one evening if you can get out of jail? And at Easter perhaps? And in the summer? While you keep on vacillating and I keep on trying to understand. I won't be any married woman's lap dog, Helen.'

The pips went. He put in more money. 'That was the last of my change,' he said.

'I do love you. You must know that.'

'No, I don't know it. And stop crying, please, because this is important. Your next letter is going to be very important, maybe the most important letter you'll ever write. If you'll come to me we'll find a place to live and I'll look after you and you needn't be afraid of Roger because I'll be with you. Roger will divorce you when he sees it's no use and then we'll get married. But your next letter's your last chance. I'm fed up, I'm sick to death of being kicked around, and it'll soon be too late.' Anger made him rash, that and the threat of the pips going again. 'There are other women in the world, remember. And when I hear you tell me your husband's so important to you that you're afraid of him seeing phone bills three months hence, like someone in a bloody French farce, I wonder if it isn't too late already!'

A sob answered him but it was cut off by the shrilling peep-peep-peep. He dropped the receiver with a crash, not bothering to say good-bye. But in the silence he leant against the wall, breathing like someone who has run a race. In his hand was one last twopence piece. His breathing steadied, and on an impulse he dialled Linthea's number.

As soon as she heard who it was she asked him

round for coffee. Anthony hesitated. His conversation with Helen had become a jumble in his mind and he couldn't remember whether he had given her this number or not. If he had and she phoned back ...? No, he wouldn't go to Linthea's, but would Linthea come to him? She would, once she had got the upstairs tenant to listen for Leroy.

Arthur had overheard it all, or as much of phone conversations as a listener can hear. Because he hadn't heard the woman's replies he wasn't sure whether or not Anthony Johnson was going out. Please let him go out, he found himself praying. Perhaps to that God whose portrait with a crown of thorns hung in All Souls' church hall where his Sunday school had been, though neither he nor Auntie Gracie had ever really believed in Him. Please let him go out.

But the light from Room 2 continued to illuminate the lichen-coated court. He heard the front door opened and closed and then he saw what he had never seen before, the shadows of two heads, one Anthony Johnson's, the other sleekly crowned with a pin-pierced chignon, cast on the lighted stone. Arthur turned away, his whole body shaking. He threw back the pink floral eiderdown and seized the pillows one after the other in his hands, strangling them, digging his fingers into their softness, tossing them and grasping them again so savagely that his nails ripped a seam. But this brought him no relief and, after an excess of useless violence, he lay face-downwards on the bed, weeping hot tears.

Linthea wore a long black wool skirt embroidered with orange flowers. The upper part of her body was covered with a yellow poncho and she had small gold pins in her hair.

'I dressed up,' she said, 'because you're expecting other guests. A party?'

He was a little disappointed because she hadn't dressed up for him. 'I'm not expecting anyone. What made you think so?'

She raised eyebrows that were perfect arcs, black crescents above white moons. 'You wouldn't come to me. Oh, I *see*. You're so fond of this exquisite little room with all its antiques and its lovely view of an old-world cellar that you can't bear to leave it. Do you know, that lampshade looks exactly like a Portuguese Man o' War?'

He laughed. 'I knew it was a jellyfish but I didn't know what kind. The fact is, I may be going to get a phone call.'

'Ah.'

'Not "ah" at all.' Anthony put the kettle on, set out cups. 'I'll tell you about it sometime. But now you tell me about you.'

'Nothing much to tell. I'm twenty-nine, born in Kingston. Jamaica, not the By-pass. I came here with my parents when I was eighteen. Trained as a social worker here in Kenbourne. Married a doctor.' She looked down at her lap, retrieved a fallen gold pin. 'He died of cancer three years ago.'

'I'm very sorry.'

'Yes.' She took the cup of coffee Anthony gave her. 'Now you,' she said.

'Me? I'm the eternal student.' As he said it, he remembered it was Helen who had dubbed him so, quoting apparently from some Chekhov play. She wasn't going to phone back. Not now. He began telling Linthea about his thesis, but took his notes gently from her when she started to read them. That sort of thing – *For his actions, cruelty to children and animals, even murder, he feels little, if any, guilt. His guilt*

81

*is more likely to be felt over his failure to perform routine or compulsive actions which are, taken in the context of benefit to society, virtually meaningless* – no, that wasn't what he wanted to talk about tonight. Pity there wasn't a sofa in the room but just the tweed-patched fireside chair and the upright chairs and the thing he thought was called a pouffe. He sat on that because he could surreptitiously, and apparently artlessly, edge it closer and closer to her. He had got quite close, and quite close too, to unburdening himself about his whole disillusionment over the Helen affair, when there came a sharp rap on the door.

Phone for him. Come to think of it, he wouldn't be able to hear the phone bell in here ... He flung the door open. On the threshold stood the new occupant of Room 3, a tall handsome man who looked rather like Muhammad Ali.

'I'm extremely sorry to disturb you,' said Winston Mervyn in impeccable academic English quite different from Linthea's warm sun-filled West Indian. He held out a small cruet. 'I wonder if you would be so kind as to lend me a little salt?'

'Sure,' said Anthony. 'Come in.' No phone call. Of course he hadn't given her the number. He remembered quite clearly now.

Winston Mervyn came in. He walked straight up to Linthea who – if this is possible in a Negress – had turned pale. She half-rose. She held out her hand and said:

'This is unbelievable. It's too much of a coincidence.'

'It is not,' said the visitor, 'entirely a coincidence. The salt was a ploy. I saw you come to the door.'

'Yes, but to be living here and in this house ...' Linthea broke off. 'We knew each other in Jamaica, Anthony. We haven't met for twelve years.'

82

# Chapter 10

On the doormat lay three letters for Winston Mervyn, a bill for Brian Kotowsky and the mauve-grey envelope from Bristol addressed to Anthony Johnson. Arthur, holding it in his hand, speculated briefly as to its contents. Had the woman decided to leave her husband or to stay with him? But he couldn't summon up much interest in it, for he was obsessed to the exclusion of all else by his need to secure absolute private possession of the cellar.

It had been frosty, the night preceding 5 November, and a thick white rime stuck like snow to walls and railings and doorsteps. The yellow leaves which clogged the gutters were each edged with a tinsel rim. He put his hand to Grainger's gate and found that it was already unlocked. For once, Barry was in before him. Arthur saw him over by a load of timber, about to set a match to a jumping cracker.

'Stop that,' Arthur said in a chilly, carrying voice. 'D'you want to set the place on fire?'

He let himself into the office. Barry came and stood sulkily in the doorway.

'When I was your age I'd have been severely punished if I'd so much as touched a firework.'

Barry blew an orange bubble gum bubble. 'What's pissing you off this morning?'

'How dare you use such language!' Arthur thundered. 'Get out of here. Go and make a cup of tea.'

'What, at half-nine?'

'Do as you're told. When I was your age I'd have thought myself lucky to have *got* a cup of tea in the morning.'

When I was your age ... Looking out of the window at the white desolation, Arthur thought of that lost childhood of his. Would he have been punished for touching a firework? Perhaps, by the time he was Barry's age, he had already been deterred from doing anything so obviously venal. Yes, he had been strictly brought up, but he had no quarrel with the strict upbringing of children.

'Until you are grown-up, Arthur,' Auntie Gracie used to say, 'I am the master of this house.'

Laxity on her part might have led to his growing up weak, slovenly, heedless about work and punctuality. And a greater freedom would have been bad for him. Look what he did with freedom when he had it – things which would, if unchecked, deprive him of freedom altogether. Like the incident with Mrs Goodwin's baby ... But before he could dwell on that one, Barry had come in with the tea.

'You see that bonfire they're going to have on the bit of ground?'

'I like my tea in my cup, not in my saucer,' said Arthur. 'No, I cannot say I have seen it. Who might "they" be?'

'People, kids, I don't know. It's a bleeding great pile of wood they got there. I reckon it'll be the best fire in Kenbourne. It's no good you looking out of the window, it's right up against them fences in Brasenose.'

Arthur sipped his tea. 'Let us hope there won't be any catastrophes. I imagine the fire brigade will have a busy night of it. Now when you've finished helping yourself to Mr Grainger's sugar, perhaps you'll condescend to empty my wastepaper basket.'

A formidable pile of correspondence awaited him. He began opening envelopes carefully. Once, hurrying, he had torn a cheque for a large sum in half. But this morning a proper concentration was almost impossible to achieve. He knew, from the images which kept moving in procession across his mental eye, from memories arising out of a past he had been used to think eradicated, from the pressure and buzzing in his head, that he was reaching the end of his tether.

Those images included, of course, dead faces; that of Auntie Gracie, those of the two girls. He saw the mouse, stiff, stretched, bloody. And now he saw the baby and heard again its screams.

Auntie Gracie had been minding that baby for its mother. There had been some sick relative, Arthur remembered, whom Mrs Goodwin was obliged to visit.

'If I have to pop out to the shops,' Auntie Gracie had said, 'Arthur will be here,' and with a loaded look, 'It will be good for Arthur to be placed in a position of trust.'

Once she was out of the house, he had gone and stood over the baby, scrutinizing it with curious desire. It was about six months old, fat, fast asleep. He withdrew the covers, lifted the woolly jacket it wore, and still it didn't wake. A napkin, white and fleecy, secured with a large safety pin, was now visible above its leggings. Safety was a strange word to apply to so obviously dangerous a weapon. Arthur removed the pin and, taut now with joy and power, thrust it up to its curled hilt into the baby's stomach. The baby woke with a shattering scream and a great bubble of scarlet blood welled out as he removed the pin. For a while he listened to its screams, watching it and exulting, watching its wide agonized mouth and the tears which washed down its red face. He watched and listened. Auntie Gracie was away at the shops quite a long time. Fortunately. He had to make things right to avoid her anger. Fortunately, too, the pin seemed to have struck no vital part. He changed the napkin which was now wet with urine as well as blood, washed it – how Auntie Gracie had congratulated him and approved of that! – and by the time she returned the baby was only crying piteously as babies do cry, apparently for no reason.

No harm ever came to the baby. It was, he supposed, a man in his mid-thirties by now. Nor had he or Auntie Gracie ever been blamed for the wound, if indeed that wound had ever been discovered. But he was glad for himself that he had known Auntie Gracie wouldn't be long away, for where else, into how many more vulnerable soft parts would he have stuck that pin had the baby been his for hours? No, she had been his guardian angel and his protectress, succeeded at her death by that other protectress, his patient white lady, garbed in her clothes ...

By one o'clock he hadn't replied to a single letter. Perhaps, when he had a good lunch inside him ... He put on his overcoat of silver-grey tweed, a shade lighter than his steel-grey silk tie, which he tightened before leaving the office until it stood out like an arch of metal. On his way to the Vale Café, he paused for a moment to view the stacked wood. The pile stood some fifteen feet high and someone had flanked it with a pair of trestle tables. Arthur shook his head in vague undefined disapproval. Then he walked briskly to the café, having an idea that the crisp air, inhaled rhythmically, would clear his pulsing head.

Returning, he was accosted by a young woman in a duffel coat who was collecting information for a poll. Arthur gave her his name and address, told her that he supported the Conservative Party, was unmarried; he refused to give his age but gave his occupation as a quantity surveyor. She took it all down and he felt a little better.

Grainger's correspondence still awaited him and, thanks to his idleness of the morning, it looked as if he might have to stay late to get it all done. During the winter, when dusk had come by five, he liked to leave the office promptly at that hour. The streets were crowded then and he could get home, safe and observed, before dark. But he comforted himself with the thought that the streets would be crowded till all hours tonight. Already he could see flashes of gold and scarlet and white fire shooting into the pale and still sunlit sky.

But from a perverse wish to see the evening's festivities spoiled, he hoped for rain and went outside several times to study the thermometer. There had been a few clouds overhead at lunchtime. Since then the clouds had shrunk and shivered away as if chilled out of existence by the increasing cold, for the red column of liquid in the thermometer had fallen steadily from 37 to 36 to 35 until now, at five-thirty, it stood at 29 degrees.

The sun had scarcely gone when stars appeared in the blue sky, as hard and clear as a sheet of lapis. And the stars remained, bright and eternal, while those false meteors shot and burst into ephemeral galaxies. Arthur pulled down the blind so that he could no longer see them, though he could hear the voices and the laughter of those who were arriving for the bonfire and the feast.

At ten past six he completed his last letter and

typed the address. Then, leaving his replies in the 'Out' tray for Barry to post in the morning. He put on his overcoat, gave yet another tug to his tie, and left the office. He locked the gates. The Guy Fawkes celebrants were making what Arthur thought of as a most unseemly din. He came out into Magdalen Hill and approached the wire-netting fence.

A small crowd of home-going commuters were already gathered there. Arthur meant to walk past, but curiosity mixed with distaste and some undefined hope of disaster, impelled him to join them.

The tables had been laid with paper cloths on which were arranged mountains of sandwiches, bread rolls, hot dogs and bowls of soup. The steam from this soup hung on the air. There were, Arthur estimated, about a hundred people present, mostly children, but many women and perhaps half a dozen men. All were wrapped in windcheaters or thick coats with scarves. Already the grass was frosted and their boots made dark green prints on the frost. The lights in the houses behind shed a steady orange refulgence over the moving figures, the silvered grass, the ponderous mountain of wood, the whole Breughel-like scene.

One of the women brought to the stacked woodpile a box barrow filled with potatoes which she tipped out. These, Arthur supposed, were to be roasted in the embers of the fire. And very nasty they would taste, he thought, as he saw a man – a black man, they all looked the same to him – tip paraffin over wood and cardboard and paper and then splash it over the guy itself. The guy, he had to admit, was a masterpiece, if you cared for that sort of thing, a huge lifelike figure dressed in a man's suit with a papier mâché mask for a face and a big straw hat on its head. He was about to turn away, sated and half-disgusted with the whole thing, when he saw something – or someone – that held him frozen and excited where he stood. For a man had come out of the crowd with a box of matches in his hand, a tall man with a blaze of blond hair hanging to the collar of his leather jacket, and the man was Anthony Johnson.

Arthur didn't question what he was doing there or how he had come to be involved in this childish display. He realized only that no man can be in two places at once. If Anthony Johnson was here – from the way the children cheered, an evident master of ceremonies – he couldn't also be at 142 Trinity Road. It looked as if he would be here for hours, and during those hours the cellar would be private and unobserved. It would be dark and very cold, solitudinous but, on this night of sporadic violent sound, sufficiently within the world to touch his fantasy with a greater than usual measure of reality.

A kind of joy that was both intense and languid filled his whole being. Until that moment he had hardly realized to the full how insistently urgent his need for the woman in the cellar was. None of his dreams, none of his frustration, had brought it home to him as the sight of Anthony Johnson, striking his first match, applying it to the timber, now did. But as he savoured his anticipation and felt it mount, he knew he must let it mount to its zenith. He had time, a lot of time. The culmination and the release would be all the greater for being sensuously deferred.

He stood there, trembling again but now with ecstasy. And he had no fear of the dark or its temptations. Happiness, contentment, was in watching Anthony Johnson apply match after match to that stack of wood until the flames began to leap, to crackle and to roar through the pyramid. As the fire

89

became established, a sheet of it licking the feet of the guy, the first fireworks went off. A rocket rose in a scream of sparks, and along the fence, under the supervision of the black man, a child ignited the first in a long row of Catherine Wheels. One after another they rotated in red and yellow flames. And those paler stronger flames climbed across the guy's legs, shooting long tongues across the black suit in which it was clothed, until they leapt to its face and head, spitting through its eye sockets, catching the straw hat and roaring through its crown.

The hat toppled off. The suit burned and fell away. There was a grotesque indecency in the way white limbs, long and smooth and glossy, lashed from under the burning material until the fire caught them and began to consume them also. Arthur came closer to the wire. His hands gripped the rusty cold wire. The mask was now a glowing mass that flew suddenly from the face and rose like a firework itself before eddying in sparks to the ground. A child screamed and its mother pulled it clear.

The flames teased the naked face. It wasn't a man's face but a woman's, pale, blank, even beautiful in its utter dead calm expressionlessness. It seemed to move and come close to Arthur until he could see nothing, no people, no cascading colour, no smoke, nothing but that familiar and beloved face. Then it was still and calm no longer. It arched back as if in parody of those burned at the stake. The great rent under its chin opened, gaped wide like a razor-made slash, and the fire took it, bursting with a hiss through the tear and roasting with a kind of lust the twisted face.

His white lady, his Auntie Gracie, his guardian angel ...

# Chapter 11

The house at 142 Trinity Road was unlit, every street-over-looking window a glaze of blackness between dim drifts of curtain. The curtains on the top floor shimmered whitely like the lacy ball gowns of women who wait in vain to be asked to dance. Inside the house there was total, breathless silence. Arthur, leaning against the banisters, his hot forehead against cold smooth wood, thought he had never known it so silent – no tap of heels, no soft giggles, mutter of words, whistle of kettles, trickle of water, throb of heaters, thud of door, heartbeat of life. It was as if it had retreated into sleep, but the sleep of an animal which is awakened at once by the smallest sound or movement. He could awaken the house by going upstairs and setting in motion all the processes of a routine evening. He could switch lights on, fill his kettle, turn on the television, turn down his bed, close the bedroom window – and look down into that court, at last unlighted, but dispossessed for ever of its lure.

Rage seized him. He put on the hall light and took a few steps towards the door of Room 2. To destroy property was foreign to his nature, property was what he respected, but now if he could get into that room, he would, he thought, destroy Anthony Johnson's books. One after another he pulled open the drawers in Stanley Caspian's desk. Stanley had been

91

known to leave duplicate keys lying about there, but they were empty now of everything except screwed-up pieces of paper and bits of string. Yet he must have revenge, for he had no doubt that Anthony Johnson had performed an act of revenge against him. All these weeks Anthony Johnson had been harbouring against him a grudge – hadn't everything in his behaviour shown it? – because he had opened that letter from the council. Now it was his turn, he who had done his best to make amends. Now some act must be performed of like magnitude. But what?

Turning away from the desk and the door of Room 2, his eye fell on the hall table. Something seemed to clutch at his chest, squeezing his ribs. All the letters were still there, undisturbed; the bill for Brian Kotowsky, the official-looking correspondence for Winston Mervyn, the mauve-grey envelope from Bristol for Anthony Johnson. No one had returned to the house since that morning, no one had removed a letter. Arthur put his hand over the Bristol envelope, covering it. A light constant tremor animated his hand, a tremor that had been there, electrifying his hands and his body with a delicate frenetic throb from the moment he had witnessed that fire and its consequences. Blood beat in his head as if it were feeding an engine.

He thought now of the telephone call he had overheard. 'Your next letter's our last chance ...' Her next letter. It lay under his trembling hand. Arthur lifted it up, holding it by its edge as if its centre were red-hot. Words of Auntie Gracie's trickled across his brain.

'Other people's correspondence is sacrosanct, Arthur. To open someone else's letter is the action of a thief.'

But she was gone from him, never more to guard

him, never more to watch and save ... He ripped open the envelope, splitting it so savagely that it tore into two pieces. He pulled the letter out. It was typewritten, not on mauve-grey paper but on flimsy such as is used for duplicates, and the machine was an Adler Standard like the one in his office at Grainger's.

*Darling Tony, I think I've changed a lot since I spoke to you. Perhaps I've grown up. Suddenly I realized when you put the phone down that you were right. I can't hover and play this insane double game any more. It came quite clearly to me that I have to choose directly between you and Roger. I would have called you back then and there, but I don't know your number – isn't that absurd? I only know your landlord's got a name like a river or a sea.*

*I have chosen, Tony. I've chosen you, absolutely and finally. For ever? I hope so. But I promised for ever once before, so I'm chary of making that vast dreadful promise again. But I will leave Roger and I will marry you if you still want me.*

*Don't be angry, I haven't told Roger yet. I'm afraid, of course I am, but it isn't only that. I can't tell him I'm leaving him without having anywhere to go or anyone to go to. All you have to do for me to tell him is to write – write to me at work – and let me know where and when to meet you. If my letter gets to you by Tuesday, you should be able to get yours to me by Friday at the latest. Of course, what I really mean is I want word from you that you aren't too disgusted with me to need me any more. I will do whatever you say. Command me.*

*Tony, forgive me. I have played fast and loose with you like 'a right gypsy'. But no longer. We could be together by Saturday. Say we will be and I will come even if I have to run from Roger in my nightdress. I will be another*

*Mary Stuart and follow you to the ends of the earth in my
shift. I love you. H.*

Arthur felt a surge of power. Just as the control of
his destiny, his peace, had lain in Anthony Johnson's
hands, so the other man's now lay in his. An eye for
an eye, a tooth for a tooth. Anthony Johnson had
taken away his white lady; now he would take from
Anthony Johnson *his* woman, rob him as he had been
robbed of his last chance.

He screwed up the letter and envelope and thrust
them into his pocket. He walked down the hall and
came to the foot of the stairs. How terrible and
beautiful the silence was! With something like
anguish, he thought of the cellar, unguarded,
unwatched. Wasn't it possible he could still get some
relief from it, from its atmosphere that had fed his
fantasy, from an imagination that could still perhaps
provide, furnishing her absence with vision and
empty air with flesh? He turned off the light, left the
house and made his way down the side passage. But
he had no torch, only a box of matches in his pocket.
One of these he lit as he passed through the first and
second rooms. He lit another and in its flare saw the
heap of clothes on the floor, Auntie Gracie's dress,
the bag, the shoes, and scattered all of them like so
much trash as if they had never clothed a passion.

It was the death of a fantasy. His imagination
shrivelled, and he was just an embittered man in a
dirty cellar looking at a pile of old clothes. The match
burned down in his fingers; its flame caught the box
which suddenly flared into a small brilliant fire.
Arthur dropped it, stamped on it. He caught his
breath on a sob in the darkness, stumbled back
through the thick darkness, feeling his way to the
steps.

Through the passage to the front he walked. He turned to the right, crossed the grass; set his foot on the bottom step. Like others before him, he would have been safe if he had not paused and looked back. The mouth of the dark opened and called him. The jaws of darkness received him, the streets received him, taking him into their arteries like a grain of poison.

The tables were bare, the fire had burned out, and the only fireworks which remained were those sparklers which are safe for children to hold in their hands. Only they and the stars now glittered over the frosty debris-scattered ground. Linthea had stacked her crockery into the barrow and now, having collected her son and Steve, left them with a wave and one of her radiant smiles.

Anthony and Winston Mervyn began dismantling the trestle tables which they would return to All Souls' hall. The last of the fire, a fading glow, dying into handfuls of dust, held enough heat to warm them as they worked. Winston, who seemed preoccupied, said something in a language Anthony recognized for what it was, though the words were unintelligible.

'What did you say?'

Winston laughed and translated. 'Look at the stars, my star. Would I were the heavens that I might look at you with many eyes.'

'Amazing bloke, you are. I suppose you'll turn out to be a professor of Greek.'

'I thought of doing that,' Winston said seriously, 'but there's more money in figures than in Aristotle. I'm an accountant.' Anthony raised his eyebrows but he didn't say what he wanted to, why was an accountant living at that grotty hole in Trinity Road?

'Easy does it,' said Winston. 'You take that end and I'll go ahead.'

They carried the tables up Magdalen Hill and along Balliol Street. A Roman Candle, ignited outside the Waterlily, illuminated in a green flash the cave-like interior of Oriel Mews. Anthony, walking behind Winston, realized that although he had been told what Winston had quoted, he hadn't been told why he chose to quote it. All Souls' caretaker took the tables from them, and Winston suggested a drink in the Waterlily. Anthony said all right but he'd like to go home first as he was expecting an important letter.

A hundred and forty-two was a blank dark smudge in a street of lighted houses. Winston went in first. He picked up his letters from the table. There was nothing for Anthony. Well, Helen's letter didn't always come on a Tuesday. It would come tomorrow.

'That's more like it,' said Winston. 'I might get along and look at that tomorrow.' He passed a printed sheet to Anthony who saw it was an estate agent's specification of a house in North Kenbourne, the best part. The price was twenty thousand pounds.

'You're a mystery,' he said.

'No, I'm not. Because I'm coloured you expect me to be uneducated, and because I live here you expect me to be poor.'

Anthony opened his mouth to say this was neither true nor fair, but he knew it was so he said, 'I reckon I do. Sorry.'

'I came to live here because my firm moved to London and now I'm looking for a house to buy.'

'You're not married, are you?'

'Oh, no, I'm not married,' said Winston. 'Let's go, shall we?'

Going out, they met Brian Kotowsky coming in.

'You look thirsty,' said Brian. 'Me, I'm always thirsty. How about going across the road and seeing if we can find an oasis?'

There was no way of getting rid of him. He trotted along beside them, talking peevishly of Jonathan Dean whom, he said, he hadn't seen since the other man moved away. This was because Jonathan and Vesta disliked each other. Brian was positive Jonathan had phoned, but Vesta had always taken the calls and refused to tell him out of spite. They walked through the mews which smelt of gunpowder and entered the Waterlily just before nine o'clock.

In another public house, the Grand Duke, in a distant part of Kenbourne, Arthur sat alone at a table, drinking brandy. A small brandy with a splash of soda. When first he had set out on this nocturnal walk he had been terrified – of himself. But gradually that fear had been conquered by the interest of the streets, by the changes which had come to them, by the squalid glitter of them, by the lonely places at which alley mouths and mews arches and paths leading to little yards hinted like whispers in the dark. He hadn't forgotten, in twenty years, the geography of this place where he had been born. And how many of the warrens, the labyrinths of lanes twisting across lanes, still remained behind new soaring façades! The air was smoky, acrid with the stench of fireworks, but now, at half-past nine, there were few people about. It excited Arthur to find himself, during that long walk, often the only pedestrian in some wide empty space, lividly lighted, swept by car lights, yet sprawled over with

97

shadows and bordered with caverns and passages penetrating the high frowning walls.

The pattern, twice before experienced, was repeating itself without his volition. On both those previous occasions he had walked aimlessly or with an unadmitted aim; on both he had entered a pub; on both ordered brandy because brandy was the one alcoholic drink he knew. Auntie Gracie had always kept some in the house for medicinal purposes. Sipping his brandy, feeling the unaccustomed warmth of it move in his body, he began to think of the next repetition in the pattern . . .

# Chapter 12

There were strangers in the Waterlily, men with
North Country accents wearing green and yellow
striped football scarves. Brian Kotowsky struck up
acquaintance with one of them, a fat meaty-faced
man called Potter, and that would have suited
Anthony very well, enabling him to discuss houses
and house-buying with Winston, but Brian kept
calling him 'Tony, old man' and trying hard to
include him in the conversation with Potter. Before
Helen's tuition, Anthony wouldn't have noticed the
way greenish-ginger hairs grew out of Potter's ears
and nostrils, nor perhaps been able to define Potter's
smell, a mixture of onions, sweat, whisky and
menthol. But he would have known Potter was very
drunk. Potter had one arm round Brian's shoulders
and, having listened to the saga of Jonathan Dean's
defection and Vesta's knack of losing her husband all
his friends, he said:

'Rude to him, was she?' He had a flat West Riding
accent. 'And he were rude to her? Pickin' on her like?
Ay, I get the picture.'

'You've got one of her kind yourself, have you?'

'Not me, lad. I never made mistake of putting my
head in the noose. But I've kept my eyes open. When
a woman's rude to a man and he's rude to her, it
means but one thing. He fancies her and she fancies
him.'

'You have to be joking,' said Brian.

'Not me, lad. You mark my words, you haven't set eyes on him because him and your missus is out somewhere now being rude.' And Potter gave a great drunken guffaw.

'I'm going,' said Anthony. 'I'm fed up with this place.' He got to his feet and glanced at Winston who replaced the specifications in their envelopes.

They turned into the mews and were very soon aware that Brian and Potter were following close behind them. It was a little after ten.

'This is going to be splendid,' said Winston in his cool precise way. 'They'll be drinking and rioting next door to me half the night.'

But as it happened, Potter was unable to make the stairs. He sat down on the bottom step and began to sing a bawdy agricultural ballad about giving some farmer's daughter the works of his threshing machine. Anthony had noticed that Li-li wasn't in and that all the upstairs lights were off. That meant Arthur Johnson must already be in bed. Sound asleep too, he hoped.

'You'd better get him out of here,' he said to Brian. 'He's your friend.'

'Friend? I never saw him before in my life, Tony old man.' Brian had brought a half-bottle of vodka back with him from the off-licence and this he raised to his lips, drinking it neat. 'Where am I supposed to put him? Out in the street? He comes from Leeds.'

'Then he can go back there. On the next train out of King's Cross.'

Brian looked helplessly at Potter who was humming now and conducting an imaginary orchestra. 'He doesn't want to go back there. He's come down for tomorrow's match.'

'What Goddamned match?' said Anthony, who

rarely swore. 'What the hell are you on about?' He knew nothing of football and cared less.

'Leeds versus Kenbourne Kingmakers.' Brian waved his bottle at Anthony. 'Want some Russian rotgut? O.K., be like that. I'd never have brought him here if I'd known he was that pissed. I suppose we couldn't put him in your . . . ?'

'No,' said Anthony, but as he was about to add something rude and to the point, Potter staggered to his feet and waved his arms, swivelling his head about.

'He wants the lavatory,' said Winston. He took Potter's arm and propelled him down the passage. Anthony unlocked the door of Room 2 and, without waiting to be asked, Brian followed him in and sat down on the bed. He was flushed and truculent.

'I didn't like what he was insinuating about Vesta.'

'He doesn't know her,' Anthony said. 'What's the use of listening to stupid generalizations about behaviour? They're always wrong.'

'You're a real pal, Tony, the best pal a man ever had.'

The lavatory flush went, and Winston came in with Potter who looked pale and smelt even worse than in the pub. Potter sat down in the fireside chair and lay back with his mouth open. Outside a rocket going off made them all jump except Potter, who began to snore.

'Give him half an hour,' said Winston, 'then we'll get some black coffee into him. In my ambulance driving days I saw a lot of them like that.'

'You've crowded a lot into your life,' said Anthony. 'Greek, accountancy, a bit of medical training. You'll be telling me you're a lawyer next.'

'Well, I did read for the bar but I was never called,'

said Winston, and taking Ruch's *Psychology and Life* from the bedside table, he was soon immersed in it.

'I didn't like what he said about my wife,' said Brian. The vodka bottle was half-empty. He glared at Potter and gave one of his shoulders a savage shake. Potter sat up, groaned and staggered off once more to the lavatory. 'He shouldn't have said that about Jonathan. Jonathan's the best friend I ever had.'

Winston looked at him severely over the top of his book. 'Make some coffee,' he snapped. 'Get on with it. You need it as much as he does.'

Brian obeyed, whimpering like a little dog. He put the kettle on while Anthony got out coffee and sugar. Feeling suddenly tired, Anthony sat on the floor because there wasn't anywhere else to sit, and closed his eyes. The last thing he noticed before he fell into a doze was that Brian was crying, the tears trickling down his sagging red cheeks.

Arthur went into the gents' where he tore the Bristol letter into small pieces and flushed them down the pan. There was a finality in this act which both pleased and frightened him. No going back now, no possibility of restoring the letter with another explanatory note. The deed was done and his revenge accomplished. Would the knowledge of that be sufficient to sustain him till he was home again? Could he get home in safety? As he emerged once more into the cocktail bar, the fear of himself began to return. But all the same, he bought another small brandy. He was deferring his departure from the Grand Duke until the last possible moment. It was twenty minutes to eleven. In his absence, someone had taken his seat and he was obliged to stand in a corner by the glass partition which divided this section from the saloon. The glass was frosted but with a flower pattern on it of clear glass. Glancing through a clear space, the shape of a petal, Arthur saw a familiar profile some three or four yards away.

Fortunately, it was the profile and not the full face of Jonathan Dean that he saw, for he was sure Dean hadn't seen him. He moved away quickly, elbowing through the crowd. Dean's mouth had been flapping like the clapper of a briskly-rung handbell, so he was obviously talking to an unseen person. Very likely, unseen *people*. Brian Kotowksy and maybe Anthony Johnson and that black man as well. Birds of a feather flock together. He must get out.

It was only when he was out in the street that he questioned that compulsion of his. If he meant to go straight home, what did it matter who saw him or what witnesses there were to his absence from 142 Trinity Road? Or didn't he mean to go straight home, but to wander the streets circuitously, the pressure in his head mounting, until the last permutation of the pattern was achieved? Arthur shivered. There was a bus stop a few yards down the High Street from the Grand Duke, but he didn't want a bus which would take him no nearer Trinity Road than the Waterlily. A taxi, on the other hand, would deposit him at his door.

Taxis came down this way, he knew, returning to the West End after dropping a fare in North Kenbourne. But the minutes passed and none came. Ten to eleven. Soon the Grand Duke would close and disgorge its patrons on to the pavement. On the opposite side of the street Arthur could see the edge of the thickly-treed mass of Radclyffe Park. Its main gate was closed, but the little iron kissing gate, the entry to a footpath which skirted the park, couldn't be closed. He saw a woman pass through this gate, her shadow, before she entered the dark path, streaming across the lighted pavement. His heart squeezed and he clenched his hands. Maureen Cowan, Bridget O'Neill . . .

At last a taxi appeared. He hailed it feverishly and asked the driver for Trinity Road.

'Where might Trinity Road be?'

Arthur told him.

'Sorry, mate. I'm going back to town and then I'm going to my bed. I've been at the wheel of this vehicle since nine this morning, and enough is enough.'

'I shall note down your number,' Arthur said shrilly. 'You're obliged to take me. I shall report you to the proper authority.'

'Screw you and the proper authority,' said the driver and moved off.

The last K.12 bus would pass at two minutes to eleven. Arthur decided he had no choice but to get on it, but at the Waterlily stop avoid Oriel Mews and walk home by the bright lighted way of Magdalen Hill. Yet it took all his self-control to remain at that bus stop and not set off on foot, to take the way the woman had taken or to follow the serpentine course of Radclyffe Lane which, passing at one point between acres of slum-cleared land, at another between terraces of squat houses and mean little shops, at last came to the hospital, the bridge and the grey-grassed embankment of Isambard Kingdom Brunel's railway. But as the temptation to do this became intolerable, the K.12 appeared over the brow of the rise from the direction of Radclyffe College.

Arthur went inside and the bus began to move. But it slowed again and stopped for the flying figure of a woman in a long black hooded cloak who had rushed from the Grand Duke to catch it. There were no more seats inside and she went upstairs.

The bus moved along fast because there wasn't much traffic at that time of night. It passed the cemetery where Maureen Cowan had plied her trade and where Auntie Gracie lay in the family plot beside her father and mother. It detoured along a one-way street and returned briefly to the High Street before turning up Kenbourne Lane. And still, all along the route, red and green and silver flashes pierced the cold dark curtain of sky, breaking at their zeniths into tumbling cascades of sparks.

They took the right-hand turn into Balliol Street and Arthur – who seldom rode on buses but who, when he did, was always ready to get off them a hundred yards before his stop – began to edge out of his seat. The black hooded shape was already waiting on the platform. Like a monk or a great bird, he thought. She was the first to alight, as if nervously anxious to get home.

The Waterlily was closed. All the shops were closed, and as he looked along the length of Balliol Street, he saw the light in the window of Kemal's Kebab House go out. But lights there were in plenty, amber squares dotted haphazardly across house fronts, street lights like wintergreen drops, the high rise tower a pharos with a hundred twinkling eyes. Scattered on the pavement were the blackened paper cases of used fireworks. But there were no people, no one but he and the cloaked woman who fluttered away across the mews entrance towards Camera Street. An occasional car passed.

Arthur stood still. He looked through the window of the public bar of the Waterlily, but he watched the woman from the corner of his eye. A cruising car had drawn up beside her, delaying her. The driver was saying something. Arthur thought he would count up to ten, by which time she would have turned into

Camera Street or gone with the man, be lost to him, he and she safe, and then he would turn and make for Magdalen Hill. But before he had got to five, he saw her recoil sharply from the car and begin to run back the way she had come. His heart ticked, it swelled and pounded. There were three white posts under the mews arch. No car could pass into it from this end. But she passed into it. The car seemed to give a shrug before it slid away down the hill, leaving her for easier, more complaisant prey.

Arthur too went into Oriel Mews, walking softly as a cat. It was dark in there, sensuously, beautifully dark. She was walking fast – he could just make out the grotesque flapping shape of her – but he walked faster, passing her and hearing the sharp intake of her breath as he brushed the skirts of her cloak.

Then, behind him, she fell back, as he had known she would. She would linger until she saw his silhouette against the lighted mouth at the Trinity Road end, until she saw him disappear. He let her see him. But instead of stepping out into the light, he pressed himself against the cold bricks of the mews wall and eased back a yard, two yards. He smelt her. He couldn't see her.

His tie was very tightly fastened and he had to wrench at it to get it off. His strength was such that if it had indeed been made of the metal it resembled he would still have possessed the power to get it free. Fireworks were hissing and breaking in his head now. The last of them fell into a million stars as the flapping hooded creature closed upon him and he upon her.

She didn't cry out. The sound she made came to his acute ears only, the gurgle of ultimate terror, and the smell of her terror was for his nostrils alone. He never felt the touch of her hands. She fell on the stones like a great dying bird, and Arthur, rocking with an inner tumult, let her weight rest heavily on his shoes until at last, precisely and fastidiously, he shifted his feet away.

# Chapter 13

When Anthony opened his eyes it was twenty past eleven. Winston was still reading *Psychology and Life*, Potter was still asleep. Both bars of the electric fire were on and the room was very hot.

'Where's Brian?'

Winston closed the book. 'He went off about half an hour ago. Said he was going to find this Dean character and have it out with him.'

'Oh, God,' said Anthony. 'Let's get rid of Potter.'

'When you like,' said Winston equably. 'I looked through his pockets while you were asleep. He's got plenty of money and he's staying at the Fleur Hotel in Judd Street.'

'Well done, sergeant. You'll go far.' A thought struck Anthony. 'You were never in the police, were you?'

Winston grinned. 'No, I never was. Shall we get him a cab?'

Anthony nodded and they managed to wake Potter. But, as always on waking, Potter had a call of nature or wanted to be sick. He departed for the lavatory and Anthony and Winston waited for him in silence. They had to wait a long time as it was fully ten minutes before Potter reappeared, green-faced, unsteady and drooling.

Arthur came through the front door of 142 Trinity

Road at twenty-five to twelve. He held his coat collar high up against his throat so that the absence of a tie wouldn't be noticed. The bitter cold made such an action natural in someone who might be thought bronchial. But there was no one to see him and he wasn't afraid.

At first the house appeared as dark as when he had left it all those hours before. No light showed in Li-li Chan's window or in that of Winston Mervyn. The hall was dark and silent, but, pausing at the foot of the stairs, he saw a line of light under the door of Room 2, and the ill-fitting lavatory door had a narrow rim of light all the way round its rectangle. Anthony Johnson. It could be no one else. Arthur moved soundlessly up the stairs, but before he reached the first landing, six steps before, he heard the lavatory door open and saw a blaze of light stream into the hall below. It seemed to him that Anthony Johnson must have paused, must be looking up the stairs – for why else should he hang about in the hall? He didn't look down and by the time he was on the landing, he heard the door of Room 2 close.

Light flooded the courtyard below his bedroom window. But it was of no importance. The only danger to him lay in his being actually caught in the act of a killing, for he had been a stranger to the woman he had strangled as he had been a stranger to Maureen Cowan and Bridget O'Neill. No one would care what time Arthur Johnson had come home that night because no one would think it necessary to enquire.

There was nothing to worry about. These were perhaps the only moments in his life when he had nothing to worry about. He savoured them, excluding thought, feeling an exquisite peace, an animal's well-being. Not bothering, for once, to wash, he stripped off his clothes, leaving on top of the heap of them the stretched twisted silver tie, and fell beneath the blue floral quilt. In seconds he was asleep.

It was always, as Winston pointed out, next to impossible to secure a taxi in Trinity Road which wasn't a through road and whose inhabitants in general couldn't afford cabs.

'We could get him up to the rank by the station.'

'No, we couldn't,' said Anthony. It had been bad enough lugging the somnolent smelly Potter from Room 2 out into the street. He must have weighed at least sixteen stone. Now he sat where they had placed him, on the low wall that divided the patch of grass from the street, his head resting against the stump of a lime tree. The heavy frost that made them shiver had no effect on Potter who began once more to snore.

'I'll go to the rank,' said Winston, 'if you'll stay here and see he doesn't fall off on to the grass.' But as he spoke a taxi cruised out of Magdalen Hill and came to a stop outside a hundred and forty-two. Li-li Chan, in a green satin boiler suit and pink feather boa, skipped out of it and thrust a pound note at the driver.

'Ninety-eight, lady,' said the driver, giving her back twopence.

'You keep change,' said Li-li, waving it away. While the driver stared after her in gloomy disbelief, she uttered a 'Hallo, it's fleezing,' to Anthony and Winston and danced off up the steps.

'You wouldn't believe it,' said the driver, 'if you hadn't seen it with your own eyes.' He scrutinized the coin as if he feared it might vanish in the wake of its bestower.

Winston grabbed Potter under one arm while Anthony took the other. They shoved him into the back of the cab. 'This one's loaded and he's in no state to argue about your tip. Fleur Hotel, Judd Street. O.K.?'

'Long as he don't throw up,' said the driver.

The night was growing quiet now and there had been no sound of fireworks for half an hour.

It took nearly an hour to air Room 2. Anthony was a long time getting to sleep and, as a result, he overslept. Waking at eight-thirty, he hadn't time to shave or wash much, for he was determined to get down to work in the college library by half-past nine. There was a stranger in the hall, a nondescript middle-aged man who nodded and said good morning in what seemed a deliberate and calculating way. Anthony had made up his mind he must be a plainclothes policeman even before he saw the police car parked outside the house, and at once he wondered if this visit had any connection with Brian Kotowsky. Brian had gone out the previous night, intent on quarrelling with Jonathan Dean – intent perhaps on fighting Dean?

But none of the occupants of the car attempted to speak to him, so he crossed the road towards Oriel Mews. Here his passage was barred. The mews entrance was blocked off by a tarpaulin sheet, erected on a frame some eight feet high, and none of its interior was visible.

The sound of knocking had awakened Arthur just before his alarm was due to go off. Someone was hammering on one of the doors, Kotowskys' or Mervyn's, on the floor below. Then he heard voices, Mervyn's and another's, but he was used to all sorts of unnecessary wanton noise, made at uncivilized

111

hours, so he didn't take much notice. Ten minutes later, when all the noise had stopped, he got up and had his bath. He cleaned bath and basin carefully, mopped the floor, plumped up the blue pillows and shook out the quilt, took a clean shirt and clean underwear from the airing cupboard.

A tramping up and down the stairs had begun. Perhaps someone else was moving out. It would be just like Stanley Caspian not to have told him. He went into the kitchen and plugged in his kettle, wondering in a detached kind of way if the body of the woman had yet been found. Imprudent of him really to have done the deed so near home, but prudence, of course, hadn't entered into it. The evening newspaper would tell him, reveal to him as to any other stranger, the known facts. And this time he wouldn't collapse and be ill from the culminating traumas of it, but would watch with relish the efforts of the police to find the killer.

A good strong pot of tea, two eggs, two rashers of bacon, two thin piping hot pieces of toast. If they had found the body, he thought as he washed up, they would in some way cordon off the mews. Its entrance was just visible from his living room window. His curiosity irresistible, he peered out between the crossover frilled net curtains. Yes, Oriel Mews was cordoned off, its arch blanked out with a big opaque sheet of something. A van had probably gone in to load or unload and the driver had found her. He scanned the area for police cars, found nothing until, focussing closer, he saw one where he least expected it, right under the window at the kerb.

Arthur's heart gave a great lurch, and suddenly his chest seemed full of scalding liquid. But they couldn't know, they couldn't have come for him . . . No one had seen him go into the mews and there was nothing to connect him with the dead woman. Pull yourself together, he told himself in the admonishing Auntie Gracie voice he kept for moments like this. Not that there ever had been a moment like this before.

He had slumped into a chair and now, looking down at his hands, he saw that he was holding the dish cloth just as he had held that silver tie last night, taut, his fingers flexed at its ends. He relaxed them. Was it possible the police car was parked outside because earlier there had been no other space in which to park? Again he looked out of the window. Anthony Johnson was crossing the road towards the closed mews. The long thrill of his doorbell ringing seemed to go through the soft tissues of Arthur's brain like a knife. He swayed. Then he went to the door.

'Mr Johnson?'

Arthur nodded, his face shrivelling with pallor.

'I'd like a word with you. May I come in?'

The man didn't wait for permission. He stepped into the flat and showed Arthur his warrant card. Detective Inspector Glass. A tall lean man was Inspector Glass with a broad flat bill of a nose and a thin mouth that parted to show big yellow dentures.

'There's been a murder, Mr Johnson. In view of that, I'd be glad if you'd tell me what your movements were last evening.'

'My movements?' Arthur had rehearsed nothing. He was totally unprepared. 'What do you mean?'

'It's quite simple. I'd just like to know how you spent last evening.'

'I was here, in my flat. I was here from the time I got in from work at six-thirty. I didn't go out.'

'Alone?'

Arthur nodded. He felt faint, sick. The man didn't

113

believe him. A blank, almost disgusted, incredulity showed in his face, and his lip curled above those hideous teeth.

'According to my information, you spent the evening with Mr Winston Mervyn, Mr Brian Kotowsky and a man called Potter.'

And now Arthur didn't understand at all. Fleeting images of the Grand Duke, of Dean's profile, appeared on his mind's eye, but surely ... Then came light.

'I think you are mistaking me for Mr *Anthony* Johnson who lives on the ground floor. Room 2.' Firmly now, as he saw he had been right, that Glass had made a mistake, he added, 'I was at home on my own all evening.'

'Sorry about that, Mr Johnson. An understandable confusion. Then you can't help us as to the whereabouts of Mr Kotowsky?'

'I know nothing about it. I hardly know him. I keep myself to myself.' But Arthur had to know, had to discover before Glass departed, why he had come to this house – why here? 'This murder – you're connecting Mr Kotowsky with it?'

'Inevitably, Mr Johnson,' said Glass, opening the front door. 'It is Mrs Vesta Kotowsky who has been murdered.'

# Chapter 14

Anthony spent the day in the college library and it was nearly five when he reached Kenbourne Lane tube station on his way home. There on the newsboards he read: *Murder of Kenbourne Woman* and *Kenbourne Killer slays again?* Though he was necessarily interested in what leads men to kill, murder itself fascinated him not at all, so he didn't buy a paper. Helen's letter would be waiting for him, and since leaving the library his whole mind had been possessed by speculating as to what she would say.

The hall table was piled with correspondence, a heap of it, for once not carefully arranged. Anthony leafed through it. Three specifications from estate agents for Winston, Li-li's Taiwan letter, a bill for Brian, a bill for Vesta, a bill that would have to be redirected for Jonathan Dean. Nothing for him. Helen hadn't written. For the first time since he had moved into 142 Trinity Road, a Tuesday and a Wednesday had gone by without a letter from her. But before he could begin to wonder about this omission, whether he had been too harsh with her, whether she was afraid to write, the front door opened and Winston Mervyn and Jonathan Dean – who as far as he knew didn't know each other, had never met – came into the hall together.

'When did they let you off the hook?' said Winston. 'We must have missed you.'

'Hook?' said Anthony.

'I mean we didn't see you at the police station.'

Anthony thought he had never seen Jonathan Dean look so grim, so spent, and at the same time so much like a real person without pose or role. 'I'm not following any of this.'

'He doesn't know,' said Jonathan. 'He doesn't know a thing. Vesta was murdered last night, Tony, strangled, and Brian's disappeared.'

They went up to Winston's room because it was bigger and airier than Anthony's. Jonathan looked round his old domain with sick eyes, and finding no hackneyed line of verse or prose to fit the situation, stretched himself full-length on the old red sofa. A freezing fog, white in the dusk, pressed smokily against the window. Winston drew the sparingly-cut curtains.

'The police came here at half-past seven this morning,' he said. 'They couldn't get an answer from Brian, so they came to me. They wanted to know when I'd last seen Brian and what sort of a mood he was in. I told them about last night. I had to.'

'You told them about all those insinuations of Potter's, d'you mean?'

'I had to, Anthony. What would you have done? Said Brian was sober and calm and went off to bed in a happy frame of mind? They rooted Potter out, anyway. He must have missed his match. Presumably, after that, they thought they wouldn't bother with you. And Potter must have remembered, hangover or not, because they got me down to the station and asked me if Brian had been in a jealous rage. I had to say he'd gone off looking for Vesta and *him*.' Winston waved his hand in the direction of the recumbent Dean.

'But it was rubbish,' said Anthony. 'It was Potter's drunken fantasy. There wasn't any foundation for it, we all know that.'

'But there was,' said Jonathan Dean.

'You mean, you and Vesta . . . ?'

'Oh, God, of *course*. That's why I moved away. We couldn't do it here, could we? In the next room to the poor old bastard. Christ, I was with her yesterday. We spent the afternoon and most of the evening together and then we went off for a drink in the Grand Duke. She left me just before eleven to get the last bus.'

Anthony shrugged. He felt cold, helpless. 'You said Brian had disappeared?'

Jonathan ran his fingers through his untidy ginger hair. 'I haven't been living in that bloody awful hole for the past week. It stinks and it's over-run with mice. My sister said I could stay in her place while she's away in Germany. She's got a flat in West Hampstead. I went back there last night from the Duke. I got there about midnight and Brian turned up around half-past. He was pissed out of his mind and he was making all sorts of threats and accusations, only he passed out and I put him to bed.'

'But how did he know you'd be there?'

'God knows. I've gone there before when my sister's been away.' Jonathan shivered. 'The thing is, Vesta could have told him before he . . .'

'Then where is he now?'

Jonathan shook his head. 'I left him there and went to work. The fuzz got hold of me at about midday and I told them everything, but when they got to my sister's Brian had gone. They're searching for him now. It's no good looking like that, Tony old man, he must have done it. Why else would he vanish?'

'He could have gone out and seen an evening

paper and panicked. I don't believe him capable of murder.'

'D'you think I do? D'you think I like thinking that way about my old pal? We were like – like two red roses on one stalk.'

Perhaps it was the crass ineptitude of this quotation, or the fact that, in these circumstances, Jonathan had quoted anything at all, which made Winston round on him. 'If he did do it, it's your fault. You shouldn't have messed about with his wife.'

'You lousy black bastard!' Jonathan turned his face into the sofa arm and his body shook. 'God, I could do with a drink.'

Not at all put out by the offensive epithets, Winston said calmly, 'I wonder how many thousand times the ears of these walls have heard those words?' He shook Jonathan vigorously. 'Why I didn't leave you on the steps of the nick for the dustmen to pick up I'll never know. Get up, if you want that drink. But we're not showing our faces in the Waterlily till all this fuss has died down.'

'They say,' said Barry, 'as that bird as was done in lived in your house. Is that a fact?'

'Yes,' said Arthur.

'Only they don't give you no number in the paper, just Trinity.' Barry spooned sugar from the basin into his mouth and crunched it. 'Here,' he said, and thrust the *Evening Standard* under Arthur's nose.

*The body of a woman, Mrs Vesta Kotowsky, 36, of Trinity Road, Kenbourne Vale, West London, was found in Oriel Mews, Kenbourne Vale, early this morning. She had been strangled. Police are treating the case as murder.*

The print swam. Other words were superimposed on it. *The body of a woman, Maureen Cowan, 24, of Parsloe Street, Kenbourne Vale, West London, was last night found in a footpath adjacent to Kenbourne Vale Cemetery. Police are treating the case . . . The body of a woman, Bridget O'Neill, 20, student nurse . . .*

Strangers to him, utter strangers. He had never even looked into their faces. Had he ever looked into any woman's face but Auntie Gracie's and Beryl's?

Beryl was Mrs Courthope's daughter. When he came home and found her there one evening, drinking tea with Auntie Gracie out of those china cups he now possessed and cherished, he had been jealous of her presence. Who was she to break in on their cloistered world? And she had been there again and again after that, sometimes with her mother, sometimes alone. It was better when her mother was there because then Auntie Gracie stayed in the room too instead of leaving Arthur and Beryl together. He had never known what to say when he was alone with Beryl, and now he couldn't remember whether he had so much as uttered a word. He couldn't remember whether Beryl was pretty or plain, talkative or silent, and he doubted whether he had known at the time. He was indifferent to her.

But she liked him, Auntie Gracie said.

'Beryl likes you very much, Arthur. Of course, that's not surprising. You're steady, you've got a good job, and though I shouldn't tell you so, you're a very nice-looking young man.'

Beryl started coming with them to the Odeon. Auntie Gracie always arranged it so that Beryl sat between them. He dared to say he had liked things better before they knew Beryl and had been alone together.

'There's no reason why we should ever be apart, Arthur. This is a big house. I have always intended you to have the top floor to yourself one day.'

He didn't know what she meant or why she was

119

hoarding her clothes coupons or examining so closely the best of the linen she had kept packed away for so long or talking of furniture being so hard to get in this aftermath of wartime. He didn't like being left with Beryl and talked about among Auntie Gracie's particular friends as if Beryl were his particular friend.

The night it had happened was the night Auntie Gracie had such a bad headache she couldn't face the Odeon and the film about American soldiers in the Pacific. Arthur said that in that case he wouldn't go either.

'You must, Arthur. You can't let Beryl down. She's been looking forward to going out with you all the week. You don't realize how fond of you she is. I know you're fond of her too, only you're shy. You haven't been friendly with any other girls, I'm glad to say.'

Friendly . . . Beryl came to the house in Magdalen Hill and they set off together in silence. But when they had to cross the road she took his arm and held on to it all the way to the cinema. Her body was warm and clinging. Suddenly she began to talk. Her talk was madness. He thought she was mad.

'I've never had a boy friend before, Arthur. Mother wouldn't let me go out with boys till you came along. I know I'm not very attractive, nothing special, but I could have had boy friends. Now I'm glad I waited. Mother's told me, you see.'

He said hoarsely, 'Told you what?'

'That you like me very much, only you're too shy to say so. I like shy boys. I've been hoping and hoping for weeks you'd ask me to go out with you alone and now you have.'

'My aunt's ill. That's why she hasn't come, because she's ill.'

'Oh, *Arthur*. You don't have to pretend any more. I know you've been trying to put her off coming with us for weeks and weeks.'

They went into the cinema. Sweets were just coming back into the shops. He bought her a bag of things called Raspberry Ruffles and muttered to her that he had to go to the gents'. 'I want to be excused,' was what he said like you said in school. There was an emergency exit between the foyer and the lavatory. Arthur walked straight out of it into the street. He walked and walked until he had put two miles between himself and Beryl, and then, for the first time in his life, he went into a pub. There he drank brandy because he didn't know what else to order.

Soon after ten he left and began to walk home along the path that bordered the cemetery. There was a girl standing near the end of the path, and as he came up to her she said good evening. Later, he had learned she was a prostitute, waiting for the pubs to turn out, though at the time he had scarcely known of the existence of prostitutes.

He went up to her and put his hand into his pocket where he had stuffed his scarf. Perhaps she thought he was feeling for his wallet, for she moved towards him and put her hand on his arm. He strangled her then, and she was too surprised to struggle or cry out. Afterwards, when he understood what he had done, he knew he would be caught, tried, hanged – but nothing had happened. The police never came to the house in Magdalen Hill, and if they had they would have discovered nothing, for Beryl told neither his aunt nor her mother that he had left her alone in the Odeon. She gave them the impression that it was she who had jilted him, left him finally at eleven that night and never wanted to see him again. Auntie Gracie was hot against her for her ingratitude and her fickleness, and of course she understood why Arthur, disappointed in love, fell ill suddenly from some virus the doctors couldn't diagnose and was off work for six weeks. He never saw Beryl again, though later he heard that she had married a greengrocer and had two children ...

'Reckon her old man done it,' said Barry.

Arthur couldn't summon the energy necessary to rebuke Barry for this slangy, coarse and ungrammatical usage. He digested the sense behind the words. They would suppose Kotowsky had done it. Glass, evidently, already supposed so. But Arthur was still unable to struggle out of the paralysis of fear in which he had been gripped since eight-thirty. Impossible to get over the fact – yet equally impossible to grasp the full significance of it – that he had not only killed a woman he knew but one who lived in the same house. Impossible too to forget or come to terms with another aspect. He had lied to Inspector Glass, that piranha-faced man, lied under the pressure of panic and forgetting that his lie could easily be detected. Anthony Johnson could show the police he had lied. Anthony Johnson, emerging from the lavatory at twenty to twelve, had seen him creeping up the stairs in the dark.

He could, of course, say he had merely been down to deposit rubbish in the dustbin. He? At that hour? In his overcoat? No, whatever he said, Anthony Johnson's testimony would be enough to draw their attention to him. And naturally Anthony Johnson would tell them. By now they would know, would perhaps be waiting for him at 142 Trinity Road.

Arthur went back there because he had nowhere else to go. No police car, no policeman in the hall. He stood in the hall, listening, wondering if they were up there on the top landing. A door above him crashed for all the world as if Jonathan Dean were back. And he was. Arthur stared. Jonathan Dean was coming downstairs with that black man and Anthony Johnson.

He managed to say good evening. Winston Mervyn said good evening back, but Jonathan Dean said nothing. He was drunk perhaps. He looked drunk, leaning on Mervyn's arm, his face grey and puffy. They went out into the street. Anthony Johnson said, 'I'll be with you in a minute,' and turned away to the hall table where he began sifting through the heap of letters Arthur hadn't felt capable of arranging methodically that morning. Arthur couldn't leave him to it and go upstairs. He edged along the hall almost shyly, but his heart was pounding with terror.

Anthony Johnson was looking annoyed. He said rather absently to Arthur, 'An awful thing, this murder.'

Arthur found a voice, a husky weak voice that came from somewhere in the back of his neck. 'Have the police – have they interviewed you?'

And now Anthony Johnson turned round to face him, his blue eyes very penetrating. 'No, they haven't, oddly enough. I'm surprised because I do have things to tell them.'

'I see.' Arthur could hear his own voice as strange, as throaty. 'Will you – will you go and tell them off your own bat, as it were?'

'I shouldn't think so. They can come to me if they want me. I don't see myself as the instrument of justice or the means of shutting a man up for life. Except, maybe, in very special circumstances. I mean, if an injury were done to me or mine, for instance.'

Arthur nodded. Relief caused sweat to break over him, flushing him with heat. Anthony Johnson's meaning was unmistakable, hardly veiled, and as if

to reinforce it, as Arthur began to walk away, he
called:

'Mr Johnson?'

'Yes?'

'I've been meaning to thank you for that note you
left me. It was weeks ago but we don't seem to have
met since. You remember? When you opened my
letter by mistake?'

'Yes.'

'It was thoughtful of you to leave that note.'
Anthony Johnson's voice was very gentle now, very
considerate. Was he imagining the hint of menace
that underlay it or was that menace really there? 'I
wouldn't like you to think I'd bear a grudge. It
wasn't as if it was a very personal letter.'

'Oh, no,' Arthur stammered. 'No, indeed. A personal letter – that would be a dreadful intrusion.' He
cleared his throat. 'An injury,' he said.

# Chapter 15

Brian Kotowsky was the only son of Polish Jews, now dead, who had emigrated to this country in the nineteen thirties. Stanley Caspian told Arthur that Jonathan Dean and Vesta's brother were the only close associates Brian had had. They had been, therefore, closely questioned by the police as to his possible hiding place. The brother-in-law remembered hearing of an aunt of Brian's, his mother's sister, who lived in Brighton, but when the police went to her house they found that she had been in hospital for a minor operation since the day before Vesta's death.

'I don't know.' By this Arthur meant he didn't know how Stanley could know so much. Some grass roots system, perhaps, that had often proved reliable in the past.

'He'll have skipped off to South America,' said Stanley, jabbing full stops into Li-li Chan's rent book. 'They must have had a fortune stashed away, him and her, considering they were both working and not paying me more than a poxy fourteen quid a week for that flat.'

'Two rooms,' said Arthur absently.

'A two-roomed flat with fridge and immersion heater. Cheap at the price. Put the kettle on, me old Arthur. Mrs Caspian's sister's mother-in-law's got a pal who knows a chap that keeps a papershop up

West Hampstead, West End Lane, and he told the pal he'd been helping the police in their enquiries on account of Kotowsky going in there Wednesday morning to get some fags and a paper. Identified him, this papershop chap did, from photos. And he's the last living soul to have set eyes on him. Have a bit of pie?'

'No, thank you,' said Arthur.

'God knows what he was doing in Hampstead. It's more than I can understand, a chap killing his own wife, me and Mrs Caspian having been a pair of real lovebirds all our married life. A cream passionate is what they call it. Thank God it wasn't under my roof. There's nothing like that to give a place a bad name. What's worrying me is when I'll be able to re-let the flat. I can't afford to take a drop in my income at this juncture, I can tell you.'

'I shouldn't wonder,' said Arthur with malice, 'if the authorities don't seal it up for months and months. And now, if I might have my little envelope?'

In his pocket was another, mauve-grey, post-marked Bristol, which he had picked up from the doormat ten minutes before. Who could have suspected that she would write again, having been turned down, or apparently turned down, and send a letter to arrive on a Saturday? However, because Stanley Caspian was already parking his car at the kerb, he had snatched it up. Now he wondered why, for he intended no further revenge on Anthony Johnson. Far from it. Just as Anthony Johnson had forgiven him for opening that letter from the council, so he would forgive Anthony Johnson for that act of destruction by fire. *Must* forgive him, because now he was entirely in Anthony Johnson's power.

Dropping the Bristol letter on his kitchen table,

Arthur forced himself to think clearly. Anthony Johnson had said plainly that he wouldn't pardon the theft of a personal letter. No letter could be more personal than last Tuesday's. Therefore, he must never know that Arthur had taken it. He would surely go to the police and tell what he had seen if he suspected Arthur of interfering with his correspondence. So Anthony Johnson must have this letter. But what if H. mentioned in it that she had written before? Arthur plugged in his electric kettle. The envelope flap reacted obediently to the jet of steam and curled easily away. With extreme care, he took out the sheet of flimsy.

*Darling Tony, Why haven't I heard from you? I couldn't believe it when the post brought me nothing from you. Letters don't go astray, do they? But the alternative is that you didn't want to write, that you're angry with me, making me wait now as I made you wait in the past. Or is it that you need time to think in, to make plans for where we shall live and so on? I see you may need time to adjust to a new life and disrupt the new one you have already made. But if you need weeks, if you want to wait till your term ends, can't you understand that I'll understand? I'm so entirely yours now, Tony, that I'll do anything you ask. Only don't let me endure suspense, don't leave me in fear.*

*But there isn't any real need to be frightened, is there? I know you'll write. Is it possible that someone living in your house would take your letters by mistake? Surely, no one who did that would keep a letter like mine, a true love letter. And yet I hope and hope this is what happened. Or that this murder in your street I've read about in the newspapers has somehow made the police take people's post.*

*Because I have to believe you didn't get my letter, I'll*

*repeat what I said in it, that I'll leave Roger and come to you whenever you like. Your most devoted and loving, H.*

Arthur read it several times. He wondered at the emotion conveyed in it. Strange that anyone could put such exaggerations, such drama, on paper. But her guesswork was correct. Her previous letter had been purloined by someone living in the house, and therefore Anthony Johnson must no more receive this one than he had received the last. He must never be allowed to receive any letter in a mauve-grey envelope, postmarked Bristol . . .

When nothing had arrived from Helen by the weekend, Anthony's attitude towards her wavered between resentful anger and the more reasonable feeling that her letter had got lost in the post. She would, in any case, write again next week. It brought him a small bitter pleasure to think she might have written to say she had made up her mind in his favour. How ironical if it were that letter which had got lost and she now be wondering if he were paying her back in her own coin. But he didn't really think she would have decided for him. The likeliest answer was that she had written with her usual ambivalence, given the letter to some colleague or friend to post, and it lay even now in that friend's pocket or handbag.

On Saturday night he phoned Linthea, but she was out and Leroy's sitter answered. However, on Sunday evening she was free and Anthony was invited to the flat in Brasenose Avenue.

The Sunday newspapers all had photographs of Brian Kotowsky, dog-faced Brian with his wild hair and his unhappy eyes. *Police Mount Massive Search for Vesta's Husband.* She was Vesta now to everyone, a household word, her christian name on the lips of strangers enough to summon up immediate images of violence, terror, passion, death. But, keeping their options open, the less genteel of the Sundays also carried whole page spread stories entitled in one case, *Was Vesta Kenbourne Killer's Victim?* and in another, echoing poor Brian's own words, *Kenbourne Killer Strikes Again?*

Linthea, in the kitchen making Chicken Maryland, talked about the murder practically, logically, like a character in a detective story. 'If Brian Kotowsky did kill her, he can't have gone straight to find this Dean because he left your house at a quarter to eleven and she didn't leave the Grand Duke till ten minutes later. So they're saying he hung about in the street on a freezing cold night on the chance she'd come that way and at that time. When she did come they didn't go home to quarrel but quarrelled in a pitch-black mews where he killed her. And that's ridiculous.'

'We don't know what they're saying.'

'The police always think murdered wives have been murdered by their husbands, and considering what I see in my work every day almost, I know why.'

He thought how Helen would have spoken of it, with intuition, using her rich imagination to clothe that night and the players in its drama. But Linthea looked coolly and prosaically at things as he did. Linthea had more in common with him than Helen had. Strange that the girl gifted with the delicate perception, the passionate imagination, should look so cool and fair, the calm and practical one so exotic. Tonight Linthea's long black hair hung loose down her back. She wore a heavy gold chain about her neck which threw a yellow gleam up against her throat and chin. He wondered about that dead husband of hers and whether she now lived a celibate life.

Later, when they had eaten and she had exhausted the subject of the Kotowskys, completed her analysis of times and circumstances and likelihood, he felt an overpowering urge to confide in her about Helen. But that brought him back to where he had been once before. Can you, if you want to make love to a woman, confess to her your present, strong and angry love for another woman? Certainly not with her son in the room, pressing you to a game of Scrabble.

'You're keeping him up late,' he said at last.

'He's on half-term. No school tomorrow, no work for me.' She had a merry laugh, evoked by very little, as some West Indians have. 'Scrabble's good for him, he can't spell at all. How will you grow up,' she said, hugging the boy, 'to be a big important doctor like Anthony if you can't spell?'

So they played Scrabble till midnight when Leroy went to bed and Linthea said very directly, 'I shall send you home now, Anthony. You must be fresh for your psychopaths in the morning.'

He didn't feel very fresh on Tuesday morning because he had awakened at four and been unable to sleep again. All day he wondered if a letter would be waiting for him when he got home, though he refused to give way to the impulse that urged him to go home early and find out. But when he returned at five there was no letter. No post had come that day for the occupants of 142 Trinity Road and the table was bare. So, on the following morning, beginning now to feel real anxiety, he waited at home until the post came, and at nine he took it in himself. Two letters, one for Li-li, one for Winston. It was now two whole weeks since he had heard from Helen.

Two of her letters couldn't have gone astray. He considered breaking her rule and phoning her at work. She was assistant to the curator of a marine art museum. But why give her what she wanted, a lover content to hang on, playing the *amour courtois* game, while she gave him nothing? No, he wouldn't phone. And maybe he wouldn't phone on the last Wednesday of the month either. By that time, anyway, he might have managed to console himself. Linthea, he thought, Linthea who had no ties, who lived in and worked for a society he understood, who wasn't effete with poetry and dream and metaphor and a jelly-like sensitivity that melts at a hard touch. Above all, this mustn't affect his thesis. He had begun to write it in earnest and it was going well. Now, having dealt in depth with the findings of various psychometric tests, he wrote:

*In the survey it was suggested that the majority of psychopaths feared their own aggression and were as guilt- and anxiety-ridden about their acts as were the normal subjects. In their manner of relating to female and authority figures, a greater disturbance was found in psychopaths than in non-psychopaths, but whereas more guilt feelings were present in the former, further analysis shows that the guilt feelings of psychopaths were indicative rather of their difficult and disagreeable situation than of true remorse. The psychopath, when offered a choice between selfish forms of conduct and those which seem self-denying and are therefore socially acceptable, may be shrewd enough to choose the latter. When obliged to be guided solely by his own judgment, his choice is directed primarily by personal need . . .*

A tap on the door, discreet and somehow insinuating, interrupted Anthony. Arthur Johnson stood outside, dressed as usual in one of his silver-sheened suits and a shirt as white as that in a detergent commercial. He gave a small deprecating cough.

'I do most sincerely apologize for this intrusion, but I have to trouble you about the little matter of the rent. Your – er, first weekly payment in advance falls due tomorrow.'

'Oh, sure,' said Anthony. 'Will a cheque do?'

'Admirably, admirably.'

While Anthony hunted out his cheque book which was sandwiched between Sokolov's *The Conditioned Reflex* and Stein's *Role of Pleasure in Behaviour*, Arthur Johnson, in a finicky manner, waved at him a small red rent book and a brown envelope on which was printed with a touching attention to detail: Mr Anthony Johnson, Room 2, 142 Trinity Road, London W15 6HD.

'If you would be good enough to place your cheque inside your rent book each Friday and the book inside this little envelope? Then I will either collect it or you may leave it on the hall table.'

Anthony nodded, wrote his cheque.

'Thank goodness, the police have ceased to trouble us.'

'They haven't troubled me at all yet,' said Anthony.

'Of course, there can be no doubt in anyone's mind that Mr Kotowsky is guilty. He's known to be in South America but he will be extradited.'

'Oh, rubbish,' said Anthony rather more roughly than he intended. 'And there's plenty of doubt in my mind. I don't believe for a moment he did it.'

Arthur had been rather perturbed during the previous week to observe that on two mornings the post had been taken in by someone else. But that hadn't happened since Saturday – thanks to his watching from his living room window for the postman to appear round the corner of Camera Street, and taking care to be down in the hall in good time. In any case, no further mauve-grey envelopes had arrived. The woman wouldn't write again. She had now been twice rebuffed and she wouldn't risk a further snub. Tuesday, 19 November, and Wednesday, 20 November, went by. Those were crucial days, but they brought Anthony Johnson only a letter from York from his mother. Arthur felt more relaxed and peaceful than he had done since the night of 5 November, and although it gave him a certain bitterness to notice, now when it was too late and unimportant, that twice this week already no light had fallen from the window of Room 2 on to the courtyard in the evenings, the cause of Anthony Johnson's absence from the house pleased him. Very little that went on escaped Arthur. He had seen that black woman call at the house with her black child. He had seen her call alone. Sometimes he had seen their silhouetted faces cast on the green stones of the yard. And when he saw Anthony Johnson depart with a bottle of wine under his arm, he knew whose home he was bound for. Much as Arthur deplored the idea of a clean fair-haired young Englishman getting involved with a black woman, it would divert Anthony Johnson's attention from Bristol.

Friday, 22 November, dawned cold and wet. Arthur saw Anthony Johnson leave the house at eight-thirty and Winston Mervyn follow him five minutes later. Then Li-li Chan emerged. She stood at the front gate under a red pagoda umbrella, scanning the cars that turned into Trinity Road from Magdalen Hill. Then the front door slammed with a Dean-like crash and Arthur heard her platform soles clumping up the stairs. He opened his door and put it on the latch.

Li-li was on the phone.

'You say you come at eight-thirty. You are over-sleeping? Why don't you buy alarm clock? I am late for my work. You would not oversleep if I sleep with you?' Arthur clicked his tongue at that one. 'Perhaps I will, perhaps I won't. Of course I love you. Now come quick before I get sack from my job.'

It was five to nine before the car came for her, an ancient blue van this time. Arthur went down to take in the post. There was nothing on the mat, so presumably the postman hadn't yet come. But as he turned back into the hall, he saw that the table which on the previous night had been bare even of vouchers, now held a pile of envelopes. The post must have come early and while he was listening to Li-li's phone conversation. She had taken it in herself.

His own new Barclaycard, two circulars for Winston Mervyn and – unbelievable but real – a mauve-grey envelope postmarked Bristol. H had written again. Was there no stopping her? Arthur held the envelope in his fingertips, held it at arm's length as if it might explode. Well, he had decided no Bristol letter must ever be allowed to reach Anthony Johnson and that decision should stand. Better burn the thing immediately as he had burned the last. And yet ... A thrill of fear touched him. Li-li had taken that letter in, might or might not have noticed it. But how could he be sure she hadn't? If Anthony Johnson began to wonder why no letter had come for him for three weeks and started asking around – following up, in fact, H's suggestion, though it had never been communicated to him – then Li-li would remember.

Again he steamed open the envelope.

*Darling Tony, What have I done? Why have you rejected me without a word? You begged me to make up my mind and let you know as soon as I could. I did let you know by the Tuesday. I told you I was willing to leave Roger as soon as I heard from you and that I'd come to you. That was November 5th and now it's November 21st. Please tell me what I did and where I went wrong. Is it because I said I couldn't promise to love you for ever? God knows, I've wished a thousand times I'd never written those words. Or is it because I said I hadn't told Roger? I would have told him, you must believe me, as soon as I'd heard from you.*

*I think I've lost you. In so far as I can think rationally at all, I think I shall never see you again. Tony, you would have pity on me if you knew what black despair I feel, as if I can't go on another day. I would even come to you, only I'm terrified of your anger. You said there are other women in the world. I am afraid to come and find you with another girl. It would kill me. You said I was the only woman you had ever felt real passion for, apart from wanting them as friends or to sleep with. You said you thought 'in love' was an old-fashioned meaningless expression, but you understood it at last because you were in love with me. These feelings can't have been destroyed because I wrote tactless silly things in my first letter. Or weren't they ever sincere?*

*Roger has gone to Scotland on business. He's to be there at least a fortnight and wanted me to go with him, only I can't get time off from work till next Wednesday. Tony, while I'm alone here, please will you phone me at home? At any time during the weekend – I won't leave the house – or next week in the evenings. I beg you to. If I ever meant anything to you in the past, if only for what we*

135

*once were to each other, I beg you to phone me. If it's only
to say you don't want me, you've changed your mind, I
want to hear you saying it. Don't be so cruel as to let me
wait by the phone all the weekend. I can take it – I think –
if you say you've changed. What I can't take is this awful
silence.*

*But, Tony, if you don't phone, and I have to face the
possibility that you won't, I shan't write again. I don't
know what I shall do, but what little pride I have left will
keep me from throwing myself at you. So whatever
happens now, this is my last letter. H.*

That, Arthur thought, re-reading the last sentence,
was at any rate something to be thankful for. But if
Anthony Johnson saw this letter he'd be on the
phone at once, tonight. And in their conversation it
would all come out, the dates she'd written and the
things she'd written. Yet Anthony Johnson must see
this letter because Li-li Chan had already seen it.

By now it was almost twenty past nine. Arthur
considered not going to work, phoning Mr Grainger
and saying he'd got this gastric bug that was going
about. He seemed to see Auntie Gracie loom before
him, shaking her head at his deceit and his coward-
ice. Besides, he'd have to go back tomorrow or the
next day. Shivering as if he were really ill, he
dragged on his raincoat and took his umbrella from
the rack in the hall. What to do with H's letter? Take
it to work and try to think of some solution. He could
come home at lunchtime, anyway, in good time to
restore it if he could find no alternative but to deliver
it and himself into Anthony Johnson's hands.

He was late, of course, late for the first time in
years. Drizzle speckled the office window, then rain
gushed in sheets against the glass. In a wretched
state that was intensely nervous and at the same time

136

apathetic, Arthur opened Grainger's post, though he felt he never wanted to see another envelope as long as he lived. The handwriting of potential customers who wanted roofs re-tiled and central heating installed danced before his eyes. He typed two replies, full of errors, but at last there was nothing for it but to take H's letter out of his briefcase and scrutinize it once more.

Should he take a chance on Li-li's having failed to notice it? The chances were she hadn't noticed it among so much other stuff. Since there seemed no alternative, this was a risk he would have to take. Destroy the letter now and hope Anthony Johnson either wouldn't bother to ask her or that she wouldn't remember. He had closed his fist over the two sheets of flimsy paper when he realized, with a new terror, that even if Anthony Johnson didn't get this latest of H's letters, he would still discover the injury that had been done him. For on Wednesday, 27 November, next Wednesday, the last Wednesday in the month, he would phone H as he always did and the whole thing would come out.

Arthur ground two sheets of paper into his type-writer and struggled with a reply to a Mr P. Coleman who wanted Grainger's advice on the conversion of his nineteenth century coach-house into a dwelling for his mother-in-law. H's letter would have to go back to 142 Trinity Road by one and it was eleven now. He'd brazen it out, that was all. He'd deny in his most severe manner ever having touched Anthony Johnson's correspondence. Useless to keep turning things over in his mind like this when there was no help for it. He glanced at the sheet on which he was typing and saw he had put an H instead of a P before Coleman and 'convict' instead of 'convert'.

The paper was torn out and a fresh sheet inserted. Anthony Johnson would go at once to the police. The police would stop hunting for Brian Kotowsky and start thinking seriously about Arthur Johnson who never went out at night but who had been out that night; who was a resident of Kenbourne Vale at the time of the murder of Maureen Cowan and at the time of the murder of Bridget O'Neill: who had unaccountably lied to them ... He flexed his hands to try and prevent their trembling.

A mammoth effort, a mammoth concentration, and a passable letter advising Mr Coleman to consult a certain firm of Kenbourne Vale architects had been achieved. But as soon as he had done it and read it through, it struck him that if this reply came to the notice of Mr Grainger he would be very displeased indeed. Mr Grainger would expect him, while possibly mentioning the architects, to suggest that Grainger's themselves would be happy to carry out the work. The displeasure of the whole world, of everyone who mattered, loomed before him. He gave a shuddering sigh. Another, and very different, letter must be composed.

Fresh sheets of paper were in the machine before Arthur realized the significance of the words he had spoken under his breath. Another, and very different, letter must be composed ...

# Chapter 16

For her letters H always used the same flimsy paper Grainger's used for their carbon copies. And she used a similar typewriter to Arthur's. Suppose he himself were to type a letter to Anthony Johnson and insert it in that mauve-grey envelope? The envelope would be the original one, the postmark and its date correct, and it could be placed on the hall table in good time for Anthony Johnson to find it. Only the contents would be different.

Arthur, who had spent half a day composing with fear and extreme care that note of apology, was appalled by the magnitude and the danger of the task. And yet the letter wouldn't have to be a long one. His purpose, already half-formulated, was to make it as short as possible. He could imitate H's hysterical style – he had seen enough of it – and make the sort of errors she made, not depressing that key properly so that it made an eight instead of an apostrophe, depressing this one too long so that the second as well as the initial letter came out as upper case. And he could make the H with his own blue-black ballpoint pen.

He put two sheets of flimsy into the typewriter. The date first: 21 November, and the O of November a capital as well as the N. *Darling Tony* – no, she wouldn't call him darling for the kind of letter he meant to write. What would she call him? The only personal letters Arthur had written in his whole life were to a certain cousin of Auntie Gracie's who had sent him five-shilling postal orders on his birthdays. *Dear Uncle Alfred, Thank you very much for the postal order. I am going to save the money up in my money box. I had a nice birthday. Auntie Gracie gave me a new school blazer. With love from Arthur.* Dear Tony? In the end, not having the least idea whether people ever wrote that way, Arthur typed *Tony*. Just *Tony*.

How to begin? She was always asking him to forgive her. *Forgive me.* That was good, convincing. *I'm sorry*, he went on, taking care that an eight instead of an apostrophe appeared, *not to have written to you before as I promised.* Why hadn't she written? *I knew you would be angry if I said I couldn't make up my mind.* Good, he was doing well. But he must get on to the nub of it. *I have made it up now and I am going to stay with Roger. I am his wife and it is my duty to stay with him.* Arthur didn't like that much, it wasn't H's style, but he couldn't better it and still make her say what he meant her to say. There ought to be some love stuff. He racked his brains for something from the television or from one of those old films. *I never really loved you. It was just infatuation.* Now for the most important thing, the point of writing this letter that was primarily designed to put an end to all further communication between H and Anthony Johnson.

Barry loafed in just before one to say he had had his lunch and would be around to answer the phone while Arthur was out. It was still teeming with rain. Arthur put up his umbrella and set off for Trinity Road via the mews. He passed the spot where he had strangled Vesta Kotowsky, feeling a tickle of nostalgia and a fretful resentment against a society which had given him the need to commit such acts yet would condemn him with loathing for yielding to them.

The house was empty. Nothing on the table had been disturbed. Arthur checked that the flap of the mauve-grey envelope was securely gummed down, and then he placed it in the very centre of the glossy mahogany table.

The house was semi-detached, with the uncluttered lines of sixties building, of pale red bricks with big windows to let in ample light. The family who had lived there since it was new had planted each January in its front garden their Christmas trees, and these Norway spruces, ten of them, stood in a row, each one a little taller than its predecessor. Anthony, as he left the house with Winston, thought of Helen and the delight she would have taken in those Christmas trees, seeing in their arrangement the almost ritualistic placing of them, evidence of domestic harmony, quietude and a sense of permanent futurity.

The street was very quiet, a cul-de-sac. Children could play there in safety. But there were no children playing now, for it was dark, dark as midnight at six o'clock.

'What d'you think?' said Winston.

'Very nice, if you've got twenty thousand pounds. But you'll have to get married. It's no place for a bachelor. You must get married, have children, and with luck you'll be able to plant at least forty more Christmas trees.'

'Do I detect a note of sacrasm?'

'Sorry,' said Anthony. Viewing the house had made him bitter. It wasn't his ideal, too bourgeois, too dull, too sheltered, and yet – could you find a better place in which to build a marriage and raise a

141

family? Relationships are hard to come by, and one woman may make a man very discriminating, very selective. He saw his youth wasted in hanging after Helen, their dream children vanishing in their dream mother's vacillations.

Winston said, 'I think I shall buy it. I shall come and live here among the nobs.' He pointed as they turned the corner to a grander street. 'Caspian lives in one of those mini-mansions, and all made out of grinding our faces.'

They walked towards the K.12 stop. A thin cold drizzle was falling. It laid a slimy sheen on pavements and on the darker tarmac of the roadway, which threw back glittering yellow and red reflections of lamps. The neighbourhood changed abruptly as London neighbourhoods do. Once again they were among the tenements, the dispirited rows of terraced cottages without gardens or fences, the corner shops, the new housing blocks.

'You can always tell council flats by the smallness of their windows,' said Anthony. 'Have you noticed?'

'And their hideous design. It comes of giving second-rate architects a chance to experiment on people who can't afford to refuse.'

'Unlike lucky you.'

'In a filthy temper tonight, aren't you? Excuse me, I'm going in here to get a paper.'

Anthony waited at the door. What was happening to him that he could be rude and resentful to this new friend he liked so much? He stood in the now fast-falling rain, feeling depression settle on him. Friday night, Friday, 22 November. He had to get through another five days of this, five days till the last Wednesday of the month. But then he would phone her, certainly he would. He thought of her face that he hadn't seen for two months. It appeared before his eyes like a ghost face in mist, delicate, sensitive, contrite, wistful. The last time he had made love to her – he remembered it now, her eyes open and watching his eyes, her smile that had nothing to do with amusement. To have that again, even impermanently, even deferred, wasn't it worth sacrificing his pride for that, his ideal of himself as strong and decisive, for that? Yes, on Wednesday he would beg and persuade all over again, he would begin again . . .

Winston came out of the shop, holding the paper up, reading the front page. He came up to Anthony, thrust the paper at him.

'Look.'

The first thing Anthony saw was the photograph of Brian, the uncompromising passport photograph that had appeared so many times already, day after day, in every newspaper. The mop of hair, the wizened yet flaccid face, the eyes that ever seemed to implore, ever to irritate with their silliness. First the picture, then the headline: *Vesta's Husband Found Drowned*. The account beneath those huge black letters was brief.

*The body of a man washed up on the beach at Hastings, Sussex, was today identified as that of Brian Kotowsky, 38, husband of Vesta Kotowsky, strangled on Guy Fawkes Day in Kenbourne Vale, West London. Mr Kotowsky had been missing since the day following his wife's death.*

*Mr Kotowsky, an antique dealer, of Trinity Road, Kenbourne Vale, was known to have relatives in Brighton.*

*His aunt, Mrs Janina Shaw, said today that she had not seen her nephew for nine years.*

*'We were once very close,' she said. 'We lost touch when*

*Brian married. I cannot say if my nephew visited my
house prior to his death as I have been ill in hospital.'*

*An inquest will be held.*

Anthony looked at Winston. Winston shrugged,
his face closed and expressionless. The rain fell on to
the newspaper, darkening it with great heavy
splashes.

On the way home they hardly spoke. With a kind
of delicacy but without communicating that delicacy
to each other, they avoided the mews and walked to
Trinity Road by the long way round. Then Winston
said:

'I shouldn't have let him go out. I should have
dissuaded him and put him to bed and then none of
this would have happened.'

'No one is responsible for another adult person.'

'Can you define an adult person?' said Winston. 'It
isn't a matter of years.'

Anthony said no more. Entering the hall, he
remembered meeting Brian there for the first time.
Brian had been sitting on the stairs doing up his
shoelaces and he had come up to him and said, 'Mr
Johnson, I presume?' Now he was dead, had walked
out into the wintry sea until he drowned. He heard
Winston say, as from a long way off, that he had a
date at seven-thirty, that he must hurry.

'And I must do some work. Have a good time.'

'I'll try. But I wish I hadn't seen a paper till
tomorrow morning.'

Winston set his foot on the bottom stair, then,
having glanced over the banisters, turned and
walked up to the table. He picked up three envelopes. 'Now I've decided on my house, I must
remember to tell these agents to stop sending me
stuff.' He handed a fourth envelope to Anthony, a

144

mauve-grey one with a Bristol postmark. 'Here's one for you,' he said.

At last, after so long, she had written. To say she wanted his patience a little longer? That she had been ill? Or, wonder of wonders, that she was coming to him? He unlocked his door and kicked on the switch of the electric fire. A single thumb thrust split open the flap of the envelope. He pulled out the sheet of flimsy. Just one sheet? That must mean she had hardly anything to say, that she had settled in his favour. On the brink of a happy upheaval of his life, of consummation, he read it.

*Tony, Forgive me. I'm sorry not to have written to you before as I promised. I knew you would be angry if I said I couldn't make up my mind. I have made it up now and I am going to stay with Roger. I am his wife and it is my duty to stay with him.*

*I never really loved you. It was just infatuation. You must forget me and it will soon be as if you hadn't known me.*

*Do not phone me. You mustn't try to get in touch with me at all. Not ever. Roger will be angry if you do. So remember, this is final. I shall not see you again and you must not contact me. H.*

Anthony read it again because at first he simply couldn't believe it. It was as if a letter for someone else and written by someone else had got into one of those envelopes whose colour and shape and texture had always held a magic of their own. This – this obscenity – couldn't be intended for him, couldn't have been written by her to him. And yet it had been. Her typewriter had been used, those distinctive errors were hers. He read it a third time, and now rage began to conquer disbelief. How dare she write such hideous cliché-ridden rubbish to *him*? How dare she keep him waiting three weeks and then write this? The language appalled him almost as much as the sentiments it expressed. Her duty to stay with Roger! And then that lonelyhearts novelette word 'infatuation'. 'Contact' too – journalese for approach or communicate. He examined the letter, analysing it, as if close scrutiny of semantics could keep him from facing the pain of it.

The truth flashed upon him. Of course. She had begun it and the remainder had been dictated by Roger. Instead of serving to pacify him, this realization only made him angrier. She had confessed to Roger and he had compelled her to write like this. But what sort of a woman was it who would let a man take her over to that extent? And when did she think she was living, she who was self-supporting and had the franchise and was strong and healthy? A hundred years ago? A deep humiliation enclosed him as he imagined them composing that letter in concert, the woman abject and grateful for forgiveness, the man domineering, relegating him, Anthony, to the status of some gigolo.

'You give that presumptuous devil his marching orders. Let him know whose wife you are and where your duty lies. And put in something about not contacting you if he values his skin. For God's sake, Helen, make him see it's final . . .'

Final.

He screwed the letter up, then unscrewed it and tore it into tiny shreds so that the temptation to read it again was removed.

# Chapter 17

The news of Brian Kotowsky's death reached Arthur at nine o'clock that night by way of the television. The announcer didn't say much about it, only that a drowned corpse had been identified and that there would be an inquest. But Arthur was satisfied. He had never even considered that honourable promptings of conscience might bring him qualms when Brian was tried for Vesta's murder. Brian Kotowsky was nothing to him, his indifference towards the dead man tempered only by a natural dislike of someone who got drunk and was noisy. But Kotowsky might have been acquitted. Nothing could now acquit him. His self-dealt death marked him as plainly a murderer as any confession or any trial could have done. The police would consider the case as closed.

He slightly regretted his forgery of the morning. So much of his life had been ruined by terror, so much of his time wasted by gruelling anxiety. All of it in vain. But he consoled himself with the thought that, at the time, he had had no choice. Undoubtedly, Kotowsky's death hadn't appeared in the early editions of the evening papers so, even if he had bought one, he still wouldn't have known in time to avoid the substitution of the letter. But now, if Anthony Johnson were to find him out, there was no damaging action he could take. The police had a culprit, dead and speechless.

And so to get on with the business of living. Arthur watched a very old film about the building of the Suez Canal, starring Loretta Young as the Empress Eugénie and Tyrone Power as de Lesseps, till eleven. He enjoyed it very much, having seen it before with Auntie Gracie when he was thirteen. Those were the days. In euphoric mood, he really thought they had been. Saturday tomorrow. The new attendant at the launderette was Mr Grainger's nephew's wife, earning a bit of pin money, and he thought he could safely leave his washing with her while he went to the shops. Maybe he'd treat himself to a duck for Sunday by way of celebration.

There are ways and ways of ending a love affair. Anthony thought of the ways he had ended with girls in the past and the ways they had ended with him. Cool discussions, rows, pseudo-noble renunciations, cheerful let's-call-it-a-day farewells. But it had never been Helen's way. No one had rid herself of him with a curt note. And yet any of those other girls would have been more justified in doing so, for he had claimed to love none of them and offered none of them permanency. A last meeting he could have taken, a final explanation from her or even an honest letter, inviting him to phone her for a last talk. What he had received was more than he could take and he refused it. There still remained the last Wednesday of the month. Tomorrow. He would ask Linthea for the use of her phone so that there wouldn't be that hassle with the change. And Helen should learn she couldn't dismiss him as if he were some guy she'd picked up and spent a couple of nights with.

Leroy was still at school when he called at

Linthea's on his way home from college. 'You're welcome,' she said, 'but I have to go out around eight, so when you've done your phoning, would you sit with Leroy for an hour or two?'

This wasn't exactly what Anthony had envisaged. He had seen himself needing a little comfort after speaking his mind to Helen. On the other hand, this way Linthea wouldn't have to know whom he was phoning and why. And there would be plenty of time later in the week, next week, the week after, for consolation. All the time in the world . . .

Linthea was ready to go out when he got there and Leroy was playing Monopoly in his bedroom with Steve and David. Because it was still only ten to eight, Anthony passed the time by reading the evening paper's account of the inquest on Brian Kotowsky. Evidence was given of the murder of Brian's wife three weeks before, of his disappearance, but not a hint was breathed that Brian might have been responsible for that murder. The body had been in the sea for a fortnight and identification had been difficult. No alcohol had been present, but the cumulative effects of alcohol were found in the arteries and the liver. The verdict, in the absence of any suicide note or prior-to-death admission of unhappiness on Brian's part, was one of misadventure. In a separate paragraph Chief Superintendent Howard Fortune, head of Kenbourne Vale C.I.D., was quoted as saying simply, 'I have no comment to make at this stage.'

Eight o'clock. He would give it till ten past. Steve and David went home, and Anthony talked to Leroy, telling him stories about a children's home where he had once worked and where the boys had got out of the windows by night and gone off to steal cars. Leroy was entranced but Anthony's heart wasn't in

149

it. At eight-fifteen he put the television on, gave Leroy milk and biscuits and shut himself up in Linthea's bedroom where she had a phone extension.

He dialled the Bristol number and it began to ring. When it had rung twelve times he knew she wasn't going to answer. Would she, after all there had been between them, just sit there and let the phone ring? She must know it was he. He dialled again and again it rang unanswered. After a while he went back to Leroy and tried to watch a quiz programme. Nine o'clock came and he forgot all about sending Leroy off to bed as he had promised. Again he dialled Helen's number. She had gone out, he thought, guessing he would phone. That was how she intended to behave if he tried to 'contact' her. And when Roger was at home and the phone rang they would have arranged it so that he answered . . . He put the receiver back and sat with a contented little boy who didn't get sent to bed until five minutes before his mother came home with Winston Mervyn.

'I don't owe you anything for the call,' said Anthony. 'I couldn't get through.'

He went home soon after and lay on his bed, thinking of ways to get in touch with Helen. He could, of course, go to her house. He could go on Saturday, it was only two hours to Bristol in the train. Roger would be there, but he wasn't afraid of Roger, his guns and his rages. But Roger would be *there*, would possibly open the door to him. With Roger enraged and belligerent, Helen frightened and obedient according to what she had the effrontery to call her duty, what could he say? And nothing would be said at all, for Roger wouldn't admit him to the house.

He could phone her mother if he knew what her mother was called or where she lived. The sister and brother-in-law? They had hardly proved trustworthy in the past. In the end he fell into an uneasy sleep. When he awoke at seven it occurred to him that he could phone her at the museum. He had never done so before because of her absurd neurosis about Roger's all-seeing eye and all-hearing ear, but he'd do it now and to hell with Roger.

He had planned to spend the day in the British Museum library but it didn't much matter what time he got there. At nine he went out and bought a couple of cans of soup at Winter's in order to get some change. On the way back he passed Arthur Johnson in a silver-grey overcoat and carrying a briefcase, the acme of respectability. Arthur Johnson said good morning and that the weather was seasonable, to which Anthony agreed absently. A hundred and forty-two was quite empty, totally silent. The seasonableness of the weather was evinced by a high wind, and little spots of coloured light cast through the wine red and sap green glass danced on the hall floor.

He went upstairs to the phone and dialled. Peep-peep-peep, and in went the first of his money. A girl's voice but not hers.

'Frobisher Museum. Can I help you?'

'I want to speak to Helen Garvist.'

'Who is that calling?'

'It's a personal call,' said Anthony.

'I'm afraid I must have your name.'

'Anthony Johnson.'

She asked him to hold the line. After about a minute she was back. 'I'm afraid Mrs Garvist isn't here.'

He hesitated, then said, 'She must be there.'

'I'm afraid not.'

Then he understood. She would have come to the

phone if he hadn't given his name, if he had insisted on anonymity. But because she didn't want to talk to him, was determined at any cost not to talk to him, she had got the girl to tell this lie.

'Let me speak to the curator,' he said firmly.

'I'll see if he's available.'

The pips started. Anthony put in more money.

'Norman Le Queux speaking,' said a thin academic voice.

'I'm a friend of Mrs Helen Garvist and I'm speaking from London. From a call box. I want to speak to Mrs Garvist. It's very urgent.'

'Mrs Garvist is taking a fortnight of her annual leave, Mr Johnson.'

How readily the name came to him . . . He had been forewarned. 'In November? She can't be.'

'I beg your pardon?'

'I'm sorry, but I don't believe you. She told you to say that, didn't she?'

There was an astonished silence. Then the curator said, 'I think the sooner we terminate this conversation the better,' and he put the receiver down.

Anthony sat on the stairs. It is very easy to become paranoid in certain situations, to believe that the whole world is against you. But what if the whole world, or those significant members of it, truly are against you? Why should Helen go away now in the cold tail end of the year? She would have mentioned something about it in her last letter if she had planned to go away. No, it wasn't paranoid, it was only feasible to believe that, wanting no more of him, she had asked Le Queux and the museum staff to deny her to a caller named Anthony Johnson. Of course they would co-operate if she said this was a man who was pestering her . . .

152

'Kotowsky's being cremated today,' said Stanley Caspian.

Arthur put the rent envelopes on the desk in front of him. 'Locally?' he said.

'Up the cemetery. Don't suppose there'll be what you'd call a big turn-out. Mrs Caspian says I ought to put in an appearance but there are limits. Where did I put me bag of crisps, Arthur?'

'Here,' said Arthur, producing it with distaste from where it had fallen into the wastepaper basket.

'Poxy sort of day for a funeral. Eleven-thirty, they're having it, I'm told. Still, I should worry. I'm laughing, Arthur, things are looking up. Two bits of good news I've got. One, the cops say I can re-let Flat 1 at my convenience, which'll be next week.'

'It could do with a paint. A face-lift, as you might say.'

'So could you and me, me old Arthur, but it's not getting it any more than we are. I've no objection to the new tenant getting busy with a brush.'

'May I know your other piece of good news?'

'Reckon you'll have to, but I don't know how you'll take it. Your rent's going up, Arthur. All perfectly legal and above board, so you needn't look like that. Up to four-fifty a year which'll be another two quid a week in that little envelope, if you please.'

Arthur had feared this. He could afford it. He knew the Rent Act made provision for just such an increase in these hard times. But he wasn't going to let Stanley get away with it totally unscathed. 'No doubt you're right,' he said distantly, 'but I shall naturally have to go into the matter in my own interest. When you let me have the new agreement it would be wise for my solicitors to look at it.' As a parting shot he added, 'I fear you won't find it easy letting those rooms. Two violent deaths, you know.

People don't care for that sort of thing, it puts them off.'

He took his envelope and went upstairs, his equilibrium which had prevailed, though declining, for a week, now shaken. He hoped that any prospective tenants of the Kotowskys' flat would come round while he was at home, in which case he would take care to let them know all. A gloomy day of thin fog and fine rain. Not enough rain, though, for his umbrella. The orange plastic bag of laundry in one hand, the shopping basket in the other, he set off for the launderette.

Mr Grainger's nephew's wife promised to keep an eye on his washing and pleased Arthur by commenting favourably on the quality of his bedlinen. He bought a Dover sole for lunch, a pound of sprouts, a piece of best end of neck for Sunday. The K.12 bus drew up outside the Waterlily and, on an impulse, Arthur got on it. It dropped him at the cemetery gates.

This was the old part, this end, a necropolis of little houses, the grey lichen-grown houses of the dead. Some years back a girl had been found dead on one of these tombs, a family vault. Arthur paused in front of the iron door which closed off the entrance to this cavern. He had been there before, had been inside, for the girl had been strangled and he had wondered if the police would regard her as the third of his victims, though he had been safe in those days with his white lady. Her murderer had been caught. He walked under the great statue of the winged victory, past the tomb of the Grand Duke who had given his name to the pub, on to the crematorium. The chapel door was closed. Arthur opened it diffidently.

A conversation seemed to be taking place inside,

for what else can you call it when one man is speaking to one other? The man who was speaking was a clergyman and the man who was listening, sole member of that congregation, was Jonathan Dean. Brian Kotowsky had only one friend to mourn him. Music began to play, but it was muzak really, as if the tape playing in a supermarket had suddenly taken a religious turn. The coffin, blanketed in purple baize, began to move, and silently the beige velvet curtains drew together. Brian Kotowsky, like Arthur's white lady, had gone to the fire.

Arthur slipped out. He didn't want to be seen. He walked back towards the gates along another path, much overgrown, this one, by brambles and the creeping ivy and long-leaved weeds the frost hadn't yet killed. Droplets of water clung to stone and trembled on leaf and twig. Presently he came to the red granite slab on which was engraved: *Arthur Leopold Johnson, 1855–1921, Maria Lilian Johnson, 1857–1918, beloved wife of the above, Grace Maria Johnson, 1888–1955, their daughter. Blessed are the dead which die in the Lord.* No room for him there, no room for his mother, though perhaps she too was dead. Perhaps that was why she hadn't come to Auntie Gracie's funeral . . .

In his best dark suit and new black tie, he had sat in the front room of the house in Magdalen Hill, reading the paper. The paper was full of some journalist's theorizing about the Kenbourne Killer and his latest victim. He had read it while he waited for the mourners, Uncle Alfred who had sent him the birthday postal orders, the Winters, Beryl's mother, Mrs Goodwin from next door. It was she who had told him of Auntie Gracie's death.

A cold Monday in March it had been. His bedroom was icy, but no one in his milieu and at that time thought of heating bedrooms. Auntie Gracie awakened him at seven-thirty – he never questioned why he should get up at seven-thirty when he only worked next door and didn't have to be there till half past nine – awakened him and left for him in the cold bathroom a jug of hot water for shaving. Then into clean underwear because it was Monday.

'If you keep yourself clean, Arthur, you don't need clean underclothes more than once a week.'

But a fresh white shirt each day because a shirt goes on top and shows. Downstairs to the kitchen where the boiler was alight and the table laid for one. Since he became a man Auntie Gracie had put away childish things for him. She ate her breakfast before he came down and waited on him because he was now master of the house. A bowl of cornflakes, one egg, two rashers of collar bacon, it was always the same. And she had been just the same that morning, her grey hair in tight curls from the new perm she hadn't yet combed out, dark skirt, lilac jumper, black and lilac crossover overall, slippers that were so hard and plain and unyielding that you could have thought them walking shoes.

'It looks like rain.' As he emptied a plate she took it and washed it. Between washing, she stood at the window, studying the sky above the rooftops in Merton Street. 'You'd better take your umbrella.'

Once he had protested that he didn't need an umbrella to walk twenty yards through light rain or a hat to withstand ten minutes' chill or a scarf against the faintly falling snow. But now he knew better. By keeping silent he could avoid hearing the words that aroused in him impotent anger and shame: 'And when you get ill like you were last time, I suppose you'll expect me to work myself into the ground nursing you and waiting on you.'

So he kept silent and didn't even attempt to argue that he might have spent a further hour in bed rather than on a stool in front of the boiler reading the paper. She bustled about the house, calling to him at intervals, 'Ten to nine, Arthur,' 'Nine o'clock, Arthur.' When he left, allowing himself ten minutes to walk next door, she came to the front door with him and put up her cheek for a kiss. Arthur always remembered those kisses when, in his introspective moments, he reminded himself how happy their relationship had been. And he felt a savage anger against Beryl's mother for a comment she had once made.

'You give that boy your cheek like you were showing the doctor a boil on your neck, Gracie.'

That morning he had kissed her in the usual way. Many times since he had wished he had allowed his lips to linger or had put an arm round her heavy shoulders. But thinking this way was a kind of fantasising, identifying with characters from films, for he had no idea how to kiss or embrace. And he blocked off the picture at this point because, after the image of that unimaginable closeness, came a frightening conclusion of the embrace, the only possible ending to it . . .

At eleven, when he was doing Grainger's accounts in the room at the side of the works – no little cedarwood and glass office in those days – Mr Grainger had walked in with Mrs Goodwin. He could see them now, Mr Grainger clearing his throat, Mrs Goodwin with tears on her face. And then the words: 'Passed away . . . her heart . . . fell down before my eyes . . . gone, Arthur. There was nothing anyone could do.'

Someone had been in and laid her out. Arthur wouldn't let the undertakers take the body till the following day. He knew what was right. The first night after death you watched by the dead. He watched. He thought of all she had done for him and what she had been – mother, father, wife, counsellor, housekeeper, sole friend. The large-featured face, waxen and calm, lay against a clean white pillowcase. He yearned towards her, wanting her back – for what? To be better than he had been? To please her as he had never pleased her? To explain or ask her for explanation? He didn't think it was for any of those things and he was afraid to touch her, afraid even to let one of his cold fingers rest against her colder cheek. The hammering in his head was strong and urgent.

Not for nearly six years had he been out alone at night. But at half past nine he went out, leaving Auntie Gracie on her own. He slipped through the passage into Merton Street and then he walked and walked, far away to a pub where they wouldn't know him – the Hospital Arms.

There he drank two brandies. A stretch of weed-grown bomb site separated the hospital from the embankment, the railway line and the footbridge that crossed it. Arthur didn't need to cross the line. His way home was by way of the long lane that straggled through tenements and cottages to the High Street. But he went on to the bomb site and lingered among the rubble stacks until the girl came hurrying over the bridge.

Bridget O'Neill, 20, student nurse. She screamed when she saw him, before he had even touched her, but there was no one in that empty waste land to hear her. A train roared past, letting out its double-noted bray. She ran from him, tripped over a brick, and fell. With his bare hands he strangled her on the ground, and then he left her, returning through the

158

dark ways to Magdalen Hill. Soon he slept, falling into a sleep almost as deep, though impermanent, as that which enclosed Auntie Gracie in her last bed.

He had never tended her grave. Thick grass grew above the sides of the slab, and her christian name was obliterated by tendrils of ivy. Death surrounded him, cold, musty, mildewed death, not the warm kind he wanted. He knew he had begun to want it again, and frightened, wearied by this urge which only death itself could end, he went back to the bus, the launderette and the eternal cleaning of the flat.

Love is the cure for love. Anthony knew that, whatever might happen between him and Linthea it could at best be a distraction. But what was wrong with distractions? His love for Helen had been deep, precious, special. It was absurd to suppose that that could be replaced at will. But many activities and many emotions go under the name of love, and almost any one of them will for a while divert the mind from the real, true and perfect thing.

So he set off for Brasenose Avenue, if not a jolly thriving wooer, at least a purposeful one. In his time he had received very few refusals. His thoughts, embittered, took a base turn. Was it likely that a widow, lonely, older than himself, would turn him down? And when he rang the doorbell it was answered almost at once by Linthea herself who drew him without a word into the flat and threw her arms round his neck. Afterwards he was thankful he hadn't responded as he had wanted to. Perhaps, even at that moment, he sensed that this was a kiss of a happiness so great as to include any third party.

Winston was in the sitting room. They had been drinking champagne. Anthony stuck his bottle of

Spanish Graves on top of the cupboard where it wouldn't be noticed.

'You can be the first to congratulate us,' Winston said. 'Well, not the first if you count Leroy.'

'You're getting married.' Anthony uttered it as a statement rather than a question.

'Saturday week,' Linthea said, embracing him again. 'Do come!'

'Of course he'll come,' said Winston. 'We'd have told you before, we decided a week ago, but we wanted to make sure it was all right with Leroy first.'

'And was it?'

Winston laughed. 'Fine, only when Linthea said she was marrying me he said he'd rather have had you.'

So Anthony also had to laugh at that one and drink some champagne and listen to Winston's romantic, but not sentimental, account of how he had always wanted Linthea, had lost her when she married and had later pursued her half across the world in great hope. Helen had once quoted to Anthony that it is a bitter thing to look at happiness through another man's eyes. He told himself that her quotations and her whole Eng. Lit. bit bored him, she was as bad as Jonathan Dean, and then he went home to do more work on his thesis.

*Though the psychopath may suffer from compulsive urges or an obsessional neurosis, his condition is related to a lowered state of cortical arousal and a chronic need for stimulation. He may therefore face the warring elements of a routine-driven life and an inability to tolerate routine in the absence of exciting stimuli . . .*

He broke off, unable to concentrate. This wasn't what he wanted to write. He wanted – needed – to do something he had never done before, write a letter to Helen.

# Chapter 18

He wouldn't send it to her home, that would be worse than useless. To the museum then? Although she hadn't a secretary, he remembered her telling him there was a girl who opened the incoming post for herself and Le Queux. Her mother would do if only he knew her mother's address. He tried to remember the names of friends she had spoken of when they were together. There must be someone to whom he could entrust a letter that was for her eyes only.

Re-reading her old letters in search of a name, a clue, was a painful exercise. *Darling Tony, I knew I'd miss you but I didn't know how bad it would be . . .* That was the one with the bit in it about an invitation to a dress show. If he'd known the name of the dress shop . . . The people she'd been to school with, to college with? He recalled only christian names, Wendy, Margaret, Hilary. Suppose he wrote to her old college? The authorities would simply forward the letter to her home. Anyone would do that unless he put in a covering letter expressly directing them not to. And could he bring himself to do that? Perhaps he could, especially as the letter he intended to write wasn't going to be a humble plea.

He wrote it. Not simply, just like that, but draft after draft until he wondered if he was as mentally unstable as the sick people he studied. The final result dissatisfied him but he couldn't improve on it.

*Dear Helen, I love you. I think I loved you from the first moment we met, and though I would give a lot to blot this feeling out and maybe be free of you, I can't. You were my whole hope for the future and it was you who gave me a purpose for my life. But that's enough of me. I don't mean to go in for maudlin self-pity.*

*This letter is about you. You led me to believe you loved me in the same way. You told me you had never loved anyone the way you loved me and that Roger was nothing to you except an object of pity. You made love with me many times, many beautiful unforgettable times, and you are not – I can tell this, you know – the kind of woman who sleeps with a man for fun or diversion. You almost promised to come away and live with me. No, it was more than that. It was a firm promise, postponed only because you wanted more time.*

*Yet you have ditched me in such a cold peremptory way that even now I can hardly believe it. When I think of that last letter of yours it takes my breath away. I don't mean to reproach you for the pain you have caused me but to ask you what you think you are doing to yourself? Have you, in these past weeks, ever asked yourself what kind of a woman can live your sort of ambivalent life, pretending and lying to a husband and lover equally? What happens to that woman as she grows older and begins to lose any idea of what truth is? Life isn't worth living for someone who is a coward, a liar and has lost self-respect, particularly when she is sensitive as, God knows, you are.*

*Think about it. Don't think about me if you don't want to but think about the damage, fear and woolly mindedness and that sort of confusion are going to do to whatever there is under that pretty exterior of yours.*

*If you want to see me I'll see you. But I won't commit*

*myself to more than that now. I think I would be wilfully*
*damaging my own self if I were ever to get back into a*
*relationship with the kind of person you are. A.*

But who could he send it to? Who could be his go-
between?

It was talking about Christmas with Winston that
brought him what could be a solution. Helen had
told him of friends in Gloucester with whom she and
her mother and, since her marriage, Roger as well,
spent every Christmas. He had never heard their
address and their name eluded him, though Helen
had mentioned it. She had told him, he remembered,
that it was Latin for a priest . . .

'Linthea and I,' Winston said, 'will still be on our
honeymoon. Lovely having Christmas in Jamaica,
only I feel a bit bad about Leroy. Maybe we ought to
take him. On our *honeymoon*? Perhaps I'm being too
conventional, perhaps . . .'

'What's the Latin for a priest?' said Anthony
abruptly.

Winston stared at him. 'Sorry if I'm boring you.'

'You're not boring me. I hope you'll have a
fabulous honeymoon. I should be so lucky. Take the
whole Merton Street Primary School with you if you
like, but just tell me the Latin for a priest.'

'*Pontifex, pontificis*, masculine.'

He knew it was the right name as soon as he heard
it. Pontifex. He'd go to the public library, the main
branch in the High Street, where they kept telephone
directories for the whole country. 'Thanks,' he said.

'You're welcome,' said Winston. 'Just a dictionary,
I am. Mr Liddell or Mr Scott.'

There were three Pontifexes (or *pontifices*, as Winston would have put it) in the city of Gloucester. But
A.W. at 26 Dittisham Road was obviously the one,

163

Miss Margaret and Sir F. being unlikely candidates. Anthony prepared an envelope: Mrs Pontifex, 26 Dittisham Road, Gloucester, and on the flap: Sender, A. Johnson, 2/142 Trinity Road, London, W15 6HD. The letter to Helen went into a blank, smaller envelope to be inserted inside it. But there would have to be a covering letter.

Anthony knew he couldn't write to a woman he had never met, instructing her to pass an enclosure to another woman without the knowledge of that woman's husband. But that wouldn't be necessary. Helen and Roger would arrive at the Pontifex home on, say, Christmas Eve. Mrs Pontifex would hand his letter over to Helen either when they were alone together – perhaps in Mrs Pontifex's bedroom immediately after their arrival – or else, and more likely, in public and full view of a company of festive relatives. Did that matter? Anthony thought not. This way, even if Roger were to demand to see it, Helen would see it first.

*Dear Mrs Pontifex, I know that Mrs Garvist will be spending Christmas with you and I wonder if you would be kind enough to give her the enclosed when you see her. I have mislaid her present address, otherwise I would not trouble you. Yours sincerely, Anthony Johnson.*

It looked, he thought, peculiar, to say the least. He had mislaid the address of someone with the rare name of Garvist whom he obviously knew well, but was in possession of the address of someone with the equally rare name of Pontifex whom he didn't know at all. If one name could be found in the phone book so could the other. He stuck a stamp on the envelope. He looked at this result of so much complicated effort. Was it worth it? Would any possible outcome

164

mitigate the depression which enclosed him? The letter need not, in any case, be sent till a few days before Christmas. Pushing it to one side with a heap of books and papers and notes, he wondered if, in the end, he would send it at all.

When Arthur spoke of 'my solicitor' he meant a firm in Kenbourne Lane who had acted for him twenty years before in the matter of proving Auntie Gracie's meagre will. Since then he had never communicated with this firm or been inside its offices, but he went there now and it cost him fifteen pounds to be told that unless there were any repairs outstanding to the fabric of his flat, he hadn't a leg to stand on against Stanley Caspian in the matter of the rent increase. Although, as he put it to himself exaggeratedly, the rest of the place was falling down. Flat 2 was in fact in good order. Almost wishing that the roof would spring a leak, Arthur managed some petty revenge by telling a young couple whom he found waiting in the hall before Stanley Caspian's Saturday arrival that Flat 1 had macabre associations and that its rent could be knocked down to eight pounds a week by anyone who cared to try it on. The young couple argued with Stanley but they didn't take the Kotowskys' flat.

The police had not reappeared. Everyone took it for granted Brian Kotowsky had murdered his wife. But Arthur remembered the case of John Reginald Halliday Christie. Christie had murdered, among others, another man's wife and that man had been hanged for it. But in the end that murder had been brought home to the true perpetrator. Arthur never relaxed his surveillance of the post or failed to put his door on the latch when he heard anyone use the telephone. Wednesday, 27 November, had been a bad evening but it had passed without Anthony Johnson making a call. No letters from Bristol had come for more than a fortnight. Surely there would be none? Arthur observed Anthony Johnson coming and going at his irregular hours, a little dejected perhaps as if some of that youthful glow and vigour which he had noticed on their first meeting, had gone out of him. But we all have to grow up and face, Arthur thought, the reality and earnestness of life. Once, passing beneath his window, Anthony Johnson raised a hand and waved to him. It wasn't a particularly enthusiastic wave, but Arthur would have distrusted it if it had been. It signified to him only that Anthony Johnson bore him no malice.

On the morning of Saturday, 7 December, he wrote a stiff letter to his solicitor, deprecating the high cost of such negative advice but nevertheless enclosing a cheque for fifteen pounds. He always paid his bills promptly, having an undefined fear of nemesis descending should he be in debt to anyone for more than a day or two. At nine he saw the postman cross the street and he went down to take in the mail. Nothing but a rates demand for Stanley Caspian which shouldn't, by rights, have come to Trinity Road at all.

Li-li Chan's rent envelope was on the hall table and so was Winston Mervyn's. Anthony Johnson's, however, was missing. Arthur listened warily outside the door of Room 2. Silence, then the clink of a tea cup against a saucer. He knocked softly on the door and gave his apologetic cough.

'Yes?'

'It's Mr Johnson, Mr Johnson,' said Arthur, feeling this was ridiculous, but not knowing how else to put it.

'One minute.'

About a quarter of a minute passed and then the door was opened by Anthony Johnson in jeans and a sweater which had obviously been pulled on in haste. The room was freezing, the electric fire having perhaps only just been switched on. From the state of the bed and the presence of the bedside table of a half-consumed cup of tea, it was evident that Anthony Johnson had been having a lie-in. And to his caller's extreme disapproval, he intended to resume it, for, having offered Arthur a cup of tea which was refused, he got back into bed fully-clothed.

'I hope you'll excuse the intrusion, but it's about the little matter of the rent.'

'You needn't have bothered. I'd have put it out before Caspian came.' Anthony Johnson finished his tea. 'It's on the table,' he said casually, 'among all that other stuff.'

'All that other stuff' was a formidable array (or muddle, as Arthur put it to himself) of books, some closed, some open and face-downwards, scattered sheets of foolscap, dog-eared notebooks and a partially completed manuscript.

'With your permission,' Arthur said, and delicately picked about in the mess as if it were a pile of noxious garbage. He came upon the brown rent envelope under a weighty tome entitled *Human Behaviour and Social Processes*.

'The rent book and my cheque are in there.'

Arthur said nothing. Under the rent envelope was another, stamped and addressed, but without his glasses he was unable, from this distance, to read the address. At once it occurred to him that this letter might be to H in Bristol. He thought quickly, said almost as quickly:

'I have to go to the post with a letter of my own. Would you care for me to take this one of yours?'

Anthony Johnson's hesitation was unmistakeable. Was he remembering that other occasion on which Arthur had posted a letter for him and the unfortunate antagonism that action had led to? Or did he perhaps suspect a tampering with his post? Anthony Johnson threw back the bed covers, got up and came over to the table. He picked up the envelope and looked at it in silence, indecisively, deep in thought. Arthur managed a considerate patient smile, but inwardly he was trembling. It must be to her, it must be. Why else would the man linger over it like this, wondering, no doubt, whether posting it would risk a violent confrontation with the woman's husband.

At last Anthony Johnson looked up. He handed the letter to Arthur with a funny swift gesture as if he must either be rid of it quickly or not at all.

'O.K.,' he said. 'Thanks.'

Once more in the hall and alone, Arthur held the envelope up to within two inches of his eyes. Then he put on his glasses to make absolutely sure. But it was all right. The letter was addressed to a Mrs Pontifex in Gloucester. He was savouring his relief when Stanley Caspian banged in, sucking a toffee. Arthur put the kettle on without waiting to be asked and handed Stanley his rents. Stanley opened Winston Mervyn's envelope first.

'Well, my God, if Mervyn's not going now! Given in his poxy notice for the first week of Jan.'

'A little bird told me he's getting married.'

Stanley munched ill-temperedly, jabbing so hard into Arthur's rent book that his pen made a hole in the page. 'That'll be the whole of the first floor vacant. Makes you wonder what the world's coming to.'

'The rats,' said Arthur, 'might be said to be leaving the sinking ship.'

'Not you, though, eh? Oh, no. Those as have unfurnished tenancies don't go till they're carried out feet first. You'll die here, me old Arthur.'

'I'm sure I hope so,' said Arthur. 'Now, if I could have my little envelope?'

He took it and set off with his laundry, pausing outside Kemal's Kebab House to drop both letters in the pillar box.

# Chapter 19

During the week which followed Arthur was oppress-
ively aware of the emptiness of 142 Trinity Road. Li-
li had never been at home much, was flying to
Taiwan for Christmas, and now Winston Mervyn
was out every night. Soon he too would be gone.
Then, if the pressure of the London housing shortage
wasn't strong enough to overcome people's semi-
superstitious distaste for a hundred and forty-two,
he and Anthony Johnson would in effect be the sole
tenants. He would once have welcomed the idea.
Once he had savoured those moments when he had
had the house to himself, when the last of them to
leave in the mornings had given the front door a final
bang. And he had dreamed of being its only
occupant, living high on the crest of silent emptiness,
while she who inhabited the depths below awaited
the attentions and whims of her master.

But now that empty silence disturbed him. For
three nights out of the seven no light fell on to the
court from the window of Room 2, and the dark well
he could see below him when he drew his curtains
brought him temptations he had no way of yielding
to. It frightened him even to think of them, but these
suppressed thoughts blossomed in dreams like
tubers which, put away in the dark, throw out sickly,
slug-like shoots. Not since he was a young man had
he dreamed of that act he had three times performed.

But he dreamed of it now and awoke one morning hanging half out of bed, his hands clenched as if in spasm round the leg of his bedside table which, unknowingly, he had dragged towards him.

The postman had ceased to call. In all the years Arthur had been there no such week as this, without a single letter, had passed. It was as if the Post Office were on strike. Of course it was easily explicable. Winston Mervyn had seldom received any post except that from estate agents; Li-li's father wouldn't write when he expected to see his daughter next week; little had ever come for Anthony Johnson but those mauve-grey Bristol envelopes. And yet this also seemed to contribute to Arthur's feeling that all the forces of life were withdrawing from the house and leaving it as a kind of mausoleum for himself.

But on the morning of Saturday, 14 December, something resembling a convulsion took place in it, like a death throe. The phone ringing wakened him. It rang for Winston Mervyn three times before nine o'clock. Then he heard Winston Mervyn running up and downstairs, Anthony Johnson in Mervyn's room, Anthony Johnson and Mervyn talking, laughing. He went down to see if there was, by chance, any post. There wasn't. The door of Room 1 was open, music playing above the whine of the vacuum cleaner. Li-li had decided, unseasonably and uniquely, to spring-clean her room. And Stanley Caspian, usually so mindful of the fabric of his property, added to the noise by slamming the front door so hard that plaster specks lay scattered on his car coat like dandruff.

Stanley detained him so long with moans about the rates, the cruelty of the government towards honest landlords and the fastidiousness of prospective tenants, that he was late in getting to the shops. Every machine at the launderette was taken. He had to leave his washing in the care of Mr Grainger's nephew's wife who was distant with him and demanded an extra twenty pence for service.

'I never heard of such a thing,' said Arthur.

'Take it or leave it. There's inflation for me same as for others.'

Arthur would have liked to say more but he was afraid it might get back to Mr Grainger, so he contented himself with a severe, 'I'll call back for it at two sharp.'

'Four'd be more like,' said the woman, 'what with this rush,' and she paid Arthur no compliments as to the superiority of his linen.

It was a June-skied day but hazeless and clearer than any June day could be, and the sunlight was made icy by a razor wind. Angrily, Arthur shouted at the children who were climbing on the statues. They took no notice beyond shouting back at him a word which, though familiar to any resident of West Kenbourne, still brought a blush to his face.

A taxi stood outside a hundred and forty-two, and as he approached, Winston Mervyn and Anthony Johnson came out of the house and went up to it. Arthur thought how awkward and embarrassed he would feel if called upon to say to a taxi driver what Winston Mervyn now said:

'Kenbourne Register Office, please.'

He said it in a bold loud voice as if he were proud of himself, and favoured everyone with a broad smile. Arthur would have liked to pass on up the steps without a word, but he knew better than to neglect his social obligations particularly as Stanley Caspian had told him this coloured fellow, obviously well-off, was buying a house in North Kenbourne.

'Let me offer you my best wishes for your future happiness, Mr Mervyn,' he said.

172

'Thanks very much.'

'A fine day for your wedding,' said Arthur, 'though somewhat chilly.'

He went indoors and passed Li-li going out, her rare effort at cleaning finished or abandoned. Again he was alone. He cooked his lunch, scoured the flat, watched Michael Redgrave in *The Captive Heart* on television. It wasn't till darkness began to close in and lights came on in the tall houses opposite that he remembered he still had to collect his washing.

Winston had engaged one of the dining rooms at the Grand Duke for his wedding reception, and there at one-thirty the bride and groom, Leroy, Anthony, Winston's brother and sister-in-law and Linthea's sister and brother-in-law sat down to lunch. Linthea gave Anthony a rose from the bouquet she was carrying.

'There, that means you'll be the next to marry.'

He felt a painful squeeze of the heart. But he smiled down at the beautiful girl in her apple green silk dress and said, 'That's only for bridesmaids.'

'For best men too. It's an old West Indian custom.'

Cries of denial, gales of laughter greeted this. Anthony made a speech which he felt was feeble, though it was received with applause. He could hardly bear to look at Winston and Linthea whose exchanged glances and secret decorous smiles spoke of happiness enjoyed and anticipated.

At four they all went back to Brasenose Avenue to collect Linthea's luggage and then to Trinity Road for Winston's. From the call box on the landing Winston phoned London Airport to check his honeymoon flight to Jamaica and was told it had been delayed three hours. By this time Leroy had already been carried off by his aunt with whom he was to stay, and Linthea felt a dislike of going back to the empty flat. At a loose end, they were debating how they should kill the intervening time when the front door, which had been left on the latch, crashed heavily, and a voice called up the stairs:

'The wedding guest, he beat his breast!'

Jonathan Dean.

'Thought I'd try and catch you before you left, old man. Wish you God speed and all that.' He showed, Anthony thought, no scars from grief over his dead friend, but seemed stouter and ruddier. Half-way up the stairs he met them coming down. 'Did I hear someone mention killing time? How about a quick one or a few slow ones up the Lily?'

'It's not five,' said Winston.

Jonathan agreed but said it wanted only ten minutes and that tempus was fugitting as usual. At this point Li-li emerged from Room 1 to be met by a look of frank lechery from Jonathan who made a joke with heavy play on her name and that of the pub which evoked screams of merriment from Winston's sister-in-law. And so, without much show of enthusiasm on the part of either bride or groom, the whole party, now swelled to seven, made their way towards the Waterlily.

When they reached the corner of Magdalen Hill and Balliol Street – by common unspoken consent, they avoided Oriel Mews – Anthony saw, standing on the other side of the street, waiting for the lights to change, a familiar lean figure in silver-grey overcoat and carrying an orange plastic laundry bag. The man's face had the sore reddish look he had noticed before, and there was something prickly and resentful in his whole bearing as if he took the persistent greenness of the traffic light and the stream of vehicles as an affront aimed personally at him. In that crowd, London working class, hippy-costumed drop-outs, brown immigrants, his clothes and his air set him apart and enclosed him in loneliness. Time and change had passed him by. He was a sad and bitter anachronism.

Anthony touched Winston's arm. 'Should we ask old Johnson to join us for a drink? It's up to you, it's your party, but it seems a bit cold not to . . .'

Before he could finish, Winston had hailed Arthur Johnson who had begun to cross the road. 'I'm glad you saw him,' he said to Anthony. 'He was rather nice to me this morning with his good wishes, and seeing everyone else in the house is here, it's the least we can do. Mr Johnson!' he called. 'Can you spare a few minutes to come and celebrate with us in the Waterlily?'

Anthony wasn't surprised to see that Arthur Johnson was flummoxed, even shocked, by the suggestion. First came the mottled flush, then a stream of excuses. 'I couldn't possibly – most kind but out of the question – a busy evening ahead of me – you must count me out, you really must, Mr Mervyn.'

It seemed definite enough. But Anthony – and evidently Arthur Johnson – had reckoned without West Indian hospitality and West Indian enthusiastic pressure. In argument, Arthur Johnson would perhaps have won, but he was given no chance to argue, the situation being managed by Winston's brother, a man of overpowering bonhomie. And Anthony who in the past had been irritated by and sorry for Arthur Johnson, now felt neither anger nor pity. It was all he could do to stop himself laughing aloud at the sight of this finicky and austere-looking man propelled into the saloon bar of the Waterlily between Perry Mervyn and Jonathan Dean. Arthur Johnson looked amazed and frightened. Still clutching his carrier bag, he had the air of some gentleman burglar of fiction apprehended by plainclothes policemen, the bag, of course, containing the spoils of crime. And now it was Li-li who took the bag from him, ignoring his protests and thrusting it under the settle on which she and Jonathan sat down with their victim between them.

It was a violation, a kidnapping almost, Arthur thought, too affronted to speak. He had never before entered the Waterlily which, in his youth, had been pointed out to him by Auntie Gracie as a den of iniquity. Bewildered, crushed by shyness, he sat stiff and silent while Jonathan Dean paid Li-li compliments across him and Li-li giggled in return. The stout and very black woman who faced him added to his discomfiture by asking him in rapid succession what he did for a living, if he was married and how long had he lived in Trinity Road. He was saved from answering her fourth question – didn't he think her new sister-in-law absolutely lovely? – by Anthony Johnson's asking him what he would drink. Arthur replied, inevitably, that he would have a small brandy.

'Claret is the liquor for boys, port for men, but he who aspires to be a hero must drink brandy.' Having quoted this, Dean roared with laughter and said it was by Dr Johnson.

Arthur didn't know what he meant but felt he was getting at him personally and perhaps also at Anthony Johnson. He wondered how soon he could make his escape. The brandy came and with it a variety of longer, less strong, drinks for the others, which made Arthur wonder if he had made a too expensive choice or even committed some gross social error. Two entirely separate conversations began to be conducted round the table, one between Li-li, Dean and Mervyn's sister-in-law, the other between the bridal couple and Mervyn's brother. And Arthur was aware of the isolation of himself and the 'other' Johnson, both of whom were left out of these exchanges. Anthony Johnson looked rather ill – had drunk too much, Arthur supposed, at whatever carousing had been going on since lunch-time – and he began turning over in his mind various opening gambits for a conversation between them. As the only English people present, for the loath-some Dean didn't count and was very likely an Irishman, anyway, it was their duty to present some sort of solid front. And he had opened his mouth to speak of the severe frost which the television had forecast for that night, when Dean, raising his glass in what he called a nuptial toast, launched into a speech.

For some moments this was listened to in silence, though Winston Mervyn seemed fidgety. Didn't like someone else stealing his thunder, Arthur thought. And Dean was certainly airing his education, spout-ing streams of stuff which couldn't have been thought up on the spur of the moment but must have been written down first. It was all about love and marriage, and Arthur actually chuckled when Dean levelled his gaze on Mervyn's stout brother-in-law and said that in marriage a man becomes slack and selfish and undergoes a fatty degeneration of his moral being. At the same time he was aware that under the table a heavily shod foot was groping across his ankles to find a daintily shod foot. He drew in his knees.

'To marry,' said Dean, 'is to domesticate the Recording Angel. Once you are married there is nothing left for you, not even suicide, but to be good.'

Only Li-li laughed. The Mervyn relatives looked blank. Winston Mervyn got up abruptly and stalked to the bar while Anthony Johnson, with a violence which alarmed Arthur because he couldn't at all understand it, said:

'For God's sake, shut up! D'you ever stop and think what you're saying?'

Dean's face fell. He blushed. But he leaned across Arthur almost as if he wasn't there and whispered on beery breath into Li-li's face, 'You like me, don't you, darling? You're not so bloody fastidious.'

Li-li giggled. There was some awkward dodging about and then Arthur realized she was kissing Dean behind his back.

'Perhaps,' he said, 'you'd care to change places with me?'

Why this should have caused so much mirth – general laughter after awkwardness – he was unable to understand, but he thought he could take it as his chance to leave. And he would have left had not Mervyn returned at that moment with another tray of drinks including a second small brandy. He edged along the settle, leaving Li-li and Dean huddled together.

It was a pity, in a way, about the brandy because it necessarily brought memories and associations. But without it he couldn't have borne the party at all, couldn't even have looked on the conviviality or withstood the incomprehensible warring tensions. Now, however, when he had drunk the last vaporous fiery drop of it, he jumped to his feet and said rather shrilly that he must go. He must no longer trespass on their hospitality, he must leave.

'Stand not upon the order of your going, but go at once,' said Dean.

Such rudeness, even if it came out of a book, wasn't to be borne. Arthur made a stiff little bow in the direction of Mervyn and the new Mrs Mervyn, gave a stiff little nod of the head in exchange for their farewells, and escaped.

The joy of getting out was heady. He hurried home through the mews, that dark throat where once, in its jaws, he had made death swallow a woman who flitted like a great black bird. A mouse, a baby, Maureen Cowan, Bridget O'Neill, Vesta Kotowsky . . . But, no. Home now, encountering no one.

At the top of the empty house he settled down to watch John Wayne discharging yet again the duties of a United States Cavalry Colonel. He leaned against the brown satin cushion, cool, clean, luxurious. The film ended at half past eight. Rather late to begin on his ironing, but better late than on Sunday. For twenty years he had done his ironing on a Saturday.

Entering the kitchen to get out the ironing board and the folded linen, he looked in vain for the orange plastic bag. It wasn't there. He had left it behind in the Waterlily.

# Chapter 20

The first to leave the party was Jonathan Dean. Anthony, aware that for the past half-hour Jonathan had been busy entangling his legs with Li-li's under the table, supposed they would remain after he and the Mervyns had gone and that the evening would end for them by Li-li's becoming Vesta's successor. Things happened differently. Li-li departed to the passageway that housed the ladies' lavatory. It also housed a phone, and when she came back she announced that she must soon go as she had a date at seven-thirty. Junia Mervyn, a woman who seemed to take delight in the general discomfiture of men, laughed merrily.

'What about me?' said Jonathan truculently.

Li-li giggled. 'You like to come too? Wait and I go call my friend again.'

'You know very well I didn't mean that.'

'Me, I don't know what men mean. I don't try to know. I love them all a little bit. You like to go on my list? Then when I come back from Taiwan I make you number three, four?' She and Junia clutched each other, laughing. Jonathan got up and without a backward look or a word to his hosts, banged out of the pub.

The men were heavily, awkwardly, silent. Anthony, suddenly and not very aptly identifyingly, felt through his depression a surge of angry misogyny. And he said before he could stop himself:

'As a connoisseur of bad behaviour in woman, I'd give you my prize.'

Li-li pouted. She sidled up to him, opening her eyes wide, trying her wiles. He wondered afterwards if he would actually have struck her, at least have given her a savage push, had Winston not interrupted by announcing it was time to leave for the airport.

He interposed his body, spoke smoothly. 'Feel like coming with us, Anthony? My brother will give you a lift back.'

Anthony said he would. In a low voice he apologized to Linthea. She kissed his cheek.

'Have women really behaved so badly to you?'

'One has. It doesn't matter. Forget it, Linthea, please.'

'I'm not to bother my pretty little head about it?'

Anthony smiled. This description of her head, goddess-like with its crown of coiled braids, was so inept that he was about to correct her with a compliment when Winston's brother said:

'Your friend left his shopping behind.'

'He's not our fliend,' said Li-li, 'and it's not shopping, it's washing.' She pulled it out from under the settle, pointing to and giggling at the topmost item it contained, a pair of underpants. 'You,' she said imperiously to Anthony, 'take it back for him.'

'Suppose you do that? I'm going to the airport.'

'Me take nasty old man's washing out on my date?'

'You've got time to take it home first,' said Winston. 'It's only a quarter past seven.' Always a controller of situations, he closed her little white hand round the handles of the orange plastic bag and placed her firmly but gently back on the settle. A fresh glass of martini in front of her, she sat silenced, looking very small and young. 'That's a good girl,' said Winston.

The night was cruelly cold, its clarity turning all the lights to sharply cut gems. Linthea took Winston's arm and shivered against him as if, now she was going home, she could allow herself to feel the cold of an English winter for the first time. As they crossed the street, Anthony saw a familiar red sports car draw up outside the Waterlily.

The contents of the bag were worth, Arthur calculated, about fifty pounds – all his working shirts, his underwear, bedlinen . . . It was unthinkable to leave them in that rough public house which would fill up, on a Saturday night, with God knew what riff-raff. But to go out at this hour into darkness?

One of them might, just might, have brought the bag back for him. He went out on to the landing, and the light from his own hall shed a little radiance as far as the top of the stairs. But below was a pit of blackness. There was nothing outside his door, nothing at the head of the stairs. He put on lights, descended. First he knocked on Li-li's door, then on that of Room 2. But he knew it was in vain. Slits of light always showed round the doors when the occupants of the rooms were in.

If only he dared forget about it, leave it till the Waterlily opened in the morning. But, no, he couldn't risk losing so much valuable property. And it was only a step to the pub, less than five minutes' walk. He went back upstairs and put on his overcoat. He walked rapidly up Camera Street, keeping his eyes lowered. But Balliol Street was full of people, corpses in brown grave clothes, their faces and their dress turned pallid or khaki by the colour-excluding sodium lamps. Yellow-brown too was the sports car parked outside Kemal's Kebab House, but Arthur recognized it as belonging to one of Li-li's young men. Only the traffic lights were bright enough to compete with that yellow glare. Their green and scarlet hurt his eyes and made him blink.

Entering the Waterlily on his own recalled to him those three previous occasions on which he had gone into a public house alone. He pushed away the memory, reminding himself how near he was to Trinity Road. The pub was crowded now and Arthur had to queue. He asked for a small brandy, though he hadn't meant to buy a drink at all. But he needed the warmth and the comfort of it to combat the agonies of embarrassment he passed through while the licensee asked the barman and the barman asked the barmaid – in bellowing amused voices – for a Mr Johnson's laundry bag.

'You were with those people who'd got married, weren't you?'

Arthur nodded.

'An orange-coloured bag? That Chinese girl took it. I saw her go out of the door with it.'

He gave a gasp of relief. Li-li was in Kemal's, and his laundry, no doubt, was in that very car he had walked past. He almost ran out of the Waterlily. He crossed the mews entrance. There were so many cars lining the street and all their paintbox colours reduced to tones of sepia. But the sports car wasn't among them. Li-li and her escort had gone.

Arthur stood shaking outside the restaurant, and the hot spicy smell that wafted to him from its briefly opened door brought a gust of nausea in which he could taste the stinging warmth of brandy. And for support he rested one arm along the convex frosted

183

top of the pillar box. All he wanted, he told himself, was to get his washing, secure it from those who, with reasonless malice, had taken it and were keeping it from him.

Where did people go when they went out in the evening? To pubs, restaurants, cinemas. Li-li had already been to a pub, a restaurant. Arthur considered, his head beginning to drum. Then he crossed the road in the direction of Magdalen Hill and the Taj Mahal.

Now the whole corner was boarded up, the waste ground as well as the area where the demolished houses had been, where Auntie Gracie's house had been. It was fenced in blankly with a row of those old doors builders save and use for this purpose. As Arthur passed close by he could see through the yellow glare that each was painted in some pale bathroom shade, pink, green, cream. Closed, nailed together, they seemed to shut off great epochs of his life. He went past Grainger's and the station. A train running under the street made strong vibrations run up through his body.

The film showing at the Taj Mahal wasn't truly Indian but something from further east. The slant-eyed faces, the heads crowned with jewelled, pagoda-shaped head-dresses, on the poster outside told him that. And this gave force to his feeling that it was here Li-li had come. But there was no parking space in Kenbourne Lane with its double yellow band coursing the edge of the pavement. Suppose she was inside? He wouldn't be able to find her or fetch her out. Still he lingered at the foot of the steps, looking almost wistfully in at the foyer, so much the same as ever yet so dreadfully changed. Hundreds of times he had passed through those swing doors with Auntie Gracie, but it was more than twenty years since he had visited any cinema except that which his own living room afforded.

He wouldn't go in there now. Behind the cinema was a vast council car park. He would go into that car park and find the red sports car. It was unlikely to be locked, for the young were all feckless and indifferent to the value of property. He made his way down the path between shops and cinema, hearing the oriental music which reached him through the tall cream-painted ramparts of the Taj Mahal. It made a huge pale cliff, overshadowing the car park which was unlit, though semicircled at its perimeter with many of those yellow lights and with silvery white ones as well. There was no one in the attendant's hut at the entrance, there was no one anywhere. Arthur passed beside the barrier, the sword-shaped arm that would rise to allow the passage of a vehicle.

Cars stood in long regular rows. Underfoot it wasn't tarmac or concrete but a gravelly mud, beginning now to freeze into hardness. He could walk on it with soundless footfalls. Slowly he crept along, scanning car after car, pausing sometimes to stare along the lines of car roofs that gleamed dully like aquatic beasts slumbering side by side on some northern moonlit coast. But it was a false moonlight, the heavy purple sky suffused only by street lamps.

When he reached the southernmost point of the great irregular quadrangle, a sense of the absurdity of what he was doing began gradually to penetrate his brandy haze. He wasn't going to find the sports car, or if he did he wouldn't dare to touch it. He had no evidence that Li-li had ever passed this way or entered the Taj Mahal. Not for this purpose had he come into the solitary half-dark of this place. He had come for the reason he always ventured into the dark and the loneliness . . .

But there were no women here. None of those creatures who threatened his liberty, were always a danger to him, was here. And he could only find one of them if he left the car park by the narrow gate behind him, impassable to vehicles, that led to a path into Brasenose Avenue. With painful lust he envisioned that little defile, but he turned his back on it, turned from its direction, and forced his legs to push him back towards the hut between the ranks of cars.

Then, as he emerged into a wider aisle, he saw that he was no longer alone. A car, one of those tinny, perched-up little Citroens, had nosed in and was searching for a space. Arthur drew himself up, narrowing and trimming his body so as to present a respectable and decorous air. Almost greater than that growing, not-to-be-permitted desire was the need to appear to any watcher as a law-abiding car owner with legitimate business here. The Citroen dived into a well of darkness between two larger cars. Arthur was only a dozen yards away from it. He saw the driver get out, and the driver was a woman.

A young girl, tallish and very slender, wearing jeans and an Afghan coat with furry edges and embroidery which gleamed a little in the light from pale distant lamps. Her hair was a golden aureole, a mass of metallic-looking filaments that hung below her shoulders. The car door open, she was bending over the interior, adjusting to the steering column some thief-proof locking device. He saw her high-heeled boots, the leather wrinkling over thin ankles, and he felt a constriction in his throat. He could taste brandied bile.

Now, soft-footed, he was a yard behind her. The girl straightened and closed the car door. But it refused to catch. She pulled it wide and shut it with a hard slam. The noise made a vast explosion in Arthur's ears as he raised his hands and leapt upon her from behind, digging his fingers into her neck.

The earth rocked as he held on to that surprisingly strong and sinewy neck, and the huge purple sky blazed at him, burning his eyes. The girl was resisting, strong as he, stronger ... She gave a powerful twist and her elbow thrust back hard into his diaphragm. He staggered at the sudden pain, slackening his hold, and a fist swung into his face, hard bone against his teeth. With a strangled grunt he fell back against the next car, sliding down its slippery bodywork. Her face loomed over his, contorted, savage, and Arthur let out a cry, for it was the face of a young man with a hooked nose, stubble on his upper lip and a cape of coarse hair streaming. The fist swung again, this time to his eye. Arthur slid down on to the frozen mud and lay there, half under the oil-blackened chassis of the other car.

He didn't move, although he was conscious. A hand turned him over, a sharp-toed boot kicked his ribs. He made no sound, but lay there with his eyes closed. The boy was standing over him, breathing heavily, making sucking sounds of satisfaction and triumph. Then he heard footsteps pounding away towards the hut and the barrier and there was a terrible deep silence.

Arthur hauled himself up, clinging to the wings of both cars. His face was wet with blood running from his upper lip and his head was banging as it had never banged from desire. He forced his eyes into focus so that he could see the shining, sleeping cars, the glittering frosted ground. No attendant coming, no one. He crawled between the cars, clutching here at a wing mirror, there at a door handle, until at last the strength that comes from terror brought him to an upright stance. He staggered. The icy air, unimpeded, was like a further blow to his face. He tasted the salt blood trickling between his teeth.

Still the hut was empty, the path between cinema and shops deserted. Covering his face with the clean white handkerchief he always carried, he made himself walk down that path, walk slowly, although he wanted to run and scream. Kenbourne Lane. No crowd was gathered, no huddle of passers-by stood staring in the direction taken by a running boy with golden hair. No one looked at Arthur. It was the season for colds, for muffled faces. He went on past the station until he came to Grainger's gates. Thank God they weren't padlocked but closed with a Yale lock. Holding up the handkerchief, he unlocked the gates, the conscientious surveyor who works Saturday nights despite a cold in the head. They closed behind him and he sank heavily against them.

But he must reach his own office. There, for a while, he would be safe. The little house of glass and cedarwood was an island and a haven in the big bare yard. He crawled to it because his legs, which had carried him so well when their strength had most been needed, had buckled now and were half-paralysed. From the ground, slippery with frost, he reached up and unlocked the door.

It was cold inside, colder than in the open air. The Adler stood on the desk, shrouded in its cover; the wastepaper basket was empty; the place smelt faintly of bubble gum. Arthur collapsed on to the floor and lay there, his body shaking with gasping sobs. He staunched the blood, which might otherwise have got on to the carpet, first with his handkerchief, then with his scarf. As the handkerchief became unusable, black with blood, he heard

188

the wail of sirens, distant and keening at first, then screaming on an ear-splitting rise and fall as the police cars came over the lights into Magdalen Hill.

# Chapter 21

West Kenbourne was populated with police. It seemed to Anthony, returning from the airport in Perry Mervyn's car, that every other pedestrian in Balliol Street was a policeman. Since they had turned from the High Street up Kenbourne Lane, he had counted five police cars.

'Maybe someone robbed a bank,' said Junia.

It was half past eleven, but lights were still on in the Dalmatian and the Waterlily and their doors stood open. Police were in the pubs and standing in the doorways, questioning customers as they left. From behind the improvised fence that shut off the waste ground, the beams from policemen's torches cut the air in long pale swaying shafts.

'Must have been a bank,' said Perry, and he and his wife offered sage opinions – they were in perfect agreement – as to the comparative innocuousness of bank robbery. It could hardly be called morally wrong, it harmed no one, and so on. Anthony, though grateful for the lift, wasn't sorry when they arrived at 142 Trinity Road.

He thanked them and they exchanged undertakings not to lose touch. Anthony supposed, and supposed they supposed, that they would never meet again. Waving, he watched the car depart, its occupants having declared they would drive around for a while and try to find out what was going on.

190

Nothing was going on in Trinity Road. A hundred and forty-two was in total darkness. He went indoors and walked slowly along the passage towards Room 2. The police hunt afforded him no interest, brought him no curiosity. Nothing was able to divert him from the all-enclosing grey misery which had succeeded disbelief, anger, pain. The wedding, the happiness of Winston and Linthea, had served only to vary his depression with fresh pain. And in the airport lounge, where they had sat drinking coffee, a horrible aspect of that pain had shown itself. For that busy place, with its continual comings and goings, was peopled for him with Helens, with versions of Helen. Every fair head, turned from him, might turn again and show him her face. One girl, from a distance, had her walk; another, talking animatedly to a man who might be Roger – how would he know? – moved her hands in Helen gestures, and her laugh, soft and clear, reached him as Helen's laugh. Once he was certain. He even got to his feet, staring, catching his breath. The others must have thought him crazy, hallucinated.

He put his key into the door lock. But before he could enter Room 2 the front door opened and Li-li came in, carrying Arthur Johnson's washing bag.

'Have you been carting that round all night?' said Anthony disagreeably.

'Is not all night. Is only twelve.' She waved the bag at him. 'There, you shall take it to him now. He will be so pleased to have it safe.'

'Knowing him, I should think he's nearly gone out of his mind worrying about it. And you can take it to him yourself.'

But, as Li-li with a pout and a giggle disappeared round the first bend of the stairs, Anthony thought he had better follow her. He caught up with her as she was mounting the second flight.

'He'll be asleep. He always goes to bed early. Leave it outside his door.'

'O.K.' Li-li dropped the bag on the landing. 'Nasty, nasty, to be old and go to bed at midnight.' She gave Anthony a sweet provocative smile. 'You like some Chinese tea?'

'No, thanks. I go to bed at midnight too.' He walked into Room 2 and closed the door firmly. It was some time before he fell asleep, for Li-li, preparing for her journey on the following day, revenged herself by packing noisily, banging her wardrobe door and apparently throwing shoes across the room, until after three.

Arthur heard the police get Grainger's doors open half an hour after he had hidden himself in the office. He saw the beams of their torches searchlighting the yard. They came up to the office and walked round it, but because the door hadn't been forced and no window was broken, they went away. He heard the gates clang behind them.

His lip had stopped bleeding. When it was safe to get up from the floor, he wrapped his handkerchief in a sheet of flimsy paper and thrust it into his coat pocket. Very little light was available to him, only a distant sheen from the lamps of Magdalen Hill. He didn't dare put the light on or even the electric fire, though it was bitterly cold. His scarf was patched and streaked with blood, but not so badly stained that he couldn't wear it. It was of the utmost importance to leave no blood on the haircord or as fingerprints. But the yellow twilight was sufficient to show him that the haircord was unmarked. He licked his fingers till they were free of the salty taste.

Then he lay down again on the floor, sleepless,

letting the long slow hours pass. His ribs ached on the left side but he didn't think the kick had broken a bone. Outside they would comb the whole area. When they couldn't find him they would leave the area and look further afield. Perhaps they wouldn't come to Trinity Road at all.

Would it never get light? Light would show any passer-by his injured face – if only he had the means to see how injured it was! – but a man walking solitary in the dark small hours would attract more attention. When the yellowness retreated into the milky grey of dawn, he dragged himself to his feet and looked out of the window on to the deserted yard. His body was stiff, every limb aching, and a sharp fluctuating pain teased his left side.

His watch had broken in the fall and the hands still showed twenty past nine. It must now be about eleven hours later than that. His watch had broken but not his glasses, which remained intact in their case. He put them on, although they were reading glasses that threw the world out of focus, but they would help disguise his eye. As to his lip – he licked a corner of his scarf and worked blindly at the cut, wincing because the rough fibres prickled the edges of the wound. But the morning was very cold and now he saw that a thin sleet had begun to fall, little granules of ice that melted as they struck the ground. The kind of day, he thought, when a man with a muffled face is accepted as normal.

Shaking a little, controlling his shaking as best he could, he went out of the office, locking the door behind him. He had left no vestige of his presence. As he approached the gates, the falling sleet thick-ened into a storm. Snow, the first of the year, swirled about him, flakes of it stinging his lip. He pulled the scarf up to cover his mouth and, with lowered head, took what was a kind of plunge into Magdalen Hill.

There was no one about but a boy delivering Sunday papers. His encounter with the girl-boy in the car park had happened too late at night for there to be anything about it in the papers, and this little boy in thick coat and balaclava didn't look at him. A man walking a retriever in Balliol Street didn't look at him, nor did the cleaning woman who was letting herself into the public bar of the Waterlily. She too had a scarf swathing the lower half of her face. Arthur entered the mews as All Souls' clock struck eight.

Someone had left a newspaper, last evening's, on top of a dustbin in the mews. He picked it up and tucked it under his arm so that anyone who saw him would think he had been out to buy it. But no one saw him. Li-li's curtains were drawn. He crept upstairs through the sleeping house. On the top landing, resting against his door, was the orange laundry bag. At some point Li-li had brought that bag up the stairs. Had she knocked on his door? And if she had, would she have assumed he was asleep? Or had she left it downstairs, and had Anthony Johnson, the only other occupant of the house, been responsible for bringing it here? There was no way of knowing. If Anthony Johnson were awake now light would show from his window on to the court, for Room 2 was dark in winter till nine. But there was no cross-barred cast of light to be seen on the green stone. Snow whirled down the well, flying against the cellar door and streaming down it as rivulets of water.

Arthur cut up his handkerchief and flushed the pieces down the lavatory. He washed his scarf and, pulling it out from the lining, washed too the pocket of his overcoat. Then, and only then, did he dare look at his face in the mirror.

His eye socket was the colour of meat that has lain exposed, a dark glazed red, and the lid was almost closed. And his lip was split, a cut running up unevenly at the centre join of the upper lip. He looked quite different, this wasn't his face, not his this sore bulbous mouth. Would it scar? It didn't seem bad enough to need stitching. He washed it carefully with warm water and antiseptic. It couldn't be stitched. Every casualty department in every hospital in London would be alerted to watch for a man coming in with a wounded mouth.

He mustn't show himself at all. At any cost, he must remain here, hidden, until his lip and his eye healed. It was hours since he had eaten or drunk anything, hours since he had slept, but he knew he could no more sleep than he could eat a crumb of bread. He drank some water and gagged on it, its coldness burning his throat.

Shrouded by the nightdress frills of the net curtains, he crouched at the window. If the police did a house-to-house search he would be lost. He watched people go by, expecting always to see the piranha face of Inspector Glass. The church bells rang for morning service and a few elderly women went by, carrying Prayer Books, on their way to All Souls'. At lunchtime he put on the television, and the last item in a news bulletin told him, as only this high authority could really tell him, what he had done and where he stood.

'A man was attacked last night in a car park near Kenbourne Lane tube station in West London ...' And there, on the screen, was the car park overhung by the ramparts of the Taj Mahal. Arthur trembled, clenching his hands. He half-expected to see himself emerge from behind a row of cars, caught by those cameras like a stalked animal. 'From the circumstances of the attack, police believe his assailant mistook him for a woman and are speculating as to whether the attacker could be the same man who, for a quarter of a century, has been known by the name of the Kenbourne Killer. A massive hunt in the area has so far been unsuccessful ...'

Arthur switched off the set. He went once more into the bathroom and looked in the mirror at the face of the Kenbourne Killer. Never, in the past, when he had thought of the things he had done, had he ever really considered that title and that role as belonging to him. But the television had told him so, it was so. Those marks had been put upon his face so that he and the world should know it. Looking at his face made him cry so he went back to his window where the nets veiled his face. The television remained off, blank, though an early Rogers-Astaire film was showing, until five when there was more news.

An Identikit picture appeared on the screen, a hard cold face, sharply lined, vicious, elderly. The subject had a hare lip and a blind eye. Was that how he, so spruce and handsome, had looked to the boy with the Citroen? He felt faint and dizzy when the boy himself appeared and seemed to stare penetratingly into his own eyes. The boy put a hand up to that deceiving hair and smiled a little proudly.

'Well, I reckon this guy thought I was a girl, you know, on account of me being skinny and having long hair.'

The interviewer addressed him with earnest approval. 'Would you be able to identify him, Mr Harrison?'

'Sure, I would. Anyway, I knocked his face about a

196

bit, didn't I? Anyone'd be able to identify him, not just me.'

And now Inspector Glass himself. Arthur shivered because his enemies were being ranged before him through this medium, once so friendly, once the purveyor of his second best delight.

The lips curled back and the great teeth showed. 'You can take it as certain that the police won't rest until we've got this chap and put him out of harm's way. It's only a matter of time. But I'd like to tell the public that this man is highly dangerous, and if anyone has the slightest suspicion of his identity, if he or she feel they're only going on what you might call intuition, they must call this number at once.'

The telephone number burned in white letters on a black ground. And the voice of Inspector Glass, the voice of a devourer of men, came heavy and grim.

'At any time of the day or night *you* can call this number. And if you hesitate, remember that next time it could be you or your wife or your mother or your daughter.'

The diesel rattle of a taxi called Arthur back to the window. Li-li came out of the house carrying two suitcases. There was another gone who might see his face and not hesitate. Snow had begun to fall again through the bitter cold darkness. He watched her get into the taxi.

And now he was alone in the house with Anthony Johnson.

# Chapter 22

That Sunday it was nearly noon before Anthony got up. Room 2 was icy and he had to use powdered milk in his tea because he had run out of fresh. The courtyard was wet, although it wasn't raining, and the triangle of sky had the yellowish-grey look snow clouds give.

It was so dark that he had to keep the lamp on all day. He sat under it, leafing through the draft of his thesis, wondering if it was any good, but into his concentration, or what passed for concentration, fragmented images of Helen kept breaking. He found himself recalling conversations they had had in the past, reading duplicity into phrases of hers that had once seemed beautifully sincere. And this obsession displaced everything else. He sat staring dully at the pink and green translucent shade that swayed with a slow gentle rhythm in the draught from the window frame crack, hypnotized by it, subdued into apathy. Soon after five, when he had heard Li-li leave, he put on his coat and set off for Winter's.

The relief barman from the Waterlily was in the shop and he and Winter were talking about the police activity of the night before. Anthony had forgotten all about it. Now, waiting to be served, he learned its nature.

'Young fellow of nineteen, student at Radclyffe

College. What I say is, if they will get themselves up like girls, they're asking for it. Not that he didn't stand up for himself. Bashed the fellow's face up something shocking. You see the news?'

The barman nodded. 'Funny thing, I got a black eye myself last week. All above board, got it at my judo. But if it wasn't better I wouldn't fancy showing myself on the street.'

'You didn't get a cut lip as well, though, did you? Mind you, that'd be a turn up for the books, all the locals finding out the Kenbourne Killer'd been serving them their booze.' Winter laughed. He turned to Anthony. 'And what can I do for you, sir?'

'Just a pint of milk, please.'

'Homogenized, Jersey or silver top?'

Anthony took the silver top. As he was closing the door behind him he heard them say something about his hair and prowling stranglers who couldn't tell the boys from the girls, and who could blame them? He went past the lighted windows of the Waterlily, for only drunks and potential pick-ups go into pubs on their own in the evenings. The snow had settled in little drifts between the cobbles of Oriel Mews where there was no light or heat to melt it. It floated thinly over Trinity Road, making a thinner webbier curtain over the draped nets at Arthur Johnson's window behind which Anthony thought he could vaguely make out a watcher.

Room 2 had grown cold again in his absence. He kicked on the electric fire, drank some milk straight out of the bottle. It was so cold it made his teeth chatter. He crouched over the fire, and into his mind came a clear and sweet vision of Helen as she had been in the summer, running along the platform at Temple Meads to meet his train when he came to her from York. He felt, closing his eyes, her hands reach up to hold his shoulders, her warm breath from her parted lips on his lips. And he felt real pain, a shaft of pain in his left side, as if he had been kicked where his heart was.

Then he lay face-downwards on the bed, hating himself for his weakness, wondering how he would get through the time ahead, the long cold winter of isolation with only Arthur Johnson for company.

Upstairs, on the landing, the telephone began to ring.

Arthur heard the phone but didn't answer it. The only people who were likely to receive phone calls had gone away. He went into the bedroom and looked again at his face. Impossible to consider going to work tomorrow. The phone had stopped ringing. He looked out of the window down to the court below. Anthony Johnson's light was on, and Arthur wondered why he hadn't answered the phone.

There was plenty of food in his fridge, including the Sunday joint he hadn't been able to face and couldn't face now. The food he had would last him for days. He managed to swallow a small piece of bread and butter. Then he looked at his face again, this time in the bathroom mirror. While he was wondering if ice would ease the swelling, if anyone would believe him if he said he had cut himself shaving – and, presumably, also knocked his eye with the razor – the phone started ringing again. He opened his front door and emerged on to the dark landing. Obscurely he felt that, whoever this might be phoning, it would be safer were he to answer it himself.

He lifted the receiver and Stanley Caspian's voice said, 'That you, Arthur? About time too. I buzzed you five minutes ago.'

Light flooded him suddenly from the hall below. He turned, covering his mouth with his left hand, and called in a muffled voice, 'It's all right. It's Mr Caspian for me.'

Anthony Johnson said, 'O.K.,' and went back into Room 2. Arthur wished the light would go out. He hunched over the phone.

'Listen, Arthur, I've got a chap coming to have a dekko at Flat I tomorrow around five. Can you let him in?'

'I'm not well,' Arthur said, sick with panic. 'I've got a – a virus infection. I shan't be going to work and I can't let anyone in. I'm going to have the day in bed.'

'My God, I suppose you can get out of your poxy bed just to open the front door?'

'No, I can't,' Arthur said shrilly. 'I'm ill. I should be in bed now.'

'Charming. After all I've done for you, Arthur, that's a bit thick. I suppose I'll have to fix it a bit earlier with this chap and come myself.'

'I'm sorry. I'm not well. I have to go and lie down.'

Stanley didn't answer but crashed down the receiver. Arthur stumbled up to his own door. It was almost closed. A slight draught, a tiny push, and he would have been locked out. He who never never neglected such precautions had forgotten to drop the latch. Shivering at the thought of what might have happened, he went into the bathroom to contemplate his lip and his eye. Tears began to course down his face, stinging the bruised flesh.

The second time the phone rang Anthony got off his bed to answer it. But the hopes he had had, hopes that were against all reason, were dissipated by the voice calling from the landing, 'It's Mr Caspian for me.'

Because the voice sounded thick and strange, Anthony, who in his disappointment would otherwise simply have drifted back into Room 2, glanced up at the figure on the landing. Arthur Johnson was covering his mouth with his left hand, and he turned away quickly, huddling over the phone, but not before Anthony had noticed one of his eyes was swollen and half-closed. The phone conversation went on for a few moments, Arthur Johnson protesting that he was ill, but from a virus infection, not some sort of facial injury. Anthony closed the door. He sat on the bed. An hour before he would have given a lot for some subject to come overpoweringly into his mind and crowd Helen out of it. But this? Did he want this and could he cope with it?

A series of images now. A man, evidently nervous, paranoid, repressed, saying, 'You are the *other* Johnson. I have been here for twenty years.' In the cellar a shop window model with a rent in her neck. Fire burning that figure, and that very night, the night of 5 November ... Anthony looked out of the window and up to that other window two floors above. No light showed, though that was Arthur Johnson's bedroom and he had said he was ill and ought to be in bed. Perhaps he was, in the dark. Anthony went out into the street and looked up. There was light up there, orange light turning the draped muslin stuff to gold, and behind that shimmering stuff a light flickering movement.

He went quickly indoors and up the two flights of stairs. He had thought of no excuse for knocking on Arthur Johnson's door, but excuses seemed base and dishonest. Besides, once he had seen, he would need no excuse. But there was no answer to his knock, no answer when he knocked again, and that told him as much as if the damaged face had presented itself to him, six inches from his own. To knock again, to insist, would be a cruelty that revolted him, for in the silence he fancied he could sense a concentrated breath-held terror behind that door.

He knew now. He would have laughed at himself if this had been a laughing matter, for the irony was that he who was writing a thesis on psychopathy, who knew all about psychopaths, had lived three months in the same house as a psychopath and not known it. So, of course, he must go to the police. Knew? Did he? Well, he was sure, certain. When we say that, Helen had once said, we always mean we are not quite sure, not quite certain. He shivered in the hot fuggy yet draughty room. It had been a shock. Presently he began looking through his books, finding Arthur Johnson or aspects of him in every case history, finding what he well knew already, that if hardly anything is known of the causes of psychopathy, even less has been discovered of ways to cure it. For ever a prison for the criminally insane then, for ever incarceration, helplessly inflicted and helplessly borne. But he would go to the police in the morning . . .

At last he undressed and got into bed. The triangle of sky was a smoky red scudded with black flakes of snow. He found it impossible to sleep and wondered if the man upstairs, lying in bed some twenty feet above him, also lay sleepless under his far greater weight of care.

At eight-thirty in the morning Arthur phoned Mr Grainger at home. He wouldn't be coming in, would have to take at least three days off. While he was on the phone he heard Anthony Johnson go into the bathroom, but the man didn't come to the foot of the stairs. Why had he knocked on his door last night? To borrow something, to get change for the phone? Still fresh with him, still aching in his bruised ribs, was the terror those repeated knocks had brought. But nothing would have made him let Anthony Johnson in to see his face. For hours he had hunched over the window ledge, intermittently leaving his post to look at his face, to listen by the door for Anthony Johnson to phone the police, watching for Anthony Johnson to go out and fetch the police. By midnight, when nothing had happened and the little court had gone dark, he had lain down, spent but sleepless.

The last of four lectures by a distinguished visiting criminologist was to be given at the college that morning. Anthony had attended them all, been rather disappointed that they were more elementary than he had hoped, and now he took notes abstractedly. He was tired and uneasy.

Still he hesitated to go to the police, although he had noted where the nearest station was, having passed its tall portals, its blue lamp, on his way to college on the K.12. One o'clock came and he was in the canteen, vacillating still, nauseated at the idea of betraying a man who had done him no injury. He seldom had much to say to the students. They were all younger than he and they seemed to him not much more than children. But now a girl who had sat next to him in the lecture room brought her tray to his table and pointed out to him a long-haired boy who was holding court at the far end of the room, surrounded by avid listeners.

'That's Philip Harrison.'

'Philip Harrison?'

204

'The guy who was attacked in the car park on Saturday.'

Anthony didn't look at him. He looked at the young girls who were his audience, one of whom was distressingly like Helen. If that girl had been in the car park she wouldn't be here now, listening with innocent relish. She would be dead. He had only to go to the police station and tell them what he knew, so little that he knew, so tenuous as it was, yet so true a pointer. Dully, he pushed away his plate. He had eaten nothing. A great weariness overcame him and he wanted nothing so much as to lie down and sleep. He remembered how, once in the summer, he and Helen had lain in each other's arms in a field in the West Country and for an hour he had slept with her hair against his cheek and the scent coming to him of seeded grass and wild parsley. Since then, it seemed, he had never slept so sweetly as during that hour. But the summer was past, in every sense, and the sweet hours of sleep. He got his coat, walked down the long hall, through the swing doors, out into the snow.

The police station was perhaps ten minutes' walk away. The college grounds were empty and barren as if the cold had shaved all vegetation away but for the clipped turf and swept up all people like so much litter. There was no one in the grounds but himself and a girl whom he could see in the extreme distance coming in by the main gates. He walked towards her and she towards him down the long gravel drive.

And now he began collecting together his knowledge and suspicions of Arthur Johnson for a coherent statement to the police. But he was distracted by the sight of the approaching girl. By now he ought to be used to the deceptions practised on him by his eyes and his mind. He wasn't going to catch his breath

205

this time because a strange girl walked like Helen, moved her head like Helen, and now that she came nearer could be seen to have Helen's crisp golden hair. He trudged on, looking down at the gravel, refusing any longer to contemplate the girl who was now only some twenty or thirty yards from him.

But, in spite of himself, he was aware that she had stopped. She had stopped and was staring straight at him. He swallowed hard and his heart thudded. They stared at each other across the cold bare expanse. As he saw her lift her arms and open them, and as she began to run towards him, calling his name, 'Tony, Tony!' he too ran towards her with open arms.

Her mouth was cold on his mouth but her body was warm. As he held her he knew he hadn't been warm like this for weeks. The warmth was wonderful and the feel of her, but he was afraid to look at her face.

'Helen,' he said, 'is it really you?'

# Chapter 23

They sat on a bench on College Green, not feeling the cold. Anthony held her face in his hands. He smoothed back a lock of hair that had fallen over her forehead, re-learning the look and the feel of her. 'I don't believe it,' he said. 'I really can't yet believe it.'

'I know. I felt like that.'

'You won't go away? I mean, you won't say in a minute that you've got a train to catch or anything like that?'

'I've nowhere *to* go. I've burned my boats. Tony, let's eat. I'm hungry, I'm starving. You know I always want to eat when I'm happy.'

The Grand Duke was crowded. They went into a café that was humble and clean and almost empty.

'I don't know whether to sit opposite you or next to you. One way I can look, the other way I can touch you.'

'Look at me,' she said. 'I want to look at you.'

She sat down and fixed her eyes on his face. She reached across the table and took his hand. They held hands on the cloth, hers covering his. 'Tony, it's all right now, it will always be all right *now*, but why didn't you answer my letters?'

'Because you told me not to. You told me never to write to you.'

'Not my last three. I begged you to write to me at the museum. Didn't you *get* them?'

207

He shook his head. 'Since the end of October I've only had one letter from you and that was the one where you told me you never wanted to see me again.'

She drew back, then leaned forward, clutching his hand. 'I never wrote such a thing!'

'Someone did. Roger?'

'I don't know. I don't – well, it's possible, but . . . I wrote and told you I was leaving him and coming to you. But how could I come when you didn't answer? I was crazy with misery. Roger went to Scotland and I waited at home alone night after night for you to phone.'

'I phoned,' he said, 'on the last Wednesday of November.'

'By then I'd gone to my mother's. I'd got a fortnight's holiday owing to me and I went to my mother because I couldn't bear being alone any more and being with Roger in Scotland would have been worse. I thought I'd never see you again.'

Just as he had thought he would never again see her. But now he had no wish to solve the mystery. It paled into insignificance beside the joy of being with her.

'Helen,' he said, 'why are you here now?'

'But you know that,' she said, surprised. 'I'm here because you wrote to me.'

'*That* letter? That stupid letter?'

'Was it? I never saw it. I only know you said you loved me in the first line of it, so I – I ran away!'

She leaned across the table and kissed him. The waitress gave a slight cough and, as they drew apart, placed their plates in front of them.

'I went to work this morning, my first day back. As soon as I got in the phone rang and it was Roger. A letter had come for me with your name and address on the flap and he – he opened it.'

'My name and address on the flap? But I . . .' He explained how he had enclosed his letter to her in one to Mrs Pontifex.

'Oh, I see. We never meant to go there for Christmas this year. She must have copied your name and address from the letter to her and forwarded it. I don't know. I told you, I didn't see it. I went out before the post came. Roger was – he was *frightening* with rage. I've heard him in some rages, I've seen him, when he's threatened to kill me and himself, but I've never heard him like that. He just read that first line, and then he sort of spat out, "From your lover." He said, "You're to go downstairs and wait outside the building for me, Helen. If you're not there I'll come up, but you'd better be there unless you want a public scene. I shan't flinch from telling everyone in that building what you are."

'He said he'd be there in the car in five minutes, Tony. I knew it couldn't take him more than five minutes and I was terrified of what he'd do. I grabbed my coat and my handbag and I rushed out and down the stairs. I remember calling out I'd had bad news and had to go.

'When I got into the street I was afraid to wait there even for a second. I crossed the road and ran down a side street, and then a taxi came and I said, "Temple Meads!" because I knew I must go to London and you. You loved me, you'd said you did, so everything was all right at last.

'I didn't bother to queue up for a ticket. I could hear an announcer saying, "The train standing at platform two is the nine fifty-one for London, calling at Bath, Swindon and Reading." It was nine-fifty then and I jumped on that train. I had to buy a ticket when the man came round and it took all the money I'd got but for fivepence. I hadn't got a cheque book or a bank card or anything. Oh, Tony, I'm entirely skint, I've got just what I stand up in.

'When I got to Paddington I found a bus going to Kenbourne Vale Garage but I hadn't got enough money to get further than to Kensal Rise. So I walked the rest.'

'You *walked*? Here from Kensal Rise?'

She smiled at his dismay. 'Out in the cold, cold snow and without any money. All I needed was a baby in my arms. I went into a newsagent's and looked up the route in a guide. I was going to go to Trinity Road but then I thought you might be here. So I came here and here I am.' Her eyes were bright, the pupils mirrors in which, at last, he could see his own face reflected. 'Are you pleased?' she said.

'Helen, I was half-dead with misery and loneliness and you ask me if I'm *pleased*?'

'I only wish,' she said, 'that I'd seen your letter. I don't suppose I ever shall now and I'd waited so long for it. Can you remember what you wrote?'

'No,' he lied. 'No, only that it was nonsense. You had the only good bit in the first line.'

She sighed, but it was a sigh of happiness. 'Tony, what are we going to do? Where shall we go?'

'Who cares? Somewhere, anywhere. We shall survive. Right now we'll go to Trinity Road.'

As he spoke the name he remembered. It was nearly three o'clock and he had delayed long enough. He put an arm round her shoulders, helped her to her feet. 'Come along, my love, we're going to Trinity Road, but we'll take in an errand I have to do on the way.'

Behind the curtains Arthur had sat all day, breaking

his vigil every half-hour or so to examine his face in the bathroom mirror. Now, at three o'clock, he saw Stanley Caspian's car draw up and park in front of one of the houses on the odd-numbered side. A man was coming to view Flat 1, and in a moment this man and Stanley would come into the house. Arthur watched the car but he could only see Stanley in it, sitting in the driving seat, his bulk and the bikini doll impeding further view. Perhaps he had brought the man with him or perhaps he was simply waiting for the new tenant to arrive for his appointment. Arthur went back to the bathroom. Already, so early, the winter light was beginning to fade. If Stanley did happen to call on him, if he had to show his face, perhaps those dreadful marks would pass unnoticed . . .

As he came out of the bathroom his doorbell rang. The sound reverberated through Arthur's body and he gave a tremendous start. He stood stock still in the hall. It was evident what had happened. Stanley had forgotten his key. Let him go home and fetch it then. The bell rang again, insistently, and Arthur could picture Stanley's fat finger pressed hard and impatiently on the push. He forced himself to go back into the living room and look out of the window. Stanley's car was empty. At any rate, it must be he. No police cars anywhere, no parked vehicles but Stanley's and a couple of vans and a grey convertible. Another long ring fetched him back into the hall. He must answer it, for it would look odder if he didn't. But he was supposed to be ill and must give the appearance of having been got out of bed. Quickly, though he was shaking, he slipped off his jacket and took his dressing gown from the hook behind the bedroom door. A handkerchief to his face, he let himself out of the flat and went downstairs.

Outlined behind the red and green glass panels was the shape of a heavy thickset man. It must be Stanley. Arthur stood behind the door and pulled it open towards him. The man marched in, looked to the right, then to the left where Arthur stood, took the edge of the door in both hands and slammed it shut as violently as Jonathan Dean had slammed it in the past.

He was youngish, dark, and he was in the grip of an emotion greater even than Arthur's fear. Arthur didn't know what this emotion was, but he knew a policeman wouldn't look like this, stand trembling and wide-eyed and wild like this. Because the hall was shadowy, lit with a misty redness and greenness, he took the handkerchief away from his face and stepped back.

'Is your name Johnson?'

'Yes,' said Arthur.

'*A.* Johnson?'

Arthur nodded, mystified, for the man peered at him incredulously. 'My God, an old man! It's unbelievable.' But he did believe and when he said hoarsely, 'Where is she?' Arthur also knew and believed.

Once it would have been threatening, dreadful. Now it was only a relief. 'You want the other Johnson,' Arthur said coldly and stiffly. 'Sit down and wait for him if you like. It's no business of mine.'

'The *other* Johnson? Don't give me that.' His eyes travelled over Arthur's dressing gown. He clenched his fists and said again, '*Where is she?*'

Arthur turned his back and climbed the stairs. He must get to his flat, shut himself in and pray that Stanley would soon come to turn this intruder out before violence drew the police. And now, realizing what could happen, he ran up the second flight to push open his own front door. A cry of dread broke from him. He had no key, hadn't dropped the latch, and the door had closed fast behind him.

He stood shaking, his back to the door, his hands creeping to shield his face. Out here what chance had he when Stanley came with the new tenant, when trouble broke out between Anthony Johnson and H's husband? And now the man had reached the head of the stairs and was facing him. Arthur looked into the barrel of a small gun – a pistol or a revolver, he didn't know which. Television hadn't taught him that.

'Open that door!'

'I can't. I've no key. I've left my key inside.'

'My wife is in there. Open that door or I'll shoot the lock off. I'll give you thirty seconds to open that door.'

His front door shattered, swinging on its hinges, would be worse than his front door locked against him. Arthur, who had moved aside when he saw the gun, brought his gaze first to the smooth circle of metal surrounding the keyhole, then, with greater dread, to the smooth metal cylinder pointed at that keyhole. A voice like a woman's, a victim's, screamed out of him.

'I can't! I tell you I can't. Go away, get out, leave me alone!' And he threw his body, arms upraised, against the door.

Something struck him a violent blow on his back, on the lower left side. The pain was unimaginable. He thought it was his heart, a heart attack, for he felt the pain long long before he heard the report as of a bursting firework, and heard too his own cry and that of another, aghast and terrified. Arthur fell backwards, his hands clutching his ribs. The pain roared in a red stream out of his mouth.

Heavily he rolled down the stairs, blood wrapping his body like a long scarlet scarf. The momentum flung him against Brian Kotowsky's door and there he felt the last beat of his heart in blood against his hand.

# The Rottweiler

## Ruth Rendell

The first girl had a bite mark on her neck but they traced the DNA to her boyfriend. But the tabloids got hold of the story and called the killer 'The Rottweiler' and the name stuck.

The latest murder takes place very near Inez Ferry's antique shop in Marylebone. Someone saw a shadowy figure running away past the station, but the only other clues are that the murderer usually strangles his victims and removes something personal – like a cigarette lighter or a necklace . . .

Since her husband died, too soon in their relationship, Inez has supplemented her income by taking in tenants. The murderous activities of the sinister 'Rottweiler' will exert a profound influence on the lives of this heterogeneous little community, especially when the suspicion emerges that one of them may be a homicidal maniac.

'In the world of contemporary crime fiction, Rendell really is top dog'
*Sunday Times*

'In Rendell's expert hands, you'll want to keep reading until dawn – without the light on'
*Red*

'Rendell skilfully crafts her characters and they breathe feverishly through her imagination'
*The Times*

arrow books

**Order further Ruth Rendell titles**
**from your local bookshop, or have them delivered**
**direct to your door by Bookpost**

| | | | |
|---|---|---|---|
| ☐ | A Guilty Thing Surprised | 0 09 923500 5 | £5.99 |
| ☐ | A Judgement in Stone | 0 09 917140 6 | £6.99 |
| ☐ | Harm Done | 0 09 928134 1 | £6.99 |
| ☐ | Live Flesh | 0 09 950270 4 | £6.99 |
| ☐ | Talking to Strange Men | 0 09 953530 0 | £6.99 |
| ☐ | The Bridesmaid | 0 09 968180 3 | £6.99 |
| ☐ | Road Rage | 0 09 947061 6 | £6.99 |
| ☐ | The Babes in the Wood | 0 09 943544 6 | £6.99 |
| ☐ | Shake Hands For Ever | 0 09 912910 8 | £6.99 |
| ☐ | A Sight for Sore Eyes | 0 09 927145 1 | £6.99 |
| ☐ | Adam and Eve and Pinch Me | | |
| | | 0 09 942619 6 | £6.99 |
| ☐ | The Rottweiler | 0 09 946024 6 | £6.99 |
| ☐ | Thirteen Steps Down | 0 09 947432 8 | £6.99 |

**Free post and packing**
Overseas customers allow £2 per paperback

Phone: 01624 677237

Post: Random House Books
c/o Bookpost, PO Box 29, Douglas, Isle of Man IM99 1BQ

Fax: 01624 670923

email: bookshop@enterprise.net

Cheques (payable to Bookpost) and credit cards accepted

Prices and availability subject to change without notice.
Allow 28 days for delivery.
When placing your order, please state if you do not wish to receive any
additional information.

www.randomhouse.co.uk/arrowbooks

**arrow books**